DEATH
BRINGS
A SHADOW

Books by Rosemary Simpson

WHAT THE DEAD LEAVE BEHIND

LIES THAT COMFORT AND BETRAY

LET THE DEAD KEEP THEIR SECRETS

DEATH BRINGS A SHADOW

Published by Kensington Publishing Corporation

DEATH
BRINGS
A SHADOW

ROSEMARY
SIMPSON

KENSINGTON BOOKS
www.kensingtonbooks.com

KENSINGTON BOOKS are published by

Kensington Publishing Corp.
119 West 40th Street
New York, NY 10018

All Kensington titles, imprints and distributed lines are available at special quantity discounts for bulk purchases for sales promotion, premiums, fund-raising, educational or institutional use. Special book excerpts or customized printings can also be created to fit specific needs. For details, write or phone the office of the Kensington Special Sales Manager: Kensington Publishing Corp., 119 West 40th Street, New York, NY, 10018. Attn. Special Sales Department. Phone: 1-800-221-2647.

Kensington and the K logo Reg. U.S. Pat. & TM Off.

Library of Congress Card Catalogue Number: 2019944837

ISBN-13: 978-1-4967-2209-6
ISBN-10: 1-4967-2209-4
First Kensington Hardcover Edition: December 2019

eISBN-13: 978-1-4967-2211-9 (ebook)
eISBN-10: 1-4967-2211-6

10 9 8 7 6 5 4 3 2 1

Printed in the United States of America

You may choose to look the other way but you can never
say again that you did not know.
—William Wilberforce (1759-1833)

When they told me my new-born babe was a girl, my
heart was heavier than it had ever been before. Slavery is
terrible for men; but it is far more terrible for women.
—Harriet Ann Jacobs (1813-1897)

Slavery is the next thing to hell.
—Harriet Tubman (c. 1822-1913)

CHAPTER 1

❧

Prudence MacKenzie watched her friend Eleanor Dickson wave excitedly toward the narrow wooden pier where her fiancé waited. Behind him stretched the coastline of Bradford Island, Georgia, a flat sweep of sun-bleached sand and gray-green live oak forest shimmering in the late-May heat. A thin veil of salt hung like mist above the water, blurring the line where foam-topped surf swept across the beach. Raucous seagulls circled overhead, calling to one another as they rode the air currents. It was a sight unlike any Prudence had ever seen before. Beautiful and utterly foreign to her Yankee eyes.

They had sailed out of New York Harbor five days ago to celebrate Eleanor's wedding on a privately owned island hundreds of miles from the city where they had both grown up. It had seemed as though her friend's new beginning signaled a metamorphosis for Prudence as well. Her Aunt Gillian, the dowager Viscountess Rotherton, who was to have chaperoned her niece during the voyage, telegrammed that her arrival in New York had been delayed for reasons she did not explain. She deeply regretted that her niece would have to cancel the trip, but there did not seem to be any other choice. Prudence had composed a dutifully respectful answer, then continued packing her trunks. She had slept long and dreamlessly every night beneath star-studded skies as the ship beat its way down the Atlantic coast, waking every morning delighted to be free of society's strictures and more certain every day that the past would no longer haunt her.

But the sight and sound of Eleanor calling out to Teddy Bennett as her family's private yacht approached the dock released an unexpected flood of memories. Resurrected the night of the Great Blizzard fourteen months ago, the hours of waiting and worrying, the death of the man she had been about to marry, and the empty days that followed. Her world had shattered into tiny fragments of self-doubt. An addiction to laudanum very nearly destroyed her future.

Until Geoffrey Hunter stepped in to save her. Steadied her as she built a new life for herself. She had never felt stronger than on the day they became partners in Hunter and MacKenzie, Investigative Law.

Where, she wondered, had this sudden rush of remembrance come from? This disturbing feeling of vulnerability? And why now? Prudence turned away from the sight of the lovers reaching out to each other and stared at the open, empty Atlantic. Blinked back tears.

Geoffrey.

There he stood, feet braced wide apart on the wooden deck, grinning into the ocean wind, black hair shining like a crow's wing, dark eyes glittering.

He smiled at her, crossed the open space that separated them, and raised her right hand to his lips. Ever the gallant Southern gentleman, Geoffrey could as easily soothe a troubled heart as sow a confusion of mixed and conflicting emotions. She wasn't sure what was happening between them, but his presence was comforting.

It also left her a little short of breath.

* * *

They set out for the Dicksons' winter retreat in a procession of two-wheeled pony traps drawn by small horses descended from Spanish stallions and mares that roamed wild on Georgia's coastal islands.

"The roads are made of crushed shells," Geoffrey told Prudence, leaning in closer than he really needed to. "Mostly oyster shells because they don't shatter into powder as easily as the others."

"They're noisy," she said, unfurling her ivory-handled silk parasol against a blindingly bright sun. "Tell me again about the Sea Islands."

"They've always been a culture apart," Geoffrey began. "A world of rice and cotton and indigo fields separated from the mainland. Subject only to their own laws and customs. Or so Sea Islanders would have you believe. Most of the plantation owners fled before Sherman marched through Georgia. They came back when President Andrew Johnson's pardon made it possible to reclaim the property they'd abandoned."

"Did the pardon include your family in North Carolina?"

Geoffrey could seldom be persuaded to talk about the South he'd left as a young man and didn't return to help rebuild.

"It did." He turned his head to make the wide-brimmed hat he wore shade his face, speaking so softly that his answer was almost lost under the crunch of spoked wooden wheels over oyster shells.

"I didn't intend to pry," Prudence apologized. "And I really only meant for you to tell me what you could about the background of the family Eleanor is marrying into." She'd had very little opportunity for private conversation with her friend aboard the yacht. Mrs. Dickson had seemed determined to stay as close to her daughter as she could during these last days before the wedding pried them apart.

"It's definite that they won't live year-round on the island.

Eleanor's father offered to buy Teddy a seat on the New York Cotton Exchange and he accepted."

"He's a lucky man. They're both lucky. To have found each other and been allowed to follow their hearts. It doesn't happen all that often in Society."

Eyes on blond Teddy and dark-haired Eleanor riding in the lead pony trap, Prudence thought them a perfectly matched couple. Thirty-two-year-old Teddy was every girl's dream of Prince Charming. Eleanor, four years younger than her fiancé, had been the acknowledged beauty of her Season. They were as at ease together as if they'd known each other all their lives instead of slightly more than seven months.

"There it is! There's Seapoint!" Eleanor called out, flourishing her parasol.

The narrow road winding through thickets of scrub live oak opened onto a broad expanse of green lawn. Before them rose the forty-room mansion Eleanor's father had designed to compete with what the Carnegies had built on Cumberland Island. It was as if someone had lifted one of the extravagant stone mansions from New York City's Fifth Avenue and set it down intact in a far different clime and era.

It didn't belong, but it was magnificent, a mass of heavy red brick and gray granite, turrets and chimneys soaring into the sky. Round-topped windows marched across the expanse of its two main stories, attic bedrooms for the staff tucked beneath sharply angled gables. Enclosed by high stone walls pierced by a tall, arched gate, Seapoint sat splendidly alone and aloof. It both beckoned and repelled, too bulky, dark, and sinister for a sun-kissed island, yet somehow the perfect expression of the new wealth that had created it.

"It's not what I expected," Prudence breathed. She had imagined white verandas and peacocks strutting beneath ancient trees hung with Spanish moss. Something out of the antebellum South of before the war, the way it had been captured in hundreds of images taken by itinerant photographers.

Geoffrey shrugged. "There's not much left of what was here before. The South is having to reinvent itself. The Sea Islands are becoming the winter playground of people like J. P. Morgan, the Carnegies and Rockefellers, the Vanderbilts and Dicksons."

"You don't sound sad about losing the past."

"It's not being lost, Prudence. Don't ever mislead yourself into thinking the South has accepted defeat. What I meant by reinventing itself is that there will be no fundamental changes to the way Southerners think and feel, but they're smart enough to have learned that survival means living behind a mask of polite deception. It's something we've always been expert at doing."

"*We*? I've never heard you talk this way, Geoffrey."

"Coming home does strange things to a man," he murmured.

Prudence's room opened onto a covered porch that stretched across the entire second floor of the mansion on its ocean side, which, she was informed, was really the back of the house. She barely had time to appreciate the view before Eleanor insisted on strolling out to the extensive rose garden heavily mulched with what looked like seaweed, adamant that Geoffrey not accompany them. It was an odd thing to do, almost as strange as Teddy's departure as soon as the pony traps had been unloaded.

"They're expecting me home at Wildacre," he'd apologized, declaring himself reluctant to leave Eleanor's company, but bound to honor an obligation. "I wish I could stay longer, but I'll be back tomorrow. I promise we'll have time together before the family dinner." He'd lingered over his fiancée's hand, then mounted his horse and ridden off with only a single backward glance.

"Father wanted the front entrance to be a grand sweep into the grounds," Eleanor explained as she and Prudence walked. "No tea tents or lawn tennis courts to mar the effect."

"It's a beautiful setting," Prudence said, breathing as deeply as her tightly laced corset would allow. The sea breezes brought a scent and taste of salt to air that grew increasingly thick and cloying the farther away from the ocean they went. Shell pathways had been laid out down to the shore and toward white stone benches at the edge of the live oak forest bordering the emerald lawns. Eleanor had already warned her not to ramble alone in the beckoning shade of the oddly twisted trees shaped by decades of strong Atlantic winds.

"Snakes are everywhere." Her friend shuddered delicately. "Rattlers, water moccasins, corals . . . and those are just the venomous ones." She gathered her skirts around her ankles. "There's a children's rhyme to remind you how to identify a coral snake, but I can never remember it."

"I'll stay on the paths," Prudence promised. The only snakes she'd ever seen had been behind glass at the Central Park Zoo. She thought she wouldn't mind not encountering one at closer range.

Eleanor stopped abruptly, then turned and grasped Prudence's arm with fingers that gripped convulsively. "This is why I brought you out here," she said, her voice trembling on the brink of panic. "Do you feel it, Prudence?"

"Feel what?"

"Eyes watching us. From somewhere deep among the trees. I've tried to find whoever it is, but I've never been able to see anyone. The undergrowth is too dense."

"I don't understand, Eleanor."

"Neither do I. Not really. But whenever I'm here, I can't shake the feeling that I'm being watched. It's happened more than once. At first, I thought it was my imagination, so I tried to ignore it. But this past winter, after Teddy and I began spending time together, the feeling grew much stronger. It frightened me."

"Have you talked to him about it?"

"I know what he'd say. That I'm a little Yankee gal who's afraid of snakes and wild pigs and raccoons and bobcats and everything else he grew up with. He loves this island, Prudence.

It's where his family put down roots when the first Bennett came over from England. He won't want to admit there's anything sinister or menacing about it."

"Geoffrey said you'll be living in New York after the wedding."

"It's a sacrifice on Teddy's part. Don't think I don't appreciate how hard it's going to be for him. But we'll still come to Bradford Island in the winter. He's not giving it up forever."

"You're shaking, Eleanor."

"Please tell me you feel it, Prudence. Please tell me I'm not letting my nerves or prewedding jitters get the better of me."

"Who do you think is watching you?" Prudence asked. She placed her hand over Eleanor's, shocked at how cold her friend's fingers felt. It was as though all the warm blood had drained out of them. Maybe if she could get her to talk about her fears, she'd see how groundless they were. From what Prudence had observed of Teddy Bennett while he was courting Eleanor in New York, he was deeply in love with her. "Teddy wouldn't bring you to a place where harm could come to you. You know he wouldn't."

"It's not Teddy I'm afraid of. He's not the one spying on me."

"Who, then?"

Eleanor didn't answer immediately. Her eyes flicked toward the live oak forest, then back to the wind-buffeted roses. "I don't know," she whispered. "Just that something or someone on this island doesn't want me here. Don't laugh, Prudence, please. You're the only one I can trust to take me seriously. Please tell me you feel it, also. I haven't said anything to anyone else. Especially not Teddy. I don't want him to be disappointed in me."

"Nothing you could do would make him think less of you. He loves you, Eleanor."

"I know. But he also secretly believes that someday I'll agree to live permanently on the island with him. To raise our children here and grow old together. My father has convinced him that he'll make his fortune in New York, but I understand Teddy better than he thinks I do. Savannah has a new Cotton Exchange. Nothing has been decided, but Teddy wouldn't have mentioned it if he weren't already contemplating an eventual move there. He tells me that Savannah is a very old and beautiful city. General Sherman occupied it briefly, but it wasn't burned the way Atlanta was. New York is a stepping stone toward what he really wants."

"Which is?"

"The Bennetts of Bradford Island restored to everything they were before the war."

"All the more reason for them to welcome you." It would be indelicate to hint that the Dickson wealth had in any way enhanced the bride-to-be's attractiveness, but Prudence knew more than most young women about marriages of convenience. "Tomorrow morning, before the day gets too warm, you and I will follow that path we saw Teddy ride away on. Who knows? We might even meet him on his way here."

"It's cool and very mysterious in the live oaks," Eleanor said wistfully. "I used to walk there often the first winter after the house was completed. Before I met Teddy, before I started feeling eyes watching me."

"Squirrels and raccoons," Prudence said decisively, "and perhaps one or two of those ponies that have run wild."

"Do you really think so?"

"The wedding is in a few days, Eleanor. That's more than enough to have on your mind. You don't need ghosts in the forest to put bags under your eyes."

"Ghosts?"

"Demons, phantoms, will-o'-the-wisps. Whatever you want to call them. Teddy loves you and you love him. Nothing else matters."

"Prudence?"

"Yes?"

"I don't feel them anymore. The eyes. They're gone." Eleanor squeezed Prudence's hand gratefully. "I don't know what you did, but the eyes aren't there any longer."

And please God they stay away, Prudence thought.

Even though she didn't for one moment believe that Eleanor was in any danger, she decided to tell Geoffrey about this oddly disturbing conversation. Pinkertons, even ex-Pinkertons, were famous for chasing down the wildest rumors and most unlikely situations.

No questions left unanswered, no bugaboos unexorcised.

"Does she have any notion of who might be spying on her?" Geoffrey asked that evening. They were strolling on the beach in the twilight, walking off the last rolling gait of their sea legs.

"None at all." Prudence was surprised by how solemnly he had taken Eleanor's fantasy of eyes peering out at her from the live oak forest. Prudence herself didn't doubt the feeling was real, but she could not read menace into it. Eleanor, she believed, had allowed herself to become fearful not so much of marriage itself as of the new world in which her fiancé had grown up but to which she was a stranger. She'd said it herself—prewedding jitters.

"There's bound to be curiosity about the newest Bennett bride," Geoffrey mused.

"Children hiding in the trees?"

"More likely some of the ex-slaves who remained on the island after the war and continued working Bennett land. It's happened all over the South. They get a shack, a bag of beans, and a few coins if they're lucky. Almost as though they'd never been freed."

"Surely not." Prudence knew next to nothing about the lives of men and women who worked from sunup to sundown to put a crust of bread in their children's mouths and a patchwork of rags on their backs. She'd grown up in a household of well-paid and well-treated servants whose loyalty to her family was real and unquestioned. Casually cruel exploitation on a grand scale was something she had never witnessed and could not imagine.

"Eleanor's father bought the island with the express intention of building an estate on it that would rival anything his competitors could come up with. This mania for constructing Fifth Avenue palaces has infected the entire Four Hundred. New York City isn't big enough for them anymore."

Prudence rarely questioned Geoffrey's arsenal of knowledge. His network of acquaintances and informants was both broad and deep, his encyclopedia of facts seemingly boundless. "What does that have to do with what Eleanor believes is happening to her?"

"Only that when Philip Dickson purchased Bradford Island, he took advantage of the near-bankruptcy of the family that had owned it for over a hundred years. Plenty of other Southerners reclaimed the lands that were confiscated from them during the war. By hard work they'll manage to hold on to them this time and eventually edge their way back to prosperity. It was unfortunate for the Bennett family that their fate fell into the hands of Teddy's father. He's the worst kind of Southerner, Prudence. A man who believes as firmly in his right to do nothing for the people who depend on him as he does in the sun's promise to rise in the east every morning." Geoffrey paused for a moment. "I asked a few questions before we left New York."

Of course he had.

"The single concession Philip Dickson agreed to was that the Bennett family would be allowed to continue to live at Wildacre for as long as they could pay the taxes on it. If they ever fail to meet that obligation, the plantation house and its immediate acreage will devolve to Dickson for whatever sum is due. It was a crafty bargain on Dickson's part."

"And Wildacre is far enough away so the two families never have to lay eyes on one another?"

"On the far northern shore of the island."

"Out of sight, out of mind," Prudence said. "Except that when Eleanor's father began to build his mansion, they had to be curious."

"It's not every day a rich Yankee invades with money instead of an army."

She hadn't expected the bitterness that soured his voice and darkened his eyes to unreadable black pits.

"I'd say every man, woman, and child on the island is obsessed with the Yankee bride. Think about it for a moment, Prudence. They all know she's her father's only child, and that Philip Dickson is not a young man. Sooner rather than later she'll be mistress of Bradford Island, but as a Bennett. Like you, I don't think she's in any danger, but I do believe she's going to have to get used to spending her every waking moment under constant scrutiny."

"Poor Eleanor. I don't think I could stand it."

CHAPTER 2

❧

Prudence slept late but fitfully the night after the Dicksons entertained Teddy Bennett's family for dinner at Seapoint. She'd had enough wine to doze off quickly when she climbed into bed shortly before eleven o'clock, but it was also enough to wake her several times out of restless dreaming. Once she thought she heard voices echoing through the night air, but she couldn't make out who they might be, and finally decided they existed only in her tense, restive mind.

She coaxed herself back to sleep by picturing Eleanor in her wedding gown, a stunning confection of white silk and Valenciennes lace, the veil so light and fine it would float cloudlike around the bride's delicate features as she walked toward her groom. They'd had such a wonderful time together during the fittings, as seam by seam and layer by layer the dress became exactly what Eleanor envisioned. Prudence hadn't had to exaggerate when she told her friend she had never seen anything more beautiful.

When the knocking on her bedroom door woke her, Prudence couldn't at first remember where she was. Strong morning sunlight streamed across her bed and a breeze of sea salt and honeysuckle perfumed the air. From off in the distance came the rhythmic swooshing sound of a rotary mower making its way back and forth through the lush green grass of the rear lawn. Then she remembered. Geoffrey had said they would scythe or mow the grass a full two days before the wedding. Any closer to the date and clouds of mosquitos and midges would be buzzing and biting around their ankles as they processed across the new stubble to the stone chapel where Eleanor and Teddy were to say their vows.

"Prudence?" Eleanor's mother stepped hesitantly into the room. "Aren't you girls awake yet? It's nearly eight o'clock."

"I'm sorry, Mrs. Dickson. I must have overslept. Too much good company last night." Prudence struggled to sit up, unbraided hair tumbling over her shoulders.

"Isn't Eleanor with you? She's not in her bed. I thought for sure she'd come in to spend a girls' night giggling and gossiping until dawn." Abigail Dickson frowned and set down the jewelry box she carried. She walked across the room and out onto the covered porch, shading her eyes against the sun. "Eleanor!" she called, twirling left and then right to sight down the length of the second-floor veranda. "She knows I don't like her to walk on the beach alone without first telling someone where she's going."

A maid carrying a morning tray of hot coffee and biscuits wrapped in a white linen napkin edged through the open bedroom door.

"Never mind," Abigail Dickson said. "You and I can have a nice chat while we're waiting." She poured coffee into two gold-rimmed cups while the maid helped Prudence into her dressing gown. "That's all for now, Lilah. You can come back later to dress Miss Prudence."

The maid closed the door softly behind her.

It was on the tip of Prudence's tongue to tell Eleanor's mother that she hadn't seen her daughter since they'd parted in the hallway late last night, but she caught herself in time. Wherever her friend had gone this morning she'd obviously wanted a few private moments before being engulfed once again in last-minute wedding preparations.

And Eleanor certainly deserved it. She'd smiled and nodded her way through a dinner that Prudence had found increasingly uncomfortable as course succeeded course and the conversation faltered and grew progressively more stilted and constrained. Teddy's two younger sisters, both unmarried and edging into irreversible spinsterhood, had seemed so awed by their surroundings that they'd said very little and rarely lifted their eyes from their plates. His father and younger brother radiated a subdued anger that seethed closer to the surface of their self-control with every glass of wine they drank. By the time the ladies adjourned to the parlor, leaving the men to their brandy and cigars, Prudence had exhausted her reserve of politely inoffensive topics. Fortunately, Abigail Dickson could chatter on for hours about absolutely nothing.

Now she was holding out the black velvet jewelry case she'd carried into the room. "This is what my beautiful Eleanor will wear with her wedding gown," she said, opening the case to display a many-coiled rope of matched pearls nestled around a large diamond clasp. "They belonged to my mother and my grandmother before her. They each wore them on their wedding day, and so did I. Now it's Eleanor's turn." Tears sparkled in Abigail's eyes. She dashed them away with a lace-trimmed handkerchief and spilled the pearls out onto the small table at which they'd sat to drink their coffee. The diamond clasp flashed like lightning as it caught the brilliant Georgia sunlight.

"They're magnificent," Prudence declared, running a forefinger along the strand of satiny white pearls.

"And this is for you, my dear," Abigail said, handing a small robin egg blue Tiffany box to Prudence. "Your maid of honor gift, but also an expression of our appreciation for the years of friendship you and Eleanor have shared. Open it."

A pair of exquisite pearl and diamond earrings twinkled up at Prudence. Tears misted her vision.

"We're a sight, aren't we?" Abigail laughed, handkerchief to her eyes again. "I'm so happy for her." Unspoken was the apprehension every mother felt on handing her daughter over to a husband whose control of her would go unchallenged once the vows were exchanged. "Her father and I couldn't have found Eleanor a better husband if we'd picked him out ourselves."

Prudence glanced toward the door leading onto the porch, sipped her coffee, and wondered where Eleanor had gone. And why. Two days ago she'd been afraid of unfriendly eyes watching her from the live oaks. Had something changed? Something happened that she hadn't shared with her friend? Surely, she wouldn't have walked into that forest of misshapen trees by herself? Not in the dark, and not this morning, either, Prudence decided. She was probably on the beach, just as Abigail had said, out of sight from the house, tiptoeing barefoot through the shallows.

Prudence decided to do her best to distract Eleanor's mother until her errant daughter returned. "You're certainly responsible for their having met."

"I suppose you're right. If Philip hadn't bought Bradford Island as a place to get away from the dreadful New York winter, they might never have been introduced. Not that they ever were, of course. Properly introduced, I mean. I'm sure Eleanor has told you the story." Without waiting for an answer, Abigail trilled on. "Philip hadn't met any of the Bennetts during the negotiations for the sale of the island. Hadn't wanted to, actually, since their situation was precarious."

"Bankrupt, is what Eleanor said."

"My dear husband does not get enjoyment from the spectacle of another man's misfortune," Abigail explained. "So he left everything to the lawyers and the bankers."

Geoffrey had had a harsher and more realistic opinion of why the transaction was handled the way it was. In his view, when men like Philip Dickson reached a certain pinnacle of financial power they preferred hiring surrogates to do the type of wrangling, bargaining, and other dirty work that had gotten them where they were in the first place.

"Eleanor has always loved to ride. She's in Central Park nearly every morning when the weather is fine. So one of the things her father impressed on the architects was the necessity to have decent stables large enough for riding stock as well as carriage horses. You should have heard the arguments, Prudence. I hardly understood a word of them myself, but Eleanor and her father knew exactly what was needed." Abigail paused for a breath and a sip of coffee.

"We visited the stables yesterday," Prudence said, thinking that was another answer to where Eleanor might have gone this morning. If she wasn't on the beach, she'd probably ridden out just as the sun was coming up. "They're as spectacular as everything else on the estate."

"Except for the wretched insects." Abigail shuddered. "It's all right as long as there's a good breeze blowing in from the ocean, but when the wind shifts or drops entirely, they're unbearable."

"You were telling me how Eleanor and Teddy met." Prudence wondered how different Mrs. Dickson's version would be from what her friend had already confided.

"So romantic. And very inappropriate. Eleanor had gone out before breakfast and refused to allow one of the grooms to accompany her. She'd ridden along the shore and at some point decided she wanted to wade in the ocean. So she dismounted, took off her boots, and walked along in the surf. But she hadn't knotted the reins around her hand. When something spooked her horse, off it went. She said it bolted so quickly and galloped so fast she hadn't a prayer of catching up to it. Being Eleanor, she continued walking along the sand in her bare feet. Can you imagine, Prudence?"

"I can."

Eleanor had a way of ignoring convention when it suited her that was both engaging and slightly scandalous. It was one of the traits the two young women shared that endeared them to each other.

"When Teddy came along leading her horse behind him, she didn't know who he was, of course. But by the time he'd accompanied her safely to the house they were talking a blue streak and laughing to beat the band. He was the first Bennett any of us had ever met."

Absent from Abigail's tale was Eleanor's account of a wild, splashing ride through Atlantic shallows, horses and riders alike glorying in the speed of the run and the feel of the spray against their skin.

"And then he followed her to New York," Prudence prompted.

"He did. We went back early, before Christmas, because it was obvious what his intentions were, long before he declared them. Philip was opposed to the match for various reasons I shan't go into, and he thought if he separated them, especially during the height of the social season, Eleanor would forget all about this odd Southerner. And he her. But they refused to remain apart. Before we knew it, Teddy was at our door, making his case for why he should be allowed to court our precious daughter. He was persistent, and eventually he won Philip over. Or rather, Eleanor did. She's always been able to wrap her father around her little finger." Abigail took a sip of cold coffee and grimaced. "Now I'm starting to get just the least little bit annoyed," she said, sweeping the rope of pearls into its velvet-covered case. She stepped out onto the veranda again, searching the beach for a slender figure dawdling along the shore.

Trying not to be obvious about it, Prudence looked quickly for a note that might have been slipped under her door or left on her dressing table when, she presumed, Eleanor decided not to wake her before going out. Nothing. "I'm sure she'll be back any moment now."

Abigail, a distracted frown puckering her forehead, patted her on the arm as she left the room.

The maid who brought a pitcher of hot water for her morning wash a few minutes later found Prudence already dressed, hair tidied into a loose bun, boots buttoned, sunhat in hand.

The maid wasn't sure, but yes, she thought Mr. Hunter might still be in the breakfast room.

Prudence sped down the stairs with the agility born of having left her hated stays on the floor of the armoire.

Eleanor's mother had said she was growing annoyed, but Prudence had begun to worry.

"You don't suppose something's happened to her, Geoffrey?"

"We'll start in the stables," he answered. "You're certain her bed hasn't been slept in? She didn't just pull the covers up herself this morning?"

"I checked before coming downstairs," Prudence told him, waving off the plate of scrambled eggs he held out to her. "The covers look just the way mine did last night. Turned down neatly, ready to climb into. But nobody slept in them. I'm sure of it. Her night clothes were folded over the back of a chair, slippers laid out in front of them."

"And you don't think Mrs. Dickson noticed that?"

Prudence shook her head. "I think she poked her head in the doorway, saw the bed was empty, and assumed Eleanor had come to my room. I don't believe she took the time to wonder if there was another possibility."

"Could she have slipped away to meet Teddy?"

Prudence thought for a moment, then shook her head. "Not in the middle of the night. Eleanor can be impulsive, but she wouldn't do anything that might worry either of her parents."

"Perhaps she was having second thoughts about the wedding. Decided to go somewhere quiet where no one would think of looking for her until she worked it out."

"She would have said something to me. And she wouldn't have left the grounds in the dark by herself. She really believed there was someone, or several someones, watching her. Spying on her from the live oaks. I wish you could have seen her face when she asked if I felt their eyes on me, too. She was frightened of those woods, Geoffrey."

"Then your first guess is probably the right one. She's gone out for an early morning ride and probably assumed she'd be back before anyone in the family was awake and up. The horse could have gone lame, she might have been thrown, or she's just lost track of time." Geoffrey smiled reassuringly at her.

By the time they stepped out onto the flagstone terrace on the ocean side of Seapoint, Prudence almost believed him.

The stable hand who was mucking out the stalls was positive Miss Eleanor hadn't been there that morning. "No, sir," he said, leading them to where her mare stood placidly pulling fresh hay from its feed box. "This horse ain't been out yet today."

The perfectly groomed animal bore no traces of a late night or early morning ride, hide gleaming from the curry comb, hoofs devoid of caked-on mud, mane lying flat and unsnarled against its neck.

Geoffrey didn't ask if any other horses were missing, but Prudence watched his eyes sweep across the row of boxed stalls, then return to meet hers. It was too early to pose the kind of questions that might set the staff to gossiping about why Miss Eleanor wasn't where she was supposed to be. And where she'd gotten herself off to.

"She's on foot, wherever she is," Geoffrey said, leading Prudence back across the wide sweep of lawn.

"The chapel?" It seemed far-fetched, but it was the only place outside the house Prudence could think of where Eleanor might feel safe. "If you're right, Geoffrey, and she started having bridal jitters after spending the evening with those horrible

Bennetts, perhaps she went out to the chapel to work out how she was going to put up with them and eventually fell asleep on one of the pews."

"It's certainly worth a look."

"If she's not there we may have to alert the household to search for her," Prudence said grimly.

"Her mother will do that for us," Geoffrey said. "I'm surprised she's waited this long."

They hurried along one of the white shell paths toward a tiny gray stone chapel nestled beneath two magnificent oak trees planted at least seventy-five years before the first brick was laid for Seapoint. Though the chapel itself was newly built, the low stone wall surrounding it had been constructed of the rubble discovered when the foundation was dug.

Geoffrey pushed open the arched wooden door and stepped inside, Prudence close behind him. Last night's cool lingered inside the thick walls, making her wish she'd thought to bring a shawl. If Eleanor had indeed fallen asleep there, she'd be chilled through.

"Eleanor?" Prudence's voice echoed into the miniature gothic arches above them. No more than a dozen wooden pews stretched on either side of the short aisle down which Eleanor would soon walk. The wood had been freshly waxed and polished; stacks of white ribboned bows and boxes of white candles lay on the rearmost seat.

But of Eleanor there was neither sight nor sound.

"She hasn't been here," Geoffrey said after a quick walk to the altar and back. Prudence knew he was looking for anything her friend might have dropped or forgotten, any clue that might indicate her presence, however brief. His features tightened the way they always did when he was about to decide that an otherwise unexceptional situation was turning serious.

"Should we walk along the shoreline?" Prudence asked. "There's a log just above the high tide mark not too far from here where she told me she likes to sit and look at the water."

"Let's take one of the dogs," Geoffrey said as they headed back toward the stable yard.

He whistled to a black lab lying on the sun-warmed bricks. The animal shook itself awake and then loped off ahead of them down the path to the beach.

"I don't have anything with her scent on it," Prudence said quietly. "I didn't think it would come to this."

"Never mind," Geoffrey reassured her. "The dog knows her. If he picks up a fresh trail and there's anything suspicious about it, he'll alert us. Labs are as intelligent as they come."

Prudence suddenly went cold with fear of what they might be about to discover.

CHAPTER 3

Teddy and Lawrence Bennett rode horseback from Wildacre to Seapoint, leading an unmounted search party of field hands and house servants along the shoreline and through once fertile fields now overgrown with saw palmetto, seedling pines, dwarf wax myrtle, and wiregrass. The searchers carried machetes to cut through undergrowth and billhooks to pull aside thorny branches and lop off snake heads. Most of them walked barefoot; May was a warm month and new shoe leather a rare and expensive commodity on the island.

"Mark my words," Lawrence Bennett said as they approached the mansion, "we are wasting our time. That Eleanor of yours is going to materialize out of the woods and have a good laugh at our expense." Younger than Teddy by sixteen months, he was close enough in looks to his brother that people meeting the Bennett boys for the first time often mistook them for twins. They were handsome men, tall and slender, with lightly bronzed southern skin, thick blond hair, and eyes as blue as the water surrounding the island on which they'd grown up.

"She's missing, Lawrence," Teddy snapped. "This isn't a prank. She doesn't know the island as we do." It tore at his heart to imagine Eleanor lost and fighting her way through the live oaks, sobbing from fear and frustration in the overgrown woods. Worst of all, if she'd gotten that far, were the interior marshlands where wiregrass flayed bare skin to ribbons. He could only imagine her horror if she stumbled into the dark brown waters of the swamp where alligators and water moccasins glided through a wasteland of rotting tree trunks. Bradford Island looked like a paradise from afar, but its reality was dangerous and unforgiving.

Philip Dickson had ordered every horse in his stable saddled and every man on the place to report to the back lawn. When he gave the command, they would form a long line and move slowly forward into the live oaks. Faces studiously impassive, those who had participated in similar searches in the past knew the chances of finding Miss Eleanor alive and unhurt after a night in the wild were slim to nonexistent. Only the grim, determined expression on her father's face kept them from voicing their worst fears.

"Stay within sight and earshot," Geoffrey cautioned Prudence, who had insisted on donning her riding habit and joining the front rank of horsemen leading the walkers through the woods. "Whatever you do and whatever you see, don't dismount until you've signaled the rest of us to join you. Wait until I get there." He was thinking of panthers and wild boar who fed on whatever fallen prey they came upon.

Prudence nodded, but didn't trust herself to speak. She knew the dreadful scenes he was conjecturing and was doing everything she could to dismiss them from her mind. Despite the misgivings she could sense all around her, she was trying to believe that Eleanor would be found safe and sound. In two days' time, wearing silk, Valenciennes lace, and ancestral pearls, she would become Teddy Bennett's bride. To admit to anything else was unthinkable. Holding her head high, Prudence forced herself to smile reassuringly at Abigail Dickson, whose stricken face was almost too painful to look at.

They set out shortly before noon, the horse brigade first, followed by a pack of hunting dogs and their trainers, last of all the walkers. The live oak forest was eerily silent, its host of creatures retreated into burrow, thicket, and den. Even the birds that normally flitted noisily from tree to tree remained hidden. The only sound was the soft thud of horses' hooves and the occasional muffled curse of a searcher who stumbled or was raked by thorns. The air was still and densely humid; sweat streaked every forehead.

At Geoffrey's suggestion, Prudence had tied a piece of mosquito netting across her face, fastening it to the black velvet English riding helmet she wore. Within minutes of entering the woods, masses of tiny insects and whining mosquitoes buzzed before her eyes, seeking moisture and blood. Waving a hand through the cloud was of little or no use. She held her breath for as long as she could, and eventually, when it couldn't reach her skin, the swarm thinned out. Eleanor, when they found her, would be covered with bites and stings. Prudence forced back a shudder and trained her eyes on the foliage through which she was passing. Geoffrey had said to watch for the tiniest thread that might have gotten snagged on a branch. She prayed that her friend had put on one of the light-colored dresses they'd packed for wearing in Georgia's warm springtime weather.

After the first hour, water carriers went from horse to horse, dog to dog, and man to man, their bottles and jugs still cool from Seapoint's deep well. Despite the urgency of the search, animals and humans alike had to pause regularly to rest if they were to last long enough to ensure success. A thin hum of conversation rose over the panting of dogs and the snorting of horses, but there was no good news to exchange. No one had seen a footprint or a hastily broken twig or branch. Nothing that might have belonged to Eleanor had fallen to the ground or been caught in a bush or shrub. The dogs hadn't picked up her scent. Yet she had to have come this way. Seapoint and its grounds and beach had been minutely searched. There was no other place on the island for her to go.

When they reached the marsh, the riders dismounted and handed their horses over to a pair of stable boys who would remain behind with them. The wiregrass grew so thickly on the flats that an animal's flanks would be sliced and bloodied before it managed to get halfway across.

Rifles were pulled from saddle scabbards and extra ammunition tucked into jacket pockets. Though Prudence had never fired anything larger than the derringer she sometimes carried in her reticule, Geoffrey had insisted she not go unarmed. Now he broke open the rifle and slipped it into the crook of her arm. Even though he smiled reassuringly, it still felt heavy and awkward. She hoped she wouldn't have to use it.

Prudence had never experienced anything like the swamp that stretched for miles in the deep interior of Bradford Island. Draperies of Spanish moss ghosted from shaggy cedars and gnarled live oaks through ground fog rising above still, dark waters where here and there a thick, rotting trunk broke the surface. Until she looked again and realized she was seeing an alligator lying in wait for unwary fish or careless frogs. Even islanders who had lived all their lives in close proximity to the beasts paused respectfully before making their way along the narrow ridges that were the only safe places to walk.

"Stay close to me, Prudence," Geoffrey said, "and watch your footing."

She felt off balance clutching the heavy rifle, but she was determined to keep the place she'd claimed as the only woman in the search party. Philip Dickson had dropped to the rear, his age and unfamiliarity with the terrain working against him. Teddy and his brother Lawrence led the way, leaping nimbly across tussocks of swamp grass to the firmer ground of small hammocks and the occasional deer walk. The afternoon sun slanted through the trees, glinting off the water, highlighting brilliant green fern banks and the deadly white of poisonous mushroom gills. It was a world of enchantment, except that the magic conjured up evil instead of wonder.

The searchers spread out as widely as they could, careful to keep within sight of one another. Occasionally either Teddy or Lawrence would raise his rifle high in the air, signaling silence. Everyone stood stock still to listen for a cry of distress. But time after time, they heard nothing.

"We brought torches," Geoffrey told Prudence at the end of one of their halts. "But I doubt they'll do us much good after dark if Eleanor is unconscious."

"How could this have happened, Geoffrey? They were so happy together, she and Teddy. What on earth made her sneak off somewhere on her own and not tell anyone where she was going? I was in the room right next to hers. She could have talked to me if something was wrong. I would have understood. I would have tried to help her."

"It's not your fault, Prudence. I remember your saying once that Eleanor often acted impulsively. I think we just have to accept that this time she made a very, very bad decision."

"But you haven't given up hope of finding her?"

"No, of course not. This is an island. We'll find her."

It was Lawrence who led them to the body.

He signaled Geoffrey to join him before Teddy, Prudence, and Eleanor's father realized what he had found.

"Keep them back," he ordered the searchers as Geoffrey hurried to his side.

Hands reached out to bar the way. The hounds whined and crouched on the wet ground. Two of the trackers rushed forward carrying a collapsible canvas stretcher.

Eleanor lay half submerged in brackish swamp water, her clothing filthy with mud. When they turned her over, Geoffrey quickly laid his handkerchief across her face. No one, especially those who loved her, should have to look at her as she was now.

Abigail Dickson's fierce self-control broke down when the search party emerged from the live oak forest bearing a stretcher on which lay the sheet-wrapped body of the swamp's latest victim. A mother's howl of pain and denial rang through the twilight mists rolling in from the Atlantic across white sand beaches and meticulously tended lawn, sending chills up the spines of those who heard it.

Her lady's maid and the housekeeper caught her as she fell. The two women supported their mistress into the house and up the staircase to the bedroom that overlooked the chapel where Eleanor was to have been married. Laudanum sent her into a deep sleep from which she would not awaken until morning. It was the only thing they could do for her.

Philip Dickson dismounted from his horse like a man gravely wounded. He, too, was caught in arms that held him up as he stumbled into the mansion built at least in part to showcase his daughter's beauty. She'd been a princess in a modern castle. Now she was a casual fatality he could not bear to contemplate.

"I'll see to her, Mr. Dickson," Prudence promised. She wasn't sure Eleanor's father understood what she meant; his eyes had glazed over and the features of his face sagged. She meant she would prepare her friend's body for burial, would do her best to make her presentable for a final viewing before the coffin lid was nailed down. Somehow, though she knew it was likely to break her heart, she knew she would. She had been preparing herself for it all during the long ride back to Seapoint. Such an intimate task could not be given to anyone who loved her less than a close friend.

"I've ordered them to take her to the wine cellar," Geoffrey said. He would not leave Prudence's side until she'd completed what she had to do, even though she had argued that his presence would be unseemly. "It's cool and private," he explained. "They'll bring warm water from the kitchen, and one of the maids will fetch whatever clothing you choose for her to wear."

"The wedding dress and veil," Prudence said automatically. They would go into the ground with the bride who never was, the only fitting destiny for garments selected with so much hope for the future.

Prudence followed the stretcher down into the damp cold of Seapoint's dark basement, refusing to leave Eleanor's body even to change out of her riding habit and boots. Lanterns were lit and hung from hooks in the ceiling, where they burned with a soft, hissing sound. When buckets of warm water, cakes of perfumed soap, and baskets of soft cloths had been brought to the wine cellar, she swallowed the hot, strong coffee Geoffrey insisted she drink. He'd laced it with bourbon to make the task before her easier to bear.

"Philip Dickson was one of my father's closest friends," Prudence informed him as they waited. "I don't remember if I told you that. He brought Eleanor to the house when my mother died. I was six; she was fourteen. She came every day for weeks, even after my mother's sister had arrived from England. Eleanor held me while I wept, played dolls and make-believe for hours on end, took me to the park when no one else could interest me in going out. She was the big sister I never had. I clung to her friendship for years afterward. I don't know how she put up with me, but she did. Even when she came out in Society she made room for me by her side. Not literally, of course, but by sharing all the excitement of her first season. Everyone thought she would be among the earliest of her group to marry, but she told me once that she didn't think she would ever fall in love."

"I think your Eleanor was that rare kind of woman who refuses to settle for second-best," Geoffrey said.

"She was. After she met Teddy, it became him or no one."

"I wonder how much of that devotion he's reciprocated," Geoffrey said.

"You mean because she was an heiress?"

He shrugged his shoulders. "I don't suppose we'll ever know. Not now. Men of our class aren't permitted to show their emotions."

He stood back from the body as a maid appeared with the dress and veil Prudence had called for. Another maid carried Eleanor's lace-trimmed undergarments, stockings, and white satin wedding slippers. A third had assembled lotions and powders, brushes and combs, scissors and files to manicure the dead woman's nails. They had not known the young mistress very long, but in the life she had lost and the children she would never bear, they were all women.

Geoffrey closed the door softly behind them. He crossed to where Prudence stood beside the decanting table on which Eleanor had been placed, still in her makeshift shroud. Touching Prudence's arm lightly, he placed his other hand on the body.

"Shall we begin?"

They cut off her clothing with a pair of silver sewing scissors, washing each limb with warm water and scented soap before proceeding to the next. The body that slowly emerged from the stained sheets in which it had been wrapped bore less evidence of Eleanor's ordeal than Prudence expected. It was as though her friend had been transported to the spot where she died, making little or no contact with the wiregrass through which she must have stumbled, though somewhere along the way she'd lost her shoes, and her stockings were in tatters.

"Could she have been on horseback most of the way?" Prudence asked, drying and powdering her friend's feet. They were scratched and bitten, but not the feet of someone who had run for miles over bramble-infested and sawgrass-covered terrain.

"The stable hand we talked to said every horse was in its stall this morning. If she did ride as far as the swamp, it wasn't on a Seapoint mount," Geoffrey said.

"What you mean is that I shouldn't jump to conclusions." Prudence hesitated before revealing more of Eleanor's body.

"Not yet."

Geoffrey's voice was so neutral and uninflected that she knew he would not be seeing her friend shamefully naked. What would lie before him, under the impartial gaze of his Pinkerton training, would be the corpse of a stranger. His compassion would not be tinged with the ordinary feelings of a man for a woman. It was both comforting and strengthening. When they finished with her, Eleanor would be herself again, but along that journey she would of necessity be someone else. It blunted the agony of what Prudence had promised Philip Dickson she would do.

It wasn't until Prudence began to wash her friend's upper torso that she felt the dislocation of Eleanor's right shoulder.

"Geoffrey!" Prudence cupped her hand around the small, hard protrusion that didn't match the smooth musculature of the other shoulder. The bone seemed to be in the wrong place.

"If I hold her arm out, then pull and twist at the same time, it will slide back into the socket," Geoffrey said. He felt around the injury with both hands, careful not to perform the maneuver he had described.

"Did she fall and pass out from the pain?" Prudence asked, imagining the horror of drowning in shallow water.

"It's possible." But there was doubt in his voice. He dipped another cloth in the warm water, wrung it out, and handed it to Prudence.

They worked in silence, gently soaking and then wiping away the mud that stained Eleanor's fair skin.

"It won't all come off," Prudence said.

"It's the tannins in the swamp water," Geoffrey explained. "They leach out from the tree roots."

"Like tea leaves left lying in the bottom of a cup." Prudence remembered a childhood fascination with the art of seeing the future in the configuration of tea leaves swirled against fine china. And how easily the leaves stained if accidentally spilled onto the white cotton of a summer dress. "There. I think that's the best I can do."

Each of Eleanor's shoulders bore a faint discoloration, as though someone had poured tea on a cloth, then neglected to rinse it out. Or rubbed too hard and inadvertently made the stain worse.

Geoffrey leaned over the body and gently laid his hands on Eleanor's shoulders. The discolorations disappeared beneath his palms and outstretched fingers.

Prudence's indrawn breath was like the rasp of a saw against metal. "Someone held her beneath the water," she whispered. Then, her voice stronger. "And looked right into her face as she struggled and choked for breath. Someone watched as she died."

Geoffrey raised the sheet they had been using to cover Eleanor as they washed the body. "He straddled her, one knee on either side. But she must have fought fiercely enough to dislocate her shoulder, and in his fury, he didn't feel the bone slip out of place."

Prudence examined one of her friend's hands, then the other. What had been done to Eleanor sickened her. She could hardly see through the tears she blinked away, but she was determined not to give in to the wave of grief threatening to overwhelm her. "If she managed to scratch him, I cleaned the evidence from under her nails when I washed away the mud."

"The nails aren't broken. It happened quickly, Prudence. She probably opened her mouth to scream and breathed in as she was pushed or thrown into the water. It's a fear reflex. You gasp for air when there isn't any."

"Can we prove she was murdered, Geoffrey?"

"There aren't any marks of strangulation around her neck. Just the dislocated shoulder and the discolorations. But remember, she was facedown in less than a foot of water when we found her, shoulders pressed by the weight of her body against the mud and broken branches of the swamp bottom."

"He turned her over because he wanted it to look as though she'd fallen. As though the drowning was accidental."

"There's nothing here to prove it wasn't," Geoffrey said, his eyes fixed on Prudence's face. It was like scanning the page of a book. Everything she was thinking and feeling flitted across her features. She wasn't attempting to hide anything from him. "Picture the spot where we found her."

"It was muddy," Prudence said, closing her eyes the better to call up the scene she would see in nightmares for months to come. "She was half submerged in the water, her hair floating around her shoulders. A log lay nearby. One of her hands was stretched out as if to reach for it."

"What else?"

"I saw mud, cattails, waterlogged branches, and tree trunks." Prudence opened her eyes. "One of the men tripped on something hidden beneath the water when he helped lift her out."

"The coroner will say it was death by mischance. That Eleanor, not familiar with the swamp and probably hysterical with the fear of being lost, stumbled blindly through the muddy water until something made her lose her balance and she fell. She isn't the first to die this way and she won't be the last."

"It wasn't an accident, Geoffrey," Prudence said, determination in her voice. Her eyes flashed in the lamplight, remembering the fear in Eleanor's voice when she'd spoken of eyes watching her from the live oaks. How monstrous to have foreseen your own death and been unable to save yourself. "The only thing I don't know is who would want to kill her."

"*Cui bono?*"

"Who profits? I can't imagine anyone profiting from Eleanor's death." Prudence wiped the remaining mud from her friend's face. She had expected horror, but beneath the grime of the swamp Eleanor's features had suffered less disfigurement than Prudence had steeled herself to find. The pale, bloated skin was mottled with reddish blotches, clusters of puncture wounds, and what could only be the tiny bite marks of shallow feeding fish.

"Water moccasins," Geoffrey said. "And probably some small catfish. " He turned Eleanor over, then pressed hard against her back, kneading his fist into the base of her lungs. A trickle of dark water flowed from between her lips. He settled the body on its back and wiped the fluid from her mouth and chin. "That's evidence of drowning, nothing more."

"We'll have to tell her parents what we suspect," Prudence said. "Are there police on the island?"

"I wouldn't think so." Geoffrey shook his head. "A county sheriff on the mainland is probably the closest law enforcement. And a local doctor or justice of the peace to act as coroner whenever there's an unexplained or violent death."

"Will they take her away?" Prudence asked. She couldn't bear the thought of a stranger's indifferent eyes examining Eleanor as though she were the carcass of a slain animal. Her friend lying alone in a makeshift morgue somewhere.

"Not if the Bennetts have the kind of influence I expect they do." Geoffrey drew a clean, dry sheet up over the body, threw another one over the pile of wedding finery. "That's all we can do for now, Prudence. It's better to leave her the way she is until after the sheriff has been here."

"Will he care, Geoffrey? Will he care enough to find whoever did this?"

"Maybe, maybe not. But it doesn't matter. We care, Prudence."

I promise you, Prudence swore silently to her friend, one

hand lightly touching the sheet that concealed Eleanor from view. *I promise you we'll find whoever did this. I'm not leaving Bradford Island until we do.*

Geoffrey's hand came down softly on her own, closed around it lightly, and joined his promise to hers.

CHAPTER 4

❧

Aunt Jessa waited in the Seapoint summer kitchen while Eleanor Dickson's body was washed and readied for the grave.

The master had locked himself in his study and the housekeeper had given the mistress enough laudanum to keep her in bed until well after sunup. By which time Aunt Jessa would have seen what she came to see and done what she'd come to do.

"Won't be long now," she was told by one of the maids the housekeeper sent scurrying from the main house to the kitchen building. The heat of roasting and baking vibrated off its brick walls and the steam of boiling pots danced in waves out the doors and windows. Open hearth kitchens were the most dangerous buildings on any southern plantation. The cooks who worked in them rolled their sleeves up as high as they would go, opened their bodices, and hitched up their skirts whenever no one was around to see and reprimand them. Their arms, legs, and chests were pockmarked with new and old burn scars. But the dishes they sent to the tables of the big house were rich, highly spiced, swimming in gravy, and delicious.

Aunt Jessa sipped a tiny cup of New Orleans coffee and

waited patiently, impervious to the noise and bustle all around her, ignoring the sidelong glances of the kitchen helpers who tried not to brush too close to her skirts as they scurried to follow Cook's orders. Nobody knew if Master Dickson would come out of his study to eat a proper dinner tonight, but the table would be laid and a meal prepared just in case. Young Miss's friend and the gentleman who'd come down from New York with her would have to be seen to in any case.

"They done," a skinny little girl announced. She hopped from one foot to the other, proud to have been given the task of informing the conjure woman that it was safe to go into the big house, jumpy as a grasshopper to be so close to a caster of spells and juju. Her eyes darted to the seagrass basket beside Aunt Jessa's rocking chair. A mat of woven swamp willow concealed the contents, but couldn't entirely mask an aroma of pungent herbs and earthy roots. She thought she detected the smell of candle wax and something dead and dried out. A frog? Was she supposed to pick up the basket and carry it inside? The housekeeper hadn't told her what else to do beyond giving her the message to deliver and a shove to start her out the door.

"Go on now, girl. You done what you sposed to." Aunt Jessa heaved her considerable bulk out of the rocking chair, chuckling as she watched the skinny little girl's legs pump her across the raked dirt yard surrounding the kitchen. She nodded her thanks to Cook for the coffee and the concealment, then picked up her basket and made her way slowly to where the housekeeper waited for her.

The narrow stairway down to the cellars was difficult to manage, but Aunt Jessa kept her eyes on the lantern held aloft by the spit boy leading the way and murmured a spell to protect herself against stumbling down it to her death. It seemed nowadays as though she lived in a cocoon of small spells, a warmly fortified place peopled by friendly spirits and the inquisitive ghosts of a host of islanders who'd passed over.

She'd never expected to live as long as she had. Despite bones that creaked and cracked in the morning and the occasional bout of forgetting who she was or where she stood, she didn't mind growing old. She had her little shack in the live oaks. There was always a spot of sunshine burning through the canopy of leaves onto the chair where she sat and rocked most afternoons.

Aunt Jessa remembered everything that had ever happened on Bradford Island. She recollected the name of every person who'd been born there, married into the place, or been bought and brought over. Black or white, it didn't matter. She knew them all.

It had been against the law to teach a slave to read and write, but Aunt Jessa had raised two generations of Bennett children, sitting quietly in a corner of the schoolroom to ensure good behavior as the youngest were introduced to their letters. None of the tutors or governesses paid her any mind. She'd absorbed every word that was spoken, every instruction on how to form the curlicue or the leaning straight line of educated handwriting, every lesson on sounding out a word until it made sense. Sometimes, when a Bennett child was slow or reluctant to learn, it was Aunt Jessa's determined coaching that saved him from a beating for laziness or stupidity. By the time the child grew up, he'd forgotten that he hadn't done it all by himself.

When freedom came, Aunt Jessa found herself too rooted in Bradford Island sand to be able to leave. She thought about it for a while, but in the end, she stayed, moving easily between the whitewashed brick walls and wide porches of Wildacre and the neat little wooden house in the live oak forest where she could breathe her own air and not have to answer to nobody. White children sat in her lap as babies, trailed at her skirts as toddlers, and brought her their troubles before they grew too self-conscious to admit to any weaknesses. When they grew up they congratulated themselves on allowing Aunt Jessa to remain part of island life after it was obvious she'd gotten too old to do much work.

What she did was preserve and pass along the secrets of the island and unlock the world of reading and writing to the young ones who wanted to learn. Every now and then she singled out for special attention a girl who might have gone her whole life without knowing what it was that made her so different from everyone else. Aunt Jessa knew how to mix remedies for stomach aches, monthly pains, and rheumatic joints. She comforted women in painful childbirths, closed the eyes of the dead, and chanted their souls to heaven.

The real juju work was done by another former Bennett slave. Queen Lula was as sweet as a ripe plum until you brought her your enemy's name and crossed her palm with silver or placed a gold coin in her long, wrinkled fingers. Then she was all business. She called up devils, threw out spells like lightning bolts, and never, ever failed to rain down destruction, heartache, and unbearable physical pain. If you could pay for it. Not being rivals, Queen Lula and Aunt Jessa drank sassafras tea together, relived moments from their shared past in the Wildacre quarters, and told outrageous stories that neither of them believed for a Geechee minute.

"I don't have any appetite, Geoffrey." Prudence ran her fork through the braised pork with apples and onions that she'd been unable to eat. The gravy had gone cold and greasy, as had the unidentifiable greens he'd told her were collards flavored with fatback. She didn't want to insult the cook or Geoffrey, who seemed to relish what they'd been served, but she couldn't help wondering who had approved tonight's menu. Surely not the fastidious Abigail Dickson whose New York table was as elegant as any to be found in the city's most exclusive French restaurants.

"This was my idea, Prudence," Geoffrey said. "I'm sorry it's not to your taste, but I told the housekeeper that we'd eat whatever was being prepared for the staff. Under the circumstances. Once I knew Philip wouldn't be joining us."

"It's not the food," Prudence lied. "I have a lump in my throat that I can't seem to swallow."

"We've done all we can for tonight. You need sleep."

What I need is what I can't have, she thought, remembering the scent of the spoon the housekeeper had used to dose Abigail Dickson with laudanum. Almost as an afterthought, she'd held the small brown bottle out to Prudence when they met in the hallway before Eleanor's body was carried into the wine cellar. Prudence had shaken her head and turned away from what was healing to some, deadly for her. What she wouldn't give now for just a few drops to help her sink into comforting oblivion.

"I think I will go up to bed," she said, getting to her feet before the sight and smell of what remained on her plate made her gag. "I don't have the right words to thank you for staying with me this afternoon, Geoffrey. I'm not sure I could have done it without you."

He leaned over and did something utterly unexpected and quite extraordinary. He very softly kissed Prudence MacKenzie on her forehead, then brushed away an errant lock of her soft brown hair. "Good night, my dear."

Giving in to a sudden impulse to visit Eleanor one last time before she started the long climb up to her bedroom, Prudence skirted the servants' dining hall quickly and quietly. The babble of conversation was loud enough to drown out whatever noise she made, and no one looked into the corridor. The knob of the door to the cellar staircase turned easily in her hand. A moment later she was alone in a soft grayness lit by a lantern from the bottom of the stairwell. Someone had thought it indecent to leave their young mistress in the pitch-black darkness of night.

Prudence crept carefully down the stairs, feeling for her footing at each step of the descent. Halfway down she paused to listen for a repetition of what she thought but couldn't believe she had heard—a steady, rhythmic chanting that was only slightly louder than a whisper. Then came the odor of something sweet, pungent, and acrid burning in the heavy, dense air of belowground. Incense?

She couldn't turn around in search of Geoffrey. Whoever was down there with Eleanor might hear her and disappear. The door had a lock, but there'd been no key in it. She remembered checking for one when she'd reached out to turn the knob. She hesitated only long enough to start feeling dizzy from the smell of whatever burnt offering was being prepared below. Then anger and indignation steadied her, made up her mind.

Throwing Pinkerton caution to the wind, Prudence stepped quickly down the final steps of the staircase, not bothering to muffle her approach, not caring if danger awaited her.

The woman who had lit a candle at Eleanor's head and another at her exposed feet glanced once in Prudence's direction without interrupting the smooth cadence of what she was crooning. Prudence thought it sounded vaguely like French, but unlike any French she had ever studied. Just when she felt she was close to grasping the meaning of a word, it slipped away from her. She didn't make a conscious decision to do nothing, but she stayed silent, mystified by what she was seeing, yet no longer afraid.

The heavyset black woman wore a full skirted black cotton dress, her hair covered by an intricately wound, snowy white turban. Thin wisps of gray smoke curled above the candle wicks, the source of the odd odor that wasn't exactly incense but something very close to it. What looked like a vial of oil lay atop the sheet with which Geoffrey had covered Eleanor, and beside it a lock of black hair and an unlit white candle with what appeared to be a name scratched into the wax just below the wick.

The woman stroked Eleanor's cheeks with the loving tenderness of a mother, then shook a drop of oil from the glass vial onto a fingertip. As solemnly as a priest, she anointed the dead woman's forehead, eyelids, and mouth. She braided the lock of black hair into Eleanor's hair until Prudence couldn't distinguish one from the other. Then she lit the white candle and let it burn until whatever had been written on it melted. Finally, she drew the sheet over Eleanor's face, extinguished the other candles and turned to smile at Prudence.

"She safe now," the woman said. "Can't nobody hurt this baby no more."

"Who are you?" Prudence murmured. "What are you doing here? Who let you in?"

"They call me Aunt Jessa. I come to see everything done right by Young Miss here." She laid a wrinkled, reassuring hand on Prudence's arm.

"She was my friend," Prudence said, choking back a sob. "Neither of us had a sister."

"Miss Eleanor gone to a better place, chile. You gotta let her go."

Tears filled Prudence's eyes but refused to spill down her cheeks; her voice shook with anger. "She was going to marry the man she loved, the man who loved her. They were planning a life together. Having children someday. How can being dead be better than being alive and happy?" She brushed Aunt Jessa's hand from her arm.

"She weren't never going to be happy like that, Miss Prudence," Aunt Jessa said. "No matter how hard she might have tried, they wouldn't have let her be happy."

"What are you talking about? Who would have stood in the way of her happiness?" Later Prudence would wonder how the woman people called Aunt Jessa knew her name.

"I'm just saying Miss Eleanor wasn't never meant for this world, not the way it is. You best hold on to your memories and go on back where you belong." Aunt Jessa picked up her basket. "It won't do you no good to stay here looking for trouble. They don't want you any more than they wanted her."

"Then she disappeared," Prudence told Geoffrey, when she found him leafing through a book and lingering over his brandy and coffee in the parlor. She wrinkled her forehead in concentration as she tried to remember every moment of the odd encounter. "She must have brushed past me when she climbed the stairs, but I can't recall the precise moment when she left. It was like I stepped into a dream. When I woke up I was still standing beside Eleanor, but I was alone and the lantern was sputtering."

He poured her a glass of sherry and insisted that she sit down and drink it, buying time to decide how much of what Prudence had seen and heard he would choose to explain to her. How much she would be prepared to accept and believe. The Yankee hardheadedness and skepticism that made it impossible for her to walk away from a puzzle without solving it would work against her in the South where so much wasn't as it seemed and far too many things defied rational explanation.

He refilled his coffee cup and topped off his brandy.

"I don't think that woman belonged here, Geoffrey. At Seapoint, I mean. She was too old to be a maid."

"From your description, I'd say she'd been some family's mammy at one time. Probably the Bennetts. You call them nannies up north. They run the nursery and look after the children until it's time to turn them over to tutors and governesses."

"She said people called her Aunt Jessa."

He nodded his head in agreement. "In slavery days, the oldest household servants who'd worked for the family all their lives were often called aunt or uncle in their final years. I had an Aunt Calla. She was the most demanding woman I ever knew, fierce as an attack dog if she caught you in some mischief, but gentle as an angel when she tucked you into bed at night. The aunties were always big women. When you sat on their laps it was like sinking into a stack of soft pillows."

Prudence stared at him. Geoffrey had grown up on a plantation in North Carolina where more than a hundred slaves toiled in the fields that had made his family wealthy for generations before the war changed everything. Prudence had never known a servant who wasn't white and often Irish. In fact, now that she thought about it, she didn't think she had ever spoken to a dark-skinned person until she'd come to Bradford Island. How odd that was. Two separate worlds in the same country, as stubbornly different and distinct as their inhabitants could make them.

"What was she doing here, Geoffrey? Eleanor couldn't have meant anything to her."

And this was where Geoffrey had to decide whether Prudence would be shocked or touched by what he believed Aunt Jessa had come to Seapoint to do. She'd gotten angry with him before when he'd tried to shield her from an unpleasant truth. With the working relationship between them warming into something deeper, he didn't dare risk jeopardizing the trust he'd worked so hard to earn.

"This is only a guess, Prudence," he began hesitantly. "But I think Aunt Jessa probably belonged to the Bennetts before the war. She might even have been Teddy Bennett's mammy. No matter how old she is now, she would have claimed the privilege of caring for any children he and Eleanor had. And Teddy would have set her up in the nursery with at least two young nursemaids to do the work."

"That still doesn't explain what she was doing putting oil on Eleanor's body and chanting something I couldn't make out no matter how hard I tried."

"Have you ever heard of voodoo? Or juju?"

Prudence shook her head.

"If you want a man to fall in love with you, you go to a voodoo queen or conjure woman and pay her to cast a spell that will get you what you want. Or if you have an enemy, you can buy a potion or a doll that will sicken or kill him. It would take me hours to explain it all to you, and there's a lot I don't know, but that's the gist of it."

"It sounds like the superstitions the Irish have about holy relics and banshees," Prudence said. "Nobody halfway intelligent believes that kind of nonsense."

"What about spiritualism? Holding séances to contact the dead? It seems to me that at one time not so very long ago half the country believed it was possible to call up the shade of a deceased loved one."

"My point exactly." Prudence's father hadn't had a very high opinion of the reasoning capacity of the plaintiffs who appeared before his bench, and he'd passed that prejudice on to the daughter he'd trained in the law. Even though, as they both knew, there was little or no chance that a woman admitted to the bar would ever be accepted on the same footing as her male colleagues.

"I think Aunt Jessa was making sure that the woman who was supposed to marry the man she'd cared for as a child was given every chance to sit with the angels. She would have done the same thing for any child of Teddy's who didn't survive his first few years or was born dead. The oil and the anointing are from the Catholic tradition, the chanting probably calls on spirits and gods whose names we don't know."

"I thought at the time that she touched Eleanor as gently as a mother. With love. And how strange and beautiful that was."

"The county sheriff is coming over in the morning," Geoffrey said, leading Prudence away from spells and back to cold reality. "From the mainland. He'll bring the coroner."

"We have to tell them what we suspect, Geoffrey."

"Don't volunteer any information until we see which way the wind is blowing."

"You're being enigmatic."

"Cautious and realistic," he said. "I know these people the way you don't, Prudence."

He was maddening when he got patriarchal with her. Then he smiled.

And a dimple she'd never noticed before appeared in his cheek.

CHAPTER 5

❧

The party of horsemen rode up Seapoint's crushed shell driveway in late afternoon of the day following the discovery of Eleanor's body. Prudence and Geoffrey watched them approach from the second-story parlor where Prudence had been impatiently pacing since breakfast.

"They've taken their time," she snapped.

"Everything takes longer when you're on an island," Geoffrey soothed, knowing she'd eventually figure out for herself that rushing headlong into a situation wasn't the Southern way. He'd rather not have to try to explain it to her.

She mumbled something he couldn't make out, then whirled from the window and started toward the curved staircase to the main floor.

"Don't," he said, blocking her way so that she almost collided with him. "Let Eleanor's father handle this."

Philip Dickson had greeted them in the dining room that morning as immaculately dressed and groomed as though he had not spent most of the inconsolable night locked in the lonely privacy of his library. The man who had inherited one fortune and made another through cold-blooded risk taking and ruthless competitiveness had risen from the ashes of his grief and once more grabbed the world by its throat. Eleanor's father got on with things; that was who he was and what he did. He looked years older than he had the day before and his eyes had the bleak emptiness of someone who has suffered overwhelming anguish and loss, but there was purpose to the set of his jaw.

It was on the tip of Prudence's tongue to demand if Geoffrey meant there was no place for a woman in the discussion that would take place once the sheriff and coroner had viewed Eleanor's remains. She bit back the sharp retort, physically exhausted and desperately miserable after a sleepless night during which she'd wrestled repeatedly with questions to which she had no answers. Worst of all was a stubborn, niggling doubt about the conclusion she'd reached and Geoffrey seemed to support. Eleanor's shoulder had appeared to be dislocated and there had been at least the suggestion of bruising, but the more she recalled what she had seen, the more she doubted the evidence of her own eyes. The uncertainty was unnerving.

Philip Dickson glanced toward the second-floor landing as he greeted his visitors, then ushered them toward the cellar where his daughter's body lay. They were out of sight before Prudence could push past Geoffrey and insist on joining them. But she wasn't a member of the family, she reminded herself. To be absolutely truthful, she and Eleanor had drifted apart, especially after Philip began to take his wife and daughter on annual trips to Europe.

For the past two years, the Dicksons had wintered at Seapoint. And there had been Teddy, of course, the determined suitor who followed her back to New York and courted her and her parents until he'd won his case. Time passed so swiftly that Prudence hadn't realized how much of it had slipped away until Eleanor asked that she be her maid of honor. She'd been surprised and immensely flattered. And for a few of the busy weeks before they left New York to sail to Bradford Island, it was as though Eleanor had once more become the older sister Prudence never had. To find her friend again and then to lose her so cruelly was unbearable.

Maybe Geoffrey was right to advise her to pull back. Her grief was too sharp, too raw. It could make her say and do things she might regret. And for Eleanor's parents, her very presence must be a painful reminder of the girl who was no longer there.

"They're coming up from the cellars," Geoffrey said quietly. He steered her toward the staircase, her arm firmly supported by his. "Now."

She really didn't understand him at times.

Eleanor's father introduced them to County Sheriff Calvin Budridge and Justice of the Peace and Coroner Thaddeus Norton.

Teddy Bennett had the look of a man who had seen his own death; his brother Lawrence was a blank slate.

"I don't think there's any doubt about it," Norton said once they had settled themselves in the library and suitable condolences had been expressed. "Miss Dickson was an unfortunate and tragic victim whose passing we must clearly blame on her unfamiliarity with the natural dangers of the island." He sighed deeply. "I'll enter a finding of accidental death by drowning." Pen poised over the death certificate, he waited for only a moment before recording his decision and certifying it with an elaborately scrolled signature. "And, of course, I release the deceased to her family. I see no need for additional formalities or procedures." By which he meant the deeply disturbing prospect of an autopsy.

Sheriff Budridge nodded in agreement. A burly, sun-browned man with deeply set brown eyes that gave away nothing, he wore his office with a casual authority that brooked no argument or challenge. He'd reduced Eleanor's shoulder dislocation with the ease born of long jailhouse practice dealing with the injuries of drunken brawlers and short-tempered hotheads. Then he'd

smiled at her father, standing sentinel over his daughter's un-
clothed body. *There,* he'd seemed to say, *she's all fixed now.
Nothing more to fret over.*

Teddy, fists clenched and eyes burning, determined to ensure
that nothing untoward was done to his Eleanor, shuddered
when the man's hands twisted her shoulder, but he did not
protest. The sheriff and the coroner spent less than ten minutes
beside the dead woman and did not roll down the sheet covering her farther than the injured shoulder. Lawrence Bennett
had told them all they needed to know during the ride over
from the Wildacre dock—where women of quality and good
family were concerned, the less invasive the examination the
better. Modesty was as much their armor in death as it had been
in life.

Prudence had had enough. She found the disingenuous, im-
personal sympathy expressed by the sheriff and coroner acutely
offensive. Then a discomfiting emotion she couldn't identify flitted across Lawrence's handsome features before assuming the
appearance of conventional grief. It seemed to her that three of
the five men in the room could barely contain their impatience
to be away and shut of Eleanor Dickson's inconvenient death.

Before Geoffrey could move to stop her, she blurted out
what no one else had said. "Eleanor didn't dislocate her shoulder by falling to the ground. She couldn't have caused that kind
of injury to herself."

Sheriff Budridge smiled condescendingly. "We see that same
problem more times than I can count on boys we have to keep
overnight in jail for their own good. They get liquored up, start
picking fights, and the next thing you know they're tripping
over their own feet. Worst thing a person can do is try to break
a fall by sticking out his arms." Heads nodded on either side of
him. "It's treacherous footing out there in the swamp. Just ask
any tracker. He'll tell you."

Furious, Prudence glared at Geoffrey, demanding that he say something. He didn't.

"There were bruises on her shoulders," she continued defiantly.

"And I'm sure Miss Dickson had injuries in other places as well," the coroner said. He folded the signed death certificate and slid it into his jacket pocket. As soon as he could get around to it, he'd file the pesky thing in the courthouse. "I've seen bodies that were black and blue all over from their encounters with floating logs." It was clear he meant to imply that the pretty little Yankee girl did not know what she was talking about. Somebody should have taught her not to stick her nose into men's business.

"You were a Pinkerton at one time, Geoffrey," Philip Dickson said. "What do you think about all this?" He hadn't gotten where he had without consulting experts when he wanted an informed opinion. He'd been shocked by the knobby protuberance on Eleanor's shoulder, relieved when the sheriff had caused it to disappear. He knew about the damage drunks and brawlers did to one another; any man who hired unskilled workers was familiar with payday mayhem. It had been easy to accept that Eleanor had tripped, then fallen heavily and awkwardly enough to pass out from the pain.

Three heads swiveled in Geoffrey's direction.

"You were a Pinkerton?" the sheriff asked.

No point denying it. "I was," Geoffrey said. He knew what was coming next. The Pinkertons had foiled a plot to assassinate President Abraham Lincoln and spied for the Union during the war. Southerners had long memories.

"And where exactly did you pink?" Lawrence used the word that in certain circles had colloquially come to mean *spy*.

Geoffrey hadn't tried to hide the remnants of his North Carolina way of speaking. To the sheriff, the coroner, and probably the Bennetts, despite the fact that he'd been a child during the war and the Reconstruction period, just having been a part of the Pinkerton organization at any time in his life condemned him. Traitor to the Cause was not a badge of honor.

He didn't answer. The details of his Pinkerton career were his own business. He shared them with no one.

Prudence broke the uncomfortable silence. "Mr. Hunter was with me when I tended to Eleanor," she said, trying not to notice Mr. Dickson's involuntary wince as his mind supplied the image of his daughter's body being readied for burial. "We both saw the dislocation and the bruising. Mr. Hunter spread his two hands over the discolorations on her shoulders." She stretched out her fingers to illustrate what he had done. "They disappeared. Someone held her down under the water until she drowned."

"Do you read novels, Miss MacKenzie?" asked Judge Norton.

"Whether or not I read novels has nothing to do with the circumstances of Miss Dickson's death." Prudence's voice trembled with suppressed rage at the implied insult to her intelligence.

"It's just that some of you ladies let your imaginations run wild. I've confined my wife's reading to the Bible and *Pilgrim's Progress*. The same for my daughters," the coroner informed her smugly.

"Miss MacKenzie is not indulging in a flight of fancy," Geoffrey said. "The dislocation is a fact. As are the bruises on Miss Dickson's shoulders."

He looked at Teddy, who so far had said nothing. Eleanor's bereft fiancé sat as if turned to stone, his mind and heart clearly somewhere else. Geoffrey wasn't sure he'd even heard any of the conversation surging around him.

"That's enough, gentlemen," Philip Dickson said, rising to his feet. "I thank you for your time and your condolences." He hadn't rung a bell, but the Seapoint butler stood in the open library doorway. "Henry will see you out. Our business here together is concluded." There was a sting to his words that

told everyone he considered the near contretemps a slight to
his daughter's memory. He wasn't obliged to suffer their company any longer than he had to.

"Teddy?" Lawrence laid a hand on his brother's shoulder.

"You go on back to Wildacre without me, Lawrence." Teddy
had a request best made in private. He wasn't sure what Philip
Dickson's reaction would be.

"Stay," Eleanor's father said when his visitors had departed
and the butler closed the library door. "We need to talk."

"Why did she do it? What drew her into the live oaks at
night and alone when she knew the forest could be dangerous?
Why? Was it to meet you, Teddy? Are you responsible and too
much of a coward to admit it?"

Hearing the knife-sharp edge in Philip Dickson's voice, Prudence finally understood why he hadn't pressed too hard against
the sheriff and the coroner when they pronounced Eleanor's
death accidental. He had his own suspicions but too much of a
care for his daughter's reputation to bring them out into the
light. Eleanor had done mischievous things when she was
younger; even as an adult she had loved to flout rules and take
chances. Her father knew this about her, and because her high
spirits and love of life were the essence of who she was, he had
never come down too hard on her. Prudence suspected that
Eleanor had been the spark of light in his mirthless world of
commerce.

"No, sir," Teddy said, standing up straight and tall, beginning to come alive again. "I would never have suggested such a
thing. Never allowed her to do it had I any suspicion what she
was planning. It wasn't me, Mr. Dickson. I swear that to you."
No one, not even her father, could be allowed to believe that his
beloved Eleanor would compromise her virtue two days before
their wedding.

"Someone lured her into the live oaks," Dickson insisted.
"Someone who wished her harm."

"Or wanted to get to you through her, Mr. Dickson," Geoffrey interrupted. "Is there anyone who hates or fears you enough to do something like this? Anyone who would profit substantially if you were unable to negotiate a contract or complete a sale or purchase?"

"We're all too vulnerable for that. Most of us have wives and children who can't be protected every moment of every day wherever they go or whatever they do. Society has rules because it is such a fragile entity. So does business. You break them at your peril."

"So you're saying that you have no enemies?" Prudence pressed.

"I have enemies. As did your father, my dear. But men of the world expect to incur rancor and bad blood. We take sensible precautions when we believe a foe is allowing his animosity to get out of hand, but we are rarely if ever in danger of our lives. Your father had to live with the knowledge that he might be targeted by a man he'd condemned to prison or the rope, but I never heard him speak of it. No, I don't think this horrific act was aimed at me, Prudence."

"Then it must have been an accident," Teddy said. "Perhaps the sheriff and the coroner and my brother are right to blame the swamp. All the time I was growing up I heard stories about slaves who had run away and died in its waters. Animals, too. Household pets that were eaten by alligators, goats and calves pulled into the murky water and held beneath the surface until they drowned. Aunt Jessa used to say that if you listened hard enough at night, you'd hear the howls of their death throes." He paled and sat down suddenly as he realized he'd just described Eleanor's final moments.

"A woman who said her name was Aunt Jessa came to Seapoint yesterday," Prudence said, responding to the puzzled look on Philip's face.

"Who is she? What was she doing here?" Dickson demanded.

"Aunt Jessa is the mammy who raised Bennett children as far

back as anyone alive can remember," Teddy explained. "She's old now, but the islanders still treat her as though she's head woman of the plantation."

"She chanted something over Eleanor," Prudence said. "Then she anointed her forehead, eyes, and lips with oil."

"And you let this crazy woman touch my child?"

"She was already in the cellar when I went down," Prudence explained. She didn't mention the odd feeling she'd had of being in a dream, of feeling powerless to challenge or interfere with what the woman in the white turban was doing. "I don't think she meant any harm, Mr. Dickson. She told me Eleanor was safe now, that nobody and nothing could harm her."

"That's what the people call white magic," Geoffrey explained. "Black magic harms. White magic protects."

"Aunt Jessa is a healer," Teddy clarified. "She may cast the occasional spell, but she isn't a voodoo priestess." He said this to Geoffrey, whom he judged to be the only other person in the room to have an inkling of what he was talking about.

"I have to know," Philip Dickson said, brushing aside women in turbans and magic of any color. "I have to know what really happened to my daughter. If you ask enough questions of enough people, you'll get answers."

"What do you want us to do, Mr. Dickson?"

"Only what you do for other people, Geoffrey. What you used to do as a Pinkerton and you and Prudence do together from that office of yours down on Wall Street. Tell me how Eleanor died. Why she went to the place where we found her. If someone did this to her deliberately, I want you to find the monster. I'll kill him myself with my bare hands if I have to."

In the strained silence that greeted his demand, Prudence looked at Geoffrey with a spark of *I told you so* in her eyes.

Neither of them had brought up Eleanor's fear of someone watching her from the live oaks. Whatever menace she had felt could no longer be proved; anxiety over a nameless, faceless threat only strengthened the argument that her own panic had caused Eleanor's death. They would keep that one vital fact to themselves for as long as they could.

Teddy raised his head from his hands and stood up again. With immense dignity he asked the man who would never be his father-in-law if he would allow his only child to be buried in the Bennett family graveyard at Wildacre.

Philip Dickson stared at him in horror and stalked from the room, slamming the door behind him so hard that books crashed down from their shelves to the floor.

CHAPTER 6

❧

"I want to go to Wildacre with Teddy when he leaves," Prudence said. "Will you come with me, Geoffrey?"

"What do you hope to find?" he asked.

"I'm not sure." Prudence's gaze swept the soaring, two-story entrance hall to the modern mansion that was Seapoint, so out of time and place on Bradford Island. "I think I want to feel what Eleanor experienced when she went there, try to understand what she was prepared to accept to make Teddy happy."

"The Bennetts." That was all Geoffrey thought he needed to say.

Prudence shuddered. "Lawrence and his father are handsome and charming, but why do I expect them to try to sell me snake oil? And those poor, washed-out sisters. Teddy isn't like the rest of his family."

"I think you'll find he has more in common with them than you might suspect. He was born and raised in a culture that's as foreign to you as a Turkish harem. It's marked him."

"I don't believe that. Teddy and Eleanor together were something new. They gave each other the strength to break away from tradition and their pasts."

Geoffrey looked skeptical and might have continued to debate the point except that the young man they were discussing joined them.

"He won't listen right now, but at least we were able to part on speaking terms." Teddy knew it was futile to attempt to argue with Eleanor's father once his mind was made up, but he was just as stubborn as Philip Dickson and just as skilled as the older man at waiting out an opponent. Where Dickson favored a blunt, heads-on approach, Teddy was prepared to meander through as many circuitous byways as it took to get what he wanted. Somehow, he had promised himself and her, Eleanor would lie in the Bennett burying ground waiting for him.

"I've ordered one of the pony traps brought around," Prudence said. "We thought we'd ride with you to Wildacre if you don't mind our company."

"I'd like that. There hasn't been much time to talk."

Teddy tied his horse to the back of the trap, then climbed in, taking up the reins with the ease of long practice. Prudence and Geoffrey squeezed in beside him. Prudence had questions to ask, and she wanted answers.

The road Teddy took wound along the edge of the live oak forest so that even though the day was warm and bright, they frequently rode in dappled shade. Prudence was mesmerized by the scintillating sunshine, intoxicated by the perfectly clear, unpolluted air. No New Yorker who ventured outside his home could escape the smoke of hundreds of thousands of coal fires and the stench of manure clumped haphazardly in every street.

Except for the crashing of waves against its Atlantic beaches and the squawk of seagulls, Bradford Island was a hushed, still place, so unlike the clamor and noisy bustle she was used to that Prudence found herself waiting and listening for some enormous cacophony of sound to break the silence.

She didn't feel completely at ease here, though Geoffrey had blended in so quickly that he seemed never to have cut his ties

with the South at all. The place might be isolated and far from
what city dwellers called civilization, but it had a breathtaking
beauty that she realized spoke to those who chose to make it
their home. Prudence could only imagine what the heat must
be like in full summer.

"I'm sorry Mr. Dickson refused your request to have Eleanor
buried in the Bennett family graveyard," she began. "It would
have been a fitting resting place, given the circumstances."

"I haven't given up hope that he'll change his mind," Teddy
said.

"Perhaps Mrs. Dickson is the one you should talk to.
Though from what the housekeeper says, she's refusing to
allow even her husband into her bedroom."

"She blames him for bringing them to what she must think is a
godforsaken place." Geoffrey's rueful tone of voice took some of
the sting out of his words. "She'll need time to forgive him."

"I don't know that she ever will," Teddy said. "Eleanor talked
about her mother often. She agonized over not being able to
please her, but they always seemed to be at loggerheads when she
was growing up. She spoke about tension between her parents,
about disagreements and arguments that often revolved around
her. Lately, with the wedding on the horizon, those earlier
problems appeared to be resolving themselves, but she didn't
fool herself into thinking they wouldn't resurface."

"Teddy, may I ask you about the wedding?"

"I don't want to have any secrets from you, Prudence. Not
now. Not if it will help find out what really happened to Eleanor.
And you, too, Geoffrey. I'll answer whatever questions you have
as honestly as I can."

"Whose idea was it to have the wedding here instead of at
Trinity Church in Manhattan?"

"I can't recall whose proposal it was originally. But once we
began talking, Eleanor and I, it seemed the better choice. Neither of us wanted a society wedding, with hundreds of guests
and a reception at Delmonico's. But if we got married in New

York, we would have been trapped into exactly that. Mr. Dickson has too many business friends and acquaintances to risk slighting any of them, and Mrs. Dickson's society circles would have been scandalized by anything less. The only way out of the dilemma was to get married far enough away so that we wouldn't be subject to anyone's dictates but our own."

"I'm surprised Eleanor's parents agreed." *Astounded*, given Abigail's society background, but Prudence was trying not to seem to find fault with either family.

"It didn't happen quickly or easily, but Eleanor has . . . had remarkable powers of persuasion. Immediate family only, was what she told them we wanted."

"Eleanor didn't have any aunts, uncles, or cousins. I remember one time she said that being the only child of only children was a very lonely life."

"I had hopes she'd find a new family here, with me," Teddy said.

"But you were going to live in New York, weren't you?"

"For the next few years at least. Until I established myself. Then I planned to transfer some of that business to the new Cotton Exchange in Savannah. All of it eventually. We would have built a town home in Savannah but spent at least half our time on the island."

"Did Mr. Dickson know of your plans?"

"Not all of them," Teddy confessed. "Eleanor and I had only begun talking about how we wanted to shape our future. It won't matter now."

The New York Cotton Exchange would be closed to him once Philip Dickson withdrew his sponsorship. Which in due course he would. To work beside Teddy every day would be a constant, stabbing reminder of the horror of his daughter's death.

They rode in silence for a while, Prudence wondering how to bring up the subject of Teddy's family without giving offense. He had seemed eager to talk about Eleanor and the life they had envisioned together, but it was a delicate topic now. With prosperous expectations tied to the Dickson name and fortune no longer a reality, he would have to fall back on the only kin left to him. The boring Bennetts, as Prudence had thought of them after the dinner party that had seemed an endless ordeal of forced smiles. Even Eleanor, though she was circumspect in her comments, had found them a trial.

Teddy pulled the buggy to a halt. "We're almost there," he announced, climbing down to unhitch his horse. He vaulted into the saddle as the animal shook its head and danced in the roadway, scenting home stables and the prospect of a good run.

"We'll follow you," Geoffrey said as Teddy moved off ahead of them. He kept the trap far enough back to avoid the dust kicked up by Teddy's horse. Unlike the road linking Seapoint to its pier, this sandy track wasn't paved with a thick layer of crushed shells.

Wildacre stood within a grove of towering oaks like a huge white ship under full sail, its balanced, classical lines perfectly proportioned and majestic. Prudence breathed in a sigh as Geoffrey turned the buggy into the long, tree-lined drive. Here was the Southern plantation hall she had expected but not found at Philip Dickson's Seapoint.

Teddy's family home was three stories tall, a double curved stairway reaching gracefully to the second floor. Slender columns rose symmetrically around the entire mansion from ground level to rooftop; every tall French window and door was placed exactly in line with the one above or below it. The brick was softly whitewashed, shutters painted black. Peacocks strutted on the green lawn, fanning their tails and calling out raucously as the pony trap intruded on their domain.

"The bottom floor is storage rooms and probably some quarters for the staff," Geoffrey said, reining the horse to a slow walk as they approached. "All of these island and riverside planters learned to accommodate flood waters and hurricane season." He swept appraising eyes over the structure.

"It's beautiful," Prudence said. "Like something out of a storybook."

"They weren't all like this," Geoffrey warned. "Not even in the glory days before the war. A fair number of plantation families made do with much more modest accommodations. Their livelihood depended on each year's harvest. Nature didn't always cooperate."

"I wonder how many acres the Bennetts were able to keep for themselves when Eleanor's father bought the island."

"Less than a hundred," Geoffrey said. He shrugged matter-of-factly. "It's public record."

"You looked up the transaction?"

"Had someone do it for me."

"Is there nothing you don't investigate?" When he didn't answer, Prudence wondered if there was anything Geoffrey didn't know about her. It was a prickly, unsettling feeling to think she had no secrets.

Teddy handed his horse off to a stable boy who had come running at the sound of hooves on the drive. Another boy held the bridle of the horse pulling the trap. By the time Prudence had stepped down and shaken out her skirts, Teddy's father was on the front veranda to greet them.

Standing as tall and straight as though still in the Confederate uniform he had once proudly worn, Elijah Bennett cast one quick, quizzical glance at his son before stepping forward to smile warmly at his visitors. Prudence had sat diagonally across from him at the Dickson dinner table two nights ago. She'd thought then that he was one of the most striking older men she had ever met; seeing him in the setting of Wildacre confirmed that opinion. The thick gold hair his sons had inherited was laced with silver, but that and sun wrinkles around his blue eyes were the only physical signs of advancing age. Time had been kind to Elijah Bennett. Eleanor must have studied him and imagined how her Teddy would look in thirty years.

"Lawrence will be sorry to have missed your arrival," he said, shaking hands with Geoffrey, bowing over Prudence's gloved fingers. "He's escorted Sheriff Budridge and Justice Norton to the landing dock. But perhaps you'll be able to stay until he returns?"

Geoffrey said something politely noncommittal, then allowed Prudence to precede him into the dim coolness of Wildacre's formal parlor, where the men were served bourbon over sugar cubes and sprigs of crushed mint. Prudence had to be content with a glass of cool lemonade.

"I've sent word up to Aurora Lee and Maggie Jane." Elijah stood before the polished bricks of the empty fireplace, legs slightly apart in the firm stance of a commanding officer about to give an order. "They'll join us shortly."

"How lovely," Prudence murmured. "I hope you'll forgive us for calling like this without warning. There wasn't time to send a note." She looked around her appreciatively. "I did so want to see the home to which my dear friend Eleanor was welcomed and where I know she hoped to become a part of her husband's family."

"Such a terrible tragedy," Elijah said. "I thought of her as another daughter since the first time Teddy brought her to meet us." He touched the black armband he wore and lowered his eyes, only raising them when the rustle of silk skirts echoed through the room.

Teddy's two sisters wore deepest mourning, even to the substitution of jet earrings for the gold that usually dangled from their ears. Aurora Lee was a forgettable faded blonde, the golden hair of her father and brothers dulled to a pale cornsilk yellow that turned her muddy skin sallow. Her nearly lashless blue eyes wore a look of perpetual dismay and her lips were narrow to the point of vanishing when she stretched them into a cold smile.

Maggie Jane, the younger of the two, was painfully thin and just as sallow of skin as her older sister. She seldom had anything to say for herself, but compensated for her lack of conversational skill by frequently erupting into nervous giggles that she attempted to stifle by pressing a fingernail-bitten hand to her mouth. In this family, all of the good looks had gone to the men. Prudence wondered what Mrs. Bennett had looked like. She remembered Eleanor telling her that Teddy's mother had died many years ago.

"We are so heartbroken to have lost dear Eleanor," Aurora Lee simpered. "And dear Miss MacKenzie, how much more agonizing for you, as close as you were to her."

"How thoughtful of you to have a care for me at such a mournful time," Prudence said, skillfully picking up the thread of condolences expected of bereaved friends and next-of-kin.

The sisters seated themselves side by side on a sofa whose faded damask upholstery was slightly frayed. In fact, as she looked around the parlor again in a fruitless search for something to say, Prudence realized that Wildacre's opulent interior was in reality rather shabby and worn at the elbows. The black of Aurora Lee's and Maggie Jane's dresses had turned rusty gray at the seams and hemlines. The Bennetts were only a few short steps away from genteel poverty. Yet not long ago they had sold their island to a wealthy New Yorker looking to compete with the Carnegies and Vanderbilts. What could have happened to the considerable sum Philip Dickson must have paid them?

Geoffrey's eyes followed Prudence's scrutiny of the parlor. He wouldn't have to tell her anything. She'd come to the same conclusion he had when he'd seen the overgrown lawn and traces of red brick showing through faded and flaking whitewash. Despite the sale of their island, this family was desperate for an infusion of ready money. Eleanor Dickson had been much more than Teddy's beloved bride-to-be. She'd been nothing less than the Bennetts' ticket back to prosperity. And now they'd lost any hope of pocketing the additional riches they'd counted on. No wonder the washed-out sisters mourned her. Without substantial dowries, a lifetime of barren spinsterhood and oft-mended out-of-fashion dresses stretched before them.

"You were going to show us some of the sights of Wildacre," Geoffrey said to Teddy, setting aside the glass of second-rate bourbon he'd been nursing. "I don't mind stretching my legs a bit."

"I'll join you," Prudence put in quickly. She still hadn't thought of a suitable topic of conversation to engage the two Misses Bennett staring blankly at her. It wasn't as if she could inquire about the latest play they had seen, the most recent lecture they'd attended, or their current choice of reading matter. Nothing happened on Bradford Island. There was no place to go and nothing to do that warranted talking about. Had high-spirited, adventure-loving Eleanor fully realized that?

Prudence kept her face politely expressionless when Aurora Lee and Maggie Jane decided not to accept their brother's invitation to accompany him and their visitors on a quick tour of the grounds.

"I'll show you where I hope Eleanor's parents will consent to bury her," Teddy said as they descended the graceful staircase and walked toward a grove of granite headstones beneath ancient oaks.

"Are you thinking the same thing I am, Geoffrey?" Prudence whispered as soon as Teddy moved ahead of them out of earshot. She hadn't told him the whole truth of why she'd wanted to come to Wildacre, but now she thought she would have to. The notion she'd had of finding some clue to Eleanor's demise in the way the Bennett family spoke of her had proved foolish and ill-thought-out. She'd imagined guilt revealed in someone's eyes, hidden jealousy, implacable hostility. Tossing and turning in her bed last night, she'd pictured a sudden and savage quarrel of unknown cause leading to a moment of overwhelming physical rage and sudden death.

"That no one in the Bennett family has a motive for wanting Eleanor out of the picture? If that's what you've decided, you're not alone."

"I can't come to any other conclusion. Whether they accepted her into the family willingly or not, they needed her." Her father's oft-repeated admonition echoed in her mind. *Facts, Prudence. Don't let your imagination run away with you.*

"They needed her fortune. What she was bringing to the marriage in the immediate future and what she stood to inherit someday," Geoffrey concluded.

Prudence had been so sure that Eleanor had been murdered. So sure. But, she now admitted, her conviction was based on the flimsiest of circumstantial evidence. Maybe she'd been wrong. Perhaps Lawrence and his despicable sheriff and coroner had the right of it after all. The swamp could have devoured Eleanor just as it had consumed countless others who had wandered into its depths and lost their way.

How sad. How unutterably sad and heartrending.

CHAPTER 7

The Wildacre graveyard had the tidy beauty of a family plot long and lovingly cared for. Located a short walk from the house, the site was nestled in a grove of ancient oaks and protected by intricately designed ironwork fencing. It reminded Prudence of the small private parks found in the most exclusive neighborhoods of Manhattan. Secluded and serenely peaceful.

As they strolled among the gravesites, Teddy recounted short biographies of some of the more colorful characters whose plots were boxed in by low walls he told them were made by mixing together crushed oyster shells, quicklime, water, sand, and ash. "It's called tabby," he explained, encouraging Prudence to run her hand along the top of one of the walls. "At one time nearly all of the buildings on Wildacre were built out of it."

"The house, too?" Prudence asked.

"The first house, which we use as storerooms now. Bricks were expensive and hard to come by in places where there wasn't any natural clay."

"The men lived longer than most of the women," Prudence remarked, gazing around her. "Except for those killed in the war." She paused by the headstone of a beloved wife at whose feet clustered six small markers, each incised with a single date beneath the name.

Neither Teddy nor Geoffrey commented. Women died in childbirth, but it wasn't a topic men talked about.

At the far end of the enclosure a wild rambling rose had taken root against the iron fence. Its thorny canes curled up and over and around the railings, masses of small white blooms among the green leaves like stars in a dark sky.

"This is where I want Eleanor to lie," Teddy said. "She loved roses."

No grave had been dug yet, nor was there any indication that the exact spot for it had been chosen. Prudence wondered if Teddy had informed his family of his plans. He'd certainly waited until Lawrence had left Seapoint before broaching the subject to Eleanor's father. Perhaps Elijah's statement that he considered his son's fiancée to be already a Bennett daughter was nothing but polite hyperbole. Some men believed women should only be told what the men wanted or needed them to hear.

As they turned to leave the graveyard, a niggling inconsistency made Prudence do a swift count of the headstones within its borders. Teddy waited politely just outside the iron fence, but Geoffrey was at her side in a few long strides.

"Where are they?" she asked quietly. "Do they have their own burial ground?"

"Slaves were never buried with the family," he said, drawing her farther away from where Teddy stood. "There's a place for them somewhere on the plantation, on waste ground that isn't fertile or can't be easily cultivated. Don't ask about it, Prudence."

There were any number of subjects that well-bred ladies didn't broach in polite company, that they weren't supposed to think about even privately. But Prudence's father had taught her that a practicing lawyer eventually came into close contact with every vile and despicable crime society could envision and legislate against. He'd had a care for her sensibilities in the way he chose to couch his descriptions, but he'd scoffed at the idea that a woman was too delicate to be able to bear the harsh realities he saw from his bench every day.

The war to end slavery was long over. The North, the Union, had won. Times had changed. Then why did Prudence feel as though she had stepped back into a living history that was suffocating her? Enveloping and imprisoning her in a cage of thorns and beautiful blooms?

Shaken, increasingly unsure what to think about this new world she did not understand, Prudence took the arm Geoffrey held out to her. She glanced back one final time at the spot where the white climbing rose glimmered in the sun-mottled shade of the oak trees.

Perhaps this wasn't the place for her friend Eleanor after all.

They could hear the vehement hiss of pent-up and abruptly expelled anger as soon as they approached the house. One of the floor-to-ceiling parlor windows had been left open after someone stepped through it from the veranda.

Lawrence Bennett, Prudence decided, returned from seeing off the sheriff and the coroner, arguing furiously with his father. The voices were distinctive and easily recognized, though she couldn't make out the words. Then someone closed the window.

Teddy frowned and shook his head apologetically. "They've been doing that a lot lately," he said. "Arguing. I wish I knew what it was about, but whenever I ask, they shut me out."

"Do you have an overseer?" Geoffrey asked.

"No. And I think that's part of the problem. Wildacre isn't large enough now to justify hiring someone. My father has never shown much interest in the day-to-day running of the place, but he won't turn the decision-making authority over to Lawrence. Until two days ago it didn't concern me; Eleanor and I were going to be living in New York for at least the next few years."

"It's too soon to decide what you'll do," Prudence counseled. She knew from sad experience the emotional and physical effects of losing someone close.

"I'm sure you're right," Teddy agreed. "I can't seem to keep a coherent thought in my head for longer than a few minutes."

Their footsteps or perhaps their voices must have penetrated to the parlor. When Teddy opened the door to usher them in, the room was silent. Aurora Lee and Maggie Jane hadn't moved from the sofa where Prudence had last seen them, and Elijah Bennett still stood by the fireplace. But a porcelain figurine lay smashed on the floor, and one of the smaller Oriental carpets had been twisted out of place by the stomp of an angry foot. Lawrence stared out the window that had stood open until a few moments ago. His rigid shoulders and the slight tremor of fisted hands were lost on no one.

Yet when he turned to acknowledge his brother and their guests, his face was composed and calm, his voice steady, welcoming, and low-pitched. Only a pinched whiteness around his eyes and lips betrayed the effort he was making to rein in his temper.

"I wonder if we could have the trap brought round," Geoffrey asked into the strained stillness. "The afternoon is wearing on and we should be getting back to Seapoint." He hesitated a moment. "I trust Sheriff Budridge and Mr. Norton got off all right?"

"Judge Norton," Lawrence corrected. "They did. The waters in the sound are usually calm this time of day." He pulled a bell cord, and when a maid appeared, pointed wordlessly at the porcelain shards on the floor. As soon as the broken bits of figurine had been swept up, he ordered the trap, then took a folded slip of paper from his jacket pocket and gave it to Geoffrey. "Thaddeus thought Mr. Dickson might want to avail himself of this gentleman's services."

Geoffrey glanced at the paper. "I'm sure he'll be most grateful for the suggestion." Undertakers had sprung up all over the country in the wake of the popularization of embalming during the war. Families had wanted to bury their fathers, husbands, and sons at home whenever they could. Arsenic in the drained blood vessels had made it possible.

"The investigation into Eleanor's death is closed, then?" Something about Lawrence Bennett made Prudence want to goad him into an ill-tempered reaction.

"That was made clear when Judge Norton signed the death certificate. He wouldn't have put his name to it otherwise," Lawrence snapped.

"I don't understand how he can be so certain when no witnesses have been identified and no questions asked," Prudence insisted. She could hear her father's voice urging her on.

"I don't believe a Yankee like yourself, newly arrived in these parts, has any idea how dangerous our swamps can be, Miss MacKenzie."

"What good would it do to go around asking questions?" Elijah added. "We all know what happened. Tragic as it was, Eleanor brought about her own death. She had no business being out in the swamp alone. And especially not at night." His jaw tightened and the muscles in his neck bunched out in righteous proclamation of an unpleasant and unwelcome truth.

"What if she *wasn't* alone?" Prudence asked.

Aurora Lee harrumphed and Maggie Jane's fingers flew to her mouth. No lady ever left her home unescorted. If she did, she deserved to have her reputation tarnished. Rules were rules.

Lawrence stepped away from the window through which lengthening shadows could be seen creeping across the lawn. "What are you insinuating, Miss MacKenzie?"

"Nothing, Mr. Bennett," Geoffrey interjected before Prudence could answer. "But Miss Dickson's parents will begin to ask questions as soon as their first grief for her has passed. Shouldn't they be provided with answers?"

"We know what happened, Mr. Hunter," Elijah said. "And from what my sons have told me, so does Mr. Dickson. He was a member of the search party that scoured the interior of the island until they found the unfortunate young woman."

One moment Eleanor was as good as another daughter, the next she was an *unfortunate young woman*. Which was it, Prudence wondered, her eyes fixed on the senior Bennett's face. He seemed to be focused on his second son rather than Geoffrey, as if it were Lawrence who had demanded reassurances.

And why hadn't Geoffrey allowed her to answer Lawrence's question? Why had he interrupted and cut off what she was about to say? Surely by now he knew that she was capable of taking care of herself.

"We don't know how she got into the swamp, Mr. Bennett," Geoffrey said reasonably. "Nor do we know what drew her outside after everyone else had gone to sleep."

"Swamp gas," Lawrence put in. "When conditions are right, it flickers blue or yellow flames that can appear as though someone is holding a lantern."

"You're saying that Eleanor looked out her window, saw what she thought was Teddy signaling to her with a lantern, and sneaked out to join him?" Prudence spoke quickly before Geoffrey could silence her with a comment of his own.

"I don't think we can discount the possibility." Lawrence wore that same look of smug superiority she had seen on his face at Seapoint.

It infuriated her.

"Eleanor's bedroom window faces the beach, not the live oak forest," Prudence informed him. "There's nothing between the house and the ocean but well-tended lawn. No swamp. No marsh. No will-o-the-wisps to be mistaken for lantern lights."

She was about to add that her room was next to her friend's and that the first night they'd arrived on the island she'd stood at her window marveling at the play of moonlight on the ocean. Definitely no swamp gas. But then she gritted her teeth and said no more. Something about letting Teddy's exasperating brother know the precise location of her Seapoint bedroom made her uneasy.

Lawrence shrugged his shoulders as if to say there was no accounting for the night ramblings of restless young women on the cusp of wifehood.

"Aunt Jessa showed up," Teddy blurted out.

Heads swiveled in his direction. The abrupt change of subject caught everyone's attention and effectively if only temporarily damped down the hostility between his brother and Prudence.

"Here?" questioned Elijah. "When?" He shot an arrow-swift glance at Lawrence, then busied himself nudging an overlooked fragment of statuary across the floor.

"She hardly ever leaves her cabin in the live oaks," Aurora Lee commented. "I can't remember the last time I saw her."

"She wasn't here," Teddy continued as if he hadn't been interrupted. "Prudence encountered her at Seapoint."

"What was she doing there?" Lawrence was plainly annoyed that the elderly woman had intruded on the island's new owners. "She's so long in the tooth and addled in the head it's a wonder she remembers where she means to go or why."

"She's not that bad, Lawrence," Aurora Lee chided.

Maggie Jane looked confused, as if she didn't quite understand what people were saying and couldn't figure out what they wanted her to contribute.

"She's old, she smells, and she has no business at either Seapoint or Wildacre," Lawrence insisted.

"Teddy said she was your nanny," Prudence maintained. "Sorry, I think the word he used was *mammy*."

"That was a long time ago," Elijah put in.

"He said a mammy sometimes got to be like a member of the family." That was an exaggeration, but Prudence was determined to find out why Lawrence had been so put out by the apparently harmless appearance of a former servant.

"That's a preposterous idea!" Lawrence flamed. "We were always fair with our people, but never did we consider any of them to be a part of the family."

"They do bear the Bennett name," Geoffrey said.

"As I'm sure your family's people adopted the Hunter name," Lawrence snapped. He didn't say *after the war* or *when freedom came* because he didn't consider the real war over and he'd never reconciled himself to the arbitrary abolition of slavery. He didn't feel he needed to explain any of that to someone whose accent was clearly North Carolinian.

"She said she came to make Miss Eleanor safe," Prudence said. And waited.

Once again Elijah and his younger son exchanged stares. There was a tension between them that Prudence found hard to fathom.

"She gave her a juju blessing," Teddy finally contributed. "She's been doing that for years, whenever there's a death on the island."

"Among the people, maybe," Lawrence corrected.

"I miss her," Maggie Jane said. Life had been so simple when there was no dearth of black hands to comply with her every whim and wish.

"None of us can live the way we did before the war," Geoffrey commented, alert for the effect his casual pronouncement would have on the Bennett men.

Lawrence stiffened and seemed about to say something. Elijah stepped away from the mantel, silencing his son with the commanding officer's glare he'd perfected on the battlefield.

"I think I hear your pony trap," Teddy announced. He looked from brother to father and back again, clearly puzzled.

"It's past time we took our leave," Geoffrey agreed. "Thank you for your hospitality, Mr. Bennett." He bowed gracefully toward Aurora Lee and Maggie Jane. "Ladies."

Then he walked closer to Lawrence and said something under his breath that Prudence couldn't catch. Teddy's brother looked surprised and then gratified. The two men shook hands.

"What did you say to him?" Prudence asked as the pony trap passed through Wildacre's gates. "To Lawrence."

"Nothing important."

"It must have been something he wanted to hear," Prudence persisted. "I watched the expression on his face change."

"I don't think you got off on the right foot with Lawrence," Geoffrey teased.

"Don't be annoying. The man's a cad and a bounder," she declared.

"I'd say he's a true son of the Old South."

"What is that supposed to mean?"

"For one thing, he likes women to know their place."

"Which means they shouldn't have any opinions contrary to his own?"

"Or at least have the sense not to voice them."

"You've changed, Geoffrey," Prudence seethed. "And you're getting worse by the day."

"I don't know what you mean."

"You know exactly what I'm talking about. Ever since we got here you've been melting into the landscape." She fumbled for exactly the right words. "You're not the same person you were in New York. You've got an accent that's getting thicker by the day, you don't seem able to look critically at anything around you, and I'd swear you feel a kinship with that disgusting Lawrence Bennett. What *did* you say to him?"

"I told him I'd see to it you didn't stick your pretty little Yankee nose in where it didn't belong."

For once, Geoffrey had left her speechless. There was absolutely nothing more Prudence wanted to say to him.

Ever again.

CHAPTER 8

Aunt Jessa wasn't surprised and she wasn't afraid.

She was too old to run and she wasn't strong enough to fight.

That made what he'd come to do quicker and easier.

It was all over before he'd gotten much of a chance to enjoy it.

Alone in her Seapoint bedroom, looking out at the vast emptiness of the Atlantic Ocean, Prudence fought against the temptation to give in. To surrender to whatever it was that had already affected Geoffrey and was gradually transforming him into someone she hardly recognized.

She tried to analyze what the difference was, but it was hard to quantify. Most of the time he appeared to be the same supportive partner upon whom she had come to rely, and yet some acutely logical and observant part of him was slipping away. No, that wasn't quite right. The sharp edges of the intelligence that made him so formidable an investigator seemed to have softened. It was as though a part of his brain had decided not to take note of certain things, to pass over others without judging or assessing them.

She realized then how often she thought of Geoffrey in terms of his Pinkerton past. Although she knew almost no details of any of the cases on which he had worked or the assignments he had undertaken, that was the side of him she knew best—the epitome of detective. Of his private life, and especially his family, she knew next to nothing. He was born in North Carolina, had been sent North to boarding school where he met and befriended her late fiancé shortly after the war ended, was independently wealthy, and at some point, had a short but successful career with the Pinkerton National Detective Agency.

That was it. The sum total of the man.

Whatever else she did or did not accomplish before they returned to New York, she decided that resolving the enigma of Geoffrey Hunter would be of crucial, pivotal importance in the life she was carving out for herself.

Or the one they might create together.

Eleanor's fate seemed to mingle with the dark shadows of Geoffrey's past.

If she could understand one, would she unravel the mystery of the other?

A soft knock roused Prudence from the reverie into which she had drifted, lulled into woolgathering by the soft sea air, the warmth of the day, and a fatigue that was as much emotional as it was physical.

Before she could call out an invitation to enter, Eleanor's mother pushed open the door and stepped inside. She looked terrible. Ravaged, desolate of eye and heart, drained of the lifeblood that was her daughter. In her hands she held the jewelry box containing the pearls worn on their wedding days by three generations of her family's women. She held the case out to Prudence, who took it from Abigail's trembling fingers and laid it on the table where they had shared early morning coffee two days ago.

"When I next see her, Prudence," her friend's mother whispered, "I'd like her to be wearing the pearls. Her father won't want her to be buried in them. He's a practical man; he'll say they're too valuable to be thrown away like that." She laid a hand on the velvet box, but didn't raise the lid. "No one but another woman would understand. Eleanor was my only child, my only daughter. I couldn't bear it if Philip were to sell them and some stranger draped them around her neck. I couldn't bear it."

"I dressed her in her veil and wedding gown this morning, Mrs. Dickson," Prudence said. "I promise I'll place the pearls on her myself. She'll be a truly beautiful bride."

"Yes, she will be. A beautiful bride." Abigail touched Prudence gently on one cheek, then drifted out of the room like a meandering ghost, one hand lightly touching a table, a chair, the doorframe as she groped her way back to her room and her empty life.

"Aunt Jessa come back while you was at Wildacre with Mr. Teddy yestidday," a skinny little girl sitting on a three-legged stool by the cellar door told Prudence. "She say give you this." On the palm of her hand lay a bracelet made of nine small shells strung evenly on a braid of seagrass. Knotted between each shell was a round white pebble painted with an elongated black oval.

"You got to wear it, miss," the skinny little girl said, slipping the bracelet on Prudence's wrist before she could protest. "It protect you 'gainst the evil eye. Aunt Jessa make it her own self and say the words. I only ever saw one other like it," she finished enviously. "You got the good juju now." Then she picked up her stool and ran off in the direction of the servants' dining room.

Prudence heard the slam of an outer door and knew she'd lost any chance of questioning her. When she tried to pull the amulet over her hand to remove it, the seagrass seemed to have shrunk. It wouldn't budge. *Never mind,* she thought, *I'll take a pair of scissors to it later.*

Carrying the jewelry box containing the precious pearls, Prudence made her way into the cellar, following the lantern light shining up the staircase. This time there was no white-turbaned woman waiting for her.

Like the effigy of a knight's lady, Eleanor lay atop the decanting table, waiting for the elaborate coffin ordered from the mainland undertaker whose card Lawrence Bennett had given Geoffrey. Prudence looped the rope of pearls around the dead woman's neck and fastened the diamond clasp.

As her mother had predicted, Eleanor was a beautiful bride.

Twilight came early that late afternoon, brought on by banks of heavy clouds rolling in across the ocean to cover the island in a soft gray pall that smelled of salt and seaweed. The air cooled, but without thunder or the threat of rain. The canopy of the live oaks wore a translucent sheen that turned the narrow dark green leaves silver.

Standing on the balcony outside her bedroom, Prudence tried to imagine Eleanor's flight across Seapoint's lawns into the shadows of the forest. She opened the French door into her friend's room, picked up a scarf left lying on a chaise longue, and pressed it to her face. Eleanor's familiar cologne enveloped her in a wave of memory and grief.

Moments later Prudence herself disappeared into the gloom beneath the twisted branches of the live oaks.

The walking was easy at first. There were no marked or raked-shell paths, but deer and wild pigs had etched out trails that wound toward springs of fresh water and dense thickets of saw palmetto and wax myrtle in which to hide and birth their young.

Prudence hadn't stopped to put on a shawl against the chill of the deep shade; now she wished she had as drops of early dew trickled onto her hair and arms. Her house shoes were delicate slippers made of thin, soft leather through which she could feel the sand and hard-as-rock acorns beneath her feet.

She had no purpose in mind other than to re-create Eleanor's odyssey, no rationale other than the conviction that if she trod in her footsteps she might somehow enter her friend's mind.

Maybe it's the cat's-eye stones in the shell bracelet working their white magic, she thought, running a tentative finger along their polished surfaces. They were as smooth as the satiny pearls that would go into the ground with Eleanor.

Prudence walked in a halo of silence as she penetrated deeper into the woods. Ahead and behind her she could hear the scuffling of squirrels and small rodents, the warbling and squawks of sea and land birds, the swish of wind through trees and grasses. She stopped frequently to look around, to listen, to wait for Eleanor's voice in her head.

But nothing happened. The small, scampering animals reminded her of the ones she saw and heard in Central Park, but the forest itself remained a collection of unfamiliar trees and plants. There were no voices in her head, nothing but frustration and a growing sense of unease to keep her company.

What had she been thinking to come out here alone? Geoffrey would be furious if he found out how impulsively she'd acted. And then, a split second later: *What right does he have to think he can tell me what to do?* She marched along to the rhythm of a mental dialogue that would probably never find voice but was immensely satisfying. The arguments she made to her silent partner were as well reasoned as any she could hope to present to a jury. And, unlike what had seemed to occur so often since they'd come to the island, her imaginary Geoffrey listened and forebore from criticizing her. It was a wonderful conversation. She won every point she attempted to make. Hands down.

It was time to turn around. She had no idea how deeply she'd penetrated the forest or how long she had been gone from the house. The only other occasion on which she'd come this way was with the search party that had hoped to find Eleanor alive. She'd been on horseback then, surrounded by islanders who knew their way through foliage that looked exactly alike in all directions. She didn't think she had anything to fear from a doe, but she certainly didn't want to encounter a wild pig on one of these narrow paths.

Her shoes were ruined, the leather sopping wet and muddy. The hem of her dress had been snagged so many times by jagged saw palmetto that it looked as though a mischievous child had taken a pair of scissors to it. She tried to twist her hair back on top of her head where it belonged, but the pins had fallen out long ago without her noticing it. Somehow, she'd have to find her way back to Seapoint, sneak into the house without anyone seeing her, then appear in the dining room for dinner as though she'd done nothing more exciting this afternoon than nap in her bedroom.

She could do it, she decided. Prudence MacKenzie had been in far worse predicaments before and come out of them unscathed. Relatively speaking.

All she had to do was retrace her steps. Keep her eyes out for her footprints in the damp, leaf-strewn sand, follow the trail she'd left behind, and hurry! No dawdling, no pretend conversations with Geoffrey, no wistful imaginings that the ghost of Eleanor would whisper in her ear. Hurry!

The eyes began to track her as soon as she took the first wrong turn toward the swamp instead of the house. By the time she realized that the scuffed footprints she could barely make out were too big to be hers, it was too late. She was well and truly lost.

Don't panic, she told herself. The rapid thumping of her heart nearly deafened her. *Find the sun. It should be sinking in the west, and the rear balconies of Seapoint face west.* But the sun was hidden behind the clouds, not a single streak of red or gold penetrating the dense gray. How much longer before true darkness descended? Prudence shuddered and then began to shake—cold, wet, and suddenly afraid of what the next few hours would bring.

The skinny little girl saw the pretty lady Aunt Jessa was protecting walk into the live oaks and knew right away she was headed toward trouble. Her kind of folk didn't have no business messing around where the swamp could reach out and pull them down. No, sir. They was things in the trees and the mud that didn't bear thinking on.

But what was she gonna do about it? You didn't go to Aunt Jessa's cabin without no invitation, and the skinny little girl had been told in no uncertain terms to stay away. Deliver the juju amulet, make sure it got on the pretty lady's wrist, then take herself out of the picture. Two out of three weren't bad. She'd just hung around the kitchen in case someone had food that needed getting rid of. The skinny little girl was always hungry.

While she was cogitating, the handsome Yankee who wasn't really what everybody thought he was came out onto the lawn and sauntered down to the beach. When he returned a few minutes later, he was walking faster and looking all around, like he'd gone out after someone and had come up short.

It didn't take but a rabbit-tail minute to make up her mind.

The skinny little girl told him what she'd seen. "She wearing the juju bracelet," she added when he dropped a coin into her outstretched hand. "Cain't nothing too bad happen to her."

But Geoffrey Hunter knew there wasn't enough white magic in the world to matter much if the black gris-gris was too strong.

He saw the shimmer of her dress through the trees and stepped off the deer path.

She was walking slowly, head down, stopping every now and then to study the trail so she wouldn't accidentally double back on herself.

Geoffrey grinned and flattened his back against a tree trunk.

It might take her a while, but it looked like she was going to find her way home without him. Probably best to let her do it on her own. Keep an eye on her, but don't interfere. She was in a prickly enough temper as it was.

The first thing he thought when he saw the shadow looming behind her was *bear*! But there hadn't been any black bears on the barrier islands since the plantation owners cleared and planted the land, driving the creatures inland toward the mountains. Panthers liked to stretch out along a thick live oak limb and wait for dinner to pass by below, and wild pigs didn't rear back on their hind legs to look like a man with outstretched arms. Then again, veils of Spanish moss hung nearly to the ground from some of the trees, twisting and turning like tattered phantom apparitions.

"Prudence," he called, loud enough to frighten away anything on four feet.

Palmetto leaves rattled noisily as something large pushed its way through them. Whatever it had been was gone before he could get a good look at it.

Prudence's head snapped up, and for a moment he saw a look of pure relief cross her face. Then her features arranged themselves into a ferocious scowl and she stamped one muddy foot. "Did you follow me?"

"No, ma'am," he said. It was the only sensible answer to give.

"Then what are you doing out here?"

"I could ask you the same question."

Stalemate. But the shadow, whatever it was, had disappeared. If something, or someone, had been stalking Prudence, Geoffrey's arrival and his shout had scared it away.

"We might as well walk back together," he said, ignoring Prudence's flyaway hair and ruined skirts. "If you don't mind the company."

"On one condition. I don't want to hear a word about how

many times you told me to be careful out here." There was a determined ring to her voice that told him she wasn't going to back down.

"I promise," he said, taking off his jacket to wrap it around her cold, damp shoulders. He thought she sagged against him for a moment in sheer gratitude at having been found. But Prudence being Prudence, the moment of weakness was brief and unacknowledged.

When they resumed walking, arm in arm, she looked straight ahead and never slowed down or faltered.

Aunt Jessa lay still and broken in the cabin where she'd strung the amulet against the evil eye. Her blood spattered the floor and dotted the walls. Beads and shells and juju dolls lay scattered around her, crushed and ground into the wood planking. The sheets and blankets had been torn from her bed, the corn shuck mattress hacked to pieces.

Somebody had looked hard and long for something.

And hadn't found it.

CHAPTER 9

Teddy came for them early the next morning.

"I got the news right after sunup," he said, gulping a cup of coffee in the Seapoint dining room. "We'll have to hurry before everything gets cleaned up. I told Jonah not to let anyone touch her or the cabin, but that may not stop them from trying to wash the body."

"Prudence?" Geoffrey was already on his feet.

"I'm coming," she said. "Give me ten minutes to get my boots and riding skirt on."

"Ten minutes. No more."

"All Jonah would say was that it was bad, real bad." Teddy kept his voice low as he and Geoffrey waited for two Seapoint horses to be saddled and brought from the stables.

"Has someone gone after the sheriff?" Prudence was slightly out of breath. She'd changed into riding clothes and run as quickly down the stairs as she could, afraid they would start off without her.

"The sheriff won't be coming," Teddy answered.

"Why not?"

"That's not the way things are done down here, Prudence," Geoffrey said quietly. He expected her to explode, and she did.

"That's the most appalling thing I've ever heard! A harmless old woman is murdered and no white person cares?"

"I care," Teddy said. "She mothered me from the time I was born until I went away to school. She was always there when I came home on vacation. We shared a life. I don't expect you to understand how that could be, but it's true."

Prudence sputtered at the effrontery and downright gall of Teddy's assertion, but she had no words to refute it.

Geoffrey watched the play of indignant emotions across her face and turned away, unwilling for her to read what he was thinking. He understood exactly what Teddy had felt for the former slave he couldn't save from a brutal death. It was the dichotomy of the South, one of the mysteries that both repelled and attracted him.

They rode out with Teddy in the lead, threading their way along a trail that was more than a deer path but less than a road. The sun flickered through the live oaks, casting dancing shadows that spooked the horses and made them prance and shy. Prudence rode with a tight rein; she'd vetoed a sidesaddle and marveled at the immediate ease with which she'd taken to riding astride. Neither Geoffrey nor Teddy seemed to have noticed that she'd violated yet another rule of ladylike deportment.

Thirty minutes into the live oaks, the track they were following widened into a fork.

"This way," Teddy signaled, and slowed his horse to a walk.

They'd been right to come as quickly as they had. A man who could only be the Jonah Teddy had spoken of was arguing fiercely with two women who were giving him no quarter. Another man stood off to one side, waiting. He was leaning on a spade.

"I tole 'em, Mister Teddy," Jonah said, standing his ground while the women glared and muttered beneath their breath. "I tole 'em not to touch nothin' 'till you got here."

"Thank you, Jonah." Teddy swung down easily from his horse as the man with the spade stepped forward to take the reins. "This is Mr. Hunter," Teddy announced to all and sundry, certain there were others within hearing distance. "He used to be a Pinkerton. You know what that means. He's a detective."

"He gonna find out who done this?" one of the women asked. Belligerent doubt and fearful respect warred in her voice and eyes.

"He'll do everything he can," Teddy confirmed. "Now you all just stand back and let him see what's happened here."

Taking their lead from Teddy, Prudence and Geoffrey dismounted and handed their reins to Jonah and the man with the shovel. Geoffrey nodded politely in the direction of the angry women, then began walking toward Aunt Jessa's open cabin door, Prudence right behind him. Ten steps from the covered front porch, he stopped.

"What is that?" Prudence asked.

A small cross had been planted in the dirt. Charred and blistered, it had clearly been set afire, burning until the fuel that had doused it was used up or the night dampness extinguished the flames. The cross was no more than two feet tall; it wouldn't have been a fire big or bright enough to draw anyone's attention.

"That's the Klan," Geoffrey said. "It was banned almost twenty years ago. According to the law, it doesn't exist anymore."

"The Enforcement Act of 1871," Prudence quoted. "Signed by President Ulysses S. Grant. There were three Enforcement Acts all told. My father considered them the most necessary legislation of the Reconstruction period." She looked down at the blackened cross. "Why is this here if the Klan was eradicated?"

"They went underground," Geoffrey said. "Most of the Klan disbanded, but a certain number of fanatics are biding their time until the political climate is ripe for them to climb out of their holes."

Teddy knocked the cross over with one booted foot. "I probably shouldn't have done that, Geoffrey," he said apologetically. "I guess you'd call it destroying evidence."

"It wouldn't have told us anything we don't already know. There was a whiff of kerosene, but that was to be expected. The sand is so scuffed up it's no use looking for footprints. There aren't any."

Aunt Jessa was lying in the center of the one-room cabin.

"Stay here by the door," Geoffrey told Teddy and Prudence. He didn't wait for an answer, moving swiftly and lightly around the body, spiraling ever closer to the dead woman until he was close enough to kneel down beside her. By then he knew nearly as much about how she died as if he'd been a witness. The blood spatters and the condition of the body told an eloquent story. Her assailant had beaten her unmercifully, probably not stopping until she was dead. There were no wounds of self-defense on her hands, no human skin beneath her nails. Her eyes were wide open, staring at eternity.

When Geoffrey nodded in their direction, Teddy crossed to kneel beside the woman he had cherished in ways outsiders could not understand. He held his hand over her eyes until they stayed closed. Prudence sidled around the bloodstains on the floor to stand beside the bed, studying the rips in the mattress, the way the covers had been flung off. She nudged the mattress up on its side and peered through the netted ropes on which it had rested. Aunt Jessa had been a meticulous housekeeper. There was no dust under her bed.

The cupboards had been emptied, their contents flung to the floor, smashed and scattered. Not a jar lid had been left unscrewed; every box had been upended. A dress, a nightgown, and an apron had been pulled from the nails on which they had hung and tossed into the mess of spilled flour, honey, and rice.

Seashells ready to be strung into necklaces or bracelets lay among round stones painted with the oval that looked like an eye. Faceless, broken dolls would never have their features painted on and hair pasted to their skulls. Bunches of drying herbs Prudence could no longer identify had been pulled down from the low ceiling and stomped underfoot.

The ruined ingredients for Aunt Jessa's white magic lay all around her.

"This wasn't a casual killing," Geoffrey said, standing to survey the damage to the cabin and its occupant's possessions. "He was searching for something she wasn't willing to give up. Not even at the cost of her own life."

"Did he find it?" Prudence asked, trying not to look at the body of the woman who had shown such tenderness toward another victim. "Was it the same person who murdered Eleanor?" Any doubts she'd had about whether Eleanor's death could have been an accident had dissolved as swiftly as the island's early morning mists.

"If he had found it, he would have stopped searching. There would be a cupboard left untouched or clothing still hanging on the wall. Something undamaged. No, Prudence, he didn't find what he came for."

"Was it the same person who murdered Eleanor?" Teddy repeated Prudence's question.

"Possibly," Geoffrey said. "It's a small island to contain two violent killers."

"Eleanor wasn't savagely beaten," Prudence said. "Her death has the air of premeditation about it." Both men listened attentively. "She was lured out of her father's house, somehow made to go to a place she greatly feared, then coldly and callously drowned. That's not at all the same as what was done to Aunt Jessa."

"You're arguing that there are more differences than similarities between the two crimes?" Geoffrey said.

"I'm thinking aloud. Trying to reason my way through two evil acts that make no sense. That's all."

"Who would want to kill Eleanor?" Teddy said.

"Exactly," Prudence agreed. "And who would commit this unspeakable abomination on a helpless old woman? I can't find a motive for either crime, let alone anything that ties them together."

"Motive, means, and opportunity," Geoffrey said. "We need answers to all three if we're to prove a case." He looked toward the open door where the two women Jonah had held back were waiting patiently. One carried a bucket, full from the way she held it, the other a handful of rags, a scrub brush, and a bar of strong lye soap. "We're done here," he said. "We'll let you all get on with what you've got to do."

Aunt Jessa's grave would be dug in the burial ground beside the small clapboard church constructed by Bradford Island's ex-slaves and their descendants. Over the years they'd used unpainted scrap lumber when nothing better could be had, and the result was a building that looked and felt humble and welcoming, open to God and the elements through shuttered but paneless windows. Sheltered, some would say *hidden*, in the live oaks.

Neither the sheriff nor the coroner would be notified of her passing. Or of the crime.

Aunt Jessa's birth had gone unrecorded except in the slave ledgers of Wildacre Plantation.

Her death was meant to be forgotten.

"I'm not sure they'll talk to an off-islander," Teddy said.

"They'll talk to me," Geoffrey asserted confidently.

"Because you were a Pinkerton?"

"That's one reason." He glanced at Prudence, who was following the conversation with an obvious effort to catch and understand what was being left unsaid. "The other is that I'm not a Bennett. They have less reason to hide anything from me."

"Times haven't changed as much as Washington would like to think they have," Teddy said. "I realize that whenever I go away and come back. Sometimes I think life isn't much different now for some of our people than it was in slavery days . . . except for the buying and selling. The fear is still there."

"Yet you and Eleanor were planning to live in Savannah eventually, and here on the island." Prudence thought she'd caught the gist of what Teddy meant. If she applied it to Geoffrey, would it begin to explain what she'd found so baffling about him lately?

"I don't belong in the North." Teddy looked off in the distance toward Wildacre and the ocean. "I'm not sure I'm entirely comfortable here either now, but it's the only place where I feel fully alive."

They'd tethered their horses and gone to stand unobtrusively beneath the low-hanging branches and sweeping Spanish moss of one of the ancient live oaks shading the burial ground where Aunt Jessa's grave was being dug. The dull thud of spades thrusting into sandy soil reverberated in the stillness. Figures had begun to materialize through the trees. Men, women, and children moving like dignified wraiths toward the clearing. One older man, holding a Bible in his right hand, waited at the church door.

"Here they come," Teddy said, taking off his hat.

Prudence shaded her eyes with one hand. The light scintillating through the leaves made it difficult to distinguish the approaching cortege.

Six men carried Aunt Jessa's sheet-wrapped body on their shoulders. There was no coffin. Women dressed head to foot in white accompanied them. They hummed as they walked, barefoot, swaying slightly from side to side. Moments after having emerged from the live oaks, they disappeared into the church. The man holding the Bible nodded in Teddy's direction, then followed inside.

"That's Preacher Solomon," Teddy said, moving out of the shade.

"Is it all right?" Prudence asked hesitantly.

"Did you see him nod at us?"

"That was an invitation to join the service," Geoffrey explained. He didn't need to add that without Preacher Solomon's nod, they would have remained outside. A white man could go anywhere he wanted, but neither Teddy nor Geoffrey would abuse that privilege.

They sat on the backless wooden bench closest to the door. There were no pews as such. The walls of the church had been whitewashed, and a small wood table stood at the front, on it a lit candle and Preacher Solomon's Bible. Hands upraised, palms facing out, he was leading the small congregation in a hymn that was also a prayer. Deep, soft voices sang and hummed a song so beautiful and melancholy it brought tears to Prudence's eyes.

No one had looked around when they'd entered.

It was as if they were invisible.

"Prudence and I will go back to the cabin," Geoffrey told Teddy when the grave had been filled, tamped down, and covered in a blanket of chalk-white seashells. By the end of the day a wooden marker with Aunt Jessa's name on it would be placed at the head.

"Will you be able to find your way back to Seapoint?"

"We'll give the horses their heads. They'll do the job for us." Geoffrey held the reins of Prudence's horse as she mounted, then took something out of his jacket and handed it to Teddy.

"What did you give him?" Prudence asked as they moved off.

"A lock of hair," Geoffrey answered. "It was in Aunt Jessa's apron pocket when I searched the body."

"Was it Eleanor's?"

"I assume so. Aunt Jessa must have taken it when she dressed her."

"I wonder why."

"If I had to guess, I'd say she was planning to make a juju doll for Teddy that would embody Eleanor's spirit and bring him comfort. But she ran out of time."

For some reason, although Prudence knew next to nothing about white and black magic, it seemed to make sense. "Why are we going back to the cabin?" she asked. "Didn't you tell the women with the bucket and rags that they could clean it? There won't be any clues left." She was tired and emotionally drained. The cool elegance of Seapoint would have been a welcome relief from the morning's heartache.

"We'll sit on Aunt Jessa's porch and wait," Geoffrey told her.

"Wait for what?"

"For the people to come and tell us what we need to know."

"I don't understand."

"There are stories that are crying out to be told, but we won't learn any of them by asking questions of men and women who have learned that silence is their best defense," Geoffrey said. "What we'll do is sit quietly and wait. First one will come, then another. Never two or more together. That way there won't be any witnesses to what each person has to say. No proof it was ever said."

"Are they that afraid?"

"You would be, too, Prudence, if you had to live in their skin."

CHAPTER 10

Jonah was the first to appear.

"What made you come by here this morning?" Geoffrey asked. He kept his eyes fixed on the man's feet or off to one side so Jonah could watch him while he was talking and judge for himself whether this ex-Pinkerton person could be trusted. No man of color dared look a white person boldly in the eye.

"I come by most ever' day, suh. Make sure she got kindling wood for the fire. Bring a squirrel or a mess of crabs for the stew pot. Aunt Jessa never did have no chirren of her own to look after her when she put on years."

"Do you know how old she was?" asked Prudence.

"No, ma'am. She didn't know her own self. She was already gettin' on when freedom come."

"But today you were here earlier than usual. Was there any special reason for that, Jonah?" Geoffrey persisted.

"She ain't been herself in a long time. Not since last winter."

"What do you mean? How wasn't she her normal self?"

"Aunt Jessa never was one to complain. She take the bad with the good and mix 'em all up together. Claimed it made life easier that way. But like I said, she changed. Got forgetful, like her mind was always somewhere else. Worked more spells than I ever knowed her do before. But she wouldn't tell no one what they was for. Then when the young miss got herself drowned in the swamp, it was like Aunt Jessa lost one of her own. She sat in that rockin' chair of hers with the tears streamin' down her face like she weren't never gonna stop cryin'."

"Did she tell you why?"

"The only thing she said was that she should have seen it comin'. Should have seen it comin'."

"But you don't know what she meant?" Geoffrey asked.

"No, suh. But she was takin' on the blame for it, whatever it was."

"You still haven't said why you came over before sunup this morning," Prudence put in. "Did you hear something that woke you up? A horse moving through the trees, perhaps?"

"No, ma'am, nothing like that," Jonah hedged. "I couldn't sleep, so I figured I'd get on with the day and see to what needed to be done."

"And after you found Aunt Jessa, you went to fetch Mr. Teddy," Geoffrey prompted. "Why was that?"

"Mr. Teddy was always her favorite. Everybody know she was partial. It was the same when he growed up. She loved that chile to death, and he loved her back."

"And you thought he'd care," Prudence said softly.

"Yes, ma'am, I did. I knowed he'd do right by her. If he could."

"Did Aunt Jessa have anything valuable in her cabin?" Geoffrey asked. "Could Mr. Teddy have given her something that somebody else would want badly enough to try to rob her? Money, perhaps?"

Jonah shook his head. "Ain't nobody got two coins to rub together most days. She the same as everyone else. Nothin' worth stealing."

"Could she have put a hex on someone?"

"She only do white magic. You gotta go to Queen Lula for the black juju."

"Can you think of *any* reason for what happened, Jonah?"

"Aunt Jessa never did have no enemies. She could walk out in the live oaks in the full moonlight and not even the panthers or the wild pigs would bother her."

"I was thinking of the two-legged variety."

"None of them neither. Not man nor woman." Jonah turned to go. "I only got one more thing to say, Mr. Hunter."

"What is that?"

"This be devil work, suh. As bad as anything I ever seen or heard tell of in slave days. And it don't get much worse than that."

Preacher Solomon spoke in biblical cadences with a solemnity that raised his every utterance above the ordinary. He was older than either Prudence or Geoffrey had at first believed him to be, but it was impossible to pinpoint his age. Like Aunt Jessa, he had been born into slavery and spent most of his life under its yoke. His hands were gnarled and scarred, his face weathered to the consistency of oiled leather, his body lean and sinewy from decades of never having enough to eat. But Preacher Solomon's eyes were bright and sharp, his teeth white and strong, his mind unclouded by the depredations of time or man.

"Seem like the women got it worse than the men sometimes," he said, then stopped, shook his head, and gazed off into the distance.

"How can that be?" Prudence asked after nearly a minute had passed with no further explanation. Images of slaves toiling in cotton and rice fields under a broiling sun rolled through her mind. Accounts published by anti-slavery factions, some of them chilling narratives by former slaves themselves, had been widely disseminated in the North. Many of them had found their way into her father's extensive library.

Preacher Solomon cast a quick glance at Geoffrey, who seemed to hesitate, then nod his permission to go ahead.

"They children got sold away more often than not. Mistress didn't want no reminders around the place."

"Reminders?"

Again Preacher Solomon looked at Geoffrey.

"Women and girls couldn't refuse their master, his male relatives, or his friends. Couldn't refuse any white man, for that matter. Still can't," Geoffrey said steadily, forcing himself to speak the unpalatable truth without using words that would shock and horrify Prudence. He knew she understood what he meant when a wave of scarlet turned her cheeks bright red and she ducked her head. "I'm sorry you had to hear that," he apologized.

"Did it happen here?" she asked, her voice shaky but undaunted. "Did it happen at Wildacre?"

"Yes, ma'am," Preacher Solomon replied. "Not Mister Teddy. He never would do nothin' like that. Not even when other young gentlemen was visiting the quarters regular-like and dippin' they wicks."

Prudence was relieved and appalled at the same time. Teddy might not have taken advantage of the ex-slave women who remained on the island, but if what Preacher Solomon said was true, other white men did so with utter impunity. It seemed that emancipation brought very little real change to their plight.

"What about the other Bennett men? Before the war?" she asked.

"All you gotta do is look around you, miss," Preacher Solomon said. "They still a few of 'em left on the island. Can't be sold off like in slavery days."

"Their own children?" Prudence's face showed anger, disgust, and revulsion. "How could they do that? What were they thinking?"

"Weren't no thought to it. No feeling one way or the other, neither. Slave woman gots to have babies. Otherwise how's master gonna make him any money off her? Women what don't have children end up in the fields or sold."

To Preacher Solomon the past was as alive as the present. The only thing that had changed was the disappearance of public auction blocks. Reconstruction was over, and with it any hope for permanent change. One at a time, the bad old days were creeping back.

"Tell us about Aunt Jessa," Geoffrey said. "We've heard that she had no enemies, that there wasn't anyone on the island who would wish her harm."

Preacher Solomon shook his head. "Ain't so. Folks don't like to speak ill of the dead, so they start forgettin' what they don't want to remember." He shifted his Bible from right hand to left, then shoved it into a pocket. "Mostly she were a good woman, but she done some things the Lord wouldn't countenance. Not hardly."

"Such as?" Prudence asked.

"Stopping babies from being born. Telling women they don't got to stay with they husbands after they been beat. Puttin' dreams into heads that didn't have no business hankering for 'em. Some of the men 'round here thought she needed to keep her nose out of they business."

"So it was mainly husbands who had grudges against her?" Geoffrey asked.

"The Bible say a woman got to obey, no matter what. Aunt Jessa didn't hold with that."

"Good for Aunt Jessa," Prudence muttered.

"Was there anyone in particular who might have wanted her dead?"

"She a keeper of secrets. Nobody could say what or how many, but if you done something you needed to hide, she knew about it."

"So people were afraid of her?"

"More like they was afraid of what she might do."

"If they crossed her?"

"Or she thought you was gonna do something bad and she needed to stop you."

"Can you give us an example?" Prudence asked.

"No, ma'am, not without rakin' up old business better left where it lie. I think mebbe I say too much as it is." Preacher Solomon clapped his hat on his head, took the Bible out of his pocket, and disappeared into the live oaks.

"I'm not sure what good this is doing us," Prudence complained when he was out of earshot. "Jonah and Preacher Solomon both stopped talking just when I thought we were on the verge of finding out something important."

"I want to take one more look inside," Geoffrey said. No one else waited in the dirt yard to talk to them; he didn't see any shadows among the trees.

"Everything will have been cleaned up and put back in place," Prudence protested.

"Exactly. The women who scrubbed the blood off the floor and walls and picked up what had been tossed around knew Aunt Jessa well. They would have put her things back where they belonged. So what we'll see is the cabin the way it was before she was attacked. Sometimes you have to step into a person's everyday life to understand him. Or her."

Geoffrey was right. As usual. Aunt Jessa's one-room home was as clean and tidy as though she had just gone out to fetch some wood or a bucket of water from the spring.

"I'm amazed," Prudence said. "You'd never know how terrible it was just a couple of hours ago."

"Those women have spent their entire lives cleaning up after other people," Geoffrey reminded her.

She could feel the warmth of an embarrassed flush creep up her neck. Why did she always seem to say the wrong thing down here? "I meant it as a compliment," she said, but even that hadn't come out right.

Geoffrey walked around the cabin corner to corner and wall

to wall, studying everything on the shelves, lifting the lids off cauldrons suspended from hooks in the fireplace, picking up pots of replanted herbs and flowers. Whatever was ruined had been thrown away, but enough remained to give a sense of what Aunt Jessa would have seen as she lay on her bed or threaded a juju amulet.

"Something's missing," Geoffrey said. "I can feel it."

Prudence was mystified. How could he tell something that should be there wasn't? As far as she knew, he'd never been inside this cabin before today.

"Everybody has a place to hide secrets," he explained. "A letter or a photograph can be slipped between the pages of a Bible, something small and valuable dropped into a flour sack or bag of sugar, a box of mementos secreted beneath a loose floorboard. Look around you, Prudence. Do you see any place where you'd be comfortable hiding your most valuable possession?"

She tried to imagine herself in Aunt Jessa's place, searching her walls and floor and everything she owned for a safe hiding place for something that was worth killing over. Remembering the thoroughness with which someone had turned everything inside out and upside down. Geoffrey had said the searcher hadn't found it, whatever it was. And so far, he'd been right about everything.

"There's no place in this cabin to hide anything," Prudence admitted. "Unless . . . ?"

"I asked Jonah to crawl underneath after they took the body out," Geoffrey said. The cabin was set on stacks of stone cemented with tabby. "He didn't find anything there either."

"Then I'm completely at a loss," Prudence said. "Maybe she never had anything to hide, after all. The killer was looking for something that doesn't exist, and so are we."

"It exists, all right. You heard Preacher Solomon. If anyone on this island had a secret, Aunt Jessa knew what it was."

"What good would it do her?"

"Power," Geoffrey said. "It gives you sway over people, but it also makes you vulnerable."

"Motive? Is that our motive?"

"It's the only one we have right now," Geoffrey said ambiguously.

They waited another hour, sitting quietly on the cabin's front porch. The day grew hotter and quieter as everything in the live oak forest succumbed to the afternoon doldrums.

It was only May. Prudence wondered again how anyone could stand the heat of August.

"Geoffrey?" She'd had a horrible thought that she couldn't get out of her mind. "What's going to happen to Eleanor? If Mr. Dickson doesn't change his mind and allow Teddy to bury her in the Bennett family plot, I mean?"

"There's an arsenic-based compound they used during the war to embalm the bodies of soldiers whose kin wanted them shipped home," Geoffrey said, understanding what she was asking. "It doesn't take a great deal of skill and I imagine every undertaker in every small town knows how to use it."

Prudence shuddered. "How awful."

"Don't think about it too much."

She lapsed into silence, but as the mosquitos continued to find her and flies buzzed over the sand where bloodied water had been tossed, Prudence grew too restless and uncomfortable to sit still. She walked to where the horses had been tethered, fiddled unnecessarily with her saddle, then stood absentmindedly running her fingers through her mount's mane. She'd had the barest tease of an idea that obstinately refused to surface where she could get a good look at it. Something someone had said today? Something she'd seen but not taken conscious note of?

"We can leave now, Prudence, if you want," Geoffrey said. "I don't think anyone else is going to show."

When had he gotten up from the porch and closed the cabin

door? Prudence had been so lost in her thoughts that she hadn't noticed. "Did they not come because of me? Because I'm so obviously an outsider?"

"Maybe." He'd decided not to pretend otherwise despite knowing the truth would sting. "It could be they need more time."

"I don't want to give up," she said. "I want to find out who murdered Eleanor and why. And I think Aunt Jessa deserves the same degree of justice."

"She does. You're right about that."

"But I've been wrong about so many other things. Is that what you're trying to say?"

"This is a world you can't be expected to understand, Prudence."

"I wasn't born and brought up thinking it's all right to own other human beings," she flared.

He stepped back as though she'd slapped him.

Then he untied his horse's reins and led the animal out from under the trees. He swung into the saddle. And waited.

They said not a word to each other all the long way back to Seapoint.

CHAPTER 11

❧

The undertaker and his assistant recruited four of Seapoint's youngest and strongest male staff to help them wrestle Eleanor's lead-lined oak coffin off the flatbed ferry that had brought it from the mainland. The wheels of the cart that hauled it to the house sank deeply into the roadbed of crushed shells. The coffin itself weighed at least three or four times more than the young woman whose body would lie within.

Philip Dickson watched from the open door of the small stone chapel where his daughter's wedding was to have taken place. Sawhorses draped in black crepe stood before the altar. The coffin would remain there, behind locked doors, until he decreed otherwise. No one, including the grieving father himself, knew when that would be.

"It's been four days," Dickson said, cutting the end off one of the Cuban cigars he favored. Whether he was smoking or not, his Seapoint library had the familiar reek of tobacco and leather that permeated the air of his New York offices.

"There's been another killing," Geoffrey began bluntly. He had reminded himself that men like Eleanor's father only showed their true emotions when hit by stark truth delivered in unembellished language. Dickson might avow that his family was safe from his business competitors, but Geoffrey was less certain. Former Pinkerton colleagues working undercover to destroy the nascent labor union movement had told him too many accounts of cold-blooded viciousness that ignored niceties of age, gender, or direct involvement with labor organizers. Dickson's response to this second death might give away an uncertainty he was anxious to hide.

Philip's hand holding the match flame to his cigar never wavered. "Tell me," he said.

"Do you remember the old woman I mentioned?" Prudence asked. She didn't know what Geoffrey was up to, but she refused to be left on the sidelines. "Her name was Aunt Jessa."

"We've managed to find out a good deal about her," Geoffrey interrupted. "She was beaten senseless."

"Savagely beaten," Prudence added.

"Who was she?" asked Philip. Prudence's effort to humanize the murder of a woman he'd never met failed to touch Eleanor's father. Except where his wife and daughter were concerned, and even then not always, he lived in a world of facts, not feelings.

"An ex-slave who had once belonged to the Bennett family," Geoffrey said in a businesslike tone, watching Dickson's face for any change of expression.

"As did every person of color on this island," Philip said. "One way or the other. Born into slavery or children of slaves. The stigma remains." He looked at Geoffrey for affirmation.

It was on the tip of Geoffrey's tongue to say that he didn't believe the stain would ever be erased, that it was as real as the color of the skin that bore it, but one look at Prudence's face and he bit back the comment.

The silence between them on the ride back to Seapoint yesterday evening had been agonizing, yet neither of them had been able to break it. They hadn't spoken to one another since.

"She raised the Bennett children until it was time to turn them over to a tutor or governess." Geoffrey was choosing his words carefully. "We were told that Teddy had always been her favorite and that he returned the affection."

Philip snorted in disbelief. He'd grown up in a family where displays of warmth or tenderness toward children were as rare as hen's teeth. "Why was she killed?" It was the same, as yet unanswered, question he had asked about Eleanor.

"We don't know," Prudence said.

"It depends on who you talk to," Geoffrey amended. "According to Jonah, the man who found the body, she was loved and respected by everyone on the island. Someone else told us that she interfered with nature and a husband's rights." He shrugged his shoulders. "One thing is very clear, though. She knew things about people, white and black alike."

"What was her connection to Eleanor? What was she doing in the cellar before you interrupted her?" Philip demanded of Prudence, who simply stared at him. "And what's that thing you're wearing on your wrist?"

She held out her arm as if it didn't belong to her and she'd only now noticed it. The amulet against the evil eye fit as snugly as ever. She'd meant to cut it off last night, but she'd been too troubled by the chill of Geoffrey's reaction to the casual remark she had thrown at him to remember. "Someone gave it to me," she said, trying to recall exactly what the skinny little girl had told her. "Aunt Jessa made it and said words over it."

"What words?" Philip demanded.

"It's white magic against the evil eye," Geoffrey explained. He had seen the amulet on Prudence's wrist the moment he'd found her in the live oak forest. Seen it and known immediately what it was, but hung back from questioning her. He seemed to be saying all the wrong things lately.

Philip waved a dismissive hand. A thin trail of smoke spiraled off the end of his cigar. "So far you've only told me what you *don't* know," he complained.

"The Bennett family, the men at least, weren't always the best of masters." Geoffrey hesitated, then said what he knew had infuriated Prudence almost more than anything else. "Especially not toward their women slaves. There were consequences."

"I've seen the pictures and read the accounts. Everyone has," Philip said.

Abolitionists had published the photographs in Northern newspapers and weekly magazines under outraged headlines proclaiming the existence of white slaves. Children and adults with no visible African features, sometimes photographed with darker-skinned half-siblings, bought or stolen from their masters, smuggled north. Some of them had appeared before abolitionist audiences to recount in person the uncertainties and horrors of a life that straddled the color line.

"I fail to see what the sins of the past have to do with Eleanor's death. Or with Teddy, for that matter," Prudence said.

She'd already argued once with Geoffrey that her friend and the eldest Bennett son were forging something new by their marriage. She hated to give up what might have been an idealized notion of the life they planned together. It had been a blow to learn that Teddy intended them to settle in Savannah. And that Eleanor had apparently agreed. Out of love and genuine enthusiasm? Or just love and resignation?

"More to the point, you still have no proof that Eleanor's death was not accidental." Philip Dickson ground out his cigar with a vicious twist of the wrist. "You've gotten nowhere."

"I don't believe it was," Prudence said quietly. "Even if the actual fall into the water was not deliberate, someone lured her out of the house and then into the swamp. Whatever happened next is on his head."

Geoffrey looked at her for a long moment, then nodded. "Prudence is right. Someone, certainly not Eleanor by herself, is responsible for her death. Our job is to find out who that person is. Anything else we learn is secondary. A distraction. We can't afford to allow ourselves to become sidetracked."

It didn't evaporate completely, but the nearly unbearable tension that had stretched tautly between Prudence and Geoffrey lessened. Softened. Lost some of its distrust and hostility. Became something else. An edginess, perhaps, that sharpened what was growing between them, imbued it with an air of urgency.

The silence lengthened until Philip Dickson sighed and pulled something from his waistcoat pocket. Eleanor's ruby and diamond engagement ring. "I will not bury my daughter with this on her finger," he declared, the muscles of his jaw set like granite. "I was told it was a Bennett family heirloom. By rights I should fling it into the swamp that took her life. But that would not be the act of a gentleman." He held the ring out across the desk. "Will you see that it's returned?"

Geoffrey stood up to take it, but Prudence was faster. "I'll make sure it is," she promised, careful not to mention Teddy by name.

Philip Dickson turned back briefly before leaving them.

"I've ordered that no more laudanum be given to my wife. She's all I have left."

Teddy stood by one of Wildacre's front windows, staring out in the direction of the family graveyard where it was now all but certain that Eleanor would not be buried. He'd slipped the ruby and diamond ring onto his watch chain, where it hung beside the fob containing a miniature of the woman who would never be his wife.

"I was against this marriage from the beginning," Lawrence said.

"You welcomed the fortune she'd be bringing," Teddy answered bitterly, swinging around angrily to face his brother.

"That was before I met her. She wasn't right for you," Lawrence insisted. "Father agreed with me."

"None of us would have wished her harm," Elijah said placatingly. "But perhaps it is for the best."

"How can you say that?" Teddy was close to losing control. "You didn't know her the way I did. You didn't want to know her."

"You forget yourself," Elijah reprimanded. "We have guests."

Geoffrey and Prudence, who should have been embarrassed and appalled at what they were hearing, made no attempt to interrupt or excuse themselves. The Bennett men had suddenly begun to reveal what they had previously been at pains to conceal.

"I think Teddy must be forgiven for his outburst," Geoffrey said. "To lose a beloved fiancée and a valued old family retainer in the same week would be a strain on anyone. He has my utmost sympathy and understanding."

Elijah stared at him. "What family retainer?" He turned to Lawrence, who shrugged his shoulders. "Teddy?"

"Aunt Jessa. Someone beat her senseless. They buried her yesterday. I paid my respects."

"Lawrence, did you know about this?"

"She left Wildacre years ago. I'd forgotten all about her."

"She raised you," Teddy said. "She helped birth all the Bennett babies, and then she took care of us until we got too big for the nursery. And even afterwards. How could you forget her?"

"She was an old woman," Lawrence said. "She'd lived longer than most."

"Can you hear yourself?" Teddy raged.

"This is not a fit topic for an argument among gentlemen," Elijah interrupted, bowing apologetically in Prudence's direction. His sons stared at one another in venomous silence. "I regret you had to be subjected to it, Miss MacKenzie."

"I find everything about Bradford Island to be endlessly interesting, Mr. Bennett," she replied, remembering to widen her eyes admiringly.

"It's a shame your first visit had to be marked by tragedy. I'm certain Mr. Hunter has told you that we Southerners pride ourselves on our hospitality."

"He has indeed."

"I suppose you'll all be leaving soon to return to New York City. Under the circumstances."

"Not immediately." Prudence smoothed her skirts, then folded her hands in demure determination. "Not until we've discovered the cause of Eleanor's accident." She paused. "If that's what it was."

"I'd forgotten that Lawrence told me Mr. Hunter was a Pinkerton at one time," Elijah said, glancing at his son.

Geoffrey smiled noncommittedly.

"We've questioned two of the islanders already," Prudence continued.

"Questioned?" Elijah asked.

"I don't like the idea of our people being interfered with by outsiders," Lawrence said.

"Your people?" Prudence queried so softly it was almost a whisper.

"Free or not, they'll always be our people." Lawrence looked to his father and brother for corroboration. "That's something you Yankees will never understand."

"Perhaps you could explain it to me, Mr. Bennett."

"I doubt it, Miss MacKenzie. We had to fight a war over the way we chose to live."

"We lost," Geoffrey stated.

"So we did," Elijah said.

Lawrence finally broke the uncomfortable silence that followed his father's reluctant admission. "It may be time to make a sweep through the woods again."

"It's been awhile," Elijah agreed.

"I don't understand," Prudence said.

"We get some hardcases hiding out in our live oaks from time to time," Lawrence explained. "They come over from the mainland to get away from the sheriff or whoever's chasing them, and mostly they're not followed. It's too hard to track anyone into the swamp. So they stay back in there and hide out. Live on fish and whatever they can steal. Wait for the stink to die down so they can get away. When we get a real bad one, we have to go in and flush him out."

"And you think that's what happened now?" Geoffrey asked.

"Could be. Our boys might fight a bit when they get liquored up, do a little cutting, but they don't usually go as far as what you say was done to Aunt Jessa." Lawrence's tone had changed, become almost neighborly in a conspiratorial way.

"Beaten to death," Teddy said. "You wouldn't do that to a dog."

"When did it happen?" Lawrence asked.

"Night before last is what we figured. Jonah brought me word yesterday morning. It was early, around sunup. Nobody else was awake. I went right out." Teddy blinked and then closed his eyes briefly, as if to erase the mental image of what he had seen.

"It was Jonah who found her?" Lawrence persisted.

"We asked him if he'd heard anything in the night, if maybe somebody passing through the trees woke him," Prudence said.

"What did he say?" Lawrence shifted his attention to the young woman he plainly disliked.

"Nothing. He didn't hear or see anything," Geoffrey said. "All he could tell us was that he'd gone over to check Aunt Jessa's woodpile. And that's when he found her."

"You believe him?" Lawrence clearly had his doubts.

Geoffrey answered before Prudence could tell them she'd thought he might be lying, probably out of fear.

"He doesn't know anything," Geoffrey repeated with finality.

"Neither does Preacher Solomon," Prudence added. She thought she understood that Geoffrey was protecting Jonah, though she wasn't sure why exactly he would think it necessary. But if Jonah had to be safeguarded, then so did Preacher Solomon.

"You've been busy," Lawrence sneered. "But I guess that's what makes Pinkertons and Yankees different from the rest of us."

Prudence didn't like Teddy's brother. She really didn't like him at all.

Chapter 1 2

⤫

The beach at twilight was as close to pure serenity as Prudence thought she had ever gotten. Despite the ugly scene at Wildacre, she had been able to dismiss the Bennett men from her mind as the setting sun filled the western sky with shades of peach and amber. When it finally slipped below the horizon, the gray wash that spilled over the water onto the land was as soft as goose down.

"Look, Geoffrey," she said, directing his attention back toward the upper-story porches of Seapoint. Abigail Dickson, wrapped in a shawl, her night-braided hair coiled over her shoulders, stood beside her husband. As they watched, Philip put one arm around his wife and drew her closer to him. She did not resist.

"Let's not go in yet." Prudence reached for Geoffrey's arm as she struggled through sand that grew harder to walk on the farther they got from the water. She had so much to say to him, but the words wouldn't come. Perhaps the conventional intimacy of walking arm in arm would open the floodgates.

"Shall we go along the sound side? The wind off the Atlantic is starting to get chilly." He'd tried several times to explain to her how deeply the comment about believing it was all right to own other human beings had hurt him. It was something against which Geoffrey had fought for as long as he could remember. It had driven a wedge between him and his family, exiled him to the North, and tortured him in those nighttime hours when conscience-stricken dreams resurrected images he'd vowed to suppress forever. That Prudence had shown herself unaware of his struggles merely proved how wide was the gulf that still separated them.

They strolled in silence until Seapoint faded into the shadows. The beach came alive at dusk as crabs scuttled out of their burrows toward the water. Tiny fish, stranded in shallow pools, darted in frantic circles. Sea oats waved gently in the soft air of the sound that stretched between Bradford Island and the Georgia mainland. Every now and then a fish leaped or a bird called out one last time before settling in for the night.

"I was glad to see Eleanor's parents together again," Prudence began. "I was afraid her mother would shut Mr. Dickson out of her grief. Laudanum does that to people. It isolates them in their own pain and addiction. The drug becomes a secret you have to hide. You always fear someone will take it away from you."

She was referring to her own battle with the contents of the little brown bottles women carried in their reticules and concealed in their bedrooms. Geoffrey had saved her from that hellish refuge. Perhaps speaking of such a private matter would tear down some of the barriers between them, which, she now admitted, had been her fault. She had lashed out in a moment of insensitive and cavalier anger. He was not responsible for his upbringing, any more than she could claim credit for hers.

Prudence waited for him to answer, but he did not. Just when she was beginning to experience the first twinges of real fear that he would never forgive her, she felt the warmth of his hand close over hers. She sighed in relief and deep contentment, confident now that he would speak when he judged the moment right. She could wait.

She turned toward him eagerly when he stopped, but he wasn't looking at her. His eyes were fixed on something or someone gliding out from the marshy reeds that grew at the mouth of a small stream emptying itself into the sound. "Look," he whispered, moving them into the darker shadow of a dune.

It was just light enough to distinguish the silhouette of a small boat, a shallow-bottomed skiff like the ones from which she'd seen fishermen casting seine nets for bait. Geoffrey's finger against her lips warned her not to speak above a whisper. The Bennett men had talked this afternoon of fugitives from the law hiding out on the island until it was safe to attempt an escape. Could this be one of them?

"He's going across on the incoming tide," Geoffrey said. His breath tickled against her neck, sending shivers to places no well-bred young lady was supposed to think about. "You can see the current out in the center of the sound. It sweeps across diagonally to a spot on the mainland. If he catches it, he won't have to use his oars and he'll be safe on the opposite shore much faster than he could manage without it. Less chance of being caught."

"Do you think he'll make it?"

"He knows what he's doing. Whoever he is, he's no stranger to these waters."

They watched as the figure pushed the boat through the last of the reeds, then hauled himself aboard. He retrieved a long pole from the bottom of the skiff, his body clearly outlined against the last fading light of the sky.

"Geoffrey, does he look familiar to you?" Prudence asked. "I can't make out any of the features of his face, but I have the feeling I've seen him before."

"Do you remember where?"

"No. And I'm not even sure I'm right. It was just a momentary impression. I'm probably mistaken. What is he doing now?"

"He has to pole himself over the shoals," Geoffrey told her. "There are sand bars all along the shore where the water is shallow."

Mesmerized, Prudence watched the rhythmic rise and fall of the man's shoulders as he nudged his boat toward deeper water. Geoffrey was right. He knew what he was doing. If he wasn't an islander, if he *was* running from the sheriff, she hoped he'd make it to safety, to a new start somewhere else. The darkness of his skin told her that if he stayed, Lawrence or men like him would hunt him mercilessly when they swept through the live oaks. She was learning the hard, unwelcome lesson that some lives counted for less than others.

A shot rang out through the clear evening air with a crack like a tree split by lightning. The man in the skiff tottered for a moment. The pole dropped from his hands. His body toppled into the water just as the boat caught the edge of the current and whirled away on the rush of incoming tide.

Geoffrey dragged Prudence to the sand as the echo of the gunfire rolled over them. Holding her so tightly she could barely breathe, he covered her body with his, forcing her to lie still beneath him.

Not another sound broke the silence. They never heard the marksman retreat, nor was there any desperate splashing from the spot where the victim had fallen overboard.

He was dead.

* * *

"Will the body wash ashore?" Prudence asked, staring at the dark waters of the sound, moonlight catching the crests of its waves.

"I doubt it," Geoffrey said. "The boat spun away into the tidal current, and I think it's likely the body was swept off also. This was a carefully calculated execution. Whoever killed him didn't want him found."

Prudence shuddered despite the jacket Geoffrey had draped over her shoulders. "Do you think we'll ever learn who he was?"

"Someone will know he's missing."

"But if he sneaked over to the island to hide out . . . ?"

"Sheriff Budridge is the kind of man who never forgets either the name or the face of anyone who manages to get away from him. He'll have a good idea who the dead man could be. But without a body or at least a description, I doubt he'll say anything."

"I don't think the sheriff approved of me," Prudence said. "He didn't come right out and tell me not to stick my nose in where it didn't belong, but he didn't hide his dislike."

"And I'm an ex-Pinkerton," Geoffrey added. "Which to some people still means Union spy." He gently turned Prudence away from the water and tucked her arm in his. "Are you all right?"

"Strangely enough, I am. Somehow nothing of what we just witnessed seems real. That's part of the barbarity of it. A man we don't know anything about is ambushed by someone we never caught a glimpse of. We have no idea why, and there isn't even a body to provide us with any clues. Do you think anyone will believe us when we tell them what happened? What we saw?"

"We're not going to tell anyone," he said.

"We have to report it to the sheriff," she argued, forgetting to keep her voice low. "He may not like either of us, but a crime has been committed in his jurisdiction. He'll have to do something about it."

"You heard what Teddy said about Aunt Jessa's murder. The sheriff wasn't summoned because Teddy knew he probably wouldn't come. Even if he did, there wouldn't be an investigation. I know it's unfair, Prudence. But that's the way it's always been down here. I don't think it will ever change."

"How horrible! As if the poor man isn't any more important than a dead animal."

"He faced hanging, or worse, if he got stopped on the mainland," Geoffrey said. "It isn't much consolation, but at least this was a clean death."

"Surely someone else heard the shot?" Prudence refused to give up. "And if they did, they'll report it."

"I doubt anyone else heard it. But if they did, and they live in the live oaks, they won't say a word. Not even to one another." He halted for a moment to order his thoughts and impress on Prudence the seriousness of their situation. "If we say nothing, then the only ones who will know what happened are you and I . . . and the killer."

"He couldn't have seen us, Geoffrey. He was in the trees."

Geoffrey held out one of Prudence's arms. The white skin shone in the moonlight.

She stared at his face, at the features starkly outlined by the same silvery light that turned the sand on which they stood luminescent.

"We can't ignore the fact that just before he fired the shooter might have sensed someone was nearby, might have heard our voices," Geoffrey said somberly. "*Might* have, Prudence. And taken the shot anyway. But he couldn't have been close enough to recognize us."

"And if he didn't know anyone was on the beach?"

"Then we were lucky. And that's the way we need to keep it."

*   *   *

She knew it wasn't right, but Prudence agreed not to say anything. For the moment. For tonight, at least. The one thing she couldn't deny was that Geoffrey was undoubtedly correct when he insisted that the sheriff would do nothing. If they went to him, they would only expose themselves. To no good end.

She felt curiously empty. Drained of emotion. It had been such a long, dreadful day.

The maid assigned to her had turned down her covers, opened the door to the veranda to let in the cool air, and laid out her nightclothes. Then she'd sat down to sew and wait, and promptly fallen asleep over her mending. Prudence shook her awake, accepted help with her corset, then sent the exhausted girl off to her narrow bed in the attic. Prudence didn't want company tonight, not even the comfort of having someone brush her light brown hair.

She thought the lamplight was picking up sunstreaks of gold as she plaited the braids that prevented painful tangles in the morning. She remembered how her mother had scolded her for romping on their Staten Island lawn when the summer sun turned her skin golden and bleached out her curls. Such a long time ago. Prudence wondered what her parents would have thought of their detective daughter who was earning a reputation in society for breaking more rules than she kept.

She was so tired it was hard to think straight, hard to marshal her thoughts. Strange to be thinking of her parents tonight. She supposed it was the sight of Philip and Abigail Dickson comforting one another that had brought them to mind. The Dicksons mourning their daughter, turning to one another under the weight of an unfathomable loss.

Enough, she told herself. *Enough. It's nearly midnight. I need sleep.*

She slipped off her night robe and draped it over a chair, started to lay her slippers where it would be easy to find them in the morning, then changed her mind. The bare wood floor was already cold underfoot. She walked over to the veranda door to close it, stepping outside for a final glimpse of brilliant stars in the deep black of the clear night sky.

She felt an odd, rolling sensation beneath her foot, as though she'd stepped on something round. A thimble dropped by the maid? She looked down, but the light was poor and she saw nothing.

Maybe I've picked up a splinter, she chided herself, aware of a slight stinging sensation. *That's what you get for wearing thin slippers, Prudence.*

But when she searched for the offending bit of wood, tweezers and needle at the ready, she couldn't find it. There was a red spot that itched when she touched it. Sandspurs, she decided, wedged into her shoe and rubbed against the skin when she and Geoffrey scurried into the shelter of the dune. She rubbed cream on the angry-looking area and decided not to worry about it. The fingers she'd touched to the irritated spot also began to itch. She rubbed more cream on them.

Almost as soon as she'd turned out her light, Prudence was asleep.

The eighteen-inch snake, brightly banded in red, yellow, and black, slithered off the second-floor veranda and down the trellis where night-blooming jessamine turned its fragrant white flowers toward the moon. It had lain inside the small woven grass basket in which it had been transported until it managed finally to dislodge the lid. A shy creature, the snake waited to make its escape until it thought it was alone.

And then something heavy had stepped on it.

Prudence couldn't breathe.

She jolted upright in her bed, gasping but unable to draw enough air into her lungs. The early dawn was barely visible through the curtains, but there was enough light to tell that there seemed to be two of everything in her room. Prudence tried to call out, but the words wouldn't come. She heard the slurred cries of a drunkard, and knew she was listening to her own desperate voice.

Sliding to the floor, hauling herself up by one of the bed's oak posters, she staggered to the door, wrenched it open, and tumbled into the corridor. She lay there, beating feebly on the Oriental carpet runner, desperately aware that she wasn't making enough noise to summon help.

Before she lapsed into unconsciousness Prudence thought she heard the sound of a door opening farther along the corridor and her name being called. Then everything went black.

Geoffrey never left her side during the first few critical hours. He held her upright in his arms when lying down proved too much for her struggling lungs and whispered constant encouragement even though it wasn't at all certain she could hear.

By mid-morning, they knew the worst. Prudence had been bitten by a coral snake. Reclusive, seldom seen outside the deep woods, it had somehow crawled into her bedroom and lain there, hidden and deadly, until her foot found it.

One of the gardeners spied the beautiful but highly venomous reptile trapped in the cape jessamine bush growing along the wall beneath her window. Injured too badly to escape, it had twined itself into the thick foliage where a ray of sunlight made its jewel-like colors gleam. He cut off its head and burned it.

Philip dispatched a man to the telegraph office on the mainland. The closest doctor was in Savannah, a full day's journey away.

Abigail came out of her seclusion to sit at Prudence's bedside, silent tears streaming down her face.

There was nothing any of them could do to stave off the inevitable.

Geoffrey sent for Queen Lula.

She was a tall woman, light brown in color, dressed in all the shades of the rainbow, enormous gold hoops hanging from her ears, arms encircled by dozens of bangle bracelets.

"Ain't nothing gonna do no good if the bite's deep enough," she said, cocking her head to one side as she listened to the convulsive, whooping breathing and ran her long, sensitive fingers over the muscles in Prudence's arms and legs. Then she examined the angry spot on her patient's foot, pushing and prodding, pinching the skin until it swelled and reddened.

It was all Geoffrey could do not to snatch her hand away, but Queen Lula was the only thing that stood between Prudence and certain death. The best of the voodoo practitioners augmented their spells with primitive but often effective medicines.

"I don't see no marks where the fangs went in," Queen Lula said.

Geoffrey pointed to a pair of delicate satin slippers lying beside the bed. The soles were made of thin Spanish leather.

Queen Lula used the handle of a hairbrush to pick them up, then laid them on a pillowcase spread across the top of the tea table. "Coral snakes got small fangs," she said. "Only reason folks survive is they cain't always bite through leather. Poison on the skin but not in the blood make you real sick, but it might not kill you." She pointed a claw-like fingernail at a rough patch on the smooth leather of one of the slippers. "See here. This where she stepped on it. Snake open its mouth and bite, but I'm not seein' no hole where the fangs got through. He squirt out his venom all right, but it stay on the leather. Little bit get on her skin."

"Will she live?" Geoffrey asked.

Queen Lula shrugged. She took a bottle of golden oil and a small pouch of dark powder from one of the pockets of her voluminous skirts and began mixing them together, muttering to herself as she stirred.

"What is that?"

She shook her head. Echinacea oil and powdered charcoal could be tried on just about anything. Sometimes it worked. Sometimes it didn't.

"Hold her mouth open," Queen Lula directed.

She spooned the blend of oil and ground charcoal between Prudence's lips, then massaged her throat to make her swallow. When it was nearly all gone, she smeared the last of it over the spot where the venom might or might not have penetrated the skin. Then she wrapped the slippers in the pillow case and stowed them in a woven grass basket she found by the veranda door.

"No sense leavin' these around where a dog might get to chewin' on 'em," she said.

"How long?" Geoffrey asked.

"Change come by the time the sun go down. One way or the other." It was the best she could do. Only a fool would try to predict the outcome of snakebite.

The long hours of the day passed with agonizing slowness, but gradually Prudence's struggle for breath eased. As she took in more air she began to be able to move her limbs. Her eyes opened and registered what she saw. The racing heartbeat Geoffrey could feel against his chest as he held her regulated itself.

He only allowed himself to hope when she fell into a natural sleep in his arms. No fever. No rattling rales in the lungs. Body slumped limply against his as though she were an exhausted child.

Queen Lula prepared to leave while the sky was still streaked with orange. "Aunt Jessa mighty fond of this chile," she said, fingering the amulet on Prudence's wrist. "You be sure she never take that off. Not while she be on this island."

"Is that what saved her?" Geoffrey asked. The question didn't seem at all odd.

"Mebbe," Queen Lula said. "Only thing is, white magic don't usually stand a chance against the black. But this be Aunt Jessa's white magic. She was a strong woman."

"So is Miss MacKenzie."

CHAPTER 13

❦

Now that she was healing, Prudence was bored. And angry. She'd had more than enough time to think about what had happened to her, and it didn't make sense.

At her insistence, Geoffrey had searched through Philip Dickson's library and found a thick volume on the flora and fauna of the Georgia coastal area. She'd paged through meticulously detailed and beautifully tinted sketches of native plants and trees, resident and migratory birds, large and small animals of woodland, sandy plain, marshes, and swamps. It was a fascinating world of dangerous beauty, utterly unlike the tamed nature she was used to in Central Park and on Staten Island.

She promised herself she'd do justice to the author's passionate erudition and all of his painstakingly accurate drawings, but for the moment the only topic to hold her interest was snakes. Specifically, the coral snake.

She read and reread the passages detailing the habitat and peculiarities of this most beautiful and reclusive of serpents. She learned the rhyme meant to teach children to distinguish between the venomous coral snake and its similarly banded but harmless imitators. *Red on yellow kills a fellow. Red on black, friend of Jack.* It had apparently leaped into widespread popularity almost thirty years ago. Easy to remember and based on the simple observation that the coral snake's black and red bands were bracketed by bands of yellow, it made identification rapid and certain.

This snake usually stayed out of sight, wasn't aggressive, and seemed inclined to bite humans only if picked up or stepped on.

Sometimes, she learned, its victim didn't realize he'd been bitten until hours later, when the symptoms began to torment him. When he saw double, found it impossible to speak clearly, experienced muscle paralysis, and couldn't breathe. Death was certain and unavoidable, though the author did reluctantly report that there had been unsubstantiated accounts of survivors who swore the snake that had bitten them had been the real thing and not the non-poisonous look-alike scarlet kingsnake. The writer was clearly skeptical.

When she finally slid a bookmark into the volume and closed its cover, Prudence lay back against the mound of pillows propping her upright in her bed, folded her hands to keep them from roaming restlessly across the coverlet, and closed her eyes to concentrate on what she had read.

It didn't make sense.

But she had been taught by her father that everything in life made sense if you could just unravel the tangled knot of why and how. Why had the snake been in her bedroom? How had it gotten there? If she could answer those two basic questions, she believed she would unlock the door to a greater mystery.

Who wanted her dead?

Aurora Lee and Maggie Jane Bennett felt trapped in an exasperating dilemma.

On the one hand, they were in polite and proper mourning for a prospective sister-in-law who never actually became a member of the family. That, they felt, was as it should be and as dictated by the etiquette books that ruled their lives.

On the other hand, that same not quite sister-in-law no longer had any use for the day dresses, evening gowns, hats, gloves, and lacy unmentionables that comprised her never-to-be-used trousseau. Which they presumed would be packed away in trunks and traveling cases to collect mildew in one of Seapoint's basement storage rooms.

Such a shame. Such a waste.

Staring into their nearly empty armoires was like sitting down to a dinner of boiled peas and cornbread when you knew that a delectable feast you'd never taste was laid out in another room. So close and yet so unobtainable.

Each of the sisters had two everyday cotton dresses, one to wash and one to wear. A mourning gown, of course, and a made-over silk evening frock that had belonged to their long-dead mother in more prosperous times. All frequently and expertly mended. What little money the family possessed was not to be wasted on a pair of spinsters. They understood why their father and brothers merited new velvet-collared coats, fawn-colored trousers, and imported English riding boots. They were men of the world, with appearances to keep up.

But oh, those trunks and armoires at Seapoint, bursting with everything they pined for.

It wasn't fair. It just wasn't fair.

Prudence had no idea why the Bennett sisters had decided to pay her a visit. She'd met them only twice before, once at the Dickson dinner party her second night on the island, and then again when she and Geoffrey had accompanied Teddy back to Wildacre after he failed to persuade Eleanor's father to allow her to be buried in his family's graveyard.

Both instances had been unmemorable. Aurora Lee spoke entirely in platitudes and Maggie Jane giggled and simpered behind ragged fingernails.

Still, Prudence reminded herself, they were Bennetts, presumably as capable of eavesdropping on the conversations of their menfolk as other women relegated to a status marginally above that of children. She had questions she was sure might never be answered unless she was able to flatter and cajole them into revealing what no one outside the family had a right to know.

Keep that thought in mind, she told herself, sitting up straighter against the tufted back of her chaise longue and composing her face in a welcoming smile. What was it her father always said? *Never ask a question in court unless you already know the answer.* Prudence wasn't in court, but if she ever got far enough in this on-again off-again investigation to accuse someone, she'd better have the answers to all the questions anyone could possibly ask. She had a feeling that Southern justice was a slippery concept at best, and she was definitely an unwelcome outsider.

"We had no idea you'd fallen ill," Aurora Lee said.

It was highly irregular to be entertained in a virtual stranger's bedroom, but it seemed there was no other choice. The formidable Mr. Dickson had explained that Miss MacKenzie was indisposed, but amenable to receiving the right sort of company. The sisters settled themselves into matching, satin-covered slipper chairs positioned opposite the open French doors to the veranda. The view of the beach and the Atlantic Ocean was breathtaking.

"I do hope you're recovering from what ailed you, Miss MacKenzie," Aurora Lee probed.

"I wish you'd call me Prudence."

Maggie Jane giggled.

"How kind of you. And of course we would be delighted if you would also address us by our Christian names."

Aurora Lee has such an odd way of speaking, Prudence thought. As though she were a character from one of Miss Jane Austen's intriguing tales.

"Our climate does take a bit of getting used to," Aurora Lee continued, when Prudence had still not revealed what exactly she was suffering from.

"I find the sea air most refreshing." Prudence declared.

"It can be so difficult to maintain one's good health after a loss like the one we all experienced. So tragic and so upsetting." Aurora Lee did not give up easily.

Maggie Jane sniffled.

"You're right, of course," Prudence conceded. She'd been of two minds about explaining what had happened to her. If someone *had* put the snake in her room, would it be wise to let him know he'd nearly succeeded? Or shrewder to allow him to think his attempt had failed? The problem was that she couldn't count on the Seapoint staff not gossiping, especially when the tidbit was so juicy.

"I encountered a snake," she said ambiguously, making up her mind on the spot. If there was a second try, she was more than prepared. There wasn't a corner of the room or a fold of her sheets she wasn't constantly inspecting.

"How dreadful!" Aurora Lee leaned forward in sympathy. "Do tell!"

"Was it a copperhead?" Maggie Jane asked, forgetting to duck her head and raise a hand to her mouth. "I saw a little one hiding under some pine straw once. I swear I didn't know what it was at first. They don't have the copperhead markings when they first hatch out."

Aurora Lee stared at her.

"At least that's what I've been told," Maggie Jane amended, sheltering behind her fingers again.

"It wasn't a copperhead," Prudence said. She was going to make them drag it out of her, alert for any indication that one of the misses Bennett might already know what type of snake someone had secreted in her room.

"You have to be careful where you walk," Aurora Lee said. "It's best to take a dog along with you if you can."

"Even in your bedroom?" Prudence asked.

The sisters immediately shook their skirts out apprehensively, eyes darting from the curtains and bedclothes that hung a good two inches above the floor to the dishes of crushed bay leaves under the bedposts. The fragrant herb was supposed to repel roaches.

"I never heard of such a thing," Aurora Lee said.

"It was a coral snake."

Maggie Jane's eyes widened and Aurora Lee shook her head in disbelief.

"I'm sure it wasn't," Aurora Lee said. "You just let yourself get scared by a kingsnake. For no good reason at all," she added with smug superiority. Plainly she thought that any Yankee who took to her bed with such a flimsy excuse wasn't half the woman a Bennett was.

"They're deadly," Maggie Jane whispered. "Nobody who gets bitten by a coral snake ever survives."

"I said I had an encounter," Prudence elaborated. "Not that I was bitten."

"You wouldn't be lying there if you had been," Aurora Lee said sharply. "I suppose somebody else saw and identified this supposed coral snake?" Somebody who knew what he was looking at, she meant.

"One of the gardeners killed him," Prudence said. "And cut off his head for good measure." Not only hadn't the two sisters believed her, they'd also expressed what seemed to be genuine shock and dismay at the whole idea of a coral snake in her bedroom. She doubted either of them was capable of acting out a lie so convincingly, but something about the way they were behaving hinted at an ulterior motive behind the unannounced visit.

"I'm glad you're all right, Prudence," Maggie Jane said shyly. "That's very kind of you."

"And speaking of kindnesses," Aurora said, taking the bit between her teeth, "Maggie Jane and I have been worried to death about poor Mrs. Dickson having to pack up all of Eleanor's clothing and personal belongings."

"I believe the housekeeper and maids will be doing that,"

Prudence said, not sure where the comment was leading. "When the time comes."

"Well, of course, they'll be doing the actual work," Aurora Lee conceded, "but I'm sure there will be decisions that only Mrs. Dickson can make. And that will be agonizingly painful for her." She turned encouragingly to Maggie Jane, who had been well rehearsed in what she needed to say.

"Oh my, yes. Very painful." Up went the hand again, but at least Maggie Jane was able to keep her eyes focused on the person she was talking to. Aurora Lee had made her practice enough. "We thought that what we might do is take that burden off her shoulders. And especially now that you're . . . the way you are."

Prudence had to fight back a smile as she suddenly understood what had really brought the Bennett girls to her bedside today. It was the thought of losing Eleanor's beautiful trousseau when it was nearly within their grasp. So close.

She looked at the tall, sallow Aurora Lee and the shorter, scrawny Maggie Jane. Eleanor had been of medium height, with the prized hourglass figure that stylish society women achieved through corsets laced so tightly they were unable to take a deep breath or walk more than a few mincing steps without feeling faint.

"I'm not sure all of the items in Eleanor's trousseau are suitable for charitable donation," Prudence said, frowning in as good an imitation of consternation as she could manage.

"We could certainly make those choices," Aurora Lee assured her.

Prudence didn't doubt for a moment that as soon as the Dickson yacht sailed northward the Bennett women would be altering Eleanor's beautiful gowns to fit themselves. One or two of the plainer dresses and perhaps a few pairs of gloves and shoes might make it to a charity, but that would be purely for form's sake. Aurora Lee and Maggie Jane were plainly hungry for what the consequences of the war had denied them.

"I wonder if you would like to glance through some of dear Eleanor's things," Prudence suggested. "I'm afraid there are a great many gowns and accessories. There may be more than you imagine, perhaps too much for you to take on by yourselves."

Aurora Lee's eyes shone with anticipation. "I wouldn't want you to overexert yourself, Prudence. If you'll summon a maid, I'm sure she'll be able to guide us."

"I wouldn't think of it." Prudence got slowly to her feet, smiling courageously. "I'm feeling a good deal stronger today." In truth, she was chomping at the bit to be out of her room, but Geoffrey had been stubbornly resistant to her demands that she no longer be treated like an invalid.

Eleanor's dressing room was a wonderland of color and delicate, expensive fabrics. Gowns were arranged by the time of day during which they were to be worn, from informal and almost comfortable morning wear to the boned silk bodices and draped skirts for dinner and dancing. Labeled boxes containing matching shoes, gloves, reticules, and hats were stacked conveniently close to the dresses they complemented. Eleanor's delicate lingerie and lace-trimmed handkerchiefs lay in neatly folded, lavender-scented piles in her dresser drawers.

The Bennett sisters said hardly a word as Prudence guided them through Eleanor's trousseau. They were clearly stunned by the sumptuous richness that not even their wildest imaginings had been able to envision.

Excusing herself to rest for a moment in the restorative air of the veranda, Prudence left them alone to marvel and coo over what would soon be theirs, wanting them to be so blinded by greed that they would readily answer any question she chose to ask. And not even wonder at the impolite intrusiveness of what she wanted to know.

"I hesitate to suggest it," Prudence said when they had settled themselves in her room again, "and I certainly don't mean to be offensive. Oh, dear, I'm not sure you'll take this in the spirit it's meant to be offered." She lowered her eyes and picked worriedly at the shawl in which she'd wrapped herself.

"Please go on," Aurora Lee urged into the prolonged silence. "Nothing you could possibly say would give offense, dear Prudence."

"I was going to propose that before you make the arrangements to donate Eleanor's things to a worthy charity, you might want to select one or two articles to keep for yourselves. To remember her by."

"One or two each?" Maggie Jane asked.

Aurora Lee frowned and made a swatting motion in her sister's direction as if to shoo off a pesky fly.

"Certainly, each," Prudence confirmed. "Perhaps a handkerchief or a bottle of scent."

Maggie Jane's eager face collapsed into disappointment. She'd clearly begun to doubt the success of the plan Aurora Lee had insisted they could accomplish.

"We may indeed," Aurora Lee put in quickly. "But not today. I think that's something I would like to give a good deal of thought to."

"Just one or two?" Maggie Jane whispered, looking toward the door leading to the corridor and the riches in Eleanor's bedroom.

"I was so sorry that your Aunt Jessa died in the tragic way she did," Prudence said, abruptly changing the subject.

Maggie Jane's perplexed face swiveled back from contemplation of Yankee dresses and bonnets.

Aurora Lee frowned. She'd never heard of anyone offering condolences on the passing of a slave. *Ex-slave.* It was so outlandish an idea that she was at a loss for words.

"Bradford Island must have been a very different world when you were children," Prudence tried again. "Before the war."

"We had just celebrated my first birthday when Georgia seceded from the Union and joined the Confederate States of America," Aurora Lee said. "Maggie Jane wasn't even born yet."

That would make her twenty-nine years old, Prudence calculated. The eldest Bennett daughter clearly considered the Confederacy a legitimate country, not the conspiracy of unlawful, rebellious states that northerners had believed it to be.

"It must have been a blow when your father decided to sell the island." Prudence threw all caution to the wind. She wasn't getting anywhere by being oblique.

Maggie Jane nodded her head vigorously and seemed about to say something when Aurora Lee plucked at her sister's sleeve, unceremoniously hauling her to her feet.

"We'll take our leave now, Prudence," she said. "But do be sure to inform Mrs. Dickson of our offer. I'm sure she'll be more than relieved to be able to pass that burden along to someone else."

"It's no trouble at all, really," Maggie Jane stammered.

They were out the door in a whirl of mended skirts.

Prudence didn't have all of the answers she'd sought, but she had confirmed at least three speculations about the Bennett family—their war had never ended, they still considered themselves the rightful owners of the island, and they were sorely in need of the money that Teddy's marriage to Eleanor would have brought them.

It wasn't much, but it was at least a beginning.

CHAPTER 14

If anyone knew who had gone missing, it would be Preacher Solomon. Geoffrey had a feeling he didn't just preach the gospel to the members of his church. When they had nowhere else to go for help, people of color went to Jesus. More than one pastor had sheltered runaways and sped them on their way when the danger of immediate recapture was past.

There was a second fresh grave in the burial ground, each one marked with a wooden cross. Geoffrey spotted them before he rode into the clearing, not surprised to find that Aunt Jessa no longer slept alone. He reined in his horse, dismounted, and walked the few remaining steps to where the freshly turned and mounded earth had been covered over with seashells.

Preacher Solomon emerged from the trees. "I heard you comin'," he said. "Horse makes a heap of noise thrashin' through the woods."

Geoffrey had made a deliberately loud approach along the track that wasn't quite a road. He'd wanted Preacher Solomon and whoever else might be at the church to know someone was on the way. Not hiding his arrival, not trying to sneak up or ambush anyone. Shotguns had a way of going off when trigger fingers got nervous. Even white men could get hurt when there weren't any witnesses.

Hat in hand, Preacher Solomon waited by the new grave as if he knew why Geoffrey had come.

"Fishin' boat pulled him out of the sound just before he was about to float out to sea," he said, motioning toward the cross that bore the name *JONAH*. "He weren't dead when he hit the water. Heaved hisself over a log and hung on. But he was shot bad. Didn't last more than a couple of hours after we got him ashore."

"Did he recover consciousness?" Geoffrey asked.

"Not so's you could make sense of what he said. Mumbled, more like it. He was out of his head, Mr. Hunter. No telling how long he was in the water."

Geoffrey and Prudence had seen the shooting on Tuesday evening while there was still enough light in the sky to make out Jonah's silhouette standing up in his boat. Today was Thursday.

"This time of year the tides can sweep through the sound like a freight train," Preacher Solomon said. "You get trapped in the channel and the next thing you know you're out in the ocean caught in a riptide. It was already full dark when he got found."

"What was he doing out on the water that time of night?" Geoffrey asked, wanting to give Preacher Solomon a chance to tell the story his way.

"Don't know why Jonah was out there, but the man who found him was having a bad turn with his nets. Ripped to shreds on a couple of crab cages that wasn't marked with floats like they supposed to be. That's why he was so late comin' back to shore. He stayed put until he got the net unsnagged and hauled aboard for mendin'. Said he nearly missed Jonah entirely. Thought at first it was just a log he was seein'." Preacher Solomon shook his head. "Didn't find no boat overturned. And Jonah didn't have family on the mainland. No reason for him to be leavin' the island."

"Was anyone asking about him in the last few days?"

"Folks been stayin' close to home since what happened to Miss Jessa. Nobody goin' nowhere."

"No strangers hiding out or crossing over?"

Preacher Solomon thought for a moment. "Leastways not that I heard tell of. Nobody since the sheriff and the coroner come for Miss Dickson."

Geoffrey smiled. He'd guessed right. The old man knew the comings and goings of the white islanders as well as what his own people were doing. He never even had to leave his church. The information came to him from the women working in the big house and the men tending the fields and stables. The Bennett family had no secrets. It was just a matter of finding someone who was willing to divulge them. Brave enough to break the code of silence and risk the consequences.

"I heard tell Queen Lula was called in over to Seapoint," Preacher Solomon said. "Not that I cotton to the idea that Miss Dickson's friend was bit by a coral snake. No, sir. Not even Queen Lula could bring her back from something that bad."

"It was a coral snake, all right," Geoffrey said. "But it didn't get its fangs into her. Just a few drops of venom on the skin."

"Well, that's all right then. Lessen you got you a cut or a scratch, that snake juice gonna make you sick but it ain't gonna kill you."

"I'll tell Miss MacKenzie you were asking about her," Geoffrey said, turning away from the graves.

Preacher Solomon hadn't mentioned Queen Lula by accident. He wasn't the kind of man to chinwag, but he had nothing against steering someone in the direction he thought they should take.

Queen Lula it was.

She was waiting for him.

Sitting in the shade of the porch that ran across the front of her one-room shack, Queen Lula was a bright beacon of color in the cool dimness of the live oaks. She held a large black cat on her lap, one hand caressing its back in slow, rhythmic strokes.

Geoffrey thought that whatever else she was, this refugee from New Orleans was as much an entertainer as any of the voodoo practitioners in the city she'd left behind. Just catching a glimpse of the black cat, instantly identifiable by true believers as her *familiar*, was enough to strike fear into the hearts of those who came seeking the power of her dark juju. There had been one like her on his family's plantation back in North Carolina all those years ago. He remembered his father telling the overseer to keep an eye on her but otherwise let her be. Superstition, he'd believed, could be almost as powerful a deterrent to rebellion as the whip.

As when approaching Preacher Solomon's church, Geoffrey hadn't troubled to muffle his approach. It was best that Queen Lula know he had nothing to hide, that he meant no harm. He'd paid her well for the concoction with which she'd neutralized the snake venom. When Prudence had fretfully picked at the amulet on her wrist and spoken of cutting it off, he'd taken the scissors out of her hand and talked her out of it. He didn't exactly believe in Queen Lula's powers, but he'd learned over the years that it was best to take no chances with the inexplicable.

She handed him a clay cup; he hesitated before drinking from it.

"Ain't nothin' but well water," she said, chuckling at his disinclination to trust her. "Nobody done crossed my palm to put a spell on you. Don't know as I'd be inclined to accept it even if they did. Some folks got a spirit what don't take kindly to spells. I figure you may be one of 'em."

"I've never heard that before," Geoffrey said, setting the cup down on the porch step. There was only one chair for sitting, fully occupied by Queen Lula and her cat. He stood, the reins of his horse held loosely in one hand.

"They be those cain't be touched by a spell. Cain't be hexed. They walk through this world protected from the power of good or evil, don't make much difference which. Carve out they own path."

"I'm going to take that as a compliment," he said, smiling his most charming grin at her. Voodoo priestess or not, she was still a woman.

She smiled back at him, enjoying the byplay. In New Orleans, white men and women of color were more open with each other than they could be in any other part of the South. As long as the woman didn't cross any of the invisible lines that kept her in her place.

Queen Lula took from her dress pocket a small doll fashioned out of seagrass.

"Who is that?" Geoffrey asked.

"Ain't nobody yet. Not till I say the words. Pass it through the smoke. Mark it with the blood."

"I heard tell you and Aunt Jessa were friends."

"Miss Jessa a good woman. Didn't deserve what they done to her."

The whites on the island might have called her *Aunt*, but to Queen Lula the title was one of the reminders of slavery, one of the soft manacles owners used to conceal the iron with which they ruled even those who might genuinely love a master's child. He'd been away for a long time, but Geoffrey understood the difference and the correction.

"I didn't know her when she was alive," he said.

"Miss Prudence did. Miss Jessa tole me 'bout meeting up with her over Miss Eleanor's body. That was a sad day."

"Is Miss Prudence one of those who can't be hexed?"

Queen Lula shook her head. "That's why Miss Jessa give her the amulet. She knowed bad juju was coming Miss Prudence's way. Felt it in her bones. But there wasn't time to do no more than what she did. And it might not be enough." She fingered the faceless, naked doll woven of dried seagrass.

"Do you know why Aunt Jessa was killed? And Jonah?" Geoffrey asked. He stood motionless, slowing down his breathing so Queen Lula could read him. Whatever mental probes she sent out should meet with no opposition.

"Keep 'em from talking."

"Talking about what? What did they know that someone was afraid one of them would bring out into the open?"

"Best you let it go. It's too late now to do any good. All the evil already been done. Onliest one you got to protect is Miss Prudence. Take her back where she belong. She don't know nothing, but mebbe somebody don't believe that. Mebbe somebody think she been told something she got no business knowing."

"She won't go anywhere until she finds out how Miss Eleanor died. Miss Prudence is stubborn that way."

"Miss Eleanor drowned in the swamp. That's all Miss Prudence ever gonna know."

"That's not enough. She doesn't believe it was an accident, and she won't give up until she's proved it."

"She that kind of woman?"

Geoffrey nodded. Smiled, because he knew what kind of woman Queen Lula meant. "Yes, she is that kind of woman."

"Ain't no changin' her?"

"Not in this life."

"You be sure she wear Miss Jessa's protection. Don't never let her take it off. I ain't sayin' it'll save her, but there's no sense takin' any chances."

And that was all Queen Lula would say. She carried herself and her cat inside the shack. Closed the door softly but firmly.

Geoffrey heard a wooden bar slide into place. He hadn't expected Queen Lula to be afraid enough to take that kind of precaution. But she was.

He wondered what or who made her anxious in the night.

It wasn't that Aurora Lee and Maggie Jane were eager to tell Lawrence and their father about the windfall coming their way. They weren't. There was always the possibility that the stern Confederate officer who lost money the way some people let water trickle through their fingers would forbid them from acquiring Eleanor's trousseau. Would find some obscure prideful reason to deny them what he could no longer provide.

But it was also useless to think they could conceal anything from him. Especially a treasure that would arrive in trunks and boxes smelling of dried lavender sachets. Once they'd altered some of Eleanor's gowns they thought he would be proud enough of their appearance to allow his newly fashionable daughters to keep them. But that would take time. The important thing was to head off any explosion of anger that brought with it a prohibition he would never rescind. Once Elijah Bennett made his feelings public, there was no changing them. He'd said many a time that only the weakest of men shilly-shallied over a decision.

They didn't know why Lawrence was interested in the goings-on at Seapoint now that Eleanor was dead and there would be no alliance between the two families, but he was. Teddy's face creased into such a look of pain whenever Eleanor's name was mentioned that neither of his sisters wanted to distress him, so they waited until they were alone with Lawrence in the parlor before telling him where they had gone and what they had done. The younger Bennett brother had more influence over his father than the other three children put together. If anyone could ensure that the trousseau would not be rejected, it was he.

"So the snake didn't bite her? You're sure of that?" he asked.

"That's what she said. It was definitely a coral snake in her bedroom. Somehow its fangs didn't penetrate through the leather soles of the slippers she was wearing," Aurora Lee answered.

"The gardener cut off its head and burned it," Maggie Jane added helpfully.

"I've never heard of a coral snake on the second floor of someone's house," Aurora Lee said. "Maybe a pygmy rattler in a basket of firewood, but never a coral snake."

"Did you tell her that?"

"She was so sure of what she was saying that I didn't insist. Really, Lawrence, I still think it could have been a kingsnake. But neither of us wanted to argue the point with her too much. She's a very insistent kind of person."

"The worst kind of Yankee female," he muttered. "Can't keep her mouth shut or her nose out of business that doesn't concern her."

"At any rate, will you speak to Father for us?" Aurora Lee pleaded.

"About what?" he answered absently.

"About the trousseau," Maggie Jane said. "How could you forget?" She looked down at the darned black mourning dress she was still wearing. "The clothes are so beautiful. And poor Eleanor doesn't need them anymore."

Lawrence looked at his two spinster sisters and saw burdens he would have to carry for the rest of his life. Aurora Lee was well past the age for a first marriage, and Maggie Jane was only two years younger. Perhaps if they dressed themselves up in the dead woman's finery and he shipped them off to relatives in Savannah or Atlanta they'd manage to find husbands who wouldn't protest the lack of a dowry until it was too late. He didn't care whether they wore silk gowns or ragged cotton dresses unless it meant the difference between securing a future out of his sight or remaining at Wildacre for the rest of their lives.

"Of course I'll speak to him," he promised, flinching at Maggie Jane's squealing giggles. "I'll point out to him your generosity in offering to spare Mrs. Dickson the sorrow of clearing out her daughter's effects and the obvious advantage to you of being able to profit from what Eleanor would certainly have wanted you to possess."

"Don't use the word *profit*," Aurora Lee chided. "It sounds like something a Yankee would say. Father will get his back up."

"I won't forget," Lawrence agreed. Profit was such a foreign concept to Elijah Bennett that he would indeed bristle if the word were used in his presence. "Was there anything else I need to know?"

Aurora Lee shrugged her shoulders. "Nothing important."

"Don't you remember, sister?" Maggie Jane asked. "Mr. Hunter sent for that voodoo woman, Queen Lula, and she came. Mixed up some kind of juju medicine and fed it to Miss Prudence. They're saying that maybe that was what saved her."

"And the amulet," recalled Aurora Lee.

"What amulet?" Lawrence queried. Dragging information out of his worthless sisters was like trying to empty the ocean with a teacup.

"Aunt Jessa gave her something against the evil eye. Some sort of bracelet made of shells and painted stones."

"And she's wearing it," Maggie Jane chimed in. "All the time, apparently. She never takes it off."

"You're sure about that?"

"We saw it with our own eyes," Aurora Lee insisted. She wanted to light into her contentious brother for the way he was picking at them, but then she remembered what he had promised to do.

Getting and keeping Eleanor's trousseau was worth any sacrifice.

CHAPTER 15

Geoffrey took his time riding back to Seapoint. He would have to tell Prudence that he'd found Jonah and that Queen Lula claimed both Jonah and Aunt Jessa were killed to keep them quiet. He was of two minds whether to insist once again that she continue to wear the amulet against the evil eye, at least until they were safely away from the island.

She'd looked so fragile this morning when he'd taken his coffee to her room. He knew she had remarkable powers of recuperation; he'd seen her rebound in days from situations that would have left other women clutching their smelling salts for weeks. But two practitioners of the arcane art of voodoo had warned that her life was in danger. Would reminding her of that make her exercise caution or irritate her into reckless, impetuous behavior? He didn't know. And he didn't want to take a chance. He had to read her mood correctly. Not always as easy a task as it sounded.

Philip Dickson called to him from the library as he went in the front door.

"Those Bennett girls were here," he said, pouring Geoffrey a whiskey. "They arrived just after you left, asking for Prudence, but obviously wanting to build bridges for their brother. I can't stand women who are obvious, Geoffrey. I have to believe that Teddy loved Eleanor, may still love her, but I don't want him hanging around my neck for the rest of my life. I've written him recommendations and introduced him to contacts on the Cotton Exchange, but I'm not willing to do any more than that. He can sink or swim on his own."

"How do Aurora Lee and Maggie Jane fit into the picture?" Geoffrey asked. He'd expected something like this from Eleanor's father, and couldn't really blame him for cutting Teddy Bennett loose. Everything he had planned to do for the young man had been for his daughter's sake. Now that was no longer necessary.

"They didn't mention him by name, but I'm sure they were trying to worm their way into my good graces so I'd see to it their brother could still make his fortune on the Exchange. Well, it won't work. Eleanor will not be laid to rest in their family burial ground and Teddy is past history. What kind of ridiculous names are those, anyway? Aurora Lee and Maggie Jane?"

Geoffrey didn't say that Southern girls were often called by two names, and that he found the lilting cadences of *Aurora Lee* and *Maggie Jane* pleasing to the ear. Philip was shaking off the immediate emotional devastation of his daughter's death and reasserting the high-handed temperament that had made him a successful businessman. Geoffrey wouldn't interfere with whatever Eleanor's father needed to do or say to heal himself. If Abigail were to have any hope of future happiness, it would only come through the strength and devotion of her husband.

"You said they asked for Prudence?"

"They went up to her room and stayed there for a good two hours. I don't see what she could have found to talk to them about."

"Perhaps they'd heard that Prudence was indisposed and they came to pay a get-well call."

"How would they know what happened?"

"Women seem to have their own ways of finding things out," Geoffrey said. "I don't think they need telegrams, the telephone, or even a newspaper. Just a cup of tea."

"You'd best go up and see if Prudence survived the visit," Philip said. "Another whiskey first?"

The smooth golden liquid slid easily down Geoffrey's throat. He knew what he was doing. Putting off the moment when he'd have to share with Prudence what he'd found out today, the warning he was feeling more and more obliged to deliver once again.

The whiskey would help.

He knocked on Prudence's door, then knocked again. No answer. No invitation to come in, though he thought she would have been expecting him to check on her by this time.

Feeling as if he were breaking some unwritten law of propriety, he knocked a third time, then turned the knob. Pushed lightly, and as the door opened, called out her name. "Prudence?"

He stepped inside the room, fully prepared to withdraw quickly if Prudence were in a state of dishabille, rather hoping that might be so.

But the bedroom was empty, the chaise longue devoid of extra pillows and the light blanket she spread over her legs. The bed was neatly made up, not a single article of clothing left out of armoire or chest of drawers.

His first thought was that she had gone to spend a quiet hour with Mrs. Dickson.

Eleanor's mother still grieved deeply and openly for her daughter, but after her husband had forbidden the continued use of laudanum she no longer lay in her bed for hours at a time staring at nothing. She moved wraithlike about the house when she could be persuaded to leave her room, but she was at least dressed and on her feet for most of the day. Prudence, recalling her own experience with laudanum, looked in on her frequently.

Geoffrey was about to leave Prudence's room for Mrs. Dickson's when he caught a glimpse out the open window of a figure walking slowly along the sandy Atlantic beach. Dressed in a cream-colored, ruffled gown and a wispy mohair shawl that fluttered in the breeze, Prudence carried a parasol against the afternoon sun and seemed to be searching the sand for shells. As he watched, she stooped once, examined her find, then tossed it aside.

Relief washed over him as Geoffrey stepped out onto the veranda. Relief, and then a surge of anger so strong it made his hands tremble. He wanted to shake Prudence's stubborn self until she realized that it wasn't safe for her to be alone anywhere on Bradford Island. Amulet or no amulet.

Aunt Jessa had claimed she was in danger. Queen Lula had reaffirmed it. And someone had put one of the deadliest snakes in North America into her bedroom! What more proof did she need?

He stood for a moment rethinking what he had almost said aloud. *Someone had put one of the deadliest snakes in North America into Prudence's bedroom.* Knowing full well that if it bit her, she would die. He leaned over the veranda railing to look more closely at the trellis on which the cape jessamine had climbed and where the gardener had spotted the trapped and wounded coral snake. The vine had been cut down, and the trellis itself would also be removed so that no other creature could gain access to the bedrooms that gave onto the veranda.

Though strong enough to support the weight of the cape jessamine, the trellis was far too flimsy for a man to be able to use it as a ladder . . . which meant that if the snake *had* been deliberately planted in Prudence's bedroom, someone who wouldn't arouse suspicion had carried it through the house.

He had to remember what Prudence constantly reminded him—women could be just as dangerous as men. And they were better at concealing their intentions.

Seapoint's staff hadn't come with the Dicksons from New

York. They were local people, a skeleton crew hired to live permanently at the house to ensure year-round upkeep, others who worked only when the Dicksons were in residence. They had no long-term ties to their employer, no history that would make them personally loyal. Any one of them could have been bribed to deliver a package to Prudence's bedroom, almost certainly not knowing what it contained.

He'd questioned each of the indoor staff once already. Nothing but shocked denials and protestations of innocence. No one admitted to anything out of the ordinary.

He wondered if, after the interrogations, one of them had given notice, perhaps simply disappeared. The housekeeper would know. He made a mental note to check with her later.

Right now, he had to get to Prudence.

Looking out to sea, the wind buffeting her ears, Prudence didn't see or hear him coming. A strong hand on her arm was the first indication she was no longer alone on the beach.

"Don't sneak up on me like that, Geoffrey," she scolded, not really angry but needing to say something. She recognized that certain look he assumed when he was annoyed with her. He wore it now.

"You shouldn't be out here by yourself."

The hand on her arm tightened. It felt as though he were about to pitch her into the waves. "I'm perfectly all right. I haven't been dizzy or felt weak all day."

"That's not what I meant and you know it."

"I don't know any such thing, Geoffrey. Perhaps you'd better explain it to me," she said, matching him remark for remark, striking back hard at the acerbic tone of his voice. She tried to shake off his hand, but the grip was too strong. It only made her more determined not to let him win whatever confrontation he had in mind.

"The amulet you're wearing was given to you for good reason," he began, not one bit less pugnacious.

"I'm well aware of that," Prudence answered. "I'm not the fool you sometimes mistake me for. And definitely not the weakling. What happened to me was no accident. Someone put that snake into my room. I know what it was meant to do. But here I am, alive and well," she finished triumphantly.

"By the sheerest combination of serendipity and good luck," he retorted.

"Don't forget the leather sole of the slippers I was wearing," she reminded him. "I had the common sense to know you don't walk barefoot anywhere in this wretched climate. Eleanor warned me about the snakes. She also mentioned spiders, roaches, ticks, midges, chiggers, deerflies, and mosquitos. Have I left anything out?"

Geoffrey stared at her, furious but unable to refute a single thing she had said. Prudence's face was inches from his own, her eyes snapping bolts of gray lightning, cheeks flushed with emotion, mouth parted to fire another riposte.

He wanted more than anything to hold her tightly in his arms and silence her lips with his own. But before he could draw her closer, she stomped viciously on his foot. When he let go of her in pained surprise, Prudence flounced off in a perfect expression of high dudgeon. He didn't know whether to laugh or swear.

Instead, he caught up with her in several long strides. But this time, he slipped his arm through one of hers with unmistakably gentle concern. "I'm sorry. I shouldn't have come down on you like that. Your room was empty. I didn't know where you'd gone. Or what else might have happened to you."

"I'm armed, Geoffrey," she said in a thoroughly disgusted voice. "Look." She held up a small cream-colored satin reticule in which he could see the outline of the derringer he'd given her. "I'm tempted to use it on you," she threatened. Then smiled.

However often they disagreed or quarreled, they couldn't stay truly at odds with each other for very long. It had always been like that, from the first time they'd met.

The derringer was only effective at nearly point-blank range, but Geoffrey decided not to point that out. Again.

"I found our ambushed man," he said. "The one we saw pitch into the sound when he was shot. It was Jonah."

"I wondered," Prudence said. "I had the strangest feeling that we'd put him in danger just by talking to him. He didn't tell us anything that would lead us to suspect someone, but whoever was responsible for Aunt Jessa's murder couldn't be sure of that."

"I think he was trying to escape the island that night. He was terrified the killer would come after him because of what he could have told us. And it turns out he was right to be afraid."

"I wonder what it was. What secret he knew. And who decided he had to die," Prudence mused.

"Aunt Jessa kept secrets, too."

"It seems that everyone we've met on this island is hiding something. Showing one face to strangers and another when we're not around."

"Preacher Solomon sent me to Queen Lula."

"He wouldn't reveal anything, but he thought she might?" Prudence asked.

"That's one way of putting it."

"Is there any other? These people are all living in fear, Geoffrey. I've never felt anything to compare with the atmosphere of this island. And I'm not talking about the midges and mosquitos this time!"

"Can you understand that people of color in the South have always lived this way, Prudence? Before the war, their sole value to their owners was the amount of work that could be wrung or beaten out of them. Then freedom came. But it was only the titular freedom of not belonging legally to another human being. Not much more than that."

"Why don't more of them leave?"

He shrugged his shoulders eloquently. "No place to go. No

money to get there. And, believe it or not, this is the only home most of them have ever known. It's been eighty years since laws prohibiting the importation of slaves were passed. These people were born into slavery right here in America. Africa isn't even a memory any longer."

They walked in silence, Prudence's hand resting comfortably on Geoffrey's arm, her skirts swishing against his legs, her body occasionally brushing against his.

"Tell me about the Bennett girls," he said. "Philip mentioned they'd come to call."

"Oh, Geoffrey, I wish you'd been here to listen to them."

"What did they want?"

"Eleanor's trousseau."

"I don't believe it."

"It's true. They made up some long story about not wanting Mrs. Dickson to have to face the agony of going through her daughter's clothes and having to decide which charity should get what, but anyone could have seen right through it."

"I hope you didn't promise them anything."

"Only that I'd talk to Abigail about their offering to take that chore off her hands. You should have seen the looks on their faces when I brought them into Eleanor's room to show them what was involved. I swear it was all they could do to keep from trying on the hats right that minute." She looked down at her own expensive skirts now damp and sandy around the hem. "They're living in near poverty, Geoffrey. Desperate for pretty things to wear. I think they still cherish hopes of catching husbands if they can only dress the part of eligible young ladies."

"Catch a husband? Shame on you, Prudence."

"You have nothing to worry about. I wouldn't stoop to anything so mortifyingly undignified."

He choked back a laugh at the thought of independent-minded Prudence landing a man like some great big fish.

"I told them about the coral snake," she said. "Not everything, but enough."

"They're sure to carry the tale back to Wildacre."

"I hope they do."

"There may be consequences."

"If anyone there wants me dead, he or she needs to know that I'm someone to be reckoned with. I don't go down easily."

Please God you don't go down at all, Geoffrey thought.

CHAPTER 16

They stayed on the beach until well past sunset, walking slowly through the crunching sand, the conversation twisting and turning its way through the events of the past ten days, but always returning to the central, unanswered questions. Was Eleanor Dickson's death a tragic accident or a deliberate murder? Who lured her into the live oaks? And why?

"We'll be leaving soon," Geoffrey said, handing a perfect, unbroken sand dollar to Prudence. It was rare to find one without at least part of its delicate rim worn away by the tumbling action of the waves.

"I thought Eleanor's father was set on remaining until we learned more about the circumstances of her death. And if it *was* murder, until we could name the killer."

"That was his first reaction. But he's had time to rethink it. The longer Eleanor's body lies unburied in that lead-lined coffin in the chapel, the worse it is for her mother. She begged a key from Philip so she could keep a vigil beside it whenever she wanted. The housekeeper says she talks to her daughter as though Eleanor were still alive."

"I thought Abigail was doing so much better." Prudence twirled the sand dollar between her fingertips.

"She is," Geoffrey confirmed. "But her progress is precarious at best. Philip feels there won't be a lasting resolution to Eleanor's death until she can be interred properly in the family vault. I agree with him."

"What will he do?"

"He's decided to send the yacht to the closest mainland port to have it readied for the return voyage to New York. The captain has told him that one of the sails needs reinforcing, and the stores have to be replenished. He's a cautious sailor, and the cargo will be a precious one."

"I wondered how he would manage it. I think I just assumed the coffin would be sent by rail."

"It would have to be shipped in a baggage car. He believes Abigail would balk at that. She needs to be able to accompany her daughter on her final journey."

"How long do we have?"

"Not more than another week. The yacht will weigh anchor tomorrow or the next day, and should be back at the Seapoint dock three or four days after that."

"It seems hopeless, Geoffrey."

"We can't stay on here by ourselves," he said, certain that was what she was going to propose.

"I know."

"You may have to let Eleanor go without ever knowing what really happened."

"We gave our word. She's gone, but we swore to her and to ourselves that we'd discover why. We've never failed before." Prudence let the sand dollar fall. Broken promises always made her angry. "I thought you were determined to get at the truth, no matter how difficult the process or how long it took."

When he didn't answer, she tried to find the reason behind his silence in the set of his jaw and the lines of his face. But the stony bleakness she read in his eyes told her that he believed she wouldn't understand, and that she would reject whatever justification he gave for abandoning the investigation.

More than anything else, Prudence needed a window into Geoffrey's mind. Not the law school and Pinkerton-trained years that formed his professional identity, but the hidden places of the private Geoffrey, where blood and family and conflicting loyalties warred for control of who and what he was. She'd been wrestling with this dilemma ever since they'd set foot on Bradford Island.

Several times now, they'd come perilously close to a more serious disagreement than they'd ever had before. Prudence feared that a calamitous quarrel might be inevitable, and she dreaded the consequences. A difference of opinion so profound it would destroy the relationship that had lately begun to seem strong and stable could mean a future without Geoffrey. People did terrible things to themselves and others without meaning to. And suffered the aftermath for the rest of their lives.

"I wish I could have told you better news," Geoffrey said, "but it wouldn't have done any good to gloss over what Philip is planning."

"A week, you said?"

"Perhaps a day or two more or less. But not much longer than that."

"Then I think what we have to do is dig in our heels and refuse to allow these people to continue to lie to us."

"Which people do you mean?"

"All of them. The entire Bennett family and every other inhabitant of this confounded island. The questions we ask are never fully answered and I keep picking up hints that there are secrets no one will reveal. It's been obvious from the first moment we arrived that they'd all be glad to see us go."

Prudence was so infuriated she found it hard to breathe. She wanted to explode in a spectacular show of unladylike emotion, but her whalebone stays wouldn't allow it. The most she could manage was gasps of frustrated rage.

"Where do you want to start?" Geoffrey asked. He'd never intended to hold out against her, but he'd had to test again how committed she was. If he was right about what he had begun to suspect, Prudence would have to face an ugliness he'd hoped she would never have to encounter. "I'll leave it up to you."

She wanted to snap at him that *he* was the trained detective, *he* was the one who had the experience to know how best to spend the brief time remaining to them. But she didn't. It was enough that she'd snatched the case from the brink of collapse. Despite his reservations, she knew Geoffrey would hold nothing back. It was always all or nothing with him.

"Let's plan out what we need to do over breakfast tomorrow," she suggested, turning back toward the house. "I need time to think it through again."

His steady steps beside her were the reassurance she needed. They might argue and spar, but they always ended up making peace with one another.

Through the not-quite-closed drapes Prudence could see the pearl-gray predawn sky lit by the palest tinge of peach. The sun hadn't risen over the horizon yet, which meant no one, not even the servants, would be stirring.

Another night of restless, interrupted sleep. And she was no closer to the plan she'd intended to formulate than she had been last night. Sighing heavily, she slipped out of bed, shrugged into a dressing gown, found her slippers, and stepped through the French doors onto the veranda.

The early morning air was clean and fresh, the lawn sparkling with a heavy ocean dew. Drops of salty moisture peppered the veranda railing. It would be at least an hour before she could ring for the maid to bring up her early morning coffee. She played with Aunt Jessa's amulet, trying unsuccessfully to slip it off her wrist and over her hand. Maybe, despite what Geoffrey had told her, now was the time to cut it off. Declare her independence from the juju superstitions that seemed to be everywhere she went.

A flash of white in the peach-streaked grayness caught Prudence's attention as she turned to go back inside. She paused. And there it was again. There, by the darker gray bulk of the chapel where Eleanor lay in her casket.

"Mr. Teddy sends someone every morning with fresh white roses," the housekeeper had told her. "Mrs. Dickson told Mr. Dickson it would break her heart if he refused to allow it. So far he hasn't."

The roses filled the narrow chapel porch, and were banked around her friend's coffin like drifts of new-fallen snow. On the one occasion she had briefly accompanied Abigail to visit her daughter, the fragrance had been overwhelming.

She thought what she was seeing was the hat or white shirt of one of Wildacre's gardeners, but as she peered through the gray dawn mist Prudence saw the wide swing of pale skirts as a young woman bent over the white roses to pluck out fading blooms. Then Prudence stiffened with shock and stepped back into the concealment of the open bedroom door.

The young woman had turned around as if half aware that someone was watching her. She raised a hand to shade her eyes against the first rays of the rising sun and looked directly toward where Prudence had retreated into the shadows.

It couldn't be. She was imagining something or someone who wasn't really there. But as the figure lowered her hand and revealed her face before turning away, Prudence knew without a doubt that Eleanor had somehow managed to cross over the great divide that separated the dead from the living. If only for the briefest of moments.

She stepped outside again and stood clutching the veranda railing, not feeling the coldness of the metal against her fingers or the wetness of the dew. Holding on to reality, to common sense, to the lawyerly reasoning that told her there were no such beings as ghosts, phantoms, spiritualist manifestations from the other side. What she was seeing wasn't there. Her imagination and her sorrow at Eleanor's loss had combined to play a trick on her sore heart and tired brain, and the sooner she acknowledged that fact, the sooner the apparition would disappear.

But it didn't.

The slender figure dressed in filmy white moved gracefully among the tall earthenware vases filled with white roses that flanked the chapel doors, plucking a bloom here and there, reaching into the basket slung over one arm to find a fresh flower to take the place of a discarded one. When the apparition approached the chapel door with an outstretched hand in which glinted something metal, Prudence came back to herself with a start of recognition. A key. The ghost who obviously wasn't a ghost was opening the chapel door with a large metal key like the one Prudence had seen Abigail take from her pocket.

No time to lose.

Prudence closed and fastened the French door, then sped along the veranda to the steps that led down to the lawn. Her slippers were soaked through and her feet were wet and chilled before she reached her destination, but she never hesitated. She had to get to the chapel before whoever was rearranging the white roses left. As she ran she tried to remember what Abigail had told her about Teddy's daily homage to his beloved fiancée.

"He won't come himself," Abigail had said. "He knows that might lead to an open confrontation with Eleanor's father."

But the flowers arrived every morning. Prudence supposed that a small cart pulled by one of the island ponies made the trek from Wildacre to Seapoint when everyone in the two big houses was still asleep. She'd never heard of a female gardener, but the young woman she'd mistaken for Eleanor's ghost might be a gardener's daughter, entrusted with the delivery and arrangement of the white roses. A woman's eye was thought to be superior to a man's when it came to the precise angle at which to place each flower in a bouquet.

Whoever she was, Prudence decided as she came to a panting halt before the chapel, she must surely know some of the Bennett family secrets that Queen Lula had hinted about to Geoffrey. And she wasn't leaving Seapoint until Prudence had had a chance to question her.

The door creaked when Prudence pushed it open, a small sound that nonetheless startled the young woman standing by Eleanor's coffin. Her arms were full of fresh white roses from which she'd been stripping some of the leaves so the stems wouldn't crowd each other in the water-filled vases arranged on either side of the small altar. A cloth had been spread at her feet to catch the falling leaves and faded blossoms.

A ray of the rising sun shone through one of the stained-glass windows, catching the young woman's face in a beam of jeweled light. One hand rose to shade her eyes, then dropped again to the roses she held as she stepped forward into pale grayness.

"Eleanor?" Prudence called out the name without thinking.

"My name Minda, miss."

It was a younger Eleanor's face that looked back at her, albeit wearing a timid, frightened expression that would have been foreign to Prudence's daring and confident friend. This girl could not be more than eighteen or nineteen years old; Eleanor had been twenty-eight.

But the black hair was the same, twined around Minda's head in two luxuriously thick braids that shone like an ebony coronet. The eyes, too, were the identical shape and rich brown color as Eleanor's, and in the center of the young woman's chin was a double of the dimple Eleanor had hated and tried to disguise with face cream and powder.

The skin was slightly darker, as though Eleanor had stayed out in the sun without her hat, but it was the way she spoke that most puzzled Prudence. The young woman standing before her looked white, but she sounded like Aunt Jessa and Queen Lula, like the maids who brought Prudence's morning coffee, made her bed, and helped her dress. How could that be?

"You all right, miss?"

"I'll just sit down for a moment," Prudence said, lowering herself slowly onto one of the elaborately carved pews. She folded her hands in her lap, accidentally fingering the juju amulet she'd been about to remove, following the girl's glance as it found and recognized what Prudence wore on her wrist. "I'm Prudence MacKenzie. I was Eleanor's friend and was to have been her bridesmaid."

"Yes, miss. I know."

"How do you know?"

"Mister Teddy. He tole us all about Miss Eleanor's life in New York City and how she was comin' back to the island to marry him. Bringin' her best friend to stand up with her. He was right proud of Miss Eleanor." Minda shook her head sadly and laid a white rose atop the coffin. "She never should've gone into the swamp like she did. Didn't nobody warn her?"

"*She* warned *me*," Prudence said, so stunned by what she was seeing and hearing that she couldn't remember the questions she had planned to ask.

"Mister Teddy say her favorite flower be white roses. We must've cut near ever' white rose on Wildacre to bring fresh ones over here every day."

How can Teddy bear to look at this girl who so closely resembles Eleanor?

"Will you come sit by me, Minda?"

"You gonna faint, miss?"

"No, I don't think so. I'd just feel better if you were closer."

Minda laid down the sheaf of flowers she was holding, then tiptoed across the leaf-strewn cloth on the stone floor and sat down gingerly beside Prudence. This close, Prudence could see that the likeness to Eleanor was not as striking as it had appeared at first glance. But close. Very close.

Wasn't there a theory that each person had a nearly identical double somewhere in the world? Her father had talked about it in relation to eye-witness testimony and suspect identifications. He'd used a German word. *Doppelgänger*, that was it.

Don't make a fool of yourself, Prudence chided. *You're tired and wrung dry by everything that's happened here.*

Somewhere outside a horse whinnied.

Minda sprang up from the bench and began gathering the wilted flowers she would take away with her. She moved quickly and neatly, leaving no trace of herself behind. "I best be going, miss. Horse whinny like that mean they's folk movin' around in the house and down at the stables."

"I wanted to ask you some questions. Can't you stay?"

"No, ma'am. I gotta get back."

Prudence didn't dare insist. If she frightened the girl, she might disappear into the live oaks where Prudence would never find her again. "I know you said your name was Minda. Will you tell me your last name, please?"

"Don't need no last names on this island, miss," Minda chuckled. "We all know who we is."

When she closed the oak door, Minda left behind a pervasive fragrance of roses and a thoroughly puzzled Prudence.

What on earth does all of this mean?

CHAPTER 17

❦

"I want to start with Queen Lula," Prudence began, pouring herself a second cup of coffee.

"I spoke to her yesterday," Geoffrey said. "Other than to repeat the warnings we already heard about, she didn't have much to add to what we already know." He stirred a lump of butter into the bowl of grits he hadn't been able to persuade Prudence to sample.

"You may have talked to her, but I haven't," she insisted. "With time as tight as it is before Philip will force us to leave, we need to split up. Why don't you go to Wildacre today and I'll ride to Queen Lula's?"

"You know that's not going to happen."

"I don't see why not." Prudence took the derringer out of her skirt pocket and laid it on the table.

"The best you can do with that in the woods is accidentally shoot yourself in the foot," Geoffrey said. "You need a rifle."

"I'll use the one I carried when we searched for Eleanor."

"I will not let you go alone," Geoffrey said, "and that's final. Rifle or no rifle, I come with you. There's no point arguing, Prudence." He poured another cup of coffee, then settled back in his chair. "I think you'd better tell me whatever it is you're hiding," he said quietly.

"I'm not sure where to begin, Geoffrey," she said, relieved that he'd brought up what she'd hesitated to talk about. "I didn't handle the situation very well." She told him about waking up before dawn, walking out onto the veranda, seeing what she at first thought was the ghost of Eleanor at the chapel door. "That sounds ridiculous now, but for just a moment I was willing to believe she'd come back from the dead."

"You were probably half asleep."

"That's kind of you. I still feel foolish. But I swear to you, Geoffrey, I never expected what I found in the chapel."

"Which was—?"

"A young woman was there arranging the white roses Teddy sends every morning. I blurted out Eleanor's name. I couldn't stop myself."

"Then what happened?"

"She told me she was called Minda." Prudence's face flushed bright red. "Geoffrey, she looks so much like Eleanor she could be her twin, but as soon as she opened her mouth I knew how wrong I was."

"What do you mean?"

"She speaks the way the Seapoint maids do."

"I think you met one of the unacknowledged Bennetts Preacher Solomon hinted at," Geoffrey said. "If she's not the only one on the island, I suspect they were given the word to stay out of sight of the Yankee wedding party."

"So embarrassing questions wouldn't be asked?"

"That would be my guess."

"I want to find out what Queen Lula knows about her and anything else she can tell us about the Bennetts. Queen Lula is the best link we have to Aunt Jessa, and Aunt Jessa leads directly to Eleanor."

"I can't quarrel with your logic," Geoffrey said. "But we'll do it together, Prudence."

"The resemblance must be coincidental, but it's made me think. My father used to say that witnesses who swore they saw someone who couldn't possibly have been where the witness placed them were the bane of a defense attorney's existence."

"It happens. More frequently than you might think."

"I've had all night to puzzle it out. What if Teddy is lying? What if he *did* send that note to Eleanor and they *did* meet the night she died? But instead of returning to the house after he left her to go back to Wildacre, she walked deeper into the woods and in the dark, someone mistook her for Minda? Someone tried to take advantage of the situation and when she ran from him, followed and killed her."

"He couldn't let her go because she'd report the incident, and that meant certain death for him. Someone like Minda would have kept quiet, but not Eleanor. And once the killer realized he'd tried to assault a white woman, he had no choice but to finish her off. He was facing a lynching or being burned alive." Geoffrey nodded his head as he fleshed out the sequence of events Prudence had proposed. "It makes as much sense as anything else," he finally said.

"If it was one of the fugitives the Bennetts talked about and he'd been hiding out in the live oaks for a while, he probably knew Minda by sight, would have seen her going back and forth from Wildacre to her mother's cabin. But he couldn't have known how much she and Eleanor resembled one another, and at night he wouldn't have seen that Eleanor was older than Minda and her skin was lighter."

"So an attempted rape turned into a murder."

"All he had to do was follow her into the swamp as she ran from him," Prudence continued. "Then when she finally turned to fight him off, he pushed her into the water and held her under until she drowned. It wouldn't have taken long. By that time she would have been exhausted."

"How does Queen Lula figure into this?"

"I'm not sure. I think all I want is for her to confirm that

Eleanor could have been mistaken for Minda. Perhaps the secret the Bennetts have been trying so hard to keep from the
Dicksons is nothing more than past sins. They have to know
what Northerners thought of men who preyed on their women
slaves before the war, and they desperately needed Teddy and
Eleanor's wedding to take place. It was the only way to secure a
piece of the Dickson fortune. Minda's existence was a mark
against them that couldn't have been ignored. That's why she
was so frightened when I found her in the chapel this morning,
and why she left in such a hurry when I began asking questions.
As you suggested, she'd been told to keep out of sight, and she
hadn't."

"Let's hope it's that simple," he said.

"She seen me, Miss Lula." Minda twisted her hands in the
folds of her skirt. "I weren't supposed to get caught bringin'
them roses, but I did. He find out, he gonna skin me alive."

"You best tell me about it, chile."

"I come this mornin' same as always. Not dark no more, but
not sunup neither. Did the outside all right, then started on the
inside. Laid down my cloth on the floor, started takin' out the
roses what wilted and puttin' in new ones. Then I heard this
creakin' noise, and the next thing I know someone's hollerin'
out 'Eleanor.' Like to have dropped in my tracks. I said, 'My
name Minda, miss.' Calm as you please. But I swear I couldn't
hardly breathe for knowin' I'd got caught."

"That don't sound smart, sendin' you over to Seapoint. That
house got a passel of windows. You bound to be found out.
Not smart at all."

"Well, it weren't me was meant to go, Miss Lula."

"How's that?"

"Mister Teddy told Limus to bring them flowers to Miss
Eleanor's coffin, but Limus don't see all that good no more.
Didn't want Mister Teddy to know he goin' blind case he say
somethin' to Mister Lawrence, so told me to do it. I said I

would, and then he warned me not to get caught over there. When I asked him why not, he tole me to go look at my face in the frog pond."

"Not a workin' brain among the lot of you," Queen Lula said disgustedly.

"What I gonna do?"

"Nothin', just plain nothin'. You don't say a word to Limus, and you get yourself away from Wildacre and back to your mama's. You stay there until Miss Eleanor's people are gone. It won't be long."

"I cain't do that, Miss Lula. Mister Bennett don't pay but when he feels like it. If I go off to Mama's, he surely won't give me what I earned. And he won't take me back. You know he won't. I need me a blinding spell, Miss Lula."

Queen Lula held out her hand, nodding in satisfaction when Minda produced a nickel from her apron pocket. "Cross my palm, chile. Now you go on to Wildacre, tell Limus you took care of the flowers for him, and come on back here this afternoon. I'll have somethin' ready for you."

"Cain't I wait, please, Miss Lula?"

"Nobody watches when I make juju," Queen Lula said. "Go on, now."

The large black cat stretched out on the voodoo queen's lap stood up, arched its back, and hissed.

Minda sped off to the patient pony waiting at the edge of the clearing. The wagon bed was strewn with wilted roses, but all she could smell as she whipped him into a trot was the rank, sulfurous stench of brimstone.

Blinding spells were among the hardest to cast and the least likely to succeed. The person to be rendered sightless wasn't physically harmed, but only made selectively unable to recognize someone who should have been familiar to him. Queen Lula had prepared one for Aunt Jessa, but judging from what happened later, it hadn't worked like it was supposed to.

Queen Lula thought that what Minda really needed was more of a changeling spell, a hex cast on her rather than on a person who needed to be made to see her differently than she really was. A changeling spell was like a veil that came down over someone's face. He or she stepped away for a while, not quite invisible, but so faded to ordinary sight as to be unnoticeable. Changeling spells were usually cast for only a day or two, just long enough to allow someone to avoid an impending disaster or convince observers that they hadn't seen the person who was right in front of them.

Queen Lula took a cornhusk doll out of the basket where she stored them. Until she gave them facial features, hair, and clothing, they were anonymous. Neither male nor female, old or young, white or black. It was all in the skill of the spellcaster and the words she spoke. Minda's changeling spell required black hair, a plain dress and white apron, the juice of a nut to darken the cornhusk to light tan, and ink made from charcoal and the blood of a dove to draw on the features.

Absorbed in what she was doing, muttering under her breath, Queen Lula ignored the black cat's angry hissing.

She didn't hear Prudence MacKenzie and Geoffrey Hunter's quiet approach until they stood at her porch staring at the work she never allowed anyone but another conjure woman to see.

Prudence held out her hand to the hissing, spitting cat. The animal butted its head into the curve of Prudence's palm, its sudden purr the only sound breaking the silence in which Queen Lula sat motionless.

"You said I was probably one of those who couldn't be hexed, so I know that doll can't be meant for me." Geoffrey smiled as he spoke, doffing his hat politely.

"I didn't hear you comin'," Queen Lula said.

"Miss Prudence is wearing Aunt Jessa's amulet," Geoffrey replied as if that explained everything.

"I've never taken it off," Prudence added.

Queen Lula rolled the cornhusk doll into a palmetto leaf, wrapped it around with a length of twine, and placed the package into the basket. She looked hard at Prudence and Geoffrey as if challenging them. They didn't ask her to explain what she'd been doing.

"Will you tell us about the white slaves who were here on the island?" Prudence asked, ignoring Geoffrey's quick intake of breath. She knew she was expected to beat endlessly around the conversational bush before getting to the point of what she wanted to find out, but Prudence had had enough of that time-wasting Southern custom.

She might be an outsider, but she'd been a voracious reader of her father's well-stocked library. One of the books that had been shelved just beyond her childhood reach had been a compendium of photographs taken throughout the prewar South by traveling photographers who sold the images to abolitionist societies. The pictures had shocked the sensibilities of antislavery factions. The subjects appeared to be entirely white, but by the laws of the Southern states, one drop of Negro blood was enough to legally enslave any man, woman, or child who could be proved to possess it. What the individual looked like didn't matter. It was that one drop of blood from the slave mother whose master impregnated her without a second thought.

And that's what Prudence believed she had witnessed that morning in the chapel where Eleanor lay. Minda was more than a descendant of former slaves who hadn't left Bradford Island after the end of the war. She was a Bennett herself, though Prudence suspected that fact could not be proved and would not be acknowledged.

If Eleanor had lived, she would have eventually discovered the identities of the light-skinned islanders whose existence the impoverished Bennetts would have kept secret for as long as they could. At least until they were sure the Dickson fortune was well and safely on its way into their depleted coffers. Prudence could only imagine what her friend's reaction would have been. "I know there must have been some," she prodded.

"You don't want to go pokin' around in nothin' like that," Queen Lula said.

"You told Mr. Hunter that Aunt Jessa and Jonah were murdered to keep them quiet," Prudence insisted stubbornly. "That means to me that they knew secrets someone didn't want revealed. Someone willing to kill to keep them hidden."

"Three people dead, miss. Ain't that enough?"

"How did it start? How far back does it go?" Prudence's resolve to get to the bottom of the mystery was single-mindedly tenacious.

Not even Queen Lula could hold out indefinitely against Judge MacKenzie's iron-willed daughter.

"Don't rightly know when it started." Queen Lula sighed deeply and settled back into her chair. The black cat jumped from beneath Prudence's hand to her mistress's lap. "Prolly the first time a new gal caught the master's eye. Or a missus was too far along in the family way to see to her husband's natural needs. Ain't that the way they always tell it?"

"It's not something any man wants to admit," Geoffrey said quietly. He'd grown up with the evidence of sexual predation all around him, never questioning the practice until education in the North opened his eyes to how different his way of life under the *peculiar institution* had been. Geoffrey changed, but when he went back to North Carolina, he found that the South had not. What he could no longer accept, he was obliged to leave. The family had not forgiven him. And he'd never managed to absolve himself of the lingering guilt at abandoning them and the society that had enriched and shaped them. He had yet to be able to explain this to Prudence.

"Go on," Prudence prompted, looking directly at Queen Lula.

"The way the stories go, the light-skinned chirren mostly

got sold off the place as quick as the slaver could take 'em. But ever' now and then a girl would turn out too good lookin' to get rid of. And her baby would be paler than she was." Queen Lula hesitated for a moment. "If the baby lucky, it got brought up in the big house right alongside the master's white chirren. The trouble started when that chile weren't a chile no more."

"It happened all over the South," Geoffrey put in. "Not just at Wildacre."

"That doesn't excuse the practice," Prudence snapped.

"I didn't mean to imply that it did. I just wanted you to know that customs were different then. The conduct you're condemning the Bennett men for engaging in was exactly what hundreds of other plantation owners did."

Queen Lula nodded. "Cain't change the past, miss."

"But you don't have to suspend moral judgment just because it's over and done with," Prudence argued. She brought her attention back to the question Minda's appearance had raised. "What happened to the mulatto children who remained at Wildacre, the ones the mistress didn't try to get rid of?"

"Nobody paid much mind if master didn't favor 'em. They worked same as everbody else, got paired off as soon as they was old enough, 'specially if they mama was dark and they was, too."

"Did any of them run away? Try to pass for white?" It was a question that had been much debated in the North when the existence of seemingly white slaves was broached. Prudence remembered reading accounts of successful runaways in the literature her father had collected. Whether a runaway was free or slave had been a thorn of contention in the courts.

"Now you hit on it," Queen Lula said. "Only one runaway from Wildacre wasn't never caught and dragged back. That was before freedom come."

"Who was he?"

"Weren't a he. Name was Selena. Light as light could be. Story goes she disappeared one day and was never heard from again.

Dogs didn't find no trace of her. Slavers, neither. Some say she drown in the swamp."

"How sad." Prudence rubbed away the moisture she could feel prickling at her eyelids. Mourning the past wasn't going to get what she wanted. "You didn't answer when I asked how many of them are on Bradford Island today." She wasn't sure what to call the descendants of those long-ago illicit couplings.

"A handful, more or less," Queen Lula said.

"I think I met one of them. She'd brought Mister Teddy's white roses to the chapel this morning. She said her name was Minda."

"Yes, ma'am. She one of 'em."

"And her mother?"

"Minda's lighter than her momma."

Prudence understood. Queen Lula hadn't had to spell it out for her. Young as she was, Minda had to have been fathered by a Bennett male of Elijah's generation. Which, according to Prudence's rapid calculations, meant she was either a half sister or a cousin to Lawrence and Teddy.

Was this the secret Eleanor's in-laws-to-be had tried so hard to keep from her? From Philip and Abigail? The Dicksons would certainly have forbidden the marriage had they known that at least one of the evil customs of slavery days hadn't changed on Bradford Island when the war ended. Eleanor's only choice would have been to elope with Teddy. But that would have meant the very real threat of being written out of her father's will. Teddy might have braved such a consequence, but Prudence was sure the rest of the Bennett family would never have accepted it. The little Yankee gal was only welcome if she came with a big dowry and even more substantial inheritance prospects.

Now the question was whether Eleanor, too, had encountered Minda sometime during the brief, happy hours before her death. Could she have understood what Minda's appearance meant and determined to confront her future father-in-law? Or Lawrence? Prudence was certain she wouldn't have wanted to speak to Teddy until she was sure of her facts. It would have hurt him too much. It might even have driven a rift between them that neither of them could navigate.

Geoffrey had a pained look on his face, as though he was following the same train of thought. And didn't like where it was leading.

"Is there anything else you can tell me?" Prudence asked.

"No, ma'am."

"Not even about Aunt Jessa?"

"Miss Jessa come to me for a spell. I give it to her. But it didn't do no good. Sometime the white and the black magic fight each other so hard don't neither one of 'em win."

"What kind of spell?"

"That be between Miss Jessa and me. Cain't never tell nobody else what spell I cast."

"Was it unusual for her to come to you for help?"

"We didn't never try to cut each other out, Miss Jessa and me. She need black juju, she come to Queen Lula. Queen Lula need white juju, she go to Miss Jessa."

Queen Lula reached into her basket and drew out the palmetto leaf–wrapped bundle. She sat quietly with it on her lap.

The juju queen and her black cat stared at the dangerous visitors, willing them to be on their way.

CHAPTER 18

❧

"They won't discuss it with you, Prudence," Geoffrey argued, trying to persuade her that it was folly to confront the Bennett men with her unsubstantiated accusations. "No lady ever refers to the existence of mixed-blood children in her household or the quarters."

"But everybody knows they're there," she insisted. "You told me yourself that it happened all over the South."

"It may have happened, but it was never mentioned in polite society. Not ever."

Prudence had been determined to ride to Wildacre after Queen Lula refused to answer any more questions. Nothing Geoffrey could say would dissuade her. She was more certain than ever that Eleanor must have realized that some of the island's inhabitants were Bennetts from the wrong side of the blanket, and that she would be expected to ignore the implications of their pale skin and Caucasian features.

Eleanor might have been so upset and distressed by what she had learned that instead of demanding that Teddy tell her the truth, she had tried to walk off her anger and disillusionment in a landscape that was as dangerous as it was beautiful.

The more she thought about it, the more Prudence wanted to believe that her friend, unable to sleep, had gotten up out of her bed and slipped outside to pace off her worries in the moonlight. Perhaps afraid that someone might see her from one of the upper-story windows, she had gone deeper into the live oak forest than she at first intended. Lost in thought, too distraught to realize how far she had gone from the safety of the house, she had worn herself out and stumbled into a situation from which she hadn't been able to extricate herself.

An accident. But caused at least in part by a long history of gravely immoral actions for which no one was willing to accept responsibility. It wouldn't change anything, but Prudence was determined to ask the questions nobody else would or could. She still wanted answers; only her focus and her suspicions had changed. She thought the theory of the possible involvement of a fugitive hiding in the swamp was probably too far-fetched an explanation of what had happened to Eleanor, though it did provide a neatly tied conclusion to the murder of Aunt Jessa. And if someone thought Jonah was leaving the island because he had seen something he shouldn't have, that was more than enough motive for killing him.

As intent as she was on unraveling the skein of the Bennett family wrongdoings, the possibility that Teddy Bennett's father or brother had conspired to keep an old woman and an old man quiet was more than Prudence wanted to face. Surely neither Aunt Jessa nor Jonah would ever have told the whole story. There were bound to be undercurrents of jealousy and bad feeling among the island's inhabitants who had nothing to do with the Bennetts and their secrets. People killed one another every day in New York City over trivial incidents that sounded ridiculous when you read about them in the newspaper.

That was the trouble with applying logic to situations that defied logic. You talked yourself out of believing in your first intuitive response. That people really could be worse than you wanted to believe them to be.

*   *   *

By the time they reached Wildacre, it had been decided that Prudence would call on Aurora Lee and Maggie Jane while Geoffrey concentrated on the men of the Bennett family.

"That's what the sisters will be expecting," Prudence agreed. "After all, they did pay me a visit at Seapoint. Even though it turned out to be more an attempt to steal Eleanor's trousseau than to console and comfort me in my illness." She didn't bother trying to hide the sarcasm in her voice or her scorn for the motives of the Bennett women.

"We don't want to put them on their guard by doing anything so far out of the ordinary that it will get their backs up."

"Honestly, Geoffrey, I'm growing heartily sick and tired of always having to say things I don't mean to people whose company I'd rather avoid."

"You've just described how detectives spend most of their days."

"This seems very different," Prudence protested.

"The main thing is to find out what, if anything, the misses Bennett know about how much Eleanor discovered before she died." Taking his cue from Prudence, Geoffrey very carefully avoided implying that the death had been anything but a tragic accident. He wasn't sure what had caused his partner to do such an about-face, but for the moment, at least, he would honor it. He had a gnawing gut feeling that their worst suspicions would eventually be confirmed.

Aurora Lee and Maggie Jane entertained Prudence on a side porch that overlooked a broad expanse of overgrown lawn and a formal garden badly in need of pruning.

Back bent, face protected from the sun by a broad-brimmed straw hat, a painfully thin man in a ragged shirt and pants clipped ineffectually at the garden's English boxwood borders. Prudence wondered briefly if he was old enough to have been born into slavery, then caught a glimpse of visibly shaking hands and filmy eyes sunken into deep sockets. Even from where she sat she recognized the signs of advanced old age. Somehow, she decided, she'd find an excuse to talk to him. Perhaps when no member of the Bennett family was around to see her do it.

She sipped the cool green tea served over crushed mint and sugar cubes, wondering if it was served liberally laced with rum or whiskey for masculine tastes. She'd never drunk cold tea before coming South, but it tasted deliciously refreshing in the warm, muggy island air.

"I wonder if you've had occasion to talk to Mrs. Dickson about our offer to help with Eleanor's things," Aurora Lee asked. "There's no hurry, of course, but we didn't want to contact any of our charities until we could tell them something definite."

"What charities would those be?" Prudence sipped her tea, trying to appear only mildly curious about where her friend's carefully chosen trousseau would end up. "Mrs. Dickson will want to know," she explained.

"We thought we'd write to the Society for the Succor of Confederate Widows and Orphans in Savannah," Aurora Lee replied glibly. "So many ladies of impeccable reputation found themselves bereft of family and fortune after the war. Our dear Eleanor's dresses would be a comforting reminder of their former station in life."

"The war's been over for almost twenty-five years," Prudence said, deliberately allowing no trace of compassion to soften her voice. "Surely the widows have remarried and the orphans grown into adulthood."

Aurora Lee's back stiffened and Maggie Jane's eyes widened into a shocked stare. An awkward silence wrapped itself around the three women, broken only by the swish of their ivory-handled fans and the occasional screech of a peacock.

"Nevertheless," Aurora Lee finally said. A slow flush reddened her cheeks.

"I'll leave it entirely in your hands." Prudence blithely pretended to ignore the tension that not even the heavily sweet-ened tea could dissolve. "When the time comes," she added. "But I haven't yet found the right moment to talk to Mrs. Dick-son about it."

"But you will, won't you?" Maggie Jane glanced defiantly at her sister.

"I suppose so," Prudence replied. "Though it might be easier on all of us to have Eleanor's trunks packed up and stored in one of the luggage rooms at Seapoint until the Dicksons decide whether or not to have them shipped north. Mrs. Dickson is active in several charities in New York City. As was Eleanor. It might be a more suitable remembrance if they were the recipi-ents of the family's generosity."

"Oh, no," Maggie Jane whimpered. "Who knows what could happen along the way? Everything could be stolen. Or ruined, if the trunks weren't properly secured." Her eyes glistened with tears of alarm as if stained and torn dresses lay strewn be-fore her on the ground.

"I suppose I'll need to talk to Mrs. Dickson today or tomor-row," Prudence mused. "Or perhaps Mr. Dickson. He intends to sail within a week."

"So soon?" Aurora Lee's feeble protest plainly implied it wasn't soon enough.

"There isn't anything to keep them here now," Prudence said softly. She'd hinted at the possible ruin of what had been a care-fully plotted scheme; now she would take advantage of the dis-appointment and dismay she could read on Maggie Jane's expressive face. "I'm sure Eleanor was as charmed as I've been by the beauty and history of the island. How fortunate you are to live in such a place. New York seems very rough and new in comparison." She didn't mean a word of what she was saying, but if it loosened tongues, she'd gush compliments and plati-tudes until the cows came home.

"Dear Eleanor. She asked so many questions," Maggie Jane said.

"Too many," Aurora Lee snapped. "Morbid curiosity is never becoming."

"I can't envision Eleanor expressing an unwholesome interest in anything ghoulish or macabre," Prudence said.

"She wanted to know all about what it was like before the war," Maggie Jane explained, ignoring her sister's glare. It was as though, having finally found a story to tell, she had decided to give it full voice.

"She told me before she went missing that hardly anyone ever left the island, even when they could," Prudence said. Remembering Geoffrey's admonitions, she deliberately did not use the terms *slaves* or *ex-slaves.* She'd heard Teddy refer to them as *our people;* she had to trust that the Bennett ladies would understand who she was talking about. "When I look out over these beautiful grounds and gardens, I can certainly see why they'd want to stay." She gestured toward the elderly gardener. Her smile implied that she was in complete agreement with the Bennett family's decision to retain his services long after he should have been dismissed. Wasn't that what considerate employers did with long-time servants?

"People not leaving the island when they could easily find work on the mainland is a sore point with Papa that we don't ever mention when he's around. It gets him riled up something fierce, and Lord knows, the doctor says he's not supposed to lose his temper," Maggie Jane confided. "Heart, you know. He and our uncle Ethan were both wounded at Peachtree Creek." She paused as if expecting Prudence to nod knowingly at the mention of one of the most decisive Confederate defeats during Sherman's Atlanta campaign.

"I don't think I've met your uncle Ethan," Prudence said, making a mental note to steer Maggie Jane back to a discussion of the Bradford islanders whose continued presence no one wanted to discuss. She was sure Eleanor hadn't spoken of an uncle when she'd given her friend thumbnail sketches of the Bennett family members she would meet at the wedding.

"He was Papa's older brother," Aurora Lee said abruptly. "He died."

"Of his wounds?" Prudence asked. "How sad."

"He was thrown."

"But Papa always said it was because he was never strong again after Peachtree Creek," Maggie Jane explained. "He wasn't supposed to be out riding the fields, but he did it every morning, just the same. I was a little thing then, but I remember being told that one of our people had to hold Jupiter's bridle while Uncle Ethan got settled into the saddle and had his boots lashed to the stirrups. When he got thrown, one leg stayed tied. Nobody knows how long Jupiter dragged him before Uncle Ethan's other foot came out of his boot. By that time, it was too late, of course." Maggie Jane's eyes glistened wetly.

Prudence wasn't sure how to get the conversation back to the topic of light-skinned slaves and what happened to them and their descendants. She thought Aurora Lee looked tense and uncomfortable, though there was nothing in what Maggie Jane had revealed about Ethan Bennett that was scandalous or embarrassing. A veteran soldier had never fully recovered from the wounds he suffered in battle. You might say his death was indirectly caused by the bullets that had plowed through flesh and undoubtedly broken bones that never knitted together properly. A sad story, tragic perhaps, but nothing to hide or be ashamed of.

"I'm sure your father was deeply saddened by the loss of his brother," she said. "But at least you had the comfort of being able to bury him in the family plot. So many of those lost in the war never came home at all."

"We don't talk about Uncle Ethan," Aurora Lee said firmly.

They don't allude to their former slaves and they don't speak of the Wildacre master whose horse dragged him to his death. Prudence wondered what topic was safe to broach without incurring someone's wrath or stubborn refusal to discuss it at all. And how on earth was she to bring up the topic of white slaves without coming right out with it? Which she was sure would earn her a polite but very prompt dismissal.

A slender young woman appeared beside the elderly gardener and began to help him down the path toward an empty wheelbarrow. She, too, wore a straw hat that shaded her face against the glare of the sun, but there was something familiar about her that pricked at Prudence's memory. She'd seen her someplace else. And recently.

Suddenly it clicked.

"Minda," she said aloud. Without thinking. And stood up.

Aurora Lee was at Prudence's side before she could say anything else. And then, while she was still asking herself if it was really the girl she'd seen arranging Eleanor's white roses in the Seapoint chapel early that morning, Prudence's arm was firmly grasped and she felt herself being turned away from the porch railing. When she looked back over her shoulder, the girl and the old gardener were gone. Vanished as quickly and mysteriously as if they'd never been there at all. Even the empty wheelbarrow had disappeared.

"Keep going," Geoffrey urged, holding tightly to Prudence's elbow as he guided her down Wildacre's broad, curved stairway toward their horses. "And smile. Try to look as though you've had a lovely, uneventful visit."

"But I told you I saw her. She's here. Minda is here."

"I don't doubt it for a moment."

"If Aurora Lee and Maggie Jane won't talk about their family's by-blows, I'll have to ask someone who will."

"By-blows? You've been reading too many English romances, Prudence," he said, standing so immovably close she had no choice but to mount the dappled gray horse she'd ridden over from Seapoint. Geoffrey put the reins into her clasped fingers and held her hands firmly in his. "Smile and wave good-bye," he ordered. "We'll talk later, I promise. But here is not the place and now is not the time."

Prudence pasted a wide grimace on her face and hoped it would pass for the smile Geoffrey had demanded. She hadn't seen any of the Bennett men as Aurora Lee and Maggie Jane ushered her along the veranda toward where Geoffrey waited. There had been an unmistakable air of urgency about the pace the Bennett women set. As though they wanted her off the premises before she could blurt out one of her unmannerly questions where either Elijah or Lawrence Bennett would overhear and be forced to respond.

Geoffrey had conveyed the same sense of immediacy as soon as he'd reached for her arm to assist her down the stairs. Which she didn't really need. She was perfectly capable of descending them on her own, thank you very much.

And she hadn't accomplished what she'd set out to do. As he could very well understand if he bothered to take the time to read between the lines of what she'd barely managed to tell him. Minda was here. And so was a gardener who had to be old enough to be one of Aunt Jessa's contemporaries. Old enough to know secrets. Perhaps close enough to the end of his life to dare to tell them.

Everywhere Prudence turned, she seemed to walk smack into an impenetrable wall.

CHAPTER 19

❧

"I told Elijah Bennett the Dicksons were planning to leave Bradford Island within a week's time," Geoffrey said as soon as they were out of sight of Wildacre.

"I'm sure he'll be glad to see them go," Prudence replied sharply, matching her mount's pace to his. She was still fuming over the unceremonious way her visit with the Bennett sisters had ended.

"He didn't try to hide it," Geoffrey agreed. "But he was polite and formal. Restrained in his reaction."

"Aurora Lee and Maggie Jane said he has an explosive temper when certain topics are raised. I got the impression they tiptoe around him, and that they're worried he might refuse to allow them to keep Eleanor's trousseau."

"Something else is going on," Geoffrey mused. "Whenever I think I'm getting close to finding out what it is, either Elijah or Lawrence deflects my questions and changes the subject. I'm positive about two things, however. Teddy's engagement to Eleanor might have brought the promise of financial rescue, but it was also perceived as a threat."

"Did they think marriage to a Yankee would ruin their social position?" questioned Prudence.

"It's more than that," Geoffrey said. He rode in silence for a while, then visibly shook off the conundrum he couldn't solve. "Lawrence wasn't at Wildacre today, but Elijah Bennett said he and his son intend to sweep the live oaks and flush out the fugitives they're convinced are hiding there. He'll enlist men from the mainland and have the sheriff deputize them. He maintains it has to be done every few years anyway, but the murders of Aunt Jessa and Jonah make it more urgent. He claims the family has always protected its people. I think it's an excuse to get rid of the ones he considers troublemakers."

"Anyone light-skinned enough to draw unwanted attention," Prudence said. "I would have thought he wouldn't bother now that Eleanor isn't here to wonder about them. Will Philip Dickson allow it? After all, he owns most of the island."

"Neither Elijah nor the sheriff will let that stop them. Dickson is well on his way to becoming an absentee landlord with no intention of ever returning to Bradford Island. Would you, in his place? He won't be able to bring himself to sell the property, but neither will he ever live here again. Once he's gone, the Bennetts will reign supreme. It will be as though Eleanor and Teddy's engagement never happened."

"I found out something else about the family, something neither Eleanor nor Teddy mentioned," Prudence said, her memory jogged by mention of their names. "It may not be important, and perhaps Eleanor was never told about him, but Elijah Bennett had an older brother named Ethan. They were both wounded at a place called Peachtree Creek, but they survived the war. Ethan was killed when his horse threw him. I don't know how many years later that was. He'd had to be tied on to the saddle, and when he was thrown, he was also dragged. I was going to press for more details, but Aurora Lee interrupted what Maggie

Jane was telling me. She said they didn't talk much about Uncle Ethan. I thought that odd."

"His portrait is hanging in the library. I saw it this morning. He and Elijah both, side by side above the fireplace. In uniform. Two young officers enshrined in Confederate gray and gold. There's a marked resemblance between the brothers. They must have been painted at the beginning of the war, before things turned bad."

"Why do you say that?"

"Portraits in defeat are never the same as likenesses captured where the future looks bright and promising."

"Maggie Jane didn't mention whether Ethan had a wife or children," Prudence said. "So I presume he didn't." She'd already wondered if the deceased Ethan Bennett had ever visited Wildacre's quarters, either before or after the war, and decided that until she knew differently, she would presume he had. Presumed guilty until proven innocent. It was a jaded reversal of the most basic tenet of American justice. Prudence didn't doubt that her father's sense of judicial propriety would have been outraged if she'd voiced such an opinion. Fortunately, he would never have to know how much Bradford Island was influencing her.

"Interesting," Geoffrey commented.

But Prudence could tell that his mind was more fixed on solving the here and now than on musing over recent history.

"I want to go back to Queen Lula's," Prudence said. "It's not far out of the way, and I told the housekeeper at Seapoint not to hold luncheon for us."

"Don't expect a warm welcome."

"She was getting ready to cast some sort of spell on that doll she wrapped in the palmetto leaf when we arrived," Prudence said. "We interrupted her."

"She won't tell you what the spell is or who she's casting it for."

"I'm more interested in what she has to say about Uncle Ethan." Prudence had a gnawing sense that the dead man about whom she knew next to nothing was important to Eleanor's story, though she didn't yet understand how that could be.

Women stayed in the parlor when men retreated to the library where the master of the house and his male guests smoked their cigars and drank their whiskey, so she hadn't seen the portraits Geoffrey described. But she could picture them in her mind's eye. Two earnest young men with that appealing blend of blond good looks and serious mien that would be unfailingly attractive to women. Lawrence and Teddy looked very much like a younger Elijah, which meant they also resembled their uncle.

"I wonder where Lawrence was this morning," Prudence said.

"I asked," Geoffrey volunteered. "Elijah didn't seem to think it was important. He said Lawrence and Teddy would have certainly been there to greet us had they known we were coming."

"But he didn't tell you where either of them had gone?"

"No, but I got the feeling he was covering for them. I saw Elijah glance out the window while we were talking." Geoffrey reined his horse to a halt. "I didn't make anything of it at the time, Prudence, but I heard someone ride out while we were in the library. I didn't catch a glimpse of the rider, but it had to have been either Teddy or Lawrence. I think the brothers must have seen us arrive at Wildacre, and for reasons of their own, decided to avoid us."

"Does it matter?"

"I suppose not. Perhaps Lawrence dislikes my company as much as I can't tolerate his."

"And Teddy?"

"Teddy gets through life by not confronting issues he can't resolve. He probably heard about your encounter with Minda in the chapel and chose not to make himself available to answer the questions he knows you want to ask. You can never forget that he's a Bennett, Prudence. First, last, and always. His instinct will be to protect the family name."

"You'll be glad to leave here, won't you, Geoffrey?" Prudence asked.

"Yes, I will. I won't pretend otherwise, though I never expected to go without finding out how and why Eleanor died. But I'm beginning to think we'll never know, and perhaps it's better if we don't. Queen Lula may be right about that."

Prudence urged her horse forward. She didn't want to argue again, so she said nothing. She understood his feelings of frustration because she shared them, but unlike Geoffrey, she wasn't weighed down by a past she'd forsworn and abandoned. She didn't feel guilty. Which might be why every time she sensed herself on the verge of giving up, she decided to try again.

The dappled gray was skittish, shying at the deep shadows along the track they were following, snorting and tossing its head in the patches of blinding sunlight. The horse needed a good run, Prudence decided, and so did she. Despair and disappointment had cobwebbed her mind and threatened to crush her spirit. She put heels to her mount's flanks and shot off down the winding path, head lowered to avoid the low-hanging live oak branches. She heard Geoffrey give a startled exclamation behind her, then the pounding of his horse's hooves. He, too, needed a good run to let out the pent-up emotions he'd been suppressing.

Trees flashed by like the blurred images of a kaleidoscope, gray-green draperies of Spanish moss waving in the breeze of their passage. *Speed is liberating*, Prudence thought, crouched down over the gray's outstretched neck, face only inches from the coarse hair of its thick mane. This wasn't at all like riding in Central Park where formal equestrian etiquette was as rigid as parlor behavior on Fifth Avenue. The Bennetts and their beautiful but decaying old mansion faded from her conscious mind as she concentrated on keeping her seat and holding firmly on to the reins. Despite the thrill of the ride, she couldn't afford to let the horse have its head; if it stumbled in the loose sand she'd go flying. Broken bones. Perhaps worse.

Something flashed across the path in front of her, a form that skittered from one thicket of trees to another, then slipped and fell, rolling over and over like a child's awkwardly thrown ball. The gray slid to a stop on splayed-out front legs, then reared on its hindquarters, letting out an ear-splitting, high-pitched neigh that echoed through the woods. Seconds later Geoffrey was out of his saddle beside her, strong hands capturing the plunging horse's bridle, gentling it as Prudence loosened the reins and slid from the saddle.

"Easy there," he crooned over and over with hypnotic persuasion and reassurance, soothing the frightened animal, asserting control. "Easy there."

Prudence knelt beside a bundle of tousled hair and disarranged skirts, listening for the sound of breathing before she reached out to touch the crumpled form. A moan and then a convulsive shudder reassured her.

Bruised and badly shaken but apparently not seriously injured, Minda looked up at her through a waterfall of black hair, lips moving soundlessly as she struggled to sit up, dark eyes flashing panic. *She'll bolt as soon as she's able,* Prudence thought, touching the girl as firmly and reassuringly as Geoffrey did the horses. "No bones broken," she murmured. "You may hurt a bit, but I don't think any serious harm was done."

She helped the girl to her feet, brushing sand from her dress while keeping tight hold of one arm. "We met this morning in the chapel at Seapoint," she said, seeing recognition register on Minda's face, feeling the trembling of her body ease as she regained her feet and her balance.

"Yes, miss," the girl whispered, her eyes darting to where Geoffrey stood with the still-nervous horses. "I didn't mean to cause no trouble."

"Why did you run out across the track like that?" Prudence asked, not letting go of Minda's arm.

"I didn't know who it was," the girl said.

"Did you think someone was chasing you?"

"Didn't know what to think, miss."

"I saw you a little while ago at Wildacre," Prudence told her, loosening her hold as she felt the muscles of Minda's arm begin to relax. Whatever had spooked her was no longer a threat.

"Yes, miss. You was sitting on the veranda with Miss Aurora Lee and Miss Maggie Jane," Minda acknowledged, her eyes skittering from Prudence's feet to Geoffrey and back again.

"Was that your father working in the garden?" Prudence asked.

A smile chased itself across Minda's lips. "That Limus. He used to be head gardener when they was a passel of 'em working the grounds. He the onliest one left now."

"He's the one who sent you to Seapoint with the roses for Miss Eleanor," Prudence guessed.

"Yes, miss. Limus don't see so good no more. He do the best he can, but he scared Mister Bennett order him off the place if he find out he goin' blind."

"Surely not after all this time?"

Minda's silence told her that Elijah Bennett had no room in his heart for ex-slaves grown too old and feeble to put in a full day's work.

"Where were you going?" Prudence asked as the girl shook down her skirts and reached with her one free hand to smooth her hair.

"Queen Lula's," she answered slowly, reluctantly.

"That was your spell she was getting ready to cast when Mr. Hunter and I interrupted her this morning." Prudence sensed Geoffrey's focused alertness, and knew she was right.

"I didn't ask for no harm to come to nobody," Minda said, her voice trembling with the fear of being accused of something for which she'd be punished. "Just needed a little time is all."

"Time for what?" Prudence pressed. "To get away from the island?"

"I cain't leave my momma." Minda's head came up defiantly. "She sick. Need someone to take care of her."

"Then what?"

Minda's face closed down stubbornly. "Queen Lula don't like folks talkin' 'bout what she do for 'em." She pulled her arm out of Prudence's grasp. "Best be on my way."

"We'll walk with you," Prudence said, starting off down the path beside a limping Minda. "I'd like to make sure you get there all right." She glanced behind her to see Geoffrey following with both horses, his eyes watchful and observant. Nothing would get through the live oaks in their direction without his seeing it.

He nodded when she raised a questioning eyebrow. Yes, he'd seen and noted Minda's remarkable resemblance to Eleanor. His agile brain was scrutinizing what few facts they had, winnowing through contradictions to sift out plausible explanations. He had read the girl's fear and was keeping his distance from her, letting Prudence take the lead.

"What's wrong with your mother?" Prudence asked quietly as they walked along. She was doing all she could not to keep glancing at the girl whose brilliant black hair and sun-kissed skin so much reminded her of the dead Eleanor, trying to picture the exact shape and size of the small cleft in her late friend's chin. Somewhere in the extensive Seapoint library there had to be a book that explained the doppelgänger theory. She'd search for it as soon as they got back. And enlist Geoffrey's help, she decided. No more going it on her own, no more arguing. They were a partnership, despite differences of temperament and background. It was time to surmount obstacles instead of letting them block progress.

She kept up a casual conversation as they walked through the live oaks, more to continue to calm and reassure Minda than in hopes of finding out anything new. The girl answered in mono-syllables, reticent but unable or afraid not to reply.

They weren't far from Queen Lula's clearing.

The bodies hung from the huge live oak that shaded the cabin from the fierce island sun.

Queen Lula and her black cat, side by side, their necks stretched by roughly woven hemp rope, their limbs motionless and elongated in the shadows of the tree branches.

Not a bird called, not an insect chittered.

The silence was profound and absolute.

Minda fell to her knees and buried her face in her hands.

Prudence stood as if struck by the curse of Lot's wife, deathly pale and unable to move.

The horses stirred restlessly as they scented death.

Would it never cease? Geoffrey wondered.

CHAPTER 20

"Cut them down," Prudence implored. She couldn't tear her gaze from the bodies, nor could she close her eyes against the horror of their stillness. "Please, Geoffrey."

He stood for a moment beneath the branches of the live oak, staring upward, registering the spot where Queen Lula's struggles had caused the rope to rub against the gray bark. "Don't look," he cautioned Prudence, unsheathing a long knife from his saddle, carrying a wooden kitchen chair from Queen Lula's porch out into the yard. If it had been a crime scene anywhere else, he wouldn't have disturbed it, but this was Bradford Island, Georgia.

He lowered Queen Lula's body to the ground as gently as he could and laid the black cat alongside her.

Prudence knelt next to Minda, cradling the girl's body in her arms. When the sobbing eased and the trembling lessened, she dipped a ladle of drinking water from the covered bucket that sat beside the door of Queen Lula's cabin. After Minda had drunk her fill, Prudence soaked her handkerchief in the remaining cool liquid. Minda pressed it against her red, swollen eyes.

"I'm better now, miss." Minda wiped her cheeks and folded

the handkerchief neatly before handing it back to Prudence. "I seen lynchin' before, but it don't never get easier to bear."

"You shouldn't ever have to see something like this," Prudence said. She could accept the idea of lawful execution, but not this vicious, wanton taking of a life.

"Did Queen Lula have family on the island?" Geoffrey asked. He covered the bodies with a coverlet taken from the dead woman's bed.

"Not a one," Minda answered, getting awkwardly to her feet.

"Then I think we'll need to get word to Preacher Solomon. Can you do that for us, Minda?"

"Yessir, I can." She glanced toward the featureless mound lying in the shade of the live oak. "She said she'd have my spell ready when I got back."

"There wasn't time," Prudence said gently. "I looked in her basket when I brought the water. The doll she was going to use is still wrapped in palmetto leaves. It hadn't been touched."

"She said it might not do no good even if she did cast me that spell," Minda said. "Might be too late. I guess she was right."

"Can you tell us what it was you were asking for?" Prudence asked.

"No, ma'am. Not if you don't already know." Minda met and held Prudence's eyes. She sighed and then turned toward the path that led from the clearing into the forest and Preacher Solomon's church.

"What did she mean, Geoffrey? *Not if I didn't already know.*" Prudence watched Minda disappear into the trees.

"I think we'd better search through Queen Lula's cabin while we have the chance," he said, not answering her question.

"Don't we need to examine the body?"

"She was lynched. Strung up still conscious judging from the marks on the tree branch. I didn't see signs of any other brutality when I cut her down. This wasn't anger or a revenge killing. Someone wanted her out of the way, pure and simple. You heard what Minda said. She's seen other hangings. Whoever did this sent a message to every soul on the island. *Keep your mouths shut or you too will end up dangling from a tree."* Geoffrey slammed one fist against the porch railing, then shook drops of blood from his skinned knuckles.

Prudence thought he looked more desolate and despairing than she had ever imagined he could be. "I'm so sorry," she whispered, reaching out to touch him.

"This is my country and these are my people," he said. "I've spent my whole adult life trying to live them down, trying to prove that I could be better than what I came from."

"You put it and them behind you," Prudence said. "Over and over again. I don't know what more could be asked of you. What more you could ask of yourself."

It wasn't enough, Prudence realized. No matter how often she tried to assuage Geoffrey's guilt for customs and practices he'd had no part establishing or maintaining, the weight of them remained squarely on his shoulders. If you didn't know him well, you might dismiss the shadows that darkened his eyes and deepened the lines on his face, but to Prudence they were easily read. She wondered how she could ever have allowed herself to become angry with this honorable man who only asked that he be allowed to keep her safe.

"We need to search the cabin," he repeated.

"What are we hoping to find?" Prudence asked, stepping onto the porch. He hadn't turned away from the comfort she was offering him, but neither had he accepted it.

"Anything that will tell us the identities of her white customers."

"I didn't realize—"

"They usually wait until they're sure no one will see them going into a voodoo woman's cabin," he told her, "but you can be sure they came."

"But there aren't any whites on the island except the Bennett family."

"I'm talking about mainlanders. If Queen Lula was the only juju woman in the area, they would have found some way to get to her. Southerners are a superstitious lot, Prudence. They read their futures in a randomly opened Bible and the stones in a bowl of peas. I'd laugh if I didn't know how seriously they take signs and portents." He winced as Prudence poured a ladle of cool water over his injured hand. "Thank you."

She wasn't sure whether he meant for the water or the consolation he'd refused to accept, but it didn't matter. The only thing that counted was that there be no more strained silences between them.

Queen Lula's cabin was almost a duplicate of Aunt Jessa's. One room with a fireplace for cooking and cold nights, a rope bed, a crudely crafted table and two chairs. Shelves had been built against the walls for supplies, hooks pounded into the wood for clothing and tools. A rag rug provided warmth for bare feet and a spot of color for the eyes. And everywhere they looked were tin cans filled with plants. Herbs spilling their leaves onto the floorboards, seedlings straining to grow large enough to be put into the ground, wild things whose flowers neither Prudence nor Geoffrey recognized. Bundles of dried grasses waited to be woven into baskets or dolls, crushed heaps of dark berries drained their juices through coarse cloth, and swags of dried leaves of all types hung from the ceiling.

"She was the real thing," Prudence breathed. She drank in Queen Lula's small kingdom with a mixture of curiosity and admiration, newly awakened to an understanding of what Geoffrey had tried to tell her about the odd customs of New Orleans that had spread far beyond the city's boundaries.

"We're looking for anything in which she might have written down her spells or the names of clients. She was literate, Prudence."

"How can you be sure she knew how to read and write?"

"When I sent for her to come to Seapoint, I wrote a note explaining what had happened. The boy who delivered it saw her open it. He said she sent him outside to wait until she got her basket ready for him to carry. But he peeked in through the window. She was holding something in her hand and muttering over it. Like Preacher Solomon praying the Bible, was how he described it. It had to have been her book of spells."

"Did he see where she put it?"

"No. He didn't want to be caught spying."

"I wish we knew what kind of spell Minda asked for." Prudence shook out Queen Lula's bed sheets, pinched their hems, then carefully folded them and laid them on the mattress she'd already examined.

"There are two good possibilities," Geoffrey said. "A blinding spell or a changeling spell."

Prudence whirled around in surprise. He'd spoken so matter-of-factly he might have been hypothesizing about the weather. "How do you know that?" she demanded.

"Look at her, Prudence. Think about her."

"Minda?"

"Of course, Minda."

"The first time I saw her in the chapel, I called out Eleanor's name. I'm still embarrassed to admit I thought for a moment I was talking to a ghost."

"But you found out very quickly that you weren't. I wish you could have been spared all this, Prudence."

"It's bad enough that husbands abuse their wives, and I know they do. There's no point denying it. But for a man to force himself on a helpless slave and then sell off his own child as if the infant were an animal—I don't believe it's the kind of sin that can be forgiven." She slammed the pillow she was holding against the knotted ropes supporting the rolled back mattress. It had already been slashed once, and most of the feathers emptied out, but now it burst wide open and the remaining feathers filled the air. Prudence coughed and batted them away.

"Oh, my God, Geoffrey," she stammered when she could

breathe again. She held a small, stitched-together stack of papers in her hand. A silver ring rolled across the cabin floor.

Geoffrey bent to pick it up, held it out for Prudence to see. "It's a man's ring. Too large for a woman." He moved to a shaft of sunlight, rolling the ring around in his fingers. "Initials and a date. *EJB. 1866.*"

"A wedding ring?"

"No. There's only one set of initials. This is a mourning ring."

"EJB could stand for Ethan Bennett," Prudence said. "And the date doesn't contradict what Maggie Jane told me about him. He survived the war."

"This would have been worn by a close male relative."

"His brother Elijah or one of his two nephews. Teddy or Lawrence."

"Lost or stolen?" Geoffrey wondered. "And when?"

"I imagine silver tarnishes quickly in this climate," Prudence said. "Humidity makes it darken much more quickly than dry air," she explained. "That's why tableware and serving pieces are kept in cabinets or velvet-lined chests."

He handed her the ring.

"I don't think this has been off the owner's finger very long." Prudence rubbed vigorously with a fold of her skirt. "Look how easily the tarnish comes off."

"How long?" Geoffrey asked.

"I'm not an expert, but I'd guess no more than six months. The thing about silver jewelry is that the more you wear it, the more it shines." Prudence gave the ring back to Geoffrey, who had no difficulty sliding it onto the fourth finger of his right hand. "Now all we have to figure out is how it came into Queen Lula's possession."

"She was using it in a spell," he declared positively. "For some of the more potent conjures, the words have to be said over an object that belongs to the person being targeted. There's a lot I don't know about voodoo, but I'm sure of that much."

"Elijah?"

"More likely than Teddy or Lawrence, I think, depending on how old the boys were when their Uncle Ethan died. Mourning rings were usually only made for the adult members of the family. Children would outgrow them too quickly."

"I could ask Aurora Lee or Maggie Jane whether their father wore a mourning ring for his brother," Prudence said. "I wouldn't have to reveal that we've found it." She was sure she could think of some way to introduce the topic of mourning jewelry into their conversation. Perhaps in relation to Eleanor's trousseau.

"We need to look at the body again," Geoffrey said, glancing up to gauge how far the sun had traveled across the sky.

"I couldn't make out exactly what she wrote on these pages," Prudence said, wrapping the homemade book in a piece of the ripped pillowcase and stowing it in the deep pocket of her skirt. "It looks at first glance like recipes, but I can't be sure."

"That can wait until we're at Seapoint," Geoffrey said. "Minda will be back here any moment with Preacher Solomon."

He lifted the coverlet from Queen Lula's body. Her face was darkened with constricted blood, tongue black and swollen, lips blue, open eyes bulging from their sockets, neck encircled by the ligature mark of the rope that had been used to string her up. Her fists were clenched, and her bowels had voided at the moment of death, soiling the bright red and yellow of her skirt. She was barefoot, and the tignon she usually wore had been knocked off as the rope was lowered over her head. Tightly curled cropped gray hair covered her skull. One of her dangling bone earrings had been ripped from her earlobe.

The black cat's neck had been wrung in someone's strong hands, the spine snapped before it was hanged beside its mistress.

Both bodies were as pliable as though they had fallen asleep from too much strong drink. Rigor hadn't had time to set in.

"I heard someone ride out from Wildacre," Geoffrey reminded Prudence.

"Do you think—"

"It's possible. The timing would be right. She hasn't been dead for more than an hour or two. Probably less." He lifted Queen Lula's hands one by one, unclenching the fingers. "No defensive wounds. Nothing under the fingernails. Just rope burns across the palms."

"The cabin wasn't as thoroughly ransacked as Aunt Jessa's. The killer may have thought he was running out of time," Prudence said, searching Queen Lula's clothing. "A handkerchief, Geoffrey. That's all that was in her pockets. But she isn't wearing the bracelets and necklaces I always saw on her. Not a single one."

"Just an earring."

"Could there have been a struggle even though her hands and fingernails aren't showing it? The necklaces and bracelets snatched off as she fought for her life?"

"Nothing about the state of her body suggests anything like that. If I had to make a guess, I'd say whoever killed her rendered her unconscious somehow, stripped off the jewelry, then hanged her. Queen Lula regained consciousness long enough to fight the rope. Her hands weren't tied, so she tried to climb it, but ran out of oxygen. The weight of her body did the rest."

Prudence sat back on her heels and looked down at the dead voodoo queen who had seemed so mysterious and invulnerable.

"Everything about a juju woman has meaning," Geoffrey said. "When the killer took her jewelry, he stole the symbols of her magic." He shrugged. "It's not the best explanation in the world, but it's the only one I have right now that makes sense."

As they covered Queen Lula, Preacher Solomon stepped into the clearing, Minda trailing behind him.

"I sent out the word," he said. "Others be comin'. We'll dig her a hole beside Miss Jessa."

"Did she belong to your church?" Prudence asked. She couldn't imagine the colorful voodoo queen singing spirituals with the congregation in the unpainted clapboard building that didn't even have glass in its windows.

"Don't matter. Ain't never turned nobody away. Not in all the years I been preachin' there."

"I'll send word to the sheriff on the mainland, if you want," Geoffrey offered. "And I'll inform Mr. Bennett of what's happened."

"I 'preciate the offer, suh," Preacher Solomon said. "But I don't expect Sheriff Budridge gonna do more 'n tell us to bury her. Ain't gonna be no investigation." He didn't have to remind them that there had been no official notice taken of Aunt Jessa's death either.

Prudence swallowed her anger. "Did Queen Lula ever work for the Bennetts?"

"Long time ago, miss. She were just plain Lula then. Born in the quarters and sold off to Old Miz Bennett's sister in New Orleans when she were about fifteen. That's where she got the juju. She come back to Bradford Island mebbe ten years ago, but all her people was long gone. She showed up one day with her baskets of spells, and slept on the floor of Miss Jessa's cabin 'till she got one built for herself. Didn't take long. She had cash money when she got here. We heard later she got run out of New Orleans, but she never would talk about it. Don't know to this day what the fuss was all about."

"She went straight to Aunt Jessa's cabin?"

"Knowed where she was goin' and who she was lookin' for. They was chirren together in the Wildacre quarters. Lula was lighter than Miss Jessa. She was one of the real pretty ones."

"Didn't anybody think at the time how strange it was that she came back here?"

"I reckon folk knowed better than to mess with a juju woman. Miss Jessa looked out for Lula as best she could before Lula got herself sold off. Seemed like Lula was gonna pay her back. There wasn't no kind of healing or magic the two of them women didn't know when they set down together. Remembered everything there was to tell about every soul ever lived on this island."

The silver mourning ring on Geoffrey's right hand caught a gleam of sunlight as he coiled the rope he'd removed from the tree.

Minda stifled a cry and turned as if to run back into the shelter of the trees, but Prudence blocked her at the last moment, both hands gripping the girl's arms.

"What is it, Minda?" she asked. When the girl refused to meet her eyes, Prudence tightened her hold. If she had to, she'd shake an answer out of her.

"That Master Bennett's ring," she muttered. "I seen him wear it."

"This ring, Minda?" Geoffrey turned his hand so the sun glinted off the silver again. "Are you sure?"

"I seen it, too," Preacher Solomon said. "Mister Bennett didn't never take it off."

"He lost it," Minda said. "We near tore that house apart lookin' for it. Didn't nobody find nothing."

"How long ago was that?" Geoffrey asked.

"Christmas time." Minda squirmed out of Prudence's loosened grasp. "Master Bennett got a letter from New York City. From Mister Teddy. Saying he was gonna marry Mr. Dickson's daughter and they'd be comin' to the island for the weddin'. It took everbody by surprise. Everbody except Miss Jessa. She said she knowed all along it was gonna happen. Ever since Mister Teddy got it in his head to go up North. Nobody else didn't suspect nothin'. But Miss Jessa knowed. Said Miss Eleanor and Mister Teddy was made for each other and couldn't nothin' keep them apart."

"How do you know all this, Minda?" Prudence asked.

"I been working the Big House since I was twelve years old, Miss Prudence. Ain't much about the Bennetts I don't know."

It was on the tip of Prudence's tongue to ask the obvious question—if Minda realized that she, too, was a Bennett. But she caught Geoffrey's eye and saw him give an infinitesimal shake of the head. *Not yet.*

Preacher Solomon gave a sigh of relief.

"Do you know when he got the ring?" Geoffrey asked. "Who gave it to him? Or why?" He removed it from his finger and held it out so Minda could get a better look at it.

"That Mister Ethan's mournin' ring," she said, recoiling from the silver circle.

"You're positive?" Prudence insisted.

"I polished it," Minda said firmly. "Got his initials inside, and a date. I seen 'em when I cleaned it. Everbody thought it mighty strange that Master Elijah would care about somethin' like that, seeing as how the brothers never did get along."

"There was bad blood between them?" Geoffrey asked.

"Bad enough so's they was talk Master Elijah weren't too broke up about it when Mister Ethan's boot got caught in his stirrup. Made Master Elijah owner of Wildacre."

"Mister Ethan wasn't married? Didn't have any children?"

Minda looked at Preacher Solomon, who shook his head.

She didn't answer.

CHAPTER 21

❦

"One of my governesses was French and an excellent teacher, so I know I should be able to understand this," Prudence said despairingly, "but I can't make out most of it." She'd undone the looped stitches holding Queen Lula's book of spells together, given half the pages to Geoffrey, and spread the rest on the large table in Philip Dickson's library. A French-English dictionary lay open in front of her, a book on voodoo customs of New Orleans beside it.

"This is Creole, Prudence. It's an oral language that evolved over time from the French spoken by Louisiana plantation owners and the African languages of their slaves. We don't know where or when Queen Lula learned how to read and write, but I'd guess she used the sounds of the English alphabet to transcribe the spells she'd memorized in Creole. The trick is to keep reading the same sentence over and over again until the rhythm of it starts to make sense. If you keep at it long and hard enough, you'll find some recognizable French roots."

"How can we ever hope to decipher all of it?"

"If we're right, and Queen Lula wrote down the most complex and least used spells, the same words will appear in many of them. We don't need a complete translation, just enough clues so we can guess at what she might have concocted for Aunt Jessa. That should point us toward whatever secret she was hiding."

"I always thought I had a good ear for languages." Prudence's lips moved as she sounded out the oddly spelled words that didn't make any sense to her.

"Don't give up yet."

She never conceded defeat, no matter how impossible a situation seemed, but she was close to throwing up her hands and escaping to the beach to walk off her frustration. Geoffrey seemed to have some particular suspicion in mind that he wasn't sharing, which made things worse. He'd mentioned two spells Queen Lula might have cast—a blinding spell and a changeling spell—but he hadn't explained what either of them entailed or how he even knew what they were.

Prudence wasn't sure how much longer she could keep her opinions about this whole voodoo notion to herself. The only thing holding her back was the fear that if she came right out and said that Queen Lula's spells were nothing but ridiculous mumbo jumbo, it would register with Geoffrey as another rejection of who and what he was. It was bad enough that she so obviously didn't fit into this world of semitropical heat and oppressive history; to question the validity of some of its obscure beliefs could translate as cruel mockery. She wouldn't do that to him, no matter how impatient she became.

"I think I've got it," he said, straightening in his chair, rolling cramped and hunched-over shoulders. He pointed to the list of words he'd copied from the pages in front of him. "*Aveugle* means 'blind' in French. What I've found is a spell that uses a variant of that word. And here's another that repeats *chanjman* several times."

"*Chanjman*," Prudence said. "Changeling?"

"I don't think it can be anything else."

"Then maybe it's time you told me what those spells are and how you know about them."

"I told you we had a voodoo woman at Sandyhill when I was young," Geoffrey began, pushing back from the table, turning away from Prudence to face the floor-to-ceiling windows that brought light and a view of the ocean into the library.

Afraid to break the stream of confidence when it had barely begun, she said nothing, hoping he would read her silence as encouragement.

"I remember Mama Flore as a whip-thin woman whose fingers wound around each other like newly hatched snakes. She had her own cabin, but most days she was at my mother's side from sunup to sundown. I suspect my father was the only individual on the plantation who wasn't afraid of her. He knew why she was there and why my mother had insisted on buying her. Mama Flore's charms and concoctions kept my mother calm. He didn't believe in voodoo, but he allowed her to heal and cast spells in the quarters without interference from the overseer. To this day I don't know why, but Mama Flore had a special affinity for the small, lost boy whose mother had forgotten she'd birthed him and whose father couldn't be bothered to rear him."

So different from Prudence's sheltered childhood. Bathed in the love of a mother who knew she would have only a few years to share with her only child, doted on by a father who did not believe a woman's mind had to remain an empty receptacle, Prudence had never known the type of loneliness Geoffrey was describing. Until her father remarried. She shook off those bitter, unproductive memories and concentrated on what Geoffrey was saying.

"I got in the habit of hiding myself in the shadow of her skirts. They smelled of herbs, crushed flowers, and candle wax. She fed me boiled sweets. I remember the tang of peppermint and the sweetness of honey. And when she cast a spell, she didn't shoo me away. It was as if I wasn't there, and yet I was. That's why I know about the blinding spell, the changeling spell, and so many others.

"The spells she cast for my mother kept her safe from unnamed threats and faceless enemies. Mama Flore brewed soothing drinks to help her sleep, whipped up creams and unguents to smooth her skin and keep age wrinkles at bay, sang mesmerizing chants to stem a blood flow that left her weak and as white as the cotton that grew in our fields. I absorbed all of that like a cat licking up warm milk. It nourished me, and I was unaware of how strange my upbringing had been until Father sent me north to school . . . where I very soon developed enough common sense to hide my differentness. I willed myself to forget, and for the most part, I did. Queen Lula brought so much of it back."

He passed a hand over his forehead and down across his eyes as though he were replacing a mask that had been temporarily lifted. "I'm sorry, Prudence. You have enough burdens to carry without my laying more on you."

"Tell me about the blinding spell, Geoffrey," she said gently.

"It's used to make a particular individual unable to recognize someone who wants to be able to approach without revealing his identity. It doesn't steal sight; it just alters it. A man or woman might use it to visit a lover if he or she fears being seen by the lover's wife or husband. A daughter who runs away from home but remains in the same city as her parents might protect herself from discovery by calling down a blinding spell on them. They could pass one another in the street with no stirring of familiarity. The parents wouldn't know who she was, and no one witnessing the encounter would be any the wiser."

"That sounds like the black magic of a fairy tale," Prudence blurted out before she could stop herself.

"I've heard it claimed that successful juju is a form of mesmerism," Geoffrey said. "For those who believe, no claim is too outrageous. For the rest of us, skepticism is the order of the day."

"Then you don't believe in voodoo?" Prudence hoped her relief wasn't too obvious.

"I believe in the power of its practitioners. But their ability to attract and control followers comes from persuasion and fear. Nothing that transcends the laws of nature."

"You spoke of a changeling spell."

"That was one of Mama Flore's favorites. She used its threat to keep misbehaving children in line," Geoffrey said. "It comes from legends of infants being replaced by the offspring of their clan's enemies, thus guaranteeing them life in hope that the stolen child would also live. Hostages to fortune. The spell exchanges one face for another, allowing the two individuals to live one another's lives, but only for a specified amount of time."

"Geoffrey, have you ever seen either of these spells at work? Do you have any proof that they accomplish what they're meant to do?"

"Stories, always told by someone else. That's as close as I've ever gotten. I told you that Father sent me north to school after the war. The last time I went back, Mother had been confined and Mama Flore was gone."

"Did you ever find out what happened to her?"

"I asked, but never got an answer."

"Who could have paid Queen Lula to cast either of those spells? Now that we know she could have done it?"

"Aunt Jessa," Geoffrey said. "If what I'm beginning to suspect is true, she's the only one who would have been desperate enough to think either of them would work." He gathered up the loose sheets of paper and the cord that had bound them together. "It's time to call on Elijah Bennett again. He needs to identify this mourning ring and we have to find out how and why it came into Queen Lula's possession."

*   *   *

"Aurora Lee has given him tincture of foxglove to regulate his heart," an exhausted-looking Maggie Jane told them. "He's in his bed, and I'm on my way up there right now."

She'd put down the tray she was carrying when Geoffrey and Prudence climbed Wildacre's front steps and knocked at the door. She picked it up again, spilling some of the beef broth in her agitation. "I'll tell him you called."

"Is Teddy here?" Prudence asked.

"He's gone to the mainland to bring back a doctor. If he can find one closer than Savannah," Maggie Jane sobbed.

"If there's anything we can do to help—" Geoffrey began.

Blinded by tears, Maggie Jane shook her head and stumbled toward the staircase to the second floor. By the time she'd steadied herself and begun the long climb, Lawrence had appeared on the landing. He whispered something to her as they passed, then hurried down to where Prudence and Geoffrey stood.

"I don't mean to be discourteous," he said, "but as my sister seems to have told you, we have serious illness in the house. I'm afraid we are not entertaining guests at the moment."

"I'm sure I speak for Philip and Abigail Dickson as well as ourselves when I say we all wish your father a speedy recovery," Prudence said. There didn't seem to be anything to do but leave.

Just as she turned back to the door that no one had thought to close, they heard a horse being ridden at speed up the oyster shell drive. Seconds later Teddy had flung himself from its saddle and raced up to the veranda. "Is he—?"

"The foxglove seems to be working," Lawrence said. His glance at Prudence and Geoffrey told them plainly that he wished them gone. "Aurora Lee thinks the crisis may have passed."

"There isn't a doctor anywhere closer than Savannah." Teddy panted. "I sent a telegram, not that I expect it to do much good."

People who lived on isolated plantations like Wildacre came into life and left it without medical help. In between they survived accident and illness by the skill of the master's wife and their own strength. Or they didn't.

"We'll be on our way," Prudence murmured.

"Please don't leave," Teddy said unexpectedly. "I'll go up for a moment to let my sisters know that a doctor won't be coming anytime soon, but there isn't much else I can do. Except wait." He fingered his watch fob and the ring he had given Eleanor.

Lawrence scowled, then turned on his heel. He disappeared down the hallway leading to the library.

"He and my father are very close," Teddy explained. He showed them into the parlor, then hurried out into the entrance hall.

They heard his rapid steps on the stairs, the sound of a door opening, quiet voices.

Geoffrey helped himself to the whiskey tray. He raised an eyebrow at Prudence, who shook her head.

"We shouldn't be here," she said.

"Men like Elijah Bennett don't die that easily."

"We won't be able to question him."

"Teddy will know if the ring we found belongs to his father. And if for some reason he's uncertain, there's always Lawrence." Geoffrey placed the silver mourning ring on the whiskey tray, positioning it so that anyone reaching for a glass would have to see it. Satisfied, he stepped away.

"It was kind of you to stay," Teddy said as he came into the parlor. "I'll just leave the doors open in case—"

"How is he doing?" Prudence asked.

"Better than when I left. He's sitting up and Maggie Jane is feeding him broth. One dripping spoonful at a time." Teddy let out a ragged sigh. "He's going to pull through. This time."

"Has he had anything like this before?" Prudence asked.

"Not that I know of. He's a great one for keeping secrets, though, especially if it's anything of a personal nature."

Teddy moved toward the whiskey tray.

Geoffrey's eyes followed him.

Prudence sat up straighter in her chair.

"Pour one for me, too, brother," Lawrence said from the doorway. "I think we've earned it."

Teddy stood frozen in place, staring down at the silver tray reflecting crystal and whiskey in a shaft of light. He reached out. Then he turned, and without saying a word, held up the silver ring.

Lawrence strode across the room, thunder in his eyes. He snatched the ring from Teddy's upraised hand and read the inscription. "EJB. 1866."

"It's Father's ring," Teddy said. "The one he always wore for his brother's memory. We have to tell him it's been found." He peered down at the whiskey tray as though other lost items would suddenly appear there.

"I wondered—" Prudence began.

"Did you have something to do with this?" Lawrence snarled. "Is this more of your meddling?"

"I don't know what you're talking about," Prudence hedged.

Geoffrey raised his glass to his lips. He wouldn't interfere. Not yet.

"I found it lying on the tray, Lawrence," Teddy said. "Someone must have put it there, but it couldn't have been Prudence. Father lost this ring at Christmastime. I remember because it was right after I wrote that I'd asked Eleanor to marry me and she'd accepted. His answer was as much about the dishonest habits of the few servants left here as it was congratulatory good wishes."

"It didn't disappear by itself," Lawrence raged. "And it didn't appear again without help."

"Perhaps it really was lost, not stolen. And whoever found it was afraid he might be accused of taking it. So he chose this way of making sure it got back to its rightful owner." Prudence's simple explanation seemed to strike a chord with Teddy.

"I'd like to believe that's what happened," he said. "I wouldn't want to accuse any of our people of theft."

"Is that the only piece of jewelry that's gone missing?" she asked.

"Lawrence? I've been away too much to be able to answer that question," Teddy said. "I don't recall either Aurora Lee or Maggie Jane saying anything about items they can't find."

"Nothing else," Lawrence said brusquely. "Father should be told we've found it. I'll take it up to him." Red-faced and still angry, he executed a stiff bow in Prudence's direction, then left the room, ring in hand.

Teddy poured his whiskey and raised his glass.

CHAPTER 22

❦

"Geoffrey told me Lawrence showed him a portrait of your uncle Ethan," Prudence began, sipping delicately from the glass of minted tea a maid had brought. "He said there was a marked resemblance between the brothers."

"They were only two years apart in age," Teddy told her. "Rather like Lawrence and me. Did he tell you they were wounded in the same battle? Peachtree Creek, it was."

"But they survived," Geoffrey said. "It was the last year of the war. Sherman was advancing on Atlanta."

Teddy nodded. "I've heard my father refight that battle a hundred times. He swears that the outcome might have been different if President Davis hadn't replaced General Johnston with General Hood at the last moment."

"The cause was already lost," Geoffrey said. "We just didn't want to admit it."

Had he noticed he'd said *we*? Prudence wondered.

"Would you like to see the portraits, Prudence?" Teddy asked.

"I would. Especially since Ethan's mourning ring has shown up again."

"It's the only one my father had made. Lawrence and I were still boys when our uncle died, and women in the South usually wear brooches with a lock of the deceased's hair." He led them from the parlor to the library, opening a window overlooking the back lawn as soon as they entered. "Father and Lawrence smoke their cigars in here when they aren't out on the veranda," he explained. "I know ladies find the smell hard to bear."

"My father liked a good cigar," Prudence said. "I grew used to the aroma on his clothing."

"Eleanor—" Teddy didn't finish what he had been about to say. He pulled back the rest of the curtains that darkened the room. "Ethan is on the left, my father on the right."

The gold hair and gold braid of the Bennett brothers leaped into stark relief against the dark gray background and the lighter gray of their uniforms. They were as handsome a pair as Prudence had ever seen. It took no effort at all to imagine them partnering two beautiful young women wearing the enormous hooped skirts of the period. There was a stubborn aura of romance about the war that not even the grim battle photographs of Mathew Brady had been able to stamp out entirely. Men in uniform were always irresistibly attractive. Until the uniforms were ripped and stained with blood.

"How old were they?" she asked.

"In their late twenties when the portraits were painted. Probably the summer of 1861, shortly after war was declared in April. Everything was being done quickly because nobody thought the conflict would last as long as it did."

"Too long," Prudence whispered. "All wars last too long."

"Ethan never married?" Geoffrey asked, probing for a lost fiancée or deceased sweetheart.

"He may have felt it was dishonorable to ask a woman to marry a man whose legs had been shattered beyond repair," Teddy said.

Prudence knew her presence stopped him from saying more than that. He couldn't have any idea what she had been exposed to in the course of the investigations she and Geoffrey had undertaken. A quick glance at her partner's face told her she had read the situation correctly. Ethan Bennett's injuries had probably been more debilitating than splintered leg bones.

"Maggie Jane mentioned the accident that took his life," she said. "I don't know when I've heard a sadder story."

"They were changed men after the war," Teddy said.

"No one escaped it," Geoffrey agreed.

"My father said he didn't think Ethan knew a pain-free day from the time he was brought home until the morning his horse threw him." Teddy looked at the half-empty glass in his hand. "Whiskey was the only thing that brought relief. The suffering and the alcohol aged him prematurely."

"He and your father must have been very close," Geoffrey said. "That's something else war does."

"Strangely, given the fact that my father commissioned a mourning ring when Ethan died, they weren't. They didn't like each other."

"I find that hard to believe," Prudence said, looking intently at the two young officers whose eyes gazed into a future neither could have imagined.

"Everyone in the family was aware of it. They didn't try to hide their mutual dislike, especially after my grandfather died and Uncle Ethan inherited. If it hadn't been for the war, my father might have taken his wife and children to one of the family's mainland plantations, but by the time of the surrender, Wildacre was all that was left of the Bennett holdings and it took both brothers to run it."

"How far back did the trouble between them go?" Geoffrey asked.

"Aunt Jessa said it started as they grew from boyhood into manhood."

"Aunt Jessa?"

"She thought the sun rose and the moon set on Ethan," Teddy said. "I never saw that woman cry until the day he came home from Peachtree Creek. I was seven years old. She knew he might keep on breathing, but his life was over. He was as dead a man as if someone had shoveled him into his grave."

"I thought you were her favorite," Prudence said.

"In this generation. It was Ethan in my father's. She was mammy to all the Bennett children, but in each set, she always cherished one of us above the others."

"Don't you want to know who killed her?" Prudence whispered, aware that anything could break Teddy's fragile mood of disclosure.

He never took his eyes from the two men in Confederate gray. "I agree with what my father believes. We've always known that fugitives from the law take refuge in our live oaks. As long as they stay hidden, we don't try to roust them out. Either the swamp will claim them or they'll move on."

"But this was different," Prudence persisted. "This was Aunt Jessa."

"And Jonah," Teddy reminded her. "I know what you're implying, Prudence. Justice is different down here. We don't expect it to be the same for people like Aunt Jessa and Jonah as it is for us. Things work themselves out without the interference of sheriffs and police. It's always been like that. It always will be." He paused for a moment, reordering his thoughts, searching for words she would understand. "Nevertheless, we'll get a posse together and clear out the vermin responsible for what was done. Our people look to us for protection."

"Queen Lula was hanged in front of her cabin," Geoffrey said harshly. "This morning. Prudence and I found her. I know you've been told about it. That makes three unexplained deaths, Teddy. Four, if you count Eleanor's drowning. The coral snake in Prudence's room would have brought the number to five. Whatever is happening on your island won't *work itself out*. Or don't you care how many more of your people have to die to safeguard the Bennett name?"

"How dare you say that to me?" Teddy whirled on Geoffrey, his face blanched, voice choking with emotion. "You of all people!"

"Say what you mean." Geoffrey slammed down his whiskey glass and unbuttoned his coat.

Prudence caught a glimpse of the butt of his Colt revolver. Of course he was armed. She should have known he would be.

"We have a name for people who betray their own. I'm sure you've heard it used over the years. *Scalawag*." Teddy spat out the word with all the force and venom of a coiled snake.

"When I left the South for good, I took nothing with me that wasn't mine," Geoffrey said. "I didn't return to prey on her misery or profit from her defeat." It was clear he was expecting an apology, equally obvious he was close to demanding satisfaction.

"So you say."

"Please, Teddy," Prudence pleaded. "You don't mean that. You know Geoffrey's history. He no more fought in the war than you did. Neither of you was old enough. It destroyed hundreds of thousands of men of your father's era. Don't let that be your legacy as well."

Neither man answered her.

"You're grieving for Eleanor," Prudence continued, desperate to strike some chord of reconciliation. "Loss does terrible things to a person's heart. It can make you bitter and so angry that you lash out at everyone, even those who care most deeply for you. I understand it because I lost two people who meant the world to me, and I nearly drowned in my own despair."

She reached out to clutch Teddy's arm, digging her fingers

into muscles knotted with rage. He wanted to hurt someone, wanted to attack the forces that had stolen his future from him. Geoffrey was the closest target.

"Please, Teddy." She felt the arm she clung to soften, the muscles loosen. Saw the fingers that had squeezed themselves into a fist open and flex.

Teddy couldn't find the words or perhaps couldn't bring himself to voice them, but he reached out his right hand. And Geoffrey shook it.

The confrontation, sudden, unexpected, and potentially deadly, had been safely navigated.

For now.

The cabin in which Minda's mother lived was deep in the live oak forest, an isolated spot where the humid air hung heavily over thick stands of palmetto and billows of deep white sand. Following the directions given by the stable boy who'd brought around their horses, Prudence and Geoffrey rode along a narrow trail for as long as they could, then led their mounts the last few hundred yards.

Minda stood on the porch, her body tense, fear in her eyes. She held the arm of a painfully thin woman whose pallor was an unhealthy jaundiced yellow. Suffering and endurance had engraved themselves into her features, but there was a hauntingly familiar beauty about her drawn face. The resemblance between mother and daughter was pronounced and unmistakable.

When she recognized them, Minda helped the woman to a cushioned rocking chair. She placed a cup of water in her hand and whispered reassurances.

"I'm glad it's you," she said, stepping down from the porch.

"Who did you think might be coming?" Geoffrey asked, not approaching too quickly or too closely.

"I wasn't sure," Minda replied.

"But you were afraid?" Prudence said.

Minda nodded.

"Did you think someone intended to do to you and your mother what was done to Queen Lula?" Prudence tied her horse's reins to the trunk of a live oak. "Is that what you thought would happen, Minda?"

"Yes, miss."

"And you didn't run?"

"I couldn't leave Mama," she said, leading Prudence to the woman in the rocking chair. "Miss Prudence, this my mama. Her name Dorcas."

"I'm please to meet you, Dorcas." Unsure whether to hold out her hand, Prudence smiled and bobbed her head. She felt Geoffrey's presence beside her, heard him say the woman's name, but nothing else.

"How'd you find us?" Minda asked.

"We were at Wildacre visiting Mister Teddy," Prudence answered, deliberately not specifying who at Wildacre had given them directions.

"He's a good man," Dorcas announced in a stronger voice than either of her visitors had expected. "Saw to Miss Jessa whenever he come home. Weren't nothin' he could do for her when he weren't."

"Was Miss Jessa having problems?" Geoffrey asked.

Dorcas looked to her daughter.

"It's all right, Mama," Minda said. "They be friends of Mister Teddy."

Still Dorcas hesitated.

"I met Aunt Jessa when she came to Seapoint to help with Miss Eleanor," Prudence said. She held out her arm. "She made this for me. Said I needed it for protection."

"You best never take it off then, miss," Minda said.

When a fit of coughing interrupted whatever Dorcas was about to say, Prudence glanced at Geoffrey. Both of them knew what the rales of consumption sounded like. Minda's mother was not long from a final crisis. A hastily concealed spot of blood on the handkerchief she pressed to her lips confirmed it.

"Aunt Jessa went to Queen Lula for a spell," Prudence began. She sat down on the porch step below Dorcas's rocking chair, her body angled so that she looked off into the live oaks. If she turned her head, she would meet Dorcas's gaze. But she did not. She folded her hands over her knees, the juju amulet prominently displayed.

And waited.

"Aunt Jessa raised me," Dorcas said, her voice only a fraction above a whisper. "I was born in the quarters at Wildacre."

"But I don't imagine you stayed there," Prudence said, continuing to gaze off into the forest.

"Master brung me into the Big House soon as I was old enough to follow orders. Give me to Young Miss for her birthday. Made Mistress so mad she swatted at me ever' time I crossed her path. I learned real fast to stay out of sight. Did whatever Miss Aurora Lee tole me to do and kept my head down."

"Were you the only one?" Prudence didn't quite know how to phrase the question.

"No, ma'am," Dorcas said bitterly, "but they mostly got sold off the place soon as they was big enough to fetch a good price. I reckon they was something special about my momma 'cause she never did get sold away. Yellow jack took her."

"Yellow fever," Geoffrey murmured. "Some years are worse than others, but it always comes back."

"Got my first chile when I was sixteen, the year before the fighting started. The babies after that all died 'till Minda come along. Aunt Jessa helped me birth her, said Minda the last chile I was ever gonna have. Tole me I'd been lucky."

"Lucky how?" Prudence asked.

"The more babies a woman had in slavery days, the more tears she gonna shed. Master sell them off one by one whenever he need the money. I only lost one chile that way. Minda born free."

"You didn't want to leave when freedom came?"

"No, ma'am. Weren't any place to go."

"She had to stay put and wait for my brother," Minda explained. "In case he ever found out where he was born and who his mama was. He'd come back here lookin' for her. Lots of folk sold off as chirren was wandering the roads lookin' for they kin after the war."

"Did he ever return?"

"Not to this day," Dorcas said. "Look like if he wait too much longer I be gone, too." She coughed again, the rough, choking sound of bloody phlegm echoing through the clearing.

"I'm so sorry," Prudence whispered.

"I know you got questions," Dorcas said when she could get her breath again. "Minda tole me all about Miss Eleanor. How she got lost in the swamp and drowned. Aunt Jessa say that chile had a hex laid on her from the day she was born. Day she come back to Bradford Island was the day it claimed her again. Weren't no escaping it after that."

"What did Aunt Jessa get from Queen Lula?" Prudence asked. "Was it a blinding spell?" She turned her head as she spoke. And met Dorcas's eyes fastened on her with a mixture of hope and despair.

"She come by here to fetch me that day," Dorcas said. "Had the ring Mister Elijah always wore for Mister Ethan in her apron pocket. Showed it to me. I asked her how she got hold of it. She said she stole it right off his finger when he sittin' in his library drinkin' hisself senseless like he do near ever' night. Didn't even feel her slide it off his finger. Made a ruckus when he couldn't find it, but Aunt Jessa had it out of the house by then."

"Did you go with her to Queen Lula's?" Prudence asked, trying to keep the threads of Dorcas's story separate and comprehensible.

"Aunt Jessa want the blinding spell. Queen Lula need some of Mama's blood to make sure it work," Minda explained.

Prudence looked at Geoffrey. He seemed to be so focused on Dorcas that she wasn't sure he'd heard what Minda had just said.

"Aunt Jessa say Mister Ethan's ring do double duty. She was real pleased at havin' it to give Queen Lula."

"Lula needed Bennett blood to bind fast the blinding spell," Geoffrey said softly, eyes still fixed on Dorcas.

She didn't answer, but after a moment her gaze drifted back from the live oaks, met his questioning stare, then sank to the worn fingers clasped in her lap.

Prudence knew better than to push any further. No one on Bradford Island would ever give voice to the truth of what Wildacre's masters had demanded from their women slaves over the years. Demanded as their absolute right. She'd seen pages of the ledgers meticulously kept by most slaveowners and reproduced by abolitionists. Light-complected children were routinely claimed to have been fathered by another slave, even one who might have been described as *exceedingly dark-skinned.*

It was clear that Dorcas must be the child of a Bennett and that Minda was also likely to have been sired by a Bennett male. The most plausible possibility, especially if Aunt Jessa needed her blood to ensure the success of the blinding spell, was that Dorcas had been fathered by the same man who had sired Ethan and Elijah.

If there were witnesses to a birth, there was no denying the identity of the mother. Would there ever be a way to tell with equal certainty who was the father?

Aunt Jessa desperately wanted Queen Lula to cast a blinding spell. For which she provided a ring worn every day by Elijah Bennett. And blood from a woman born into slavery but white enough to pass. An unacknowledged Bennett.

What was the connection?

And what was the link to Eleanor?

CHAPTER 23

Two days after his apparent heart attack, Elijah Bennett was out of bed, ignoring the pleadings of his hovering daughters to lie back down and let himself be dosed with more tincture of foxglove.

He felt fine, he informed them, and he'd prove it by going ahead with the plan to lead a posse of mainlanders to sweep the trash out of his live oaks. Sheriff Budridge had been notified; a group of twenty armed and mounted volunteers was eager to cross the sound and roust out the fugitives and lowlifes hiding on the island.

And yes, since they wouldn't stop yammering about it, Aurora Lee and Maggie Jane had his permission to help Eleanor's mother with the disposal of her daughter's trousseau. The sooner that was done, the sooner the Dicksons would go back to New York. As the girls had pointed out more than once, the yacht was being prepared for the homeward voyage. He agreed that they needed to hurry up and get those trunks packed.

Women's business bored him. Elijah had more important things to do than listen to their whining.

* * *

Philip Dickson charged Prudence with seeing to it that Eleanor's things were transported from Seapoint to Wildacre as quickly and efficiently as possible. He had acquiesced to Abigail's plea that their daughter's bedroom remain as it was, but drew the line at retaining any of her clothing. Nor would he consider transporting Eleanor's trousseau back to New York for donation to charities there when it could be given to needy and deserving women in nearby Savannah. Pleading and weeping did no good. He had made up his mind.

In a rare moment of emotional frankness, he confided to Prudence his fear that if Abigail were allowed to ship Eleanor's effects to their home, she would be unable to part with them. And that, he believed, would ultimately destroy her fragile hold on life and sanity. "Death is like an amputation," he'd said. "The pain is intense, but it's best not to dwell upon it."

Prudence promised that Abigail would not be disturbed by Aurora Lee and Maggie Jane's presence in the house. Mrs. Dickson would be welcome in Eleanor's room during the sorting and packing, of course, but she could also choose not to be a part of it. Prudence had already spoken to the maids who would be doing the actual work. They understood what was expected of them.

"In and out on the same day," Philip commanded. "Not a minute longer." He planned to shut himself into the quiet of his library while Teddy's sisters were in the house. He didn't want to have to thank them for what they were doing and he didn't want to see trunks being carted down the stairs and loaded onto the carts that would carry them to Wildacre. It would be too much like repeating the journey out of the swamp behind Eleanor's body.

Strong as he was, he didn't think he could bear it.

Aurora Lee's plan was simple. "We pack our immediate choices into one trunk," she instructed Maggie Jane as they arrived at Seapoint. "And when everything is unloaded at Wildacre, we have that one taken upstairs. The rest of them can be stored down below in the tabby rooms."

"What will Father say when we appear in new gowns?" Maggie Jane asked, her face flushed with excitement and apprehension. "He's bound to notice."

"He may remark when we transition out of mourning, which we can do as soon as the Dickson yacht clears the dock," Aurora Lee said. "But aside from realizing we're not wearing black anymore, I doubt he'll say a thing unless you're stupid enough to provoke him."

"And Lawrence can calm him down, if necessary." Maggie Jane was so used to being belittled that it hardly hurt anymore.

"Our dear brother probably can't wait to ship us off to relatives in Atlanta or Savannah," Aurora Lee guessed shrewdly. "And now that we have a wardrobe that won't disgrace the family name, I won't mind it at all."

"Won't you miss the island? And Wildacre?"

"Not if it means finding a husband and having a home of my own." Aurora Lee had resolutely kept her bitterness in check when it seemed there was no alternative to barren spinsterhood, but now she didn't trouble to hide it. "I'm sick to death of taking orders."

"You'll have to obey a husband," Maggie Jane said, climbing down from their pony cart.

"A husband can be manipulated," Aurora Lee replied smugly. "Hush now, here comes Miss Yankee Prudence."

She pasted a wide smile on her face that wasn't entirely insincere.

Abigail Dickson elected to stay in her room. "I don't think I can face seeing anyone else handling my daughter's clothes," she told Prudence. "I know I should be the one supervising the packing, but I simply can't."

"I understand," Prudence said, holding Abigail's cold hands. Despite the warmth of the day, Eleanor's mother had wrapped herself in a cashmere shawl. "I'll see that everything is done properly."

"And with respect," Abigail directed.

"Of course. With your permission, I'll tell Aurora Lee and Maggie Jane that the family would like each of them to choose something of Eleanor's that they can keep to cherish her memory."

Abigail's lips tightened. "I removed her jewelry case from her room yesterday, and I'm taking it back to New York with me. Bracelets, earrings, necklaces. Philip doesn't have to know."

"What will you do with them?" Prudence asked.

"I'll wear them, even if it's only when I'm alone." She touched one finger to the earrings half hidden beneath loops of her hair. "These are Eleanor's. We gave them to her for her sixteenth birthday."

"I remember," Prudence said. "I asked my father for a pair of cameos just like hers."

"Did he get them for you?"

"He always gave me anything I wanted." Prudence smiled.

"Losing someone you love is worse than dying yourself," Abigail said.

Prudence bent to kiss her friend's mother on the cheek.

"It's so difficult to choose," Maggie Jane simpered, gesturing at the dresses arranged in neat piles on Eleanor's bed.

"Perhaps a hat?" Prudence suggested. "Or a pair of gloves?"

Maggie Jane looked disappointed.

"You can always choose later," Aurora Lee said. "When we do a second sorting. We can't send everything off willy-nilly to the Society for the Succor of Confederate Widows and Orphans," she explained to Prudence.

Prudence interpreted that to mean Aurora Lee and her sister would be picking and choosing the best items for themselves. Or keeping all of them, if they thought they could get away with it.

She'd mulled over what she suspected the Bennett girls of planning and decided not to interfere. Eleanor had been one of the most generous people Prudence had known, always eager to share whatever she had, sincerely interested in the welfare of the women and children served by the charities for which she volunteered. Prudence knew exactly how Eleanor would deal with the situation. She'd throw back her head and laugh at the absurdity of it, then consider the need that drove the Bennett sisters. "If it makes even one day of their lonely lives easier to bear, let them have it all," she'd say. She wouldn't begrudge a single handkerchief. And she'd forget about what she'd given as soon as it left her hands. Eleanor hadn't believed in charity with strings.

"Did I tell you that I met someone from Wildacre at the chapel the other day?" Prudence asked casually, not taking her eyes from the scarf she was folding. "Actually it was the same young woman I saw talking to your gardener. She told me her name was Minda."

Aurora Lee and Maggie Jane froze in place.

As she deposited the neatly folded scarf in one of the half-packed trunks, Prudence caught a glimpse of the guarded look that flashed between the sisters. She sensed that the two maids who were bringing garments out from Eleanor's dressing room also stopped what they were doing. It was as though a collective breath was being held.

"She reminds me of someone, but I can't think who it is," Prudence continued. She frowned as though considering the puzzle, then shook her head. "She certainly does a good job with Teddy's roses."

"Teddy's roses?" echoed Maggie Jane.

"Surely you know that he sends fresh white roses every day to be placed around Eleanor's coffin?" Prudence sighed as though it were the most romantic thing she had ever experienced. "Wait. I just remembered." She looked Aurora Lee and Maggie Jane full in the face, her eyes pinned to theirs. The maids had backed into the dressing room, out of sight. "When I first saw Minda in the chapel I thought I was seeing a younger Eleanor's ghost. Isn't that the strangest thing you ever heard?"

"Minda doesn't look a bit like Eleanor," Aurora Lee said stiffly. "I don't see how you could have mistaken her for the woman Teddy was going to marry." Her color was high and her voice shrill.

"She's not white, Prudence," Maggie Jane explained in a whisper, glancing at the empty dressing room doorway.

"She looks white."

"No, she doesn't," Aurora Lee snapped. "You need to stay out of things you don't understand."

"What things don't I understand?" Prudence prompted.

Aurora Lee glared at her sister before the helpful Maggie Jane could volunteer more information. "I think we need to pay attention to what we're doing." She flounced toward the dressing room, emerging with her hands full of lavender-scented shirtwaists.

The two maids skittered out behind her and began to carry the clothing on the bed to the waiting trunks. They worked in silence, exchanging nervous glances, but not once meeting Prudence's eyes.

"Geoffrey told me you wouldn't want to talk about it."

"You'd do well to listen to him," Aurora Lee said.

"Not talking about something makes the situation worse," Prudence insisted.

"There is no situation." Aurora Lee's patience was at the breaking point.

"Did Eleanor ask you about her? About Minda? Or any of the others?"

"I don't know what you're talking about, Prudence. And neither do you." Aurora Lee snapped shut the lid of one of the trunks. "The subject is closed. I don't want to hear another word about what you think you know. Because you don't."

Maggie Jane stood with nail-bitten fingers pressed against

trembling lips, tears about to spill down her cheeks. "Please don't fight," she murmured.

Despite herself, Prudence couldn't help but feel sorry for the miserable Maggie Jane. She handed her one of Eleanor's monogrammed handkerchiefs.

"Miss?" Lilah held out a wrinkled piece of paper. "This fell out on the floor when I was wrappin' up Miss Eleanor's shoes."

"What does it say?" Prudence asked.

The maid shook her head. "Cain't read, miss."

Chiding herself for not stopping to think before she asked the question, Prudence smoothed out the paper and glanced at what was written there.

"What is it?" Aurora Lee demanded.

Maggie Jane wiped her eyes and dabbed delicately at her nose.

"I'm not sure," Prudence said. She felt a hollow, sinking feeling in the pit of her stomach. She started to read the message aloud, then stopped abruptly. "It's nothing." She slipped the note into the cuff of her left sleeve. "We do need to move more quickly if we want to finish all of this today."

"I insist you tell me what's written on that piece of paper," Aurora Lee demanded. Her sharp eyes focused intently on Prudence's wrist as if they could pierce through the sleeve of her gown.

"Please, Prudence," Maggie Jane begged. "If it has anything to do with what made Eleanor leave the house that night, we deserve to know." Her fingers came up to her mouth again. "Even if it's not what we want it to be," she whispered.

Aurora Lee's threatening tone of voice hadn't moved her, but Maggie Jane's plaintive pleading did. Prudence laid the note facedown on the table that stood near the French doors to the veranda. She smoothed out the wrinkles as best she could, Aurora Lee and Maggie Jane peering over her shoulders. When she could delay no longer, she turned it over.

"'*Meet me in the live oaks,*'" Aurora Jane read aloud. "'*You won't be sorry.*' There's no signature."

"That's Teddy's handwriting," Maggie Jane blurted out.

"No, it's not."

"It is, sister. I'd know it anywhere."

Aurora Lee's palm cracked against Maggie Jane's cheek. A large red welt stained the younger girl's skin. She shrank back and seemed to curl into herself like a whipped dog.

Prudence stared at the two sisters. Aurora Lee neither apologized nor made any move to comfort the weeping Maggie Jane.

"I don't know what's got into you, saying something like that," Aurora Lee snapped. "You know good and well that's not Teddy's handwriting."

"That's easy enough to prove or disprove," Prudence said, handing Maggie Jane another one of Eleanor's handkerchiefs. "I'm sure we'll find letters from Teddy in Eleanor's correspondence."

When she moved toward the leather portfolio Eleanor had carried with her from New York, Aurora Lee snatched up the note, ripped it into tiny pieces before Prudence could stop her, and threw the fragments from the balcony into the Atlantic wind.

Maggie Jane darted out as if to snatch the whirling bits of paper from the air, but it was too late. Nothing remained of the note someone had written to lure Eleanor into the live oaks.

"We'll see to the rest of the packing, and my sister and I will make sure that Eleanor's things go where they will do the most good," Aurora Lee spat. "But as soon as we're finished with the trunks, we're leaving. I no longer feel welcome in this house."

Dumbfounded, Prudence watched as the two Bennett sisters grabbed up armfuls of Eleanor's clothing and accessories, dumping them unceremoniously into whichever trunk was closest. The maids, prodded relentlessly by Aurora Lee, worked even more quickly. In less than an hour the hastily packed trunks had been carried down to the wagon that would follow them back to Wildacre. Eleanor's bedroom was forlorn and empty, the coverlet on her bed rumpled, rugs askew, a pair of overlooked shoes kicked beneath a chair.

Grabbing Maggie Jane's hand, Aurora Lee dragged her down the mansion's central staircase to where their pony cart waited outside the front door.

"Maggie Jane said it was Teddy's handwriting," Prudence told Geoffrey and Philip Dickson. She had watched Aurora Jane furiously whip the pony cart along the oyster shell drive and out Seapoint's massive front gates, then knocked on the library door where Eleanor's father had waited out the packing of the trousseau. Not surprisingly, Geoffrey had chosen to join him there. Both men held half-drunk glasses of whiskey.

"I don't suppose there's any point asking if she's sure?" Philip asked.

"She insisted that Teddy wrote the note," Prudence explained. "Aurora Lee was so angry she slapped her across the face. You could see the mark of her hand on her sister's skin."

"Did that make Maggie Jane change her mind?" In Geoffrey's ex-Pinkerton world, unreliable witnesses were to be expected.

"She didn't have time to say anything else. Aurora Lee ripped up the note and tossed the pieces off the balcony before I realized what was happening."

"What's your feeling about it, Prudence?" Geoffrey had learned to value and trust his partner's instincts.

She showed him a letter from Teddy that she'd retrieved from the portfolio where Eleanor had kept recent correspondence. "The handwriting looks similar if not the same. But I only had a few moments to look at the note, and I was more interested in what it said than in the shape of the letters."

"That's good enough for me," Philip said. "I'll leave you two to argue it out, but my mind's made up. I don't need to hear any more. I said from the beginning that Teddy had a hand in what happened to Eleanor. I don't know what made her walk deeper into the live oaks when he left her, and I'll never forgive him for not making sure she was safely back inside the house before he went on his way. I doubt you'll find out, Geoffrey, no matter how good an investigator you are. He may not be guilty of murder, but he's damned sure to blame for carelessness." He drank off the rest of his whiskey with the grim look of a juror who's decided on a defendant's guilt and won't be persuaded otherwise. "I'm going upstairs to see to my wife. Thank you for helping persuade her to stay in her room, Prudence. It must have been difficult enough for her to know what was going on without being forced to participate."

He closed the library door softly behind him.

They waited until they heard his footsteps recede into the carpeted hall of the upper floor.

"I think we can presume that Eleanor believed the note came from someone she could trust," Geoffrey began. His habit was to examine and then pick apart both sides of whatever evidence was presented to prove or disprove a client's case. Prudence often called him his own best devil's advocate. "Teddy would fit that description, though he's not the only one."

"Who else?" Prudence had followed this style of reasoning with him many times.

"Almost anyone with whom she'd had a conversation since her father started bringing the family to the island. You told me that Eleanor didn't make or see enemies."

"But she *was* afraid, Geoffrey. She thought eyes were watching her from the live oaks."

"I remember. But think about it for a moment. How afraid could she have been if she left the house late at night entirely on her own? And presumably on the strength of an unsigned note. Repeat it to me again."

"As best I can recall, it was brief and to the point," Prudence said, closing her eyes as she concentrated. " 'Meet me in the live oaks. You won't be sorry.' "

"Someone is promising to give her something she wants," Geoffrey said.

"Information?" questioned Prudence, her mind immediately summoning up Minda's face. Maggie Jane had whispered that she wasn't white. Aurora Lee had vehemently refused to acknowledge that the girl even *looked* white.

"It doesn't sound like a lover's plea to join him in the moonlight," Geoffrey agreed. "Too brusque and businesslike. But that doesn't automatically rule out Teddy. It just makes him a little less likely candidate."

After an hour's discussion, they were no closer to determining who had written the note that had lured Eleanor to her death.

If it wasn't Teddy, Prudence wondered what hive of hornets her friend could have stirred up.

Geoffrey kept his opinion to himself.

"It wasn't Teddy's handwriting, was it?" Maggie Jane asked. She'd cried most of the way from Seapoint to Wildacre. "I was wrong, wasn't I?" She glanced at Aurora Lee's hard face and somehow found the courage to continue. "The boys always shared the same tutor growing up. They were made to practice a gentleman's penmanship until every letter was perfectly formed. I remember teasing them about it."

"Father warned them that if they tried to fool the tutor into thinking Teddy's essays were written by Lawrence, he'd have both their hides."

"So it wasn't Teddy who wrote that note to Eleanor." Maggie Jane's eyes ached, she could hardly breathe, and her head throbbed.

"That's just it, you little fool. It *might* have been Teddy. But it could just as easily have been Lawrence. The only way we'll know is if we ask them."

"I don't want to do that," Maggie Jane said.

"Do you want to live the rest of your life not knowing?"

"There are a lot of things I don't know. They don't hurt me unless I think too hard about them. The best thing to do is not ask questions." Maggie Jane had chewed on her fingers until the skin around the cuticles bled.

"You wouldn't mind asking Teddy," Aurora Lee said as the white brick façade of Wildacre appeared through the green of its towering oaks. "It's Lawrence you're afraid of."

"Aren't you? Aren't you afraid of him, too?"

Aurora Lee never admitted to being frightened of anything. But after a moment, she nodded her head.

She knew her brother. And his temper.

CHAPTER 24

Teddy asked Geoffrey to join the Bennett men and the sheriff's posse on their sweep of the island. Instead of objecting, Lawrence instructed his brother to add his voice to the invitation. Teddy obligingly passed along the information.

"I distrust what Elijah Bennett says is the reason for the sweep," Geoffrey told Prudence. "He says it's to clear out the nests of fugitives hiding in the swamp and the live oaks. But there's no proof anyone is actually there. A posse like this can degenerate very quickly into a dangerous mob, especially if most of its members are Ku Kluxers gone underground. If that's who the sheriff has recruited, there won't be any moderate voices in the group."

"What was Teddy's rationale for wanting you to come along?"

"He didn't say it in so many words, because he doesn't want to appear disloyal to his father and brother. But he implied that he didn't want to be the only voice of reason if the posse doesn't find what it's looking for and decides to take it out on the people who've been living on the island all their lives."

"Suppose they do find the fugitives they say they're looking for?" Prudence asked. "What will they do to them?"

"That may be what Teddy is most worried about. With the sheriff along, fugitives should be arrested and transported back to the mainland, theoretically to the jail or prison they escaped from."

"But—" Prudence looked confused.

"But this sheriff is partial to summary justice," Geoffrey said. "Lynching."

"Queen Lula was—" Prudence couldn't bring herself to use the word *lynched*.

"Apparently the sheriff maintains that the fugitives he'll be looking for killed both Aunt Jessa and Queen Lula in the course of raiding their cabins for food and whatever they could sell. Then they burned the cross in Aunt Jessa's yard and strung up Queen Lula to give the impression that white men were responsible because the law doesn't usually bother investigating that kind of murder."

"Does he have a theory about who shot Jonah? And why?"

"He says Jonah was known to help harbor fugitives, but that this time he was going to turn them in because of what had been done to Aunt Jessa. So they followed and shot him when he set out to row across the sound."

"What proof does he have for this?"

"He doesn't need any."

"I think Teddy's right, Geoffrey. You do need to be a part of this posse." Prudence laid a land gently on his sleeve. "But please be careful."

They set off as soon as the sheriff and the twenty men he'd brought with him had unloaded from the flat-bottomed barges that ferried them and their horses from the mainland. All were armed with rifles scabbarded on their saddles and pistols holstered on their hips. Perhaps a quarter of them were grizzled veterans of the war, toughened survivors of hand-to-hand combat, near-starvation, forced marches in brutal heat, and the misery of humiliating defeat. Some of them were barely in their twenties at the surrender, but the experience had shaped every day of their lives thereafter.

Alongside them rode equally grim-faced younger men, whose fathers and uncles had never come back. Just as scarred as the veterans, they cherished grudges born in the aftermath of war and advocated quick, brutal justice. Coils of rope hung from their saddles.

"We'll push from this side of the live oaks," Elijah Bennett directed. It was his island, his land. Sheriff Budridge would command the men, but it was Elijah who knew every feature of the dangerous terrain through which they would be moving. "Drive them toward the swamp. Into it if they're stupid enough to chance quicksand, moccasins, and gators. If they get through, which I doubt they will, there's only ocean on the other side. Either way, we'll have them."

"Some of our people may be caught up," Teddy said. "We'll identify them for you."

"Won't matter whose people they are if they've been givin' 'em food and helping 'em hide out," a voice called.

There were plenty of men on the mainland whose families had never owned a slave. Planters considered sharecroppers and anyone but the successful merchant and professional classes poor white trash. Indigent they might be, but their skin color guaranteed them immunity from any viciousness they chose to visit on people of color. Nothing made them madder than a rich white man coddling his negroes.

"We know all our people. We'll tell you who to let go," Teddy repeated.

This time there were smirks and shoulder shrugs, but no outright defiance.

Geoffrey guided his horse toward Teddy's. He wouldn't be obvious about it, but he'd have Teddy's back.

The posse fanned out into a straight line, the same maneuver that had been used in the search for Eleanor. Over the years the trees along the fringes of the forest had thinned out, buffeted by storms and salty winds, chopped down for firewood, cleared for roads. Where once there had been rice and sea island cotton fields, now there were open expanses of sawgrass, seedling pines, and straggling young oaks twisted into fantastic shapes.

Not until the hunters reached the section of the forest that had never been cleared because the land was too poor to be worth the trouble did they come upon individuals and small family groups trying to eke out a living running fishing nets and crab traps, planting gardens of okra, squash, Indian corn, and runner beans. Children in ragged shirts huddled in doorways or clung to their mommas' skirts, wide-eyed and frightened. Women hid their daughters and hoped they were dark and ugly enough to escape notice. Very few men showed themselves. Most were out on the water. The few who weren't faded into the forest to wait until the posse had passed. The very old remembered slavery days, dropped their eyes, and said nothing.

Every time the sheriff and his men rode into a clearing, Teddy dismounted. He made a point of walking up to the cabin, where he propped one foot on the porch and started talking. He asked how things were going, commented on the weather, complimented the gardens, commiserated at meager catches. These were his people, his actions said, and don't let anybody forget it. And because Geoffrey nudged his horse up to the front of the posse and loosened his rifle in its scabbard, men who might have been ripe for trouble-making in the miserably bug-ridden heat and humidity of the island's interior did nothing. Sat their mounts, wreathed their faces in cigar smoke to foil the mosquitoes, and hoped the sheriff would eventually lead them to where they could have some fun.

"They're taking cover in the swamp," Lawrence said. "Sneaking out at night to do their mischief, and crawling back before sunup." It was the only explanation that fit the case he and Elijah had built to bring Sheriff Calvin Budridge across the water. There was bound to be somebody laying low out there. Hiding from his wife or an angry husband or from the man he'd cheated at cards or cracked over the head with a whiskey bottle. Always someone. *Innocent scapegoat* wasn't in Lawrence's vocabulary. Everybody was guilty of something if you looked at him long and hard enough. Eleanor's death had to be an accident because the possibility of interference was something no one would tolerate. A white woman's reputation had to be protected.

A lynching would make everybody feel better.

Deep in the swamp they found an abandoned lean-to and signs of recent habitation.

"Looks like one man on his own," Sheriff Budridge said, sweeping aside gnawed squirrel bones and the ashes of a small firepit. A ragged blanket lay beneath the sheet of tin that had been clumsily fastened to a tree trunk, shelter from the rain but not much else. "Looks to me like he took off in a hurry."

"Probably swam the sound back to the mainland," Elijah contributed.

"None of our people said anything about a missing boat," Teddy confirmed.

"Could be your man," the sheriff continued. "Like you said, starving and desperate enough to kill those women and ransack their cabins, but crafty enough to try to make it look like they were guilty of something that caught up with them. He counted on you all thinking some rough justice had been dispensed. Figgered on it buying him some time, and he was right. He's gone now."

The horses danced as a burst of wind and rain hammered on the tin lean-to, then swirled away.

Clouds had been building all day, the air growing heavier and harder to breathe. Sometimes it had been so still you could hear the man next to you panting in the heat. Storms were a fact of life along the Georgia coast. After they passed, everything sparkled for a day or so. But they could turn dangerous. Only a foolish man ignored the warning signs.

"We got us a blow coming," Budridge said, pulling his hat down tighter on his head. "I think we'll head back, Mr. Bennett. We're gonna need to get across the water before the first squall line hits."

They made good time out of the swamp and back toward the live oaks and the dock where the barges waited. A sense of satisfaction spurred them along; they weren't looking for anyone anymore, and it was just possible whoever he was had drowned himself trying to swim the sound. After a while that version of events would take on the ring of truth.

The clouds massed darker and more menacing above them as they rode, slowing to pick their way more carefully where the live oaks met the edge of the swamp. There were quicksand bogs to trap the unwary and indications that the forest creatures were restless and on the move to safety in the interior's deep thickets.

Deer flashed by along narrow tracks, alert to the presence of horses and humans, but unafraid for once. The men heard the growl of a panther above them, but no one glanced into the tree limbs from which it would pounce if challenged. A reek like a kitchen waste pit told them a pack of wild hogs was passing through the brush, out of sight but announced by the rank stench and the light patter of sharp hooves. Panthers usually avoided any but easy prey, but wild pigs were fearless and driven by a kind of unpredictable madness akin to lust. The horses rolled their huge eyes, poised to stomp furiously at whatever rushed out of the tangled undergrowth.

With the stench of wild hog still in the air, Geoffrey found himself cut off from the rest of the posse. One moment they were strung out along the track, each rider close behind the man in front of him for safety, the next he was alone. The silence behind him was the only warning he had. A quick glance showed him empty trail. He glimpsed a hint of ghostlike riders through the trees. No birds sang or squawked, no leaves rustled at the passage of deer or the scamper of squirrels. No snakes sought their burrows, no panthers coughed.

When the boar burst into sight, it was with the rush of a freight train barreling too fast along a familiar track. Geoffrey's horse whinnied and screamed in fright, rearing repeatedly on its hind legs, lashing out with front hooves. Caught half-turned in his saddle, looking behind him for the men who had been so close just a few minutes before, Geoffrey barely managed to grab his rifle from its scabbard and pull his boots from the stirrups before he was pitched from the saddle. The fall was inevitable. His only hope of surviving was to manage it as best he could.

He rolled as he landed, a thick layer of mulch cushioning the impact and keeping him from losing consciousness. Before he slid to a stop, his trigger finger was in place, and as the boar's foul odor bore down on him, he fired. Blindly. Guided only by the memory of where the hog had been and his instinctive sense of the direction from which it was charging.

He fired once, then again, impervious to the spatter of blood and brains that rained down on him, seeing only the yellow ivory of curved tusks and the glow of enraged red eyes. Two hundred pounds of murderous ferocity caught him a glancing blow as the animal fell, its coarse, bristled hide scraping against him, deadly sharp hooves scrabbling wildly for a purchase they would never find.

He lay still, listening, while the forest came back to life around him. The stink of the dead boar lodged in his nostrils and coated the inside of his mouth. When the soft patter of tiny hooves on decaying leaves moved off into the distance, he knew the small herd had left its erstwhile leader behind. Another, younger male would take its place.

Teddy flung himself from his horse, letting the reins trail, pulling out his pistol as he cautiously approached the boar's carcass, falling to his knees beside Geoffrey when the beast did not move.

"I'm all right," Geoffrey said, pushing himself up. "Winded, but all right." He took his finger off the rifle's trigger and slipped the safety back on. His nerves screamed at him to be ready for the next attack, but his brain told him it was too late. Whoever had separated him from the rest of the posse had had only one chance at killing him. And he'd missed it. There were too many potential witnesses churning up the forest floor to take the risk again. Geoffrey was a white man from an old plantation family. If he went down, somebody would want to know why.

"I don't remember when I've seen a boar this big," Teddy said admiringly. "You got him right between the eyes. Twice. Good thing, too. They don't stop easily." He reached out to help Geoffrey to his feet.

Lawrence had already gone after Geoffrey's fear-maddened horse. Without a rider to guide him, the animal would run until he sensed he was out of danger.

Elijah Bennett sat his horse a little apart from the others, hands crossed over the pommel of his saddle, leaning forward the better to assess the boar Geoffrey had killed. One of the younger men had taken out a long knife and was cutting off the animal's tusks and ears. He stuffed them into a leather draw-string bag and held it out to Geoffrey.

"The rest of the carcass is too tough to butcher," Elijah said reluctantly. "And this storm seems to be picking up speed. We'd best be on our way as soon as Lawrence brings back that horse of yours, Mr. Hunter."

"There's no point holding everyone up," Geoffrey said. "Sheriff Budridge and his men have to get back to the mainland before the sound gets too rough. You need to lead them out, Mr. Bennett. We don't want anybody getting lost."

"My horse will carry two if we don't push him," Teddy volunteered. "And I can walk for a while. We're bound to run into Lawrence on the way."

"We'll get going then." Sheriff Budridge waved his men on, waiting until the last of them had passed before touching one finger to his hat. "Much obliged."

At Teddy's insistence, Geoffrey heaved himself stiffly into the saddle.

"You're sure nothing's broken?" Teddy asked. He stood beside the horse, one hand on the animal's bridle to gentle him.

"I'll be sore tomorrow, but I've been hurt a lot worse."

"What made you go off like that on your own?" Teddy asked, running a reassuring hand along the horse's neck.

"I didn't," Geoffrey answered. "Didn't go off on my own. First time I knew what was going on was when I looked behind me and could barely see you all through the trees. Then the boar came crashing out at me, my horse reared and bucked, and I felt myself flying through the air."

"I thought maybe you saw one of our people in the woods and tried to warn him off before the posse could spot him."

Geoffrey shook his head. "I didn't ride on ahead that far by myself, Teddy. The rest of you all hung back. Who was setting the pace for the posse?"

"Father was riding with Sheriff Budridge and I was at the tail end to catch up any stragglers. The last time I looked, Lawrence had the lead, with you right behind him."

"The trail was well marked so I kept on going when he turned his horse around and rode back past me. I thought he wanted to say something to your father or the sheriff," Geoffrey said. "I was watching the clouds and feeling the air, trying to figure out how soon this storm was gonna hit. I smelled that old boar before he charged me, but it was a second too late. Those are the kind of mistakes raw recruits make, Teddy. And I almost paid with my life."

"Lawrence should have called for you to wait when he saw how far ahead you'd gotten," Teddy said. "I'm sorry for that."

"Maybe he thought it was time I learned a lesson."

"All of this has hit him harder than I would have thought possible. Wildacre is his whole life."

Meaning, Geoffrey thought, *that without the influx of Dickson money, what is left of the once-grand Wildacre plantation is in greater danger of being lost than anyone else knows.*

Fear made people do strange things. Take chances that made no sense. Imagine threats where none existed. Suspect mortal enemies lurking behind every tree.

By every measure, today's clearing out of the swamp and the live oaks had been a bust. The only thing they'd found had been a piece of tin fastened to a tree, a ragged blanket, and the remains of a camp that looked as if it had been abandoned weeks or months ago.

Disappointed and in the absence of a real culprit, Lawrence might have decided to liven up the posse's homeward trek. Had he, too, smelled the attack odor of the boar? If he had, he could have made sure, on the spur of the moment, that when it burst from cover, Geoffrey would be alone. Its sole and therefore very vulnerable target. Was he so warped that he could find death or serious injury amusing?

Geoffrey wondered how the two of them, Lawrence and Teddy, could possibly be brothers.

CHAPTER 25

❦

Lawrence never returned with Geoffrey's spooked horse.

Hours later, when Teddy and Geoffrey finally emerged from the live oak forest, the first heavy squall lines were moving swiftly over the Atlantic. Teddy's mount had gone lame and the wind made it hard to walk; they hunched their shoulders, ducked their heads, and tried to ignore the sting of swirling sand and gusts of salty rain.

"You'll never make it back to Wildacre," Geoffrey shouted.

Teddy didn't argue. He'd been through too many Atlantic storms to take chances. There might be uncomfortable moments when he faced Philip Dickson, but he'd get through them as best he could.

The brick bulk of Seapoint loomed substantial and solid in its acres of manicured grounds. Gas lights gleamed reassuringly through the darkening afternoon, beckoning them to safety. As they approached the side drive that led to the stables, a boy raced out to lead away Teddy's limping horse.

Tall specimen trees swayed and tossed their canopies, oleander leaves whirled along the ground, and the white roses on the porch of the stone chapel lay scattered among overturned baskets and broken vases. In the distance, huge, frothy ocean waves pounded the shore, resculpting the beach.

Their jackets and pants were drenched and their hair plastered to their skulls when they stumbled into Seapoint's elegantly tiled entrance hall. The stillness was like suddenly going deaf.

"We're not hurt," Geoffrey reassured Abigail and Prudence, who rushed from the library as the front door slammed open. He struggled to close it against the force of the wind. "Wet and dirty, but otherwise all right."

Stiffly polite and correct, Philip did not turn Teddy away. But neither did he pretend that his presence was welcome. Abigail had argued convincingly that the young man's grief was profound and genuine, refusing to believe he could have done anything to endanger her daughter. If Philip couldn't bring himself to treat Teddy with the warmth of family, she told him, he must at least extend him the formal courtesies due a guest. For his wife's sake, Philip had agreed.

Thirty minutes after their arrival, their wet clothes exchanged for dry, Teddy and Geoffrey met in the upstairs hall. The vista from the second floor windows was both breathtaking and sinister. In just half an hour the sky had darkened to an ominous dark gray, the wind roared against the glass panes, and the booming of the sea was like thunder.

They walked down the curved staircase together, while behind them servants battened down the last row of outside shutters. As each window was barred against the storm, the noise grew a little more muffled. The house had been designed and built to withstand coastal hurricanes. Geoffrey wondered how the inhabitants of the live oaks would fare.

Despite the day's heat and humidity, a fire had been laid in the library and crackled brightly. Candles supplemented the gas lamps so that a comforting light bathed the room against the dark menace of the storm. Prudence stood beside the shuttered windows, tensely alert to what was happening outside. Abigail clasped both their hands in hers. She had fiercely reminded her husband of his promise to be civil to Teddy, and she expected him to keep it.

Philip poured whiskey. "I don't suppose you found anyone hiding out?"

"There were signs that someone had been camping in the swamp. But he was long gone," Teddy explained.

"I hope your father and brother are satisfied that they've made the island safe from marauders again." There was no mistaking the sarcasm of Philip's remark.

Torn between family loyalty and his private opinion that there had never been any dangerous fugitives to begin with, Teddy said nothing. More than anything, he wanted to be beside Eleanor's coffin in the gothic chapel at the foot of the garden. Too late. He hadn't thought of it in time.

"I suppose the yacht is moored in one of the inlets on the mainland," Geoffrey said into the silence.

"The captain sent a note over on the same barge that brought Sheriff Budridge and his posse," Philip answered. "He'll stay there until the storm passes and the waters calm down. He thinks we can track its progress up the coast via telegraph reports. I'm anxious to be off, but I'm deferring to his judgment."

"I don't mind spending a few extra days here," Abigail said. She sipped from a glass of Portuguese sherry. Her eyes, like Teddy's, were drawn in the direction of the chapel where Eleanor lay.

Everyone knew that as soon as they reached New York, Philip Dickson would arrange to have his daughter's coffin placed in the family mausoleum. Until then Abigail could sit by Eleanor's side as often and as long as she pleased, comforting herself with the illusion that her only child could still hear the endearments she whispered. Keeping vigil was not quite saying good-bye.

She fingered her earrings and the narrow gold bracelet encircling one slender wrist. "Teddy, won't you come sit here beside me?" The loveseat on which she'd ensconced herself had just enough room for two people. Conversation could be low-voiced and intimate.

Whiskey glass in hand, Teddy settled himself next to the woman who would have been his mother-in-law.

Watching them, Prudence thought how right it was for Abigail to have sought Teddy's company. They were perhaps the two people on the island who most wanted to talk about Eleanor. Before she turned away, Prudence heard Abigail's soft voice. "Do you remember—?" she was saying. Her eyes lit up with a happy memory.

Teddy nodded and leaned in to share it with her.

Philip had pulled out a map of the Atlantic coast and spread it across his desktop. One finger traced the route the yacht would take once the weather broke and it became safe to put to sea again. They'd sailed fifty miles out from land on the way down to avoid the dangerous waters off North Carolina. He assumed the captain would take the same precautions on the way home.

As soon as the storm passed he'd get a message to the mainland telegraph office. It would be hard on Abigail, but for the best if Eleanor's coffin could be taken straight from the dock to the mortuary and then to the house. Two days should be enough. A closed casket vigil at home, the service at Trinity Church, and then the entombment.

He'd find a quiet moment during the voyage to ask Prudence to see to the removal of Eleanor's clothing from the New York City house. Her room there, too, could be preserved as Abigail would wish it to be, with some few personal items remaining, but the bulk of the dresses, shoes, and hats would go to charity. More hard choices, but they needed to be made.

And there was a final conversation to have with Teddy. Business ties had to be severed, arrangements canceled, the young man's position made clear. Philip would not move against him, but neither would he continue to act as either active mentor or sponsor.

It helped a man get through the pain if he remained strong enough to ensure that everything that should be done was taken care of.

The storm made Prudence restless and filled her mind with island images. She pictured Eleanor wandering alone through the live oaks on a moonlit night and today's posse riding with malign purpose toward the swamp. Aunt Jessa's beaten body lying on the floor of her cabin, the lurch into the water when a bullet struck Jonah, the horrifying sight of Queen Lula and her black cat hanging from a tree. The classic whitewashed façade of Wildacre hiding generations of abuse. The faces of islanders whose Bennett blood would never be acknowledged.

Her head ached with the heaviness of the air and a whirling kaleidoscope of scenes endlessly repeating themselves. She yearned for cool dry breezes and a cultivated city park where she could walk without worrying about stepping on a venomous snake or being stung into near insanity by mosquitos and midges. She couldn't imagine Eleanor living year-round on Bradford Island, but perhaps that was the reason Teddy had spoken of a house in Savannah. Maybe that was the compromise that would have made everything else possible.

I wouldn't know, Prudence thought. *I've never been in love like that.* And felt no guilt in admitting that while she had been prepared and even eager to marry her late fiancé, she had not been in love with him. Not in the way that Eleanor had fallen head over heels for Teddy and he for her. Which was better? To remain emotionally independent enough to take charge of one's own destiny? Or to lose oneself in a delirium of happiness and delight that might be short-lived and never come again?

Geoffrey caught her eye, then glanced toward the library door, a clear signal that he, too, was restless. Abigail, unshed tears pooled in her eyes, had left the loveseat to look over her husband's shoulder as he calculated the yacht's projected route back to New York. Teddy stood as far away from the desk as he could get while remaining in the same room. When the Dicksons sailed, they would be taking Eleanor's mortal remains with them. All he would have left would be his memories.

Prudence touched Teddy's sleeve, then slipped her arm through his, guiding him toward the door where Geoffrey had one hand on the knob. As they stepped out into the foyer and closed the library door behind them, the Dicksons didn't seem to notice their departure.

With no fire burning, the foyer felt damp and chilly, its two-story height soaring into darkness above their heads. Geoffrey lit two of the gas lamps lined up on the table where outgoing mail was stacked and handed one to Teddy, leaving Prudence's hands free to hold on to the banister and gather her skirts as they climbed to the second floor. One of the shutters had been blown off the Atlantic-facing windows.

Outside, everything was pitch black. If there was a moon, it was well hidden behind mountains of dark clouds. In the brief moment that the landscape was lit up by a flash of lightning, Prudence's eyes were drawn to the chapel where a marriage was to have been celebrated.

How strange it was to be on this island she had never heard of until her friend decided to wed the eldest son of the family who had once owned it. Waiting out a ferocious storm for the second time in her life, Prudence remembered what it felt like to be trapped by circumstances utterly beyond her control. What if she had been born into a situation where her whole life was a trap? Where there was never any hope of escaping the cage that imprisoned her?

Staring at the rain-lashed darkness beyond the window pane, she remembered the slave Queen Lula had said was the only one ever to disappear from Wildacre and never be found. She wondered if the pale girl had taken her chances on a night like this one. When pursuit would be unthinkable until the storm blew itself out. By which time there might not be a scent trail for the dogs to follow. What had Queen Lula called her? *Sally?* No. The name started with an *S*, but it was an unusual one. Prudence didn't think she had ever heard it before.

"Geoffrey, do you remember the name of the runaway Queen Lula told us about?" she asked as the three of them settled into the upstairs parlor's comfortable overstuffed chairs.

"Selena," he said promptly. "She claimed the girl was the only slave from Wildacre who was never caught and brought back. What made you think of her?"

"If I were desperate and planning a run for freedom, I'd take a storm like this as a sign. Nobody would be likely to come after me for hours, perhaps days. And maybe by then I would have reached a place of safety. A station of the Underground Railroad or perhaps a kind farmer willing to give me a ride on his wagon. Queen Lula said she was light enough to pass for white." Again Prudence stared at the dark window, imagining a young woman's struggle through wind and rain, a small bag with food and everything she owned on her back. "I wonder what she looked like."

"Stories were told about her," Teddy said unexpectedly. "We weren't supposed to know about them, but we did. I was no more than four years old at the time, but every runaway was talked about in the quarters for years afterward, usually because the punishment for trying to escape was so brutal. My grandfather believed in public whippings with all of us gathered around to witness what was done. Anybody who cried out in sympathy or refused to watch would feel the sting of the lash."

"How terrible."

"What can you tell us about her? About Selena," Geoffrey asked.

Prudence glanced at him curiously. She hadn't expected him to pursue the topic. They had agreed to discuss something else with Teddy when the three of them were alone. That was one of the reasons for leaving the library together.

"Almost nothing," Teddy answered. "Except that Aunt Jessa was the one who raised her up after her own mother died. I imagine they were all shocked when she made a run for it. Big House slaves never ran; they were devoted to the family."

Prudence stared at him. Could he really believe what he was saying? That someone who couldn't even lay claim to her own life would feel anything but hatred for the people who had taken it from her?

"I don't expect you to understand, Prudence," Teddy said, catching the look on her face. "But that's the way it was back then. At least that's the way I remember it. What I was told." He looked at Geoffrey for confirmation. "I can't imagine why Queen Lula told you that story."

"I was asking about the light-skinned islanders," Prudence said. "I talked to Minda when she brought the white roses to the chapel. In fact, when I first saw her, I called out Eleanor's name." She paused.

"We do have ghosts on the island, you know," Teddy said, ignoring the mention of Minda. "Lawrence and I used to dare each other to go out alone into the live oaks when it grew dark. You could see blue lights dancing above the ground sometimes. In the direction of the swamp. It was gas escaping from the mud bogs, of course, but it was more spine-chilling to think they were the restless souls of the dead rather than believe our tutors' scientific explanations."

"Selena's escape would have been before the war." Geoffrey seemed intent on gathering all the details of the long-ago break for freedom.

Teddy nodded, obviously puzzled at Geoffrey's interest in a topic that planters avoided talking about in the presence of ladies. For fear of causing them distress. No Southern male of his father's era had wanted to admit that he lived his life on the knife's edge of constant vigilance against the threat of a slave uprising. But neither could he deny it. Ownership was no longer an issue after the war, but it would take generations for the fear of a bloody revolt to work its way out of everyday life. "I'd tell you to ask my father about that period of Wildacre's history," he said, "but I know what his response would be."

"He'd tell me my curiosity wasn't the act of a gentleman," Geoffrey said.

"You've heard that phrase before." Teddy smiled ruefully.

"More times than I care to remember. Sandyhill had its secrets, too." Geoffrey seemed to accept that Teddy had told him all he could about the elusive Selena. He nodded at Prudence. It was time.

"Teddy," Prudence began. "Something happened the other day when your sisters were here. Did they tell you about it?"

"Does it have to do with Eleanor's trousseau?"

"Not directly."

"Then I'm at a loss." He looked quizzically at Prudence.

"One of the maids brought me a note that had been hidden inside a shoe she was packing."

He raised an eyebrow, but said nothing, waiting for her to continue.

"The note read, '*Meet me in the live oaks. You won't be sorry.*' When Maggie Jane saw it, she said it was your handwriting."

Teddy's face went pale. "I would never have arranged a clandestine meeting at night with Eleanor. You know that, Prudence. I had too much respect for her. And we were going to be married in a few days." His features contorted in pain. How many times would he have to deny that he'd been complicit in the death of the woman he loved? "I don't understand. Where is this note?"

"Aurora Lee ripped it up. She threw the bits and pieces from the balcony."

"That sounds like her," Teddy said bitterly. "Out of sight, out of mind. My sister doesn't like truth to cloud her reality."

"Did you write it?" Geoffrey pressed.

"No. I did not," Teddy snapped.

"Then someone else did. Someone who knew your hand-writing well enough to fool Maggie Jane into believing that's what she was seeing. It was the proof we needed that Eleanor was lured out into the live oaks the night she disappeared. That she didn't go entirely on her own to walk off prewedding jit-ters," Prudence said.

"I never believed that theory," Teddy claimed. "Though per-haps I allowed myself to be talked into accepting it because the alternative was too terrible to contemplate." He drew a hand down over his face as if to wipe away suspicions that could no longer be avoided.

"Aunt Jessa is the key to all this," Geoffrey said. "I thought so from the beginning. I'm even more certain now." He began ticking off on his fingers the points he had already made to Pru-dence. "Aunt Jessa kept the island's secrets. She confided at least one of them to Queen Lula because she needed a spell to ward off some calamity she feared was coming. The spell didn't work. We know that from what Queen Lula implied. The tragedy she was trying to deflect was Eleanor's death. After that, it was a matter of cleaning up loose ends, getting rid of the two women who might reveal what the killer desperately wanted to hide. I was puzzled by Jonah's death. It didn't seem necessary. Until I realized that his bid to leave the island wouldn't be allowed because his silence could no longer be as-sured."

"And the coral snake?" Teddy asked.

"We don't think the attempt on my life was because of any serious threat I posed. It was the act of an angry, vengeful indi-vidual who harbors slights and grudges until he eventually acts on them," Prudence said. "It was the kind of malicious trick you play on someone out of pique, the uncertainty of whether the snake will strike absolving you of guilty intent."

"Someone was determined that you and Eleanor would not

marry," Geoffrey said. "No matter what lengths he had to go to in order to prevent it."

"Hence the note," Prudence said.

It was obvious from the look on his face that Teddy knew where their suspicions had led them.

"Lawrence," he breathed.

CHAPTER 26

Prudence woke to sunlight streaming in through the French doors of her bedroom and the aroma of freshly brewed coffee. Lilah, the maid who had brought up her tray, hummed as she pulled back the curtains, a huge smile on her face.

"We come through it all right, miss," she said cheerfully. "Didn't nobody get hurt and from what I hear tell, there ain't much damage neither. Leaves and branches all over the place, but that's about it."

If she'd been an Irish servant, and Catholic, Prudence thought, *Lilah would have crossed herself.*

"It be cool now, Miss Prudence, but the heat's gonna come on somethin' fierce before too long. That's always the way of things after a storm like we had last night. And you gotta watch out for the mosquitos. They get all stirred up by the wind and start bitin' like fury. Best you take a shawl if you go out."

"Is breakfast laid on downstairs?"

"Cook was just startin' in on the eggs when I got your coffee, miss," Lilah said. "Mrs. Dickson sent word she wanted a tray, so I reckon it'll be just the gentlemen in the dining room this mornin'."

"Then we'd better hurry up and get me dressed," Prudence said.

A strange kind of chemistry had bloomed last night, as though she, Teddy, and Geoffrey were bound one to the other by a common purpose. It had begun when Teddy uttered his brother's name with dawning recognition that Lawrence had never wanted his marriage to Eleanor to take place, no matter how much he pretended to welcome it. She thought they had been on the point of uncovering something vital when Teddy had abruptly excused himself and gone back downstairs to the library. When they looked for him there later, Philip told them he had retired to the guest room.

Abigail had looked bewildered. "He seemed ill."

Not ill, Prudence thought. Stunned by a misgiving that could destroy the bonds of brotherhood and devastate a family already shattered by war and its aftermath.

It was obvious Teddy hadn't had more than a few hours of sleep. If that. His face was drawn, the skin dull and as if pulled too tightly over the skull beneath. Patches of beard had escaped his razor; his hair, though neatly combed, was peculiarly lifeless. He hadn't touched the food on his plate except to poke at it with a fork that never reached his mouth.

He's a man in mortal mental agony, Prudence thought.

Geoffrey, holding her chair as she seated herself at the table, whispered into her ear. "He can't be allowed to go back to Wildacre like this. Not alone, especially if he intends to confront Lawrence."

She nodded in agreement, unfolding her napkin slowly to stall for time. She had no idea what to say to him. "Has Mr. Dickson already eaten?" she finally managed.

"He took coffee into the library," Geoffrey said. "Something about double-checking his charts."

Teddy laid his fork squarely across his untouched plate, lining his knife beside it, folding his pristine napkin. "I think I know what we have to do next," he announced.

Neither Geoffrey nor Prudence said a word. They waited.

"Geoffrey said yesterday that Aunt Jessa was the key to everything that's happened," Teddy began. "I thought about that all night. Along with other things." He took a sip of his cold coffee. "When I was six years old, my grandfather hired a tutor for us. For Lawrence and me. I had a collection of shells and arrowheads and other things I'd picked up here and there. Aunt Jessa had told me about talismans, so I carried some of them in my pockets. For luck and protection against evil spirits. When I tried to explain, the tutor said they were unchristian fetishes and that I had to get rid of them. I refused, so he beat me. With Grandfather's approval, of course. And then the tutor confiscated everything. What he didn't burn, he buried in the outhouse. I was terrified, convinced that I was defenseless. That I would fall ill and die the way I knew bad children did. Coffined and put into the ground."

Prudence poured hot coffee into a clean cup and set it within Teddy's reach.

"Aunt Jessa saved me. She had me put my few remaining treasures into one of the tin boxes that Grandfather's cigars came in, and together we took it into the live oaks. We dug a hole beneath a huge tree and buried the box there. Covered it over with leaves until you couldn't tell the ground had been disturbed. She lit a candle and said words over our hiding place. She told me it was a spell she'd concocted just for me, that I'd always be safe from harm because my spirit totems would never be found by anyone else. I believed her."

"What happened to the tutor?" Prudence asked.

"It was during the war. He left Wildacre to join the fighting."

"Did you dig up the box after he was gone?"

"It's still there," Teddy said. "Aunt Jessa made me promise that whenever I had a painful or frightening secret, I would breathe my trouble into some small object and bury it in the tin box. That way, she said, I would exercise power over the demons that were threatening me."

"I wish I'd had an Aunt Jessa," Prudence said.

"The thing is, she called it *our* secret place. Her secrets were there as well as mine. When we buried the box the first time, she put something of hers in it, too. A lock of black hair. I remember wanting to find out whose hair it was, but not having the courage to ask such an ordinary question. If Aunt Jessa had a secret that she wanted me to know, that's where she would have hidden it. Not in her cabin, Geoffrey. Whoever searched for it there found nothing."

"Who else knows about the tin box?" Geoffrey asked.

"No one."

"Not even Lawrence? You're sure?"

"Especially not Lawrence. We grew apart as we got older. Became something less than friends, perhaps even less than brothers."

"How many times did you go there? To where the box was buried?" Prudence asked.

"Not many. The magic of it was that just knowing I had hidden juju working for me kept other fears at bay. I was twelve or so the last time I put something in the tin box. I hadn't thought of it in years, not until last night when you said Aunt Jessa was key to what happened to Eleanor. When I realized that if she wanted to leave me a message, that's where she would put it."

"Do you think you can find the spot again?" Geoffrey asked.

"I know I can. If I close my eyes I'm able to retrace every step of the way. It's not the kind of thing you forget."

"But the trees have grown and some of them must have died." Prudence couldn't imagine having to retrace such a long-ago pilgrimage.

Teddy stood up, stepped away from the table. "Shall we go? I'd like you to come with me."

* * *

They drove a pony cart along the sound road until the roof-line of Wildacre came into view through the trees. Then Teddy veered into the live oaks and dropped a feedbag over the horse's head as he tied off the reins.

"It's not a long walk from here," he said, taking a small hand shovel from the back of the cart.

The air was so clear that everything appeared newly washed and brighter than the day before, but all around them on the ground lay evidence of the storm. Dead leaves and branches had been stripped from the trees by the wind and left to fall where they might. Even new growth had been no match for the force of the blustery rain; piles of green lay scattered among the deadfall as though a giant's hand had flung them there like a deck of cards. The sand squeaked beneath their boots, but the water that had pelted down with such force only hours before had nearly all been absorbed. Only here and there did a puddle remain, clouds of tiny insects buzzing busily across the surface.

Prudence swatted at what she could feel but not see, then draped her shawl over her head, covering exposed neck and shoulders against the onslaught of voracious no-see-ums. Geoffrey, guiding and supporting her through the debris-strewn sand, seemed impervious to the assault. Prudence felt the outline of the Colt he wore in a holster beneath his arm when she stumbled against him.

"Something else I realized last night," Teddy was saying. "Lawrence wasn't opposed to my marriage to Eleanor at first. He welcomed it." His voice turned bitter. "I should say he liked the idea of a Bennett coming into Dickson money. So did my father. It wasn't until after I brought Eleanor to Wildacre that they changed. My father first, then Lawrence. I've never understood what it was that turned them against her. Certainly not Eleanor herself. Everyone who ever met her, loved her. You remember how she was, Prudence?"

"I do. And you're right, Teddy. Eleanor didn't have an enemy in the world."

"Walk us through those early days," Geoffrey said. "I would have thought the Dicksons were familiar figures once Seapoint was built and they began coming here to spend their winters."

"It wasn't like that," Teddy said. "They weren't neighbors. They were conquerors. That's how my father saw them. You have to remember that all of the negotiations for the sale of the island were carried out by Philip Dickson's lawyers. And then an architect and a building foreman oversaw Seapoint's construction. I remember we heard that Eleanor's father came to the island from time to time while the house was going up and the grounds being laid out, but none of us met him. It was clear from the beginning that he wanted nothing to do with anyone who lived at Wildacre. It was as though we existed in a different world, and that's how the Dicksons wanted it."

"You must have hated them," Prudence said.

"In the abstract, I suppose we did," Teddy answered. "The South was still a bitter place when people like the Dicksons began coming down here to build their winter palaces on our islands. They were wealthy beyond our wildest imaginings, especially after the hardships of the war years and Reconstruction. They were the victors, we the vanquished."

"Eleanor described to me how you met," Prudence said.

Teddy's face brightened. "It was only the second winter they'd spent on the island," he said. "Eleanor told me later that she loved wandering through these woods, and she'd done a lot of it, anytime she could manage to get out of the house and away from her mother's supervision. But she never ventured as far as the swamp. She'd been warned about its dangers."

"I was told she helped her father design the stables." *Later,* Prudence thought, *I'll tell Teddy what Eleanor confided about the eyes she felt watching her from deep in the live oaks. About the fears that had begun to haunt her.* For now it was important not to interrupt his flow of memories.

"She and Philip rode every morning. I'd see them sometimes in the distance when I was crossing over to the mainland, cantering along the shoreline as though they hadn't a care in the world. They were very close, father and daughter. That may have been the only reason he finally agreed to our marriage. Eleanor convinced him that I did truly love her for herself and not the fortune she would someday inherit."

"But you didn't meet until that second winter," Geoffrey pressed.

"When her horse got away from her and I managed to grab his reins and lead him back toward Seapoint. I think we fell in love the moment we first looked into one another's eyes. We knew. It was as simple as that."

"And when did you take her to Wildacre?"

"That was odd. It was just before the Dicksons sailed back to New York, right before Christmas. I already knew that I would follow them, and that I'd stay there until we got her father's permission to marry. No matter how long it took. Eleanor was curious about my family, but she understood that their opposition might be as strong as her father's. She agreed to wait to meet them until everything was official."

"What happened to change that?"

"We got careless, the way happy people often do. There's a small, spring-fed pond on the island, not far from Wildacre. We boys used to swim there when the weather got unbearably hot. The water is crystal clear and always cool. It bubbles up from somewhere deep below the surface. From the moment I first took Eleanor there, it became our special place, where we thought we could be private and safe. And we were. Until the day Aunt Jessa found us."

Teddy paused to get his bearings. "This way," he said, pointing toward a narrow deer path through a dense growth of palmettos.

"Wait, Teddy," Prudence pleaded. "You can't leave it like that."

"Aunt Jessa promised to keep our secret. And when she left us, she folded Eleanor into her arms as though she were a long-lost Bennett child. I should have known then that if Aunt Jessa had seen us, it was more than likely someone else had also."

"Who?"

"I never managed to find that out. But whoever it was told my father. He prides himself on knowing everything that happens on the island. So when he informed me that he'd learned I'd been meeting secretly with some woman and that he had a good mind to ship her to the mainland, I told him everything. Who Eleanor was and that I planned to follow her to New York and win her father's permission to marry her. You would have thought I'd handed him a pot of gold. He insisted that I bring her to Wildacre.

"Two days later I did. They were all in the parlor, waiting for us. My father, Lawrence, Aurora Lee, and Maggie Jane. A wall of Bennetts. The girls were polite and welcoming. So was Lawrence. I thought things were going as well as could be expected, and then suddenly my father stormed out of the room. No explanation. The next day the Dicksons sailed for New York.

"That was when my father began to put pressure on me to give her up. Abandon this wild idea that I was going to save the Bennett fortunes by marrying the heiress to what had been our little kingdom for generations. I told him it wasn't like that, and that nothing he could say or do would make me change my mind. He stopped berating me, but then Lawrence joined the fray, delivering ultimatums far more threatening and bizarre than Father's.

"The atmosphere at Wildacre was poisonous, so I traveled to New York earlier than I'd planned and I didn't come back until a week before all of you arrived. I don't know what happened during the months I was gone, but on the surface, at least, my father and Lawrence seemed to have come to terms with what I was doing. You know the rest."

They'd broken through the undergrowth into a sandy clearing over which loomed one of the largest live oak trees on the island, its dense shade cooler by several degrees than the air along the path they'd been following.

"This is it," Teddy breathed.

"It's beautiful," Prudence said.

"Majestic," Geoffrey agreed.

"Aunt Jessa said a tree like this is sacred, and that when it finally dies, as everything must, all the souls who found release from pain by seeking its protection are set free forever. She said it was a good place to hide our secrets."

"And easy to find when you wanted to add to them," Geoffrey said.

"That, too," Teddy agreed. He walked to the foot of the tree and paced three steps out from the trunk, kneeled down, brushed aside a thick carpet of decaying leaves, and began to dig in the sand. "We didn't bury it very deep."

"Can you tell if someone has dug here recently?" Prudence asked.

"Aunt Jessa, you mean?" He paused for a moment. "Sand is very forgiving. It leaves no traces. Unless you mark a spot, you'll never find it again."

Geoffrey and Prudence watched as Teddy dug. When his shovel made a clunking noise, all three of them caught their breath and then laughed aloud. Prudence could feel her heart racing as the outline of the box was uncovered, and then the box itself, its lid scoured by time and sand. With one quick jerk, Teddy wrenched the box from its hiding place and sank back onto his heels.

"I'm almost afraid to open it," he said, brushing sand and leaves from his hands. "Prudence, will you do the honors?"

"No, Teddy. If Aunt Jessa left something here for you, she'd want your eyes to be the first to see it."

But she sat down as close to him as she could get, Geoffrey on his knees beside her.

Slowly Teddy pried at the metal lid until he felt it move. He laid it upside down on the ground and lifted out a small package neatly wrapped in a piece of cloth and tied with kitchen twine. "I didn't put this here," he said, handing it to Prudence while he rifled through the items that lay beneath. "But the rest of these things *are* mine." He held a perfectly oblong rock between his fingers, its surface as smooth and shiny as glass. "I found this on the beach one day. I don't know where it came from, but I used to imagine it had been spewed out of a volcano. And this," he said, fingering the peeled, hollow stem of a thumb-width piece of live oak, "is my first attempt at carving a flute." He counted out half a dozen wickedly sharp arrowheads. "You used to be able to find these all over the island," he reminisced.

"It feels like a book, Teddy," Prudence said, her fingers tapping impatiently along the sides of the calico-wrapped package.

"Open it," he directed.

Geoffrey slipped the blade of his pocket knife beneath the tightly knotted kitchen twine.

"It's someone's diary," Prudence said, paging quickly through the leather-bound journal whose pages were covered with a man's spiky handwriting. She held it out to Teddy without attempting to read any of the entries.

"*'This book belongs to Ethan Bennett and recounts his journey into manhood from the eve of his eighteenth birthday until the Lord shall please to call him Home,'*" Teddy read.

"The uncle whose portrait hangs in the Wildacre library," Prudence whispered. She pictured the handsome, earnest young man bent over his journal in the light of a single candle, his blond hair curling on the nape of his neck and hanging over his forehead. He would have eight or nine good years left before war was declared, forever altering the course of his life.

"I wonder why she put these here," Teddy said, holding out a photograph he'd slipped from between the pages of the journal. "It's a picture of Eleanor, though I can't imagine where Aunt Jessa got it."

It was indeed a posed photograph of Eleanor, but not the Eleanor Prudence had known. This Eleanor wore the crocheted collar, lace-inset sleeves, and wide-skirted, tight-bodiced dress of thirty years ago. Her hair was braided and looped around her ears, an expression of infinite sadness on the fine-featured face looking into the camera lens.

Prudence turned the photograph over. A name was written on the back in the same spiky handwriting she had seen in the journal.

Selena.

She handed it to Geoffrey, who closed his eyes as if the image and the name were too painful for him to bear. "I suspected something like this, though I couldn't tell you why. It was just a feeling."

"I don't understand." Teddy stared at the photograph of his Eleanor, turning it over to read the name written on the back.

"The answers lie in that journal," Geoffrey told him. "And back at Seapoint." He put the lid on Teddy's childhood treasure box. "Do you want to keep it, or shall I bury it again?"

"No more secrets," Teddy said, tucking the box under one arm, sliding the photograph into the inner pocket of his coat where it would lie against his heart. "No more secrets."

CHAPTER 27

"I don't know much about my uncle Ethan," Teddy said when he, Prudence, and Geoffrey had settled themselves into the library at Seapoint. "He was rarely talked about."

Philip Dickson was out with his estate manager inspecting the damage done by last night's storm and Abigail had gone to the chapel to spend the afternoon beside Eleanor's coffin, leaving orders that she was not to be disturbed.

"You knew him as a child, Teddy," Prudence admonished.

"Yes, and that's how I remember him. As a child would." Teddy shrugged. "He was a very somber man. Rarely smiled, never laughed. Something about his nieces and nephews made him deeply melancholy. I used to catch him watching us. The intensity of his stare was unnerving. Aunt Jessa cautioned us against making too much noise when he was around. We knew he was frequently in pain and that we had to be careful not to bump into him or leave a ball or a toy out where he might trip. It was as if he lived inside a fenced enclosure that no one else was allowed to enter."

"How old were you when he died?" Prudence asked.

"It was within a year of the war ending," Teddy said. "So I was nine."

"That's old enough to have accurate memories," Geoffrey commented.

"I recall so much about those days after my father came home. But Uncle Ethan is never in the foreground of what I see when I close my eyes. There was a sense that he wouldn't last very long. Some veterans didn't. They might appear to be in good health, but the heart had gone out of them. They sickened and died of nothing but the absence of hope. Tough men who had survived the worst days of the war were defeated by the peace."

"Aunt Jessa still lived at Wildacre then?"

"She was never far from my uncle's side. My father recovered within a few months but by that time Sherman had laid waste to most of eastern Georgia. Uncle Ethan's wounds were more severe; he kept to his bed and then to a chaise longue on the veranda until just before the surrender. Aunt Jessa hovered over him the way she did my mother. He was a long time coming back to himself, and then I think it was only because she chivvied him into it."

Teddy held the calico-wrapped journal in one hand as if uncertain what to do with it. He looked pleadingly at Prudence.

"If it becomes too difficult," she said gently, "we can take turns reading from it."

Teddy nodded. He unwrapped the calico and opened the journal to the first page. "'*This book belongs to Ethan Bennett and recounts his journey into manhood from the eve of his eighteenth birthday until the Lord shall please to call him Home,*'" he read again, in a thin voice that shook with anticipation.

Prudence smiled encouragement.

Teddy skipped rapidly through the early pages, reading a line here and there that described daily life at Wildacre and a growing tension between the brothers. When Elijah married at age twenty-one, Ethan made an oblique reference to visits to the quarters that he imagined the new husband would have to manage more discreetly in the future.

Teddy's face flushed. He glanced despairingly at Geoffrey and then apologetically at Prudence. "I can't read any more of this. Not out loud."

"I can," Prudence reassured him, reaching for the small book. "It won't be any worse than some passages from one of Mr. Dickens's novels."

She continued as Teddy had begun, silently skimming whole pages, choosing a sentence or a paragraph here and there to read aloud. It was beginning to seem as though the diary would tell them nothing of what they had hoped to discover. Why then, had someone taken such care to hide it?

None of them expected the secret that Ethan confided to his most private self a little more than a year before Georgia seceded from the Union.

> *Her name is Selena and I have never known anyone as beautiful. She could pass for white, but she is not. She is one of us, though I do not know which Bennett man first sired her line. And therein lies the second sin. She is enslaved and the same blood that runs through my veins runs through hers.*

"He writes that he has known her all her life and yet he hasn't," Prudence said, lowering the journal to her lap for a moment, putting into context the fragmentary entries she had just read. "It would seem that Aunt Jessa managed to protect the girl for a while by keeping her largely out of sight. She covered her straight hair with a turban and her body with the loose-fitting clothing of a much older woman. And because she became her invalid mistress's personal body servant, even to sleeping on a pallet at the foot of her bed or outside her bedroom door at night, Selena escaped the kind of depredations other young women in the quarters were prey to."

Geoffrey had risen to his feet as soon as Prudence stopped reading. He poured whiskey for himself and Teddy, then, at a nod from his partner, for Prudence also. She wondered if this was the scandal he had been hinting at. If so, it seemed rather tame, given what she had learned about how the Bennett family ruled its isolated kingdom. Even Teddy didn't seem as shocked as she would have expected him to be.

"Wildacre was a much different place in the days before the war," Teddy said, raising his glass as though to toast that never-to-be-forgotten era. "I remember how full of people it always seemed when I was a child. Relatives and family friends from other plantations often came and spent weeks with us on the island. They brought their own servants, so the quarters were full to bursting when there were guests in the Big House. My grandfather was a fierce and frightening man, but he instructed his overseer to relax some of the rules that governed the quarters whenever there were visitors. I remember not realizing until I was much older what he had meant when he said it brought new blood into the mix."

It was a matter-of-fact statement that Prudence thought he would never have voiced if Eleanor had been there to hear it. She would have been incensed at the license to sire mulatto children on slave women helpless to resist the casual lust of a master. But Teddy sipped at his whiskey as though the journal had catapulted him from his painful present into a past where he felt more comfortably at home.

When Geoffrey sat down again and neither man said anything to break the silence, Prudence picked up the journal and continued reading aloud. Gradually it became clear that Ethan Bennett and the slave Selena chose to delude themselves into believing their stolen time together went unnoticed. Aunt Jessa had taught her how to read and write, a crime in itself, and she encouraged the girl to mimic the speech of the white family she served.

It was a dangerous game the two young people played, but as Prudence read each revealing entry, it became apparent that they got away with it for nearly a year. Then Selena found herself in the family way, and nothing could be hidden any longer.

> *My father has stipulated that she is to occupy a small cabin at the far end of the row, and that she is no longer to show herself in the Big House. The child, if it lives, will be sold off the place as soon as it is weaned. As will she. I have begun to plan their escape.*

"Hopeless," Teddy said. "It could never be done."

"Yet Queen Lula named Selena as the only runaway who was never found or brought back to Wildacre," Prudence reminded him.

"Because she died in the swamp," Teddy maintained.

"Perhaps not." It was the voice Prudence had heard Geoffrey use in court when it was time to focus a jury's attention on the turning point of a case.

It seemed inconceivable, but Teddy did not appear to have connected long-ago Selena and the Eleanor he had hoped to marry. He was reacting to the unfolding story as though it were entirely the tale of his uncle's doomed love. Nothing to do with him at all.

> *I have found someone who will take her North for me. It will have to be soon because I fear war may be coming. If the man from Illinois is elected, the South will not remain in the Union. If, God willing, he is defeated, I must still see her and my unborn child to safety. They cannot live where I am unable to protect them.*

As she continued to read, Prudence felt herself sharing the anguish of a young man steeped in misery and nearly devoid of hope. Whoever it was who had agreed to escort Selena to freedom changed his mind; despite what Ethan was prepared to pay, the danger was too great. Weeks passed. As Selena's time approached, Ethan's entries grew increasingly desperate. Until, finally, when it was almost too late, another rescuer appeared on the scene.

> *My prayers have been answered. I will not name him, for his own protection and that of my beloved. Selena will travel North with him; she will pretend to be his wife as they journey to safety.*
>
> *If I could take her myself, I would gladly abandon everything to do it, but Father has set a watch on me and I am too easily recognizable in this area to be anything but a danger to her.*
>
> *What we are about to do is perilous. All I can think of is that in chasing freedom, she may find death. And it will be on my head, for it is I who have insisted she and the child she carries must go. Six months ago, when a traveling photographer came to the island, he captured her image for me. I pray God that photograph is not all that remains of her when this is over.*

"He was right about the war. Georgia seceded three months after Lincoln was elected," Teddy said. "If Selena did make it to the North, there would have been no communication between her and Uncle Ethan for the next four years."

"It looks as though he hid his journal in the tin box while he was fighting in the Confederate Army," Geoffrey said. "He must have wanted to be certain that if he was killed, it wouldn't be found on his body."

"The next entry is dated May 1, 1865," Prudence announced.

"Peachtree Creek was in July of 1864," Teddy reminded them.

"Uncle Ethan and Father spent months in a Savannah hospital, but my grandfather brought them home well before Sherman took the city at Christmas that year. He must have had Aunt Jessa dig up the journal right after the surrender."

"Will you read the rest of the entries, Teddy?" Prudence asked, handing him the diary. She thought he seemed strangely detached from what had happened at Wildacre all those years ago. Perhaps having to decipher his uncle's handwriting and breathe in the musty scent of the long-buried pages would awaken him to what Prudence suspected had to be Selena's hidden truth.

> *As soon as I am able, I shall go North in search of them. If such a thing is possible in this new world where slavery no longer exists, I shall find my Selena and we will marry. I will sign over my inheritance rights in Wildacre to Elijah; he has no interest in living anywhere but here. If necessary, I shall quit these United States. Canada or Europe, perhaps France. Somewhere not exhausted from the struggle of brother against brother.*

"He doesn't write again until months later." Reluctantly, more slowly now, Teddy continued reading Ethan Bennett's journal.

> *All hope is lost. The cotton factor disappeared before the war ended and is probably dead, according to the detective I hired to find him.*
> *He was a man of means and a gentleman, loving the South but abhorring slavery. As did I. The detective will continue to look for Selena, and for our child, but he fears the trail has gone cold. I had given the factor funds to purchase a house for my beloved and establish a bank account from which she could draw whatever she needed, but there is no record of*

any such transactions. I refuse to believe the detective's suggestion that he kept the money for himself and sold the two loves of my life back into slavery, though I have heard of such a thing being done.

"He never finds out whether the child is a boy or a girl," Prudence said. "Or whether it lived or died."

Teddy turned the pages of the journal, skimming his uncle's final words. "He writes that he has decided he must remain at Wildacre because if she is alive, Selena will write to him there. The detective continues to send him reports, but every lead that appears promising comes to nothing. He is able to get about with the use of two canes, but then he says that he is determined to ride again, as he once did."

"That must be when he had himself tied into the saddle so he could ride his acres," Geoffrey speculated.

"The last entry is in a different hand," Teddy said.

Ethan Bennett was dragged to his death yesterday. He was buried near the graves of his father and his mother in the family burying ground at Wildacre. He had one love in his life and fathered one child. I swear to the truth of this statement because I knew them all. And loved each of them.

"Aunt Jessa?" Prudence asked.

"The entry is signed with the letter *J*," Teddy answered. "She must have retrieved the diary from Ethan's bedroom and buried it in the tin box again before anyone else could discover it. Along with the photograph of Selena. She wrote that she knew them all. Not just both of them. She knew them *all*. Loved each of them."

Teddy ran his thumb over the face of his uncle's great love, obscuring the features, then revealing them again. "It's Eleanor. It's why she was killed."

*   *   *

Prudence walked to the chapel and convinced Abigail to come back to the house with her.

"I don't see what could be so important that it won't wait," Eleanor's mother complained.

Prudence waited patiently but neither explained nor left Abigail's side until they entered the library.

Philip, just as puzzled and annoyed, had given up trying to get answers out of Geoffrey and Teddy. He'd dismissed his estate manager to write up a report of what they had seen and taken out his Atlantic charts again.

"Is this your doing, Philip?" his wife asked petulantly. She settled herself on the sofa she had shared with Teddy the night before as the storm raged across the island.

"I have no idea why I'm being held captive in my own house," he retorted.

Geoffrey and Teddy had insisted that he remain with them in the library until Abigail joined them.

"I'm sorry for the questions we have to ask you," Prudence began, enfolding one of Abigail's hands in hers. "Believe me, if there was any other way to do this, we would."

Eleanor's parents stared at her. The worst thing either of them could have imagined had already happened. Nothing, they thought, could compare with the death of a beloved child.

"We know that Eleanor was not your natural daughter," Geoffrey began, using the reassuringly firm tone of voice that never failed to coax difficult testimony out of reluctant witnesses.

"Philip?" Abigail's panicked protest was as good as an admission.

"We wouldn't need to inquire if it weren't vital to learning how and why she died," Prudence said.

"Nothing you tell us will in any way change my feelings for Eleanor," Teddy promised.

"We lost children," Philip said, head bowed, one hand circling aimlessly over the Atlantic chart on his desk. "Before Eleanor."

"They all died," Abigail murmured, "all of my children died, some of them before they could be born. One girl lived for three months. When I found her lifeless in the bed I tried to join her. Philip wouldn't let me go." She peeled back the cuffs of her black mourning gown. Threads of silver scarring criss-crossed her wrists. "I couldn't even do that well."

"Eleanor was older than our girl by several weeks," Philip said. "A beautiful, healthy child whose mother had recently died. The man in whose care she had been placed was unmarried. He was a business associate who was looking to solve his own dilemma. He could not raise the infant entrusted to him, nor did he wish to place her in an orphanage. I brought her home that same day to Abigail. Our daughter's death was not yet known outside the confines of our own house, so we decided there would be no notice placed in the newspapers, no funeral. The servants would be told that Abigail had found the child unresponsive, and, in a moment of hysteria mistakenly thought her dead. The individual who gave her to us had terms, of course, and we agreed to them."

"What were those terms?" Geoffrey asked.

"That Eleanor would never be told she was not our natural child and we would not attempt to learn her true parentage."

"Didn't that seem strange to you?"

"He told us that her mother had been an otherwise virtuous young woman of good family who had allowed herself to be taken advantage of by a man not worthy to be called a gentleman. That when he abandoned her she was sent away to bear the child in secret. I don't know what would have happened had she not died. Perhaps a way would have been found for her and the child to return home."

"Not in this case," Teddy said. He handed Philip the photograph of Selena.

"I've never seen this portrait of Eleanor before," Philip said.

"May I?" Abigail rose from the couch and joined her husband at his desk. The hand she reached out for the photograph trembled visibly. She turned it over, then collapsed into Philip's arms, shaking her head in denial. She had recognized, as he had not, that the clothing worn by the woman who was the image of her daughter had been fashionable thirty years ago.

"What was the name of the man who brought you your daughter?" Geoffrey asked.

"He was a cotton factor on the New York Exchange who had represented many fine Southern families for years," Philip said, evading the question. "Not revealing his name was the third condition he demanded and to which I agreed. I gave my word as a gentleman."

"Is he still alive?"

"No. He disappeared during the last year of the war. Those of us who knew him speculated that he was apprehended during a mission he undertook for President Lincoln. He had unusually free passage back and forth across the lines. We made inquiries, but no trace of him was ever found."

"Your word as a gentleman no longer binds you," Geoffrey said. "Death breaks the contract."

"There are some who would disagree with that," Philip said.

"Please," Prudence pleaded.

Abigail eased herself from her husband's embrace, her tear-stained face as set and determined as he had ever seen it. "You never told me his name, either. After all this time, and now that she's gone, I want to know who my daughter really was. If giving up this man's identity will help to solve the mystery, then I beg you to tell us. You owe me that, Philip."

Dickson removed a leather wallet from his coat pocket, undid the strap, and extracted a business card softened by time. "I've carried it with me ever since the day we made our agreement. Stephen Aycock was an independent agent, as you can see, working several of the exchanges. That's probably what made him valuable to the Union cause."

"Did he spy for Allan Pinkerton?" Geoffrey asked.

"There's no way of knowing, unless he appears in the agency's records."

"It doesn't matter," Teddy said, staring fixedly at the card. "There was a Mr. Aycock who came to Wildacre twice a year. Sometimes more frequently. He brought small gifts for us children, toys he picked up in the course of his travels. Sweets, too. Not the homemade sugar treats made on the plantation, but real chocolate that melted on your fingers before you could get it into your mouth."

"You're sure, Teddy?" Prudence asked.

"We had to compose thank-you notes for the toys and the sweets," he said. "I remember our father writing out his name for us to copy. He was very insistent that we get it right."

"Are there expense and income records from before the war?" asked Geoffrey, remembering the voluminous notations of every transaction that took place at Sandyhill.

"Union troops came through all of the islands at one time or another," Teddy said, "but Wildacre was never in danger of being burned down. So, yes, as far as I know, the plantation books still exist. Stephen Aycock's name will be there."

"You'd better tell us what this is about," Philip demanded.

Teddy held the photograph of Selena where everyone could see it, then laid it atop the Atlantic chart.

"This is Eleanor's mother. She was born into slavery on Wildacre Plantation. Eleanor's father was my Uncle Ethan, who fought for the Confederacy. He arranged for Selena to be smuggled North when she was expecting their child. Stephen Aycock was the factor who transacted business for the Bennett family. He was also the man who posed as Selena's husband during her escape and the guardian who gave you her child when she died."

"No," Abigail cried out. "That's not possible."

"It is," Philip said. He looked around him at the opulent mansion he had built for the child he had lost forever. "Stephen

Aycock wrote me a letter during the war about a beautiful sea island off the coast of Georgia where land was sure to become available when the South was defeated. As he knew it would be. I never forgot his descriptions. He seemed to be envisioning a paradise. Purchasing Bradford Island when it was put up for sale and building Seapoint was no accident. He had already primed me for it."

He tapped Selena's photograph lightly with the tip of one finger. "She was a beautiful woman."

"So was her daughter," Teddy agreed. "So was her daughter."

CHAPTER 28

❧

"It's best that you not go alone." Geoffrey followed Teddy to the Seapoint stables where the head groom saddled a horse for him.

"I appreciate the gesture, but this isn't your quarrel." Teddy had turned as cold and implacable as stone. "It had to have been Lawrence who wrote the note luring Eleanor into the live oaks. The only thing I don't know is whether he did it with or without my father's knowledge. A Bennett is responsible for Eleanor's death, and a Bennett will pay the price."

"You're not leaving me here," Prudence called out. Panting from the short run over the lawn, she ordered that her horse, too, be saddled.

Abigail had fled to the chapel. The sound of her frenzied sobbing carried out onto the covered porch. Philip, afraid she would do herself harm, dared not leave her. But he was adamant about quitting the island as soon as the yacht returned from the mainland and could be readied for the return sail to New York. "Two days at the most," he warned them.

Teddy set a punishing pace to Wildacre; Prudence and Geoffrey pushed their mounts as fast as they dared down the road that ran alongside the sound. It was the same track where Teddy had been riding the day Eleanor's horse bolted, leaving her walking the beach empty-handed until he caught the animal and returned it to her.

The day they met for the first time. And fell in love.

Sunlight shining through the towering live oaks surrounding Wildacre bathed the grounds in tones of green and gold, heralding one of the spectacular sunsets for which the Georgia sea islands were famous. The Bennett family had gathered on the veranda, Elijah and Lawrence drinking whiskey over crushed mint and sugar lumps, Aurora Lee and Maggie Jane sipping cold tea sweetened with peach nectar. Both women wore hastily refitted gowns from Eleanor's trousseau.

When Teddy galloped up the drive, closely followed by Prudence and Geoffrey, he shattered the late afternoon calm. Lawrence rose to his feet as his brother's horse skidded to a halt at the foot of the curved staircase, fragments of crushed shells exploding upward from beneath its hooves.

Geoffrey caught his arm while Teddy was still only halfway up the stairs. He jerked him unceremoniously to a halt, reminding him in a low, urgent voice that questions had to be asked and answered before accusations could be made. And that there were ladies present.

Aurora Lee paled. Maggie Jane turned crimson. There was no doubt in either of their minds that Prudence would recognize the dresses they wore.

"You may wish to retire inside," Teddy choked out, wondering how and when the sisters he had last seen in ancient mourning gowns had found cream and blue afternoon frocks that reminded him of the lace-trimmed gowns Eleanor had liked to wear. He had no illusions about their supposed ignorance of the way white planters had used their female slaves, but the subject was never even hinted at in polite company where ladies were present. What he had to say to Lawrence and to his father would go far beyond the bounds of propriety.

Maggie Jane nodded and gathered her skirts, but Aurora Lee pushed her back into her chair.

"I can't imagine what brings you charging in here like a wild man," she said, including Geoffrey and Prudence in her scathing look, "but since we're bound to hear about it eventually, we might as well stay."

Lawrence and Elijah exchanged looks, then Elijah shrugged. He poured himself more whiskey, not bothering with the dish of crushed mint and the bowl of sugar lumps. "Let's have it out then," he muttered, so low that Prudence wasn't sure she had heard him correctly.

"Do you recognize this woman?" Teddy asked, handing the photograph of Selena to his father.

Elijah glanced at it, then set the stiff cardboard down on the table as though it burned his fingers.

Aurora Lee and Maggie Jane craned their necks to make out the image. When Maggie Jane reached to pick it up, Elijah snarled at her to leave it lay. Lawrence glanced down as if indifferent to whatever it was Teddy had brought into their midst.

"Do you recognize her?" Teddy repeated, his hands clenched into tight fists, his voice harsh and threatening.

"Why should I answer such an impertinent question?" Elijah asked.

"I'll know if you lie to me," Teddy said. "I've read Uncle Ethan's diary. The one Lawrence was looking for when he or someone he paid tore apart Aunt Jessa's cabin." He fixed his brother with an accusatory stare. "How did you know about the journal? Did Father tell you? Did he turn to you when he couldn't do his own dirty business?"

Lawrence swirled the whiskey in his glass, looking out at the expanse of shadowy green where peacocks strutted and unfurled their iridescent tails. "I think that's enough, Teddy. You don't want to say things you won't be able to take back."

Geoffrey's arm across his chest was all that kept Teddy from hurling himself at his brother in an incoherent rage. Prudence clung to one arm, whispering in his ear, pleading with him to listen to her. Every lawyer knew that leaving the accused to stew in edgy quiet was one of the surest ways to obtain a confession.

The silence stretched on, interrupted only by the occasional nervous hiccup from behind Maggie Jane's fingers. Aurora Lee edged closer to where Selena's photograph lay. When she saw the face clearly enough to know that it was Eleanor's, she gasped and then turned away to whisper into her sister's ear.

"It's over," Elijah finally said, speaking to Lawrence. "I don't suppose there's any point denying it. Not if they have the journal." He sat back in his chair as if what must happen next was as ordinary as any conversation at the end of a pleasant day. "I always wondered what became of it. I found keeping a journal to be a boring pastime, but Ethan wrote so much and so often that I teased him about composing a novel to rival those of Mr. Dickens. When we didn't find it after he died, I assumed he'd had the sense to burn the thing. At least the pages in which he undoubtedly confessed his great and illicit love.

"Father suspected him of smuggling the girl North, but he denied the charge and nothing could be proved. We put it out that she'd drowned in the swamp. And then Georgia seceded and war was declared."

"Did he never doubt on which side he would fight?" Prudence asked before she could stop herself.

"Whatever else he did, Ethan was a Bennett," Lawrence said, as if that answered her tactless and insulting question.

"He wasn't the first man a woman of color seduced into forgetting who he was," Elijah said. "I blame her, not him. My brother was as soft toward our people as our father could be harsh. Selena saw a chance to trick him into getting her to freedom and she took it."

"When did you know?" Teddy asked.

"I suspected, the day you brought Eleanor here to Wildacre," Elijah said. "The resemblance was so strong there couldn't be any other explanation. But we had to be certain."

"Father set me to combing through the plantation record books from right before and after the war," Lawrence contributed. He seemed to relish telling the tale. "I found mention of sums of money that didn't seem to buy anything, then bills from a detective, and a letter that came after Ethan's accident stating that the agency had closed the case and would no longer pursue the investigation requested by Mr. Bennett."

"That agency had gone out of existence by the time Eleanor appeared," Elijah continued, "but the country is full of ex-Pinkertons setting up on their own. The girl was never formally adopted because Philip Dickson simply used his dead child's birth certificate. Our operative found a woman who worked in the Dickson house during those years. She remembered hearing of the passing of a female child, but then being told there had been a mistake, the baby was alive after all. The servants were told that while the girl had come close enough to dying to catapult the parents into premature mourning, she had survived. The notice of her birth had already appeared in the newspapers. We assume the nanny must have been aware of the substitution, but that she was well paid for her silence.

"Given what we knew, we couldn't allow the marriage to take place," Elijah finished matter-of-factly. "I did my best to talk you out of it."

"And then you did an about-face," Teddy interrupted. "While

I was still in New York you wrote that you would welcome Eleanor into the family and that your initial opposition had only been to test my determination. I've never been happier than on the day I received that letter. But it was all lies, wasn't it?"

Elijah shrugged as if to ask what difference it could possibly make now that the bride-to-be was dead.

"I don't know exactly what your plan was, but I'm sure the Dickson wealth played a role in it. You realized that if I married Eleanor I would come into a fortune that could be directed to the restoration of Wildacre and the settling of whatever debts remained unpaid after you sold the island to her father. I don't doubt you've accumulated more obligations. You were never good at managing what few resources we had."

"It's not necessary to be insulting, Teddy," Elijah reprimanded his son.

"And you," Teddy said, turning to Lawrence. "What did you say to her after your note persuaded Eleanor to meet you in the live oaks that night? There's no point denying it. Your own sister recognized your handwriting."

"She was filth, Teddy," Lawrence snarled.

"What did you say to her?" With Geoffrey close beside him and Prudence still holding tight to one arm, Teddy refused to be baited. He wanted an answer to his question, and he thought he could put up with anything Lawrence threw his way in order to get it.

"Only the truth of who and what she was. And that she was bound to be found out. She'd been raised among Yankees, but we have an instinct for things like that down here. I told her exactly what she could expect to happen if she insisted on going through with a so-called marriage. We have laws against that kind of abomination."

Geoffrey unobtrusively moved one hand beneath his coat where it rested within inches of the shoulder holster that held his Colt revolver.

"How could one brother do that to another?" Teddy asked, wrenching himself free from Prudence's hold.

"You became too much like a Yankee for your own good," Lawrence retorted. He emptied his glass, poured more whiskey. "The Bennetts have always been gentlemen. You seem to have forgotten that."

"No gentleman worthy of the name forces himself on a woman," Teddy retorted. "No matter her condition. He has an obligation to deal fairly with those who serve him. Slavery didn't have to be the cruel institution we made it."

"You're confusing obligation with privilege," Lawrence insisted. "There is no such thing as obligation toward a chattel. And the privilege of ownership is a sacred trust between God Almighty and those He has elevated to exercise its rights over the lesser creatures He created. Any man of the cloth worth his calling will tell you that."

She had stepped into a different world, Prudence realized. She felt as dazed and confounded as though she were trying and failing to fight her way out of a bad dream.

"I tried to convince Lawrence that we could deal with the situation," Elijah interrupted. "Reasonably and in a way that would benefit everyone. Unfortunately, you had already made known your intentions to too many people to simply change your mind. That would have invited speculation and possibly scandal."

"What did you have in mind, Father?" Teddy's contempt for the man was obvious and scathing.

"Simply that we allow the union, Teddy. For a time. I trusted you would come to your senses when we deemed the time was right to tell you the truth about her."

"Then what?"

Once again, Elijah shrugged. Plainly he didn't feel it necessary to put into words what Eleanor's fate would have been once her fortune had been secured. A sanatorium for six months, perhaps a year. A lingering, wasting death that would leave her widower free to remarry. No one the wiser and the Bennetts all the richer.

"But you wouldn't agree, would you, Lawrence?" Menace was as clear in Teddy's voice as though he'd suddenly pulled a weapon.

"I told Father and I told Eleanor exactly what I'm telling you," Lawrence said, repugnance written across his features. "Only a fool thinks he can hide that kind of obscenity. What if a dark child had been born?"

"And you couldn't sell it off the place?" Teddy mocked.

Aurora Lee and Maggie Jane's skirts rustled, but neither sister rose to leave the veranda.

"Eleanor should have cooperated," Lawrence declared righteously.

"You counted on that, did you?" Geoffrey asked.

"Stay out of this," Lawrence growled.

"You obviously did not know my Eleanor," Teddy said.

"Or her mother," Prudence whispered, thinking of the immense courage it must have taken for a heavily pregnant Selena to trust herself and her unborn child to the cotton factor who claimed to be able to smuggle her North. How hard she must have struggled against death after the infant was born. How despairing the moment when she realized that there would be no life with Ethan in a place where they and their child could thrive.

"I sat across the dinner table from her that night at Seapoint," Lawrence continued, "and the gorge rose in my throat as I watched her pretend to be white. I could not swallow the food on my plate for knowing I was expected to accept, even for a little while, that she was something she wasn't."

"He would not be dissuaded," Elijah said mournfully, as though he was once more feeling the wealth Eleanor represented slip from between his fingers. "I begged him to be sensible. He called it compromising his principles. In the end, I had to agree that perhaps he was choosing the more honorable course."

"I might have allowed her to pass," Lawrence said reasonably. "But not here. Not as a Bennett."

"She was already a Bennett," Prudence whispered, more and more horrified at every one of Lawrence's rationales for what he had done.

"She turned down my offer," he said as if he had not heard Prudence's comment. "At first she refused to accept the truth of who she was. She ran from me, deeper into the live oaks. There was a moon that night; I could see her clearly as she passed beneath the trees. I caught up with her, told her again the story of Ethan's obsession, of how he'd paid Stephen Aycock to steal Selena. I told her that my father remembered Selena, and that he'd immediately recognized her mother's face in her. Even before we had proof of what we now knew had happened all those years ago."

"You should have come to me instead of her," Teddy agonized. "I would have taken her away. No one would have ever known."

"No," Lawrence said bitterly. "You might think now that's what you would have done, but I know you, Teddy. You would never have been able to abandon Wildacre. Have you forgotten that you confided your hopes of building a life in Savannah once you'd established yourself on the New York Cotton Exchange? You talked about returning to the island someday for good. She had to disappear. It was the only way."

"You let her drown in the swamp. You knew she could never make her way out of it alone."

"Unfortunately, your Eleanor was not that cooperative," Lawrence said brusquely. "She had to be persuaded."

Prudence saw again the hand-sized bruises on Eleanor's shoulders, imagined the terrified shock when her friend realized that the man looming over her would hold her beneath the swamp's murky water until she drowned. Did she close her eyes as it happened? Did her heart call out to Teddy in those final, searing moments of life?

"No Southern jury will convict me," Lawrence said smugly. "No judge will sentence me. I did what had to be done."

Teddy stared at his brother in excruciating horror.

Then he stripped the leather riding glove from his right hand and struck it across Lawrence's face.

CHAPTER 29

The sharp crack of leather against bare skin echoed in the shocked silence.

"I shall be your second, Lawrence," Elijah Bennett said, rising slowly to his feet.

"And I yours, Teddy," Geoffrey stated firmly.

The popularity of duels fought in the name of one's honor after a real or imagined slight had declined markedly after the war. No one quite knew why, but many blamed the bloodbath from which the nation emerged united once more, but badly damaged. Even in the South, where dueling had always found more favor than in the North, life after the slaughter of the battlefields was too precious to waste on a gentleman's adherence to the exaggerated ritual of the *code duello*.

But for Teddy Bennett, who knew the truth of his brother's statement that no jury would convict him and no judge would sentence him for the killing of a black woman, it was the only way to exact retribution for Eleanor's death.

Geoffrey's swift commitment to act as his second was further proof, if any were needed, that justice would have to be bought at the risk of Teddy's own life.

Prudence, stunned at the prospect of formalized violence in place of a court of law, could not believe what had happened. She understood now why Geoffrey had insisted on accompanying Teddy to Wildacre, why he had stayed at his side from the moment they climbed onto the veranda to confront the assembled Bennetts. He had told her once that brutality lay close beneath the polished veneer of Southern plantation life. She hadn't understood its all-encompassing nature, hadn't realized that the barbarity of coldly taking a life occurred in the Big House as well as in the quarters.

"Pistols at ten paces," Elijah said after conferring briefly with his younger son. "Tomorrow at dawn. Your principal knows the spot." He spoke directly to Geoffrey as if Teddy were invisible or not standing within arm's reach. Until the duel played itself out, the duelists would ignore one another's existence. All communication would be between the seconds.

Geoffrey knew the intricacies of the code duello as well as Elijah. All four of the men now inextricably bound together in this exquisite dance of death had been raised on it, though perhaps the younger ones had thought of it as a revered relic of the past. Yet the moment Teddy knew that every other avenue was closed to him, it had suddenly come alive again with unarguable logic and irresistible force.

"Tell Philip and Abigail what's happened," Geoffrey urged as he shepherded Prudence toward her horse. "The dueling ground will be somewhere in the live oaks. Even on a plantation as remote as Wildacre, it was always in an isolated spot." He didn't have to explain that the women of the family clung to one another as they listened for the sound of measured shots reverberating through the woods.

"Can't you talk them out of it?" Prudence begged.

"We're obliged to try," Geoffrey said. "That's the first duty of a second. But I don't hold out much hope of success. Teddy is determined and Lawrence has tradition on his side. Neither of them will offer or accept an apology."

"You're not coming back with me to Seapoint?"

"I'll stay here with Teddy."

"How can they bear to be in the same house when they plan to kill each other in the morning?" Prudence asked. As romantic as the idea of a duel might sound in a novel, she thought the reality of it was pure insanity such as only men mesmerized by costly and elaborately constructed weapons could dream up.

"There's a code of behavior to all this," Geoffrey explained to a mystified Prudence. "Teddy and Lawrence won't speak to one another; they won't even allow their eyes to meet. They'll retire early, each to his own room, and in the morning, they'll ride separately to the dueling ground."

"Philip will want to be a witness," she predicted.

"The servants know where the dueling ground is," Geoffrey said, his mind already drifting toward the young man whose impetuous action had set everything in motion.

Perhaps not so impetuous, he decided. Teddy might have worked it all out during that mad dash from Seapoint. Perhaps he had always suspected that he would have to kill his brother to avenge Eleanor's honor. And his own.

"I'm not going to stay away, either," Prudence declared. "Just so you know, Geoffrey."

"It's not customary for women to be present," he told her.

"Custom be damned!" she said vehemently.

Elijah and Geoffrey met that evening to work out final arrangements.

"Lawrence has chosen these matched sets of dueling pistols," Elijah reported, leading Geoffrey toward the library table where the weapons lay nestled in velvet-lined leather cases. "Each of my sons received a set on his twenty-first birthday. Their initials are carved into the stocks."

As he was expected to do, Geoffrey lifted each gold-filigreed pistol from its nest and examined it carefully. Checked the long, smooth bore barrel, the firing pin, the action of the trigger, and the size and weight of the lead bullets stored beside the mold that had created them. He fingered the immaculate tools used for cleaning, and nodded in satisfaction when the inspection was completed.

"They're French," Elijah said.

"I recognized the style," Geoffrey told him. "Beautiful."

"Unless there is an objection, Lawrence will use one of the pistols bearing his initials, and Teddy will do likewise."

"No objection," Geoffrey said, wondering if the father had ever envisioned his sons squaring off at one another when he commissioned the dueling pieces.

"The count will be ten paces. Turn and fire at will."

"I've discussed this with Teddy. He agrees in advance to all of Lawrence's conditions."

"No apology is tendered."

"None is expected."

"There's not time to send to Savannah for a surgeon," Elijah said.

"It is understood that there will be no delay in order to secure a medical presence." Teddy had told Geoffrey to acquiesce to whatever Lawrence, the aggrieved party, demanded. But protocol required that the seconds formally announce and accept every condition that would govern the conduct of two gentlemen in conflict with each other. And every time a constraint was stipulated, there was the slightest possible chance that a refusal might lead to the kind of arbitration that satisfied honor without jeopardizing life or limb.

"One round?" Geoffrey asked. Each participant would fire a single shot at his opponent.

"Lawrence has no wish to fight *à l'outrance*," Elijah confirmed.

Not to the death, then, although any bullet taken in the center of the body usually proved fatal. Perhaps not on the field of honor, but agonizing hours or days later. Geoffrey did not doubt that both brothers would aim to do the most damage one to the other.

There would be no deliberate misses in the early gray light of dawn.

"It's barbaric," Abigail declared.

"Teddy is convinced that it's the only way to obtain justice for Eleanor," Prudence explained again.

Somewhere on the road from Wildacre to Seapoint, she had smacked up hard against the logic of Teddy's reasoning. And been unable to deny it. If Lawrence was right in his assertion that no judge or jury in the state of Georgia would pronounce sentence on him, then there was no point debating the fine points of the law. They ceased to have any meaning in this case. A more primitive code had taken over, one the Bennett men recognized, accepted, and were prepared to administer. Firing pistols at point blank range with the intent of killing one another made perfect sense to them.

In the absence of any alternative, it had also begun to make sense to Prudence.

Philip Dickson instructed the head groom to have a carriage ready in time to make it to the dueling ground well before the sun was up. Abigail, despite her scorn for the way Teddy was choosing to obtain justice for Eleanor, refused to be left behind. Prudence declared that she, too, intended to be a witness to whatever happened beneath the live oaks. She'd already told Geoffrey to expect her.

As she climbed the stairs to her bedroom, certain she would not be able to sleep a wink, Prudence wondered if a second coffin would join Eleanor's in the Seapoint chapel.

And then what? Eleanor to the Dickson family mausoleum in New York, Teddy to the Wildacre burying ground?

Briefly together in life, would the lovers be forever separated in death?

*　*　*

Geoffrey couldn't sleep.

He ran over in his mind everything he and Elijah had discussed and agreed upon, the arguments he had used in a futile attempt to make Teddy change his mind about dueling with his brother, the careful inspection of the weapons to be used. Everything had been accomplished according to the strictest injunctions of the code duello. Nothing had been slighted or omitted.

He had insisted on sleeping on a valet's couch in Teddy's dressing room so as to be nearby if either duelist had second thoughts during the night. He could hear Teddy's steady breathing and light snore through the door he had left cracked open to the bedroom. The prospect of his own death or the deliberate murder of his only brother did not seem to be interfering with Teddy's slumber.

Geoffrey lit the candle lantern sitting on the floor beside his narrow bed.

Perhaps a small whiskey would help.

Padding barefoot over Wildacre's wide-planked flooring, Geoffrey eased himself into the second-floor hallway and down the stairs to the main floor. Not a sound disturbed the stillness of the house. He wondered if Aurora Lee and Maggie Jane slept, then remembered that most ladies resorted to laudanum in difficult times. And Elijah? What kind of father turned such a seemingly indifferent eye when mortal conflict erupted between his sons? Or perhaps it was just one son who would be sincerely mourned if the worst were to happen.

The nighttime whiskey tray was in the library.

So was Lawrence. Asleep or passed out in his father's great armchair, one hand curled around an empty glass resting on his knee. Above him, over the fireplace, Ethan and Elijah Bennett, stiffly handsome in their braid encrusted gray uniforms, stood watch. Except that their eyes weren't cast downward at the slumped figure below. Whatever their blank eyes were seeing, it wasn't the tragedy to be played out in the morning.

Careless, Geoffrey thought, watching Lawrence for signs of consciousness as he poured himself the whiskey he'd come downstairs to find. Depending on how much he'd had to drink, Lawrence could have a shaky hand and blurred vision when he faced Teddy. There would be shadows under the trees; the dim, ethereal predawn light made outlines uncertain and the placement of a bullet difficult to calculate. Still, it wasn't his place to wake him up and hustle him off to bed for what remained of the night. Only his second could do that.

Geoffrey had half a mind to knock on the door of Elijah's bedroom on the way back to the hard couch in Teddy's dressing room. He couldn't remember anything in the code duello that addressed this precise situation, but common courtesy and fair play should cover it.

Elijah and Geoffrey had locked the matched sets of dueling pistols inside a glass-fronted cabinet in the hallway once both seconds were satisfied that the pistols were of exactly equal range and caliber. Each of them pocketed a key. There were, Elijah said, only two.

As he headed toward the staircase, Geoffrey glanced at the cabinet. With one foot already on the first step, he paused, turned around. Something was not as it had been.

He stood in front of the cabinet, eyes tracking the precise angles at which the two leather cases were aligned. One of them was off by less than a finger's width from where he was sure it had been placed. A barely discernible difference, but enough to jolt his Pinkerton-trained powers of observation.

Before he did anything else, he had to make sure he would not be interrupted. It took only a moment to check that Lawrence was still unconscious, then close the library door.

Geoffrey had pulled on his trousers before shrugging into the borrowed dressing gown that was too tight across the shoulders but better than nothing. The key to the cabinet was still in his pocket.

He opened the lid of the case that seemed out of alignment. Teddy's gold inlay initials winked up at him in the flickering light of the candle lantern. He saw no finger smudges on the pistols' gleaming barrels, and every one of the small tools and molded bullets lay in its velvet bed.

Perhaps, when they closed and locked the cabinet door, either he or Elijah had accidentally nudged the pistol case. He tried to remember which of them had last touched the boxes. *Both*, he thought. Elijah had placed Lawrence's set of pistols on the shelf, and Geoffrey had done the same with Teddy's. The door had swung closed on well-oiled hinges, Elijah had locked it, pocketed his key, then waited while Geoffrey tested the key he had been given. Unlocked, then locked the cabinet again.

How then, had one case been moved?

And why?

Because someone, not he, had moved it. Elijah? The elder Bennett's careful adherence to the role of second, as prescribed by the code duello, made that seem unlikely. Yet the case had definitely been moved. Just a fraction of an inch, but not accidentally.

By someone who had a key. Or who had been given a key.

Geoffrey lifted one of Teddy's pistols from its bed. The greatest, perhaps the only flaw in its design was the absolute need for the firing pin to strike the cartridge precisely in its center. In no other way could the lead ball be made to streak with deadly speed and accuracy down the length of the barrel and through empty air to find its target. The firing pin. Loose, it would wobble, lose its tensile strength. Too long and it would scrape rather than strike. Too short and it would flail uselessly against nothing.

Geoffrey opened the case containing Lawrence's pistols. He laid Teddy's weapon beside Lawrence's, compared the length of the firing pins. Saw clearly the duplicity, the tampering that would not be obvious to the casual eye. One pin would strike true; the other had been filed short by perhaps an eighth of an inch.

Both of Teddy's pistols had been tampered with. So that whichever he chose in the morning would misfire. Leave him the exposed victim of his brother's aim. Which Geoffrey did not doubt would be true and lethal.

Working quickly, using the precision tools fitted into their velvet beds, he removed the useless firing pins and replaced them with the spares that lay beneath the bullet mold. No experienced dueler neglected to carry extra firing pins; his life depended on them.

When he had finished, Geoffrey checked Teddy's pistols carefully for other signs of tampering, but found none. Lawrence's strategy had been the essence of simplicity. And it would have succeeded, too, if he hadn't taken that one additional drink of whiskey that made him nudge the closed case out of line and never notice the discrepancy.

For the briefest of moments, Geoffrey considered what would happen in the dawn stillness of the live oak forest. Teddy and Lawrence would each fire one shot. Whether either or both would find their mark was out of Geoffrey's control. Out of Lawrence's now, too. The match was once again as equal as it had been when Teddy struck his brother across the face with a leather riding glove.

One or both of them might die.

The odds were even.

As they should be in a combat of gentlemen.

CHAPTER 30

Until the early morning sky turned pearly gray, the only light illuminating Wildacre's dueling field came from half a dozen lanterns marking its perimeters. The flat, sandy ground was covered by a thin layer of last year's live oak leaves, sodden underfoot from the storm that had raked the island. Immensely tall, twisted trees encircled the open area, embracing the men who had come to redeem their honor in bloody courage.

The saddle horses were led away from the shooting area and hobbled. The carriage in which the Seapoint witnesses had traveled stood nearby. Empty. Prudence and Abigail had chosen to wait in the open air, Philip beside them. All three wore unrelieved black, stark acknowledgement that one or both of the Bennett brothers would be dead before the sun dried last night's dew. In somber silence they waited as Elijah and Geoffrey completed the rituals entrusted to seconds by the code duello.

When each of the seconds had counted off ten paces, he drove a sword into the ground to mark the spot at which a duelist would turn and fire. Elijah had provided the swords he and

Ethan had worn when they fell at the battle of Peachtree Creek. Polished to a high gleam, the steel of both blades shone, dented and nicked by bone and bullets. Below each pommel hung a gold bullion sword knot, dulled by the mud and blood of combat.

Fitting, Prudence thought, since what brought them to this beautiful, desolate spot this morning was rooted in the conflict for which those swords had been struck. She saw Abigail slip her hand into the crook of her husband's arm, heard the faintest of whispers as Philip bent to say something to her. A bouquet of slightly wilted white roses lay on the seat of the carriage out of which they had climbed. In memory of Eleanor, Abigail would strew the flowers on the bloodied dueling ground when it was all over.

Teddy and Lawrence met in the center of the field. It was the first time they had come face-to-face since Teddy had deliberately provoked the duel. Both men wore blindingly white shirts, open at the throat, billowy sleeves cuffed at the wrist. It was traditional to wear white above the waist so the location and severity of chest wounds became immediately apparent. Blood would bloom, is how it was sometimes described.

The seconds asked one last time if honor could be served in no other way. Then Geoffrey, whose role as spokesman had been determined by the toss of a coin, outlined what would happen next. Weapons would be loaded by the seconds in full view of each other and the duelists. In this case, since the brothers had agreed to use pistols marked by their initials, Teddy would choose one of the matched set he had received on his twenty-first birthday; Lawrence would do the same. They were to stand back-to-back and then each walk ten paces from the other in cadence with Geoffrey's count.

At ten, when they reached the swords that marked the farthest limit of the agreed-upon distance, the command would be given to turn and fire. One shot each. If only one man loosed a bullet, he must remain immobile on the field until his opponent retaliated or it was determined by the seconds that he was inca-pable of discharging his weapon. At that point, honor would have been served.

And someone would almost certainly be dead or fatally wounded.

Prudence clasped her gloved hands together to control their trembling.

Geoffrey caught her eye as if to reassure her that although he couldn't be at her side, he was standing there in spirit. She straightened her spine, holding herself as rigidly upright as any governess could wish. Thinking to herself even as she did so how ridiculous all of this ritual was. Wanting it to end. Wishing fervently there was some way to stop it.

The lanterns were extinguished and carried from the field. Curtains of gray Spanish moss waved in the freshening morn-ing breeze. It had grown light enough to make out the features of Teddy and Lawrence's faces—grim, determined, devoid of any trace of fear. Mechanical men, ready to be wound up and set on their automated march.

Geoffrey's voice echoed across the sand and into the trees. Deep and profoundly solemn, it counted off the paces.

"One. Two. Three. Four."

The sand squeaked beneath the duelists' boots, oak leaves wet and slippery.

"Five. Six. Seven. Eight."

Prudence's nerves screamed with silent tension.

"Nine.

"Ten.

"Turn and fire."

Lawrence might have raised his weapon a fraction of a sec-ond earlier than Teddy. It was enough. Bright red blood bloomed on Teddy's white shirt and he fell to the ground, still clutching the pistol he had not discharged.

No one moved. It wasn't over yet.

Lawrence stood facing his brother, the full width of his body

exposed to the shot Teddy had yet to take. Slowly, with infinitesimal movements, Teddy raised the long-barreled pistol, propping it on his wrist. All eyes were on the finger wrapped around
the trigger. But it didn't move. His head drooped on his neck,
slipping downward until his eyes closed and he seemed to lose
consciousness.

Was it over?

Lawrence looked at the seconds as if to ask their authoriza-
tion to leave the field. Seeing their heads bent toward each
other to confer, he smiled in satisfaction and glanced toward
where Philip and Abigail Dickson stood. Then he whirled and
bowed a mocking salaam in the direction of Eleanor's parents,
his back turned rudely to where Teddy lay.

*Your mulatto daughter is dead. I killed her, and there is noth-
ing you can do about it.*

Teddy's bullet caught him full in the base of his spine with an
earsplitting crack of lead entering bone.

The pistol flew from Lawrence's hand.

He fell facedown in the sand.

And did not move.

Prudence rushed to where Teddy had collapsed as soon as
Lawrence fell. Each man had discharged his one bullet. There
was no longer any danger of a wild shot being fired. With Philip
and Abigail beside her, she ripped open Teddy's bloodstained
shirt. Lawrence's bullet had passed cleanly through the flesh
and muscle of his lower left side, missing bone and vital organs.
The hole it left pulsed blood, but slowly. No artery had been
nicked, no vein ripped apart. As long as putrefaction didn't set
in, he would probably live.

If there were onlookers to the white men's duel watching
from deep in the live oaks, they chose not to make their presence known.

Philip unstoppered the flask he always carried with him and
poured whiskey into the wound and down Teddy's throat.

Abigail had ordered a basket of ripped linen bandages and lint before she left Seapoint. She packed the wound and, as Philip propped Teddy's upper body into a seated position, wrapped the linen strips tightly around his torso.

Satisfied that Teddy was not gravely wounded and was receiving good care, Geoffrey turned his attention to where Elijah knelt over his unconscious younger son.

The muscles of his face convulsing with the effort to hold back his anguish, the Bennett patriarch stared at the spot where Teddy's bullet had entered Lawrence's body. There wasn't much blood. It had been as clean a shot as it was calculated. Of the two brothers, Teddy had always been the one with the more precise and perfect aim.

Lawrence's eyelids fluttered and his fingers clawed weakly at the ground.

"We won't know for sure until a surgeon can get a probe in him," Geoffrey said, "but my guess is that the bullet is lodged in bone."

"I've seen this kind of wound before," Elijah said. "If he lives, the slug will have to be left where it is and he'll never walk again." He got slowly to his feet. "I expect he'd rather be dead."

"We'll take them both back to Wildacre in the Dicksons' carriage." Geoffrey signaled the coachman to bring the vehicle out from under the trees. "We can tie the extra horses onto the back."

Elijah looked toward where his other son was sputtering whiskey as he regained consciousness. "I don't guess Teddy and I have much to say to each other. He'll hold me responsible, seeing as how I was the one who recognized her for what she was. Can't say that I blame him, but I don't see that there was anything else I could do."

He was so wrong that Geoffrey knew there was no point trying to change his mind.

* * *

The doctor who came from Savannah two days later confirmed that the bullet Teddy fired had embedded itself in Lawrence's spine. "We saw this frequently during the war," he told them, packing up his instruments and declining an invitation to remain overnight on the island. "Have your blacksmith put wheels on a chair to roll him around in. That's the best you can do. Your son is paralyzed throughout his lower extremities, Mr. Bennett. He'll need someone attending him night and day. And I'd make sure he doesn't have access to a pistol." He saw no point hiding the truth, either from a patient or the family.

"Will the bullet stay where it is?" Elijah asked.

"It could shift. But without his being able to move, I doubt that will happen." He spoke directly to Lawrence, who hadn't said a word or uttered a single groan during the doctor's examination. "You won't feel anything either way." And because he thought the man deserved to know exactly what lay ahead of him, he added, "There's no reason you won't live your allotted span of years. Your heart seems sound and your lungs are clear."

Lawrence stared at him. He hadn't felt the touch of the doctor's hands on his body or the probe he'd heard clink dully against the flattened bullet that was depriving him of all sensation below the waist. He'd seen enough veterans of the war to recognize a future he didn't want to live. He'd have to bide his time, though. Teddy would see to it that he got the best of care. Day after long day Lawrence would stare at the four walls of whichever room he was deposited in or stew in the heat of the veranda, wondering if curious eyes watched from the live oaks. Torturing himself imagining the whispers that he'd gotten what he deserved.

"Thank you, Doctor," he said, wondering how long it would be before the body servant who shaved him left the razor within reach when he emptied the slop bowl.

"I'll be on my way, then."

"One more thing to ask of you, Doctor," Elijah said as they left Lawrence's room.

"What's that, Mr. Bennett?"

"My daughters are going to spend some time with family in Savannah. Their trunks are packed, and they're waiting in the parlor. I wonder if you would undertake the task of chaperoning them on the journey?"

"I shall consider it an honor, sir." From what he'd observed of the Misses Bennett, they were two swiftly withering candidates for the marriage market. Unfortunately, though the doctor chose not to share the information, there were more spinsters in Savannah than men willing and able to marry them. He himself was supremely uninterested.

Teddy had himself driven to Seapoint the morning the Dickson yacht left the island. He was pale and obviously in pain, but the wound had closed and the skin around it showed no deadly streaks of red. The whiskey Philip poured into it on the field of honor had staved off infection.

Eleanor's coffin was the last item to be carried aboard the sailing craft. Six men shouldered it from the chapel onto the cart that rumbled over the narrow sand track to the dock. She had traveled the same road two weeks earlier, chattering happily with the fiancé who had won her heart and with whom she confidently expected to exchange vows of lifelong love and devotion.

They had all been so happy that day, Prudence recalled, spirits buoyed by the sea voyage down from New York City and the anticipation of the quiet, private ceremony Eleanor and Teddy had insisted on. The couple was going to carve out a new life for themselves, choosing to retain the best of both of the worlds from which they came, trusting implicitly in each other to keep promises already made and those yet to be vowed.

Of them all, perhaps only Geoffrey had seen through the joy to the darkness beyond, but even he had not envisioned how impenetrable it would be. He and Prudence had talked well past moonrise last night, walking the beach in the clear white light that illuminated everything in shades of black, white, and gray. It had become the custom at Hunter and MacKenzie, Investigative Law, to dissect every case before it was consigned to the office's meticulously kept files. The too-short life and cruel death of Eleanor Dickson was no exception.

"When did you know?" Prudence asked him. She'd taken off her shoes to wade barefoot in the warm shallows. Physically tired and emotionally drained, she grieved more for the heartache of the man who walked beside her than for herself. They had both suffered painful losses, but the passage of time did not seem to have healed Geoffrey's sorrow. It wasn't a single person he mourned, but the entire culture in which he'd grown up, the way of life that remained a part of him no matter how much he struggled against it.

"I'm not sure," he answered. "I think it was seeing Eleanor against the background of the island that first disturbed me. Her place in New York society was so well established by her family connections that when you introduced me to her there I don't think she registered as anyone but another pretty and accomplished debutante about to embark on marriage. But here, where there were no distractions, she took on an exotic quality I recognized but was reluctant to name.

"Aunt Jessa's murder told me there were secrets on this island that Eleanor's death was an attempt to conceal. That was the beginning. From that point on it was a matter of unraveling the past and tying it to the present." He reached for her arm when she stumbled in the shifting sand. And didn't relinquish it as they continued walking. "Do you remember the portrait of Ethan Bennett hanging in the Wildacre library?"

"How could I forget it? They looked so much alike, he and Elijah. Two sides of a coin, but one side badly damaged."

"There was a single, significant difference," Geoffrey said.

Prudence frowned, trying to picture the faces of the two

young men, searching for whatever it was Geoffrey had seen but she had missed.

"Ethan had a slight cleft," he said, touching a finger lightly to Prudence's chin. "So did Eleanor. It's a trait that runs in families, though no one knows why. Not every child inherits it, but when one does, it's recognizable."

"Maggie Jane has it," Prudence said. "It was the first thing I noticed about her because she so often hides her mouth with her fingers. She doesn't realize that it draws attention to the cleft." She stopped abruptly, sand and seawater pooling around her toes. "Minda has it also."

"I suspect she's Elijah's child."

"Oh, Geoffrey."

"Never to be acknowledged in any way, but everyone on the island will know."

"Do you think Teddy suspects?"

"He turned a blind eye to that type of thing long ago. He sees but his mind refuses to accept the evidence. Most Southern men prefer it that way. It might seem cruel, Prudence, but it's been going on for so long that no one questions it. There may be moments of bitterness when the child realizes who he or she is, but they pass. If there is no possibility of entry into the white world, there is comfort and acceptance to be found in the other."

"It breaks my heart," Prudence said.

"You can't fix all of society's ills in one lifetime."

"Teddy won't go to Savannah, will he?"

"No. He'll stay here on the island. Elijah won't last much longer, and when he dies, Wildacre passes to Teddy. He'll run it with the same dedication and efficiency he would have demonstrated on the Cotton Exchange, and he'll gradually bring the plantation back to some semblance of what it once was. But he won't leave it. And every evening he'll have his brother wheeled out onto the veranda where they'll drink whiskey together over crushed mint and sugar lumps. He won't say a word to Lawrence about what happened, but the silence will do its work, and eventually Teddy will be alone with his memories."

"How will Lawrence do it?" Prudence asked.

"It's surprisingly easy to kill oneself," Geoffrey said. "A razor across the wrists or throat, laudanum saved until the dose is large enough to be fatal, a bullet to the brain. Lawrence will never regret what he did, only the consequences of it."

"He meant to kill Teddy, didn't he?"

"He aimed for the belly," Geoffrey said, "but his hand was shaky. He had sat in the library into the early hours, drinking himself into oblivion."

"How do you know that?"

"Sometime in the middle of the night I went downstairs in search of whiskey myself. Teddy was snoring and the valet's couch was so hard and uncomfortable I couldn't sleep. I saw Lawrence slumped in a chair before the fireplace, empty glass still in his hand." He hesitated, then clamped his lips so tightly together that a thin white line appeared above them.

"Before I went back upstairs I glanced at the cabinet where Elijah and I had locked the dueling pistols. One of the cases was crooked, and I knew that we had left them precisely aligned. So I unlocked the cabinet door and checked them. The firing pins in both of Teddy's guns had been tampered with. I replaced them, relocked the cabinet, and said nothing. When Lawrence turned his back on his brother after he had fired his shot, he believed Teddy's pistol would misfire."

"Have you told him?"

"Teddy? No. And I won't. The code duello only requires that both gentlemen face each other with equal odds. They did, insofar as those odds could be determined by their seconds. The other elements that influence a duel's outcome—a man's previous experience with the weapon of choice, the amount of whiskey he drinks to shore up his courage, the calculating coldness it takes to kill when the passion of the moment has cooled—those things are individual traits over which only the duelist has any control. I don't know why Lawrence drank himself insensible the night before he faced Teddy across a dueling ground, but it proved to be his undoing."

"Lawrence's weaknesses were overweening pride and arrogance," Prudence said. "He truly believed he had the right to kill Eleanor and that he would escape any retribution for the taking of her life."

"It's as good an explanation as any." Geoffrey shrugged. "His punishment will be to spend whatever miserable years remain to him trapped in a body he can no longer control, tormented by a mind that won't let him forget he brought it on himself. A creature to be scorned and perhaps pitied, then forgotten."

"You're a hard man sometimes, Geoffrey."

"I believe in justice, Prudence."

And that's where they had left it.

CHAPTER 31

❧

The small cabin where Eleanor's casket would lie during the northward voyage had been stripped of its furnishings except for a single chair in which Abigail sat, one hand resting on the polished oak as though it touched the living child who had been so cruelly taken from her. She would spend every waking moment with her daughter's remains until the wrought iron doors of the Dickson family mausoleum locked them away from her.

Philip had had a final, bitterly candid conversation with Teddy Bennett, who had implored him, one last time, to allow Eleanor to rest in the Wildacre burying grounds. Philip hadn't hesitated for a moment. Eleanor might have thought she loved him, her father informed the wounded man, but she would have come to her senses eventually. She could never have lived in the world Teddy represented; the affection he claimed they shared would have turned into rancorous resentment. Sullen anger. Harsh words and ill treatment. Philip would not surrender any part of his daughter to the place that had destroyed her.

When Eleanor's father turned his back on the man who had hoped to marry her, he erased him from his mind as though

Teddy Bennett had never existed. To deny him even the half-life of memory was the only vengeance he could exact. It would have to be enough. At least until he determined how to dispose of Bradford Island in the new will he would write.

Perhaps, he thought, feeling the swell of the Atlantic beneath his braced legs as the yacht moved away from the dock, *perhaps I needn't wait that long.* There was a growing movement in the country to preserve huge tracts of land in some of the western states, to afford them by legislative act the same protection Ulysses S. Grant had approved for the Yellowstone area some seventeen years ago. He smiled to himself at the thought of ordinary citizens taking picnic baskets into the Bennett family's live oaks and digging for crabs along the shores of what had once been their private beaches.

Philip Dickson would not return to the island that had taken his daughter's life, but he could ensure that never again would it be the isolated kingdom of the family that had both spawned and killed her.

"You said you wouldn't be sorry to leave Bradford Island, Geoffrey," Prudence remarked. They stood together at the yacht's port railing, watching the broad, sandy beach and the twisted branches of the live oak forest recede into the distance. What she was really asking was whether his ties to the South of his youth had strengthened or been further weakened by their experience on one of Georgia's most beautiful sea islands.

"I'm not," he replied, covering the hand gripping the railing with his own. "I don't regret one moment of its beauty, but I won't dwell on any of the rest of it. I shall always deplore Eleanor's death, as much for why Lawrence killed her as for the deed itself, but I number her as one of the late casualties of the war. There are countless victims of its cruelty throughout the country. You and I, Prudence, have seen a face of blind hatred up close, and we'll never forget it. This crime was unlike the others we've investigated, and I hope to God we never have another one to match it."

He lapsed into silence, eyes turning to the Atlantic horizon that lay ahead of them. Telling her that the subject was closed. He would no longer welcome her questions. When Geoffrey put something behind him, he wanted it to stay there.

So Prudence did what she had so often done before. She tackled the mystery of who he was with the lawyerly concentration in which her father had trained her. They would have five days together in close quarters before the yacht sailed into New York Harbor. More than enough time to unpeel another layer of the protective defenses in which he'd wrapped himself. Just when she thought she had grasped the essence of Geoffrey, he changed. Again.

The duel seemed to have toughened him in some new way she had not seen before. He hadn't questioned its rightness nor any of the arcane dictates of the code duello. It was as though all of the loose threads of his boyhood and what came after had suddenly resolved themselves into a knot he didn't care to untie.

Neat and deadly. It was as close a description of Geoffrey himself as any that had ever crossed her mind.

Five days, she thought. With nothing to do but sleep long and dreamlessly at night and drink in the beauty of sun and sea by day.

And turn her formidable intellect to the mystery standing beside her.